LUSH

CALIFORNIA KINGS  BOOK ONE

tinia montford

This is a work of fiction. Names, characters, places, and incidents either are the product of the author's imagination or are used fictitiously. Any resemblance to actual persons, living or dead, events, or locales is entirely coincidental.

First Edition: March 2025

Editor: Lopt & Cropt Editing
Proofreader: Beth Attwood
Cover Designer: Deranged Doctor Designs

To Grandpa Willie-
The best man I've ever known. No one, now or ever, can hold a candle
to the greatness you bring into my life. You are the epitome of
everything good and kind.

Playlist

Who is She ? – I Monster
Glory Box – Portishead
Anger Management – Lovage
Liquid Smooth - Mitski
Flawless – The Neighbourhood
I Hate Myself for Loving You – Joan Jett & the Blackhearts
I Can't Quit You Baby – Led Zeppelin
My Tunnels Are Long and Dark These Days – Asaf Avidan
After Dark – Mr.Kitty
Fire of Love – Jesse Jo Stark

Want the full Laurene & Reese experience? Listen at: https://
shorturl.at/thznH

Would you like to see deleted scenes, character interviews and
exclusive character art? Sign up for my newsletter at: https://
tiniamontford.com/newsletter/

You can also connect with me on:
Website | Facebook | Instagram | Pinterest | Tik Tok

I wonder if I could take back every 'I love you' ever said
to you, would I do it?

FARAAZ KAZI

AN HOUR BEFORE THE ACCIDENT

THE LAUGHTER SPILLED from the main hall of the yacht club, bright and careless, tangled with the relentless thump of music. I should've been out there, smiling, toasting, pretending.

Instead, I'd been hiding in this bathroom for nearly twenty minutes, like it could stop the slow, sinking dread pooling in my chest.

Smile, Laurene! Smile!

Conrad's great.

Really? my conscience said. He was great. Great for the family, great for appearances, great for everything except *me*.

The door opened and shut softly behind me.

"It's over."

I refused to look behind me. I couldn't. If I did, I'd crack.

Instead, I focused on putting on my lipstick, the motion mechanical. I looked immaculate—*perfect*—the kind of woman my mother would smile at with pride. But I *hated* the color.

This fucking burgundy.

The same shade she shoved at me for every *happy* occasion, every moment she wanted to control. A color that *screamed* her. Everything she expected me to be. Everything I despised.

I met his gaze in the bathroom mirror.

He loomed there, his suit rumpled and tie slightly askew, his dark hair rebelliously unkempt. He looked the exact opposite of his brother—wild, unapologetic, dangerous. Everything I wasn't supposed to want.

"Don't look away." Every word wrapped around me like a challenge, and that rebellious part of me strained beneath my skin. But he wasn't asking. He was demanding.

And I obeyed.

"You shouldn't be here."

I wanted him here. I *needed* him. But I couldn't have him.

"I could say the same to you." In the dim light, his green eyes seemed almost black. "Shouldn't you be outside? Smiling for the cameras? Pretending you don't hate every second of this?"

"This"—I pointed between us—"ends now. Get out before somebody sees you."

His eyes held mine, and the way he *saw* me, like he was stripping away every layer, every excuse, was almost too much.

I turned. "This isn't a game, Reese. My mama would burn the entire town to the ground if she knew about us."

"She doesn't know." He stepped closer. "I was careful. No one saw me. We still have the plan."

"*Please.*" I had to get through this night without more tears. "Let's...let's just cut our losses. I—I don't know if I can do it now."

He was behind me before I knew it, his weight trapping me against the counter. I closed my eyes, my breath catching as his exhale grazed the sensitive skin of my neck, hot and tantalizing.

"Can we think of something else?" A bitter laugh escaped my lips. "She always knows, Reese. You don't understand—"

"What I understand," he said, his voice sharp, "is that you're *miserable*. You're about to marry my brother, and you're standing here trying to convince yourself it's what you want. Believe in our plan or is that what you want, Laurene?"

My reflection stared back at me, every detail curated by Mama. I wasn't the heir; that was Erik. I was the one Mama had molded into perfection—beauty, poise, intelligence, social grace. I was her trophy. But now, with everyone watching, with Mama's grand plans hanging over me like a guillotine, the plan we came up with didn't seem like a grand idea. I just wanted Reese safe.

"What I want doesn't matter."

Reese's hand, calloused and warm, cupped my chin, forcing me to meet his gaze in the mirror. "It matters to me."

Smile, Laurene.

Smile and nod. Smile and comply. Smile and marry Conrad Ashbourne.

And I was so fucking tired of it.

Mama told me what to do, so I did it. I was marrying Reese's older brother. A man I barely knew.

A man I didn't want.

"Look at me," Reese said, his voice low and intense.

A bruise marked his jaw, and I wondered how he'd gotten it. My chest tightened with a familiar mix of anger and worry, a combination that always left me off-balance. I hated how much I still cared.

His fingers skimmed down my throat, his lips barely grazing my ear. I shivered as his hand danced over my collarbone, drifting dangerously toward my breasts.

"Reese." I tried to pull away from the spell he always seemed to cast on me. But his mouth found the sensitive spot on my neck, and I bit my lip to stop the moan that rose in my throat.

He released my flesh, a mark already forming. "You know you belong to me, Laurie."

This was killing me. I could manage the rest of the world, but Reese? He was an uncontrollable wildfire. The way Reese touched me, the things he did—they clung to me, burned me, *marked me.*

Hating him would have been easier.

But I loved him, hopelessly, with everything I had left.

"I... Reese, mm-hmm—we can't!"

"I *need* you."

The footsteps outside the door cut through my thoughts and chilled me.

"This is dangerous."

We were in public. *Anyone* could find us like this. Our families already hated each other. This would be a scandal.

Reese's hands slid up my thighs, lifting my dress, exposing my bare skin to the cool air. My fingers wrapped around his wrists, a feeble attempt to stop him.

"I hate you," I said, my voice trembling.

"You don't."

His lips pressed softly against mine before he sucked on my bottom lip. I shuddered, felt myself weakening, my head falling back, throat exposed. His hands moved with an urgency that stole what little air I had left.

"Tell me you don't feel it," he murmured as he kissed me, his hands inching my dress up and over my ass.

"I…" The word stuck in my throat, and I hated myself for the hesitation. "I don't."

A lie. A weak, pitiful lie that didn't fool either of us.

Reese didn't wait for an answer. He spun me around, gripping my hips. His eyes locked on to mine—I saw anger, regret, and all the things we couldn't fix.

"I've tried to forget you," he murmured, "but I can't. Stop lying to me, stop lying to yourself. I've been drowning without you."

"You'll ruin me."

His hands slid over my ass, and I felt him squeeze before giving it a firm slap and I gasped. I trailed my hands up his chest and he caught one, lifting it to his lips to kiss the center of my palm.

Just one more time.

Words fell apart as his hand slipped between my thighs, pulling my thong aside. I felt him dip a finger into my wetness and breach my tight walls. My nails dug into his shoulders, and he gently pumped before, in one fluid motion, he hoisted me onto the counter. I tightened a hand on the edge of the counter, my other clutching his shoulder as he rocked me against him.

"Marry me."

I had to remember why we were all here tonight.

"I'm engaged now. To *Conrad*," I said. "Your *brother*."

"You don't belong to him!" His voice thundered. I flinched, but it wasn't fear—it was frustration. "You belong with me."

This marriage was a merger carefully crafted by our parents. My feelings didn't matter, and neither did his.

"You're the only thing that makes sense," he whispered.

My pulse hammered in my ears, drowning out the sound of reason.

"You don't love him."

Conrad and I… We barely existed in the same space outside of the public eye. There were no romantic illusions between us. No promises of love. Just a duty to uphold, a role to play. Over time, I'd get used to a loveless marriage.

Women in this town did it all the time.

I'll find a way to survive and thrive because I was a *King*.

I felt his hands tremble slightly as he held my face.

Be strong, Laurene. "I have a responsibility—"

"Trust me." His voice was so sure, like he knew my heart better than I did. And maybe he did. "How many more years are you going to smile and pretend and keep up that goody-two-shoes shit? You were made to create, get dirty and sexy… *with me.*"

I shook my head. Reese didn't *get it.*

"I've loved you through every storm, every moment of doubt. I see you—the real you. And I love every part of you, even the parts you think are unlovable and broken. Just be with me. I don't care if Dad disowns me. Let Conrad and Jennie take the company—I'll give up everything just to keep you by my side. Please, just give us a chance."

I wanted to believe him, but I knew better. I knew how my

family would handle him. Mama's threat was clear. If I defied her—if I didn't marry Conrad—she'd disown me. No trust, no family, nothing.

"You want that art gallery? It's done, sweetheart. We could disappear. Bali, Santorini, Paris? Just name the place, and I'll get us there."

"Millions of dollars are on the line, Reese. Our families won't just let us disappear." I slapped his shoulder.

"Should I just stand by? Watch them own you, *own us*?" His voice cracked, raw and furious. "Hell no. They don't get to take you from me."

I wanted to run with him and never look back. "Running won't solve anything."

"Giving in is not the answer either!"

I can't desert my family. Reese's gaze softened, and he gently wiped away my tear.

"We'll figure it out. But we fight, Laurie. We fight for us."

"Kiss me." *Just one more time. Before I break his heart completely.*

His lips were on mine in an instant, and the world disappeared. All the guilt, the shame, the fear of what would come next melted away. There was nothing but Reese—the heat of his breath, the way his hands clutched me like I might vanish, the desperate press of his body against mine.

A moan escaped my lips, and I felt his tongue teasing mine and I opened my mouth. He grunted when I wrapped my legs around him and felt his hardening length against my core.

"I love you," he gasped out when he broke the kiss. "Seeing him with you, it tears me apart. Conrad can have the money and the company, but he can't have you. Not you, *please*."

He slid his hand beneath my dress, forcefully tearing away my thong, and I spread my legs.

"Fuck, you're soaked already." His gaze flickered over my face as I squirmed under his touch, and his mischievous smirk returned. "Let me love you forever."

Our clothes fell away in a frenzy of need, even knowing that outside the door, everyone we cared for waited with my fiancé. He reached into his pocket to grab a condom and rolled it on. Using my wetness, he ran his dick between my slick lips as he kissed me, capturing my gasp as he slid in, and I stretched to accommodate him.

"Reese!" I cried out.

"Good girl." Reese moved with me. "Just take it like you always do."

I clung to him, desperately trying to memorize every touch, every kiss, every inch of his skin against mine.

"*Yes.*" I hoped this temporary surrender would bring Reese peace when he saw me walk down the aisle. "Yes!"

Our bodies moved in a familiar, frantic rhythm. He repeated my name as I felt my body tighten, heat curling and building in my gut with each thrust as he fucked me with no mercy.

"*I love you,*" he murmured, repeating it like a chant. "You're under my skin, deep in my heart. I'll never let you go."

He will hate me forever for what I'm going to do.

Reese was so thick; I felt him everywhere, his thrust sloppy against me in his desperation, and I leaned back, moving his hair from his face.

"I love you," I allowed myself to say finally. I hated it was too late.

He played with my throbbing clit, shifting my leg over his shoulder. His intensity suffocated me, leaving me breathless. I touched his cheek and felt his steady spirit.

"Don't ever doubt how I feel about you," I whispered.

Reese leaned closer, slowing his strokes, but making sure to keep hitting my G-spot. My mind short-circuited as he brought us closer to the end. I panted heavily, lifting my hips, winding them in a circular motion as I came down to meet him.

"You gotta trust me. Trust the plan. Now cum for me. Only me."

It was sudden—almost violent. I screamed Reese's name and scratched at his suit, wishing I could leave marks on his skin. He came right after, crashing into me, and I savored his moans as we tried to catch our breath.

"You'll never get rid of me. I'm here." He placed a finger on my chest above my heart. "I'm in your heart, *forever*."

Someone knocked on the door.

CHAPTER 1

Laurene

PRESENT DAY—SIX YEARS LATER

"WELCOME BACK, MISS KING." She had a plastic smile, but her voice was cold and formal. She knew my name, *everyone* here did, but the way she said it made my skin prickle.

The flight from Paris was awful; leaving my little sanctuary only to return to… What? My mess?

Bags in hand, I stepped out of the jet.

The cold northern California air hit me like a wall, salty and familiar. There was a bone-chilling silence, like the world was holding its breath.

No crowd. No welcoming committee. No angry pitchforks or protesters, like I'd half expected.

All I heard was the hum of the engines slowing and my pulse thudding in my ears.

I was finally home.

"Mrs. King, we need to ask your daughter a few questions," the detective said.

The police station smelled like burnt coffee and mildew. My skin was damp, sticky with ocean water, motor oil, and sweat. The wool blanket wrapped around my shoulders scratched at my neck, but I clutched it tighter, trying to stop the shaking.

"You don't need to talk to my daughter!" Mama snapped. "You're

supposed to be helping us. But here you are, dragging us down here. I will be talking to the mayor about this shit. Her fiancé is hurt. We need to be at the hospital."

The overhead fluorescent lights buzzed. The chair beneath me was hard. My wet hair puffed at the ends and roots. My throat burned — either from the water I'd swallowed or the bile rising every time I thought about Conrad's body sailing over the railing, crashing against the rocks, then sinking into the dark water.

This wasn't our plan.

"I'm giving you the courtesy of being here because of your standing in this town." The detective barely looked at her, voice flat. "Your daughter is an adult."

"My daughter is a King. Our family built this fucking town you're paid to protect, and you will respect us."

Mama was beside me, her hand cold and tight against my wrist. Too tight. I tried not to flinch.

The detective pulled out a notepad and clicked his pen. "We have reason to believe there was a fight tonight. Between Conrad and Reese Ashbourne."

My stomach dropped.

I kept seeing it.

Reese's punch to Conrad's face. The way the waves slammed against the boat. The deck tilted. Conrad's voice slurred, twisted into something mean.

The snap of wood. The shattering of glass.

The splash.

"We also have witnesses placing Laurene with Reese before the crash."

Mama's fingers released me. I felt her staring at me. Hard. Sharp. Calculating.

"What are you implying? Conrad is her fiancé; she wouldn't be caught dead with his brother."

I couldn't look at her. I couldn't look at anyone.

"Miss King," the detective pressed, "was Reese involved in the fight that led to this?"

My head was pounding, a drumbeat that felt like it was splitting my skull in half.

"Are you asking me...if Reese killed—I mean...hurt h-his brother?"

Tell the truth. Let them dig. Let them find out everything.

Or—

"Laurene, tell him what he wants to hear, so we can go. You have nothing to hide," Mama sneered the words at the detective, then turned to me.

Even here, in this mess, she still needed me to be perfect. I had to be careful. I had to keep everything she'd built safe. My life wasn't just mine. What had I been thinking? That Reese and I were really gonna have a happily ever after?

Had I ruined everything? Had I ruined my family? King was my last name, but it was her legacy, her perfect image. The daughter who'd always been so good.

One answer would keep me safe.

Mama was watching me, her eyes pinning me in place, judging.

"They fought tonight." *The words slid out too easy. Like I wasn't setting Reese on fire and walking away.*

No! What are you doing, Laurene! Keep your mouth shut. Don't say a damn thing—

The detective's pen scratched against the paper as he scribbled something down. "Did Reese hurt Conrad?"

No. Reese protected me. We had a plan. It went horribly wrong.

I couldn't say that. If anyone in this town found out what I'd done—that I was sleeping with Reese, what we'd planned—Mama would be disgraced. Mama would disown me.

I could already hear the whispers, the headlines if the truth got out. Laurene King, the daughter of the powerful Yvonne King, destroyed over a hundred years of the King family's prized legacy here in Lush.

I'd be the tarnish. The black blip. The outcast.

Mama's image of me was everything. The town respected me.

Everyone wanted to be me. I couldn't lose that. If I crumbled, so did she. So did my sibling. So did our companies.

"Miss King," the detective said, his voice breaking through my thoughts.

I glanced at Mama. I could feel the anger and the fear radiating off her. She wanted me to protect us.

"Reese was jealous." I almost gagged on the words.

Mama inhaled sharply beside me.

Screams and shouts—the music cutting off as the speaker went over the edge. The sound of fists hitting skin. The boat rocking, a body slipping—

"Jealous of what?" the detective pushed, and I could feel his eyes drilling into me. He wasn't buying it.

The blanket around me suddenly felt too tight, too heavy. My head was pounding, and my nails were digging into my palms.

"Reese didn't want me with Conrad." I swallowed hard, my breath coming in short gasps. It was easier this way. Reese wasn't the victim here. He was the villain. I'd make him the villain.

"Why wouldn't Reese want you with Conrad?"

Don't do this, Laurene. Reese loves you. You love him. Stand up to your mother for once in your fucking pathetic, privileged life.

"Because Conrad was everything Reese couldn't be. He was always better than Reese—more successful, more liked. Reese couldn't stand it. He was...frustrated."

And just like that, I betrayed the love of my life.

Mama didn't say anything, but I could feel her relief. But she didn't know the truth. She didn't know my plan with Reese, and if she knew the truth of the relationship, this moment could have gone differently.

Mama stood abruptly. "Can we go now?"

I'd saved us. And I was still the perfect daughter.

The beach city of Lush stretched out before me like a postcard —too perfect, too idyllic. My hometown, the rich's last-kept secret. Tucked away in the cliffs, the place where my great-great...maybe seven times great-grandfather had made his mark.

Augustus King. The man who'd fled the Black Wall Street massacre with only scraps of his wealth.

And here I was, standing in the aftermath of everything that he had been built, that now my mother maintained. The Kings' history here was covered in blood and secrets and lies—mine included.

The memory of that night had been replaying nonstop in my brain for six years. The fucked-up truth of it I couldn't escape. I'd gotten exactly what I wanted. I remained the perfect, innocent King daughter. I'd secured my family's status and wealth. I didn't have to answer for betraying Conrad.

And then—before Reese could come after me, before he could demand answers or turn on me for what I had done—I ran.

I left for Paris, untouched by the fallout, while Reese was left to rot in the mess we'd created together.

But now I was back. In the distance was a stunning collection of pastel-colored mansions, beachfront villas, and low-rise condos, their smooth stucco walls warmed by the sun. The air vibrated with the sounds of seagulls and distant boat horns as luxurious yachts passed in the marina; the scent of grapes hung heavy in the air from the nearby vineyards.

The wind whipped my hair, carrying the scent of jet fuel as I surveyed the array of luxury cars—Rolls-Royces, Bentleys, and a couple of Ferraris—lined up by the hangar with my family's huge sign.

King Enterprises.

The empire we'd built. The empire I was a part of, for better or worse.

My grandfather's initial textile venture merged into a conglomerate sprawling across industries: real estate, luxury goods, media, tech startups. If it could be bought, built, or leveraged for power, we owned a piece of it.

There was a sleek black SUV sitting in front of the jet. A familiar figure leaned casually against the door. "Erik?"

"Wassup, Lulu."

I ran down the steps toward my big brother. The last one on my side. Erik stayed in touch, even when others didn't. All those late-night calls, the random check-ins. He always showed up when I needed him most, miles or oceans away.

He enveloped me in a bear hug and spun me around like we were kids again.

Erik, the oldest, ran King Crown Aviation, our company that built luxury planes for the rich, the famous, and, when needed, the government. He would inherit King Enterprises when Mama retired. It was the family tradition—the firstborn always inherits.

That didn't mean Mama didn't put the rest of us to work the moment she could.

Serena, the middle child after me by six years, ran King Developments.

It was our real estate company, and even though Serena had cut me off after I left, Erik had let me know she ran it ruthlessly.

Gigi, the baby of the family, was…well, Gigi. I'd spoken to her about a month ago. Now she decided she wanted to be a social media model.

"I've missed you!" I said between laughter. "Mama let you out the dungeon?"

"Somebody has to keep the empire running smoothly." He chuckled, and set me back down. "You know how she is. One wrong move or deal, and I'm up all night in meetings or worse, getting a lecture about 'letting the family down.'"

Yvonne King was tough on her good days, but hellish on her bad ones.

Erik was thirty-five now, two years older than me. He was taller, broader, his frame more solid than I remembered—but worn. A strong jaw, streaked with some gray hairs, told a different story. That stubble over his gleaming dark skin gave him a tough edge, but it couldn't hide the exhaustion lurking just beneath the surface.

Six years all alone dealing with Mama—I bet that had been tough on him.

"I was surprised when Mama said I needed to pick you up. You didn't say nothin' about coming back home. Since when was y'all choppin' it up again?"

I caught sight of a few staff members in crisp uniforms standing at a discreet distance. The gossip was probably already circling—*Laurene King, the runaway bride back in Lush like nothing had ever happened.*

"It was last-minute," I said, swallowing the bitter taste of the lie. It hadn't been last-minute at all. Everything in Paris had started to dry up—my gallery job was mysteriously gone. I was living paycheck to paycheck, barely scraping by. My apartment was too expensive.

It was like the universe—or Yvonne King—had conveniently shut every door until I had no choice but to come back to Lush.

Erik frowned. "Imma be honest, you might wanna rethink this. People ain't forgot what happened."

Being away made it crystal clear: I was done with this town. Their feelings weren't my problem anymore. What did I owe them? The same they'd given me. Nothing.

A sleek limo came speeding down the tarmac, skidding to a stop in front of us. My heart raced. Was it him? Did Reese know I was back?

"Fuck," Erik said under his breath.

A driver stepped out, smoothing his uniform before opening the back door to reveal Mama.

"What does Mama have planned? I know she didn't call me back here just 'cause she missed me. She's got something up her sleeve." I looked at Erik.

"She's...Mama. You know how she is. She wants you here because you're family."

"Bullshit. You know something, don't you?"

"Make the right choice, Lu."

I wasn't the same anymore. And this town—this family—

would never see the old Laurene again. I wasn't going back. Freedom felt too good.

"Laurene." Mama's hair, a deep, vibrant black, was perfectly silk-pressed, gleaming under the light, a testament to her stylist's skill—not a single gray hair in sight. She sashayed over in a sharp suit, pushing down her big sunglasses. "Glad you made it back in one piece. Did the new plane treat you well? Your brother designed it, I'm not sold on it."

Mama cut me off when I left. Totally. Not a word. No cash. No calls. Not even a damn messenger pigeon. Just silence. Like I didn't exist. For six years.

Out of nowhere, staff emerged to minister to my mother, swiftly collecting her bags and loading them onto the jet I just exited.

"Give us a minute, Erik," Mama commanded him.

He met my gaze, his eyes holding that old, reassuring look— a quick flick of his thumb across his nose, his way of saying he was on my side before he headed to the SUV.

"Are we going to talk business, or just pretend it's all fine?" I crossed my arms.

"I need to be in Palm Springs in an hour." Her voice was smooth as she flicked dirt from under her nails.

"Why am I here, Mama?"

"I can't want my daughter home?"

I was tired of the games. The schemes. I'd loved Paris, and here she was pulling me back into this shit.

"No. I have a life in Paris. Which is where I should be."

"Did you forget what happened?"

"You kicked me out."

"*You* decided to leave. It was your choice."

"A choice?" I scoffed. "You're gonna pretend like I really had one?"

The truth was such a twisted thing in this family. It could save or destroy you—and everyone had their own warped relationship with it.

"This new attitude, Laurene, you need to *fix* that."

I thinned my lips as Mama scowled and continued, "We will have this discussion later. Have your brother take you to the mansion and say hello to your father."

She pulled her purse higher on her shoulder, brushing past me to the jet and snapping at staff, "Handle those bags like they're worth more than your life. They're Hermès."

"Just tell me what you want so I can decide to stay or to go."

"I heard things weren't going well for you in Paris."

I narrowed my eyes on her, "You just 'heard' about that?"

She didn't look at me, but I caught the corner of her mouth twitching. "Everyone talks. I keep my ear to the ground, Laurene."

"Have Erik get me another jet back to Paris. I'm leaving."

I started to brush past Mama, but she grabbed my arm, spinning me around.

"Did you conveniently forget how you fucked us over? My reputation—*our* family's reputation—was dragged through the mud for years because of you. Not a scandal since we *founded* this town, and look what you did!"

"A life was lost, Mama. You can't just ignore that."

Conrad didn't deserve what happened. It wasn't a part of the plan.

There were so many things I needed to say to her. But I knew who I was dealing with, and she wouldn't give a damn. "Why did you call me home then? You want me in my old position?"

I had run King Investments, a small firm specializing in high-end art, luxury goods, and collectibles. I had a knack for numbers and an eye for art. I didn't get to run galleries or host exhibitions then, though, even though I'd wanted to. Mama just wanted me to find the overlooked gems and make them shine.

Erik told me Mama tried to find a replacement for me after I left. They weren't me. They couldn't be me. I was *great*, and everyone knew it.

Mama had shut the company down out of spite.

"I called you home because you have a place in this family and I'm feeling *generous*. I can send you back to Paris and try again in ten years, if you want? But by then you'll be living in a cardboard box outside of the Eiffel Tower."

When I left home, I didn't know where the hell I was going. No guarantees, no safety net—I just needed to escape everyone and everything. Paris was my chance for a fresh start.

Paris was rough at first. No family, no friends, nothing. The entire world seemed to be against me. I really needed money, and the art world, with all its power and pretentiousness, was my way back in.

I learned from Mama to rely on my old contacts from King Investments; they knew my family name but didn't treat me differently or shun me when Mama disowned me.

It also helped with the occasional emails from Daddy. He couldn't outright fight back against Mama, but he did text or email me to take a jog on the Seine. Or do some shopping around Galeries Lafayette Champs-Élysées. I always ran into some old clients—art dealers, curators, even some big-name collectors. It was easy to work as a freelance consultant for galleries, curating exhibits, and managing emerging artists.

The hours were long, the pay was low, but I built a reputation. And I would be damned if I lose everything I've worked for.

"What's the catch, Mama? What do you want me from me? Money? Ideas? I know last quarter was good. I reached out to Grandpa's old partners—"

"They turned their backs on us," Mama snapped. "Like hell I'll ask those traitors for anything ever again."

Next idea: give her what she wants.

"I'm prepared to be the CFO then. Bring back King Investments, teach whatever I know. Clean exchange."

That role wasn't what I ever wanted. It was quick, but I could see the blueprint she'd sketched out for me reappear in her eyes now.

Her eyes narrowed as if the very thought insulted her. "I've got the best of the best on my board, and you sure as hell ain't one of them."

Get messy, she loves dirt.

"I have valuable information," I said. "Secrets. People forgot you had a daughter in Paris. They talk when they think you're out of reach. Your partners, your enemies, even your friends."

"Secrets are dangerous. You sure you wanna do that again?" Her eyes didn't flicker, but I caught the slightest twitch in her brow.

"When haven't you been able to turn secrets into profit?"

Reese would hate this. He'd want me to fight back, escape it all. I was asking the very person who'd locked me in this cage to help me survive it.

But Paris taught me the harsh realities of survival. I battled to get what I wanted. I got good at seeing people's weaknesses and using that to my benefit. I became well-known, not only in Parisian art galleries, but also in the city's social scene. I got to know some powerful collectors; I helped them get access to the artists they wanted, and they promoted me.

I did well because I was good, not because of who I am. I made it on my own. People either loved or hated me, but everyone respected me. But I had my eyes on the prize. My own gallery. That was always my dream.

Till it got taken away.

She dug through her purse and pulled out a photo.

"What is this?"

It was a version of me I'd buried, smiling beside Conrad at my engagement party.

"It's part of our family's history," she said. "You can't run from your past, no matter how much you try to bury it."

My gaze shifted to the figure next to Conrad in the photo: *Reese*. His face was grim, unlike our fake smiles.

Mama snapped her fingers and all the staff disappeared.

"When I took on this role after your grandpa Ben," she

began, her voice cold, "I expanded this empire—*not* for me, Laurene, but for you, for your siblings, for our legacy. Every decision, every sacrifice I made, was not for you to throw it all away on your petty little *feelings*. You think I stifled you, but I wanted you to *thrive*. I wanted you to have the choices I never had."

I figured I could outrun the guilt, but it just got worse.

"Love's complicated. It ain't always soft. Sometimes it means pushing you to be better, even if it hurts. Despite all this, I do love you."

I took a peek at the engagement photo. I'd put duty before love, and it had messed everything up.

"You are here to remind this town why the Kings are indispensable. We made this fucking town, and our mayor, Dante is forgetting it. People are now threatening that."

"How is our power being threatened?"

"He's bringing in outsiders, cutting us out of deals, making the economy less family-dominated. He and others are trying to erase the past. Erase *us*. I will not let that happen. Augustus King's legacy will remain intact."

"And why would they trust *me*?"

She smirked, but it didn't reach her eyes. "You're my *daughter*. That still carries weight. Serena doesn't have the same… charm as you do to help me with this. It requires finesse."

"What do I get out of helping you?"

Mama's smirk deepened. "The money your grandfather left. It's all yours once you've proven you can still deliver."

I stiffened. When I left, Mama all but scrubbed me from the family's websites, boards, and social connections. The money I had saved wasn't a fraction that was left in my trust.

That money could fix everything for me. It could finally get me the gallery I'd been saving and working for.

"Deliver what?"

"I need you to get close to Dante. Make him trust you. Find out who he's working with, what he's planning—where he's vulnerable," she said simply. "I taught you to be the best, and only you can do this for me, Laurene."

She paced in front of me.

"He won't talk to me. I need to stay ahead of Dante. So, our only option is the Ashbournes," Mama said sullenly, as if the words themselves left a bad taste in her mouth.

I stared at her. "The Ashbournes? You're telling me we need to team up with them? Again?" I scoffed. "You've hated them for decades."

She didn't flinch. "I hate them, but right now, they're the only ones who can help us. Dante's carving up our territory—securing votes, locking in contracts, flipping our allies. The Ashbournes have connections we don't. Leverage we need."

"We've got to cozy up to the Ashbournes to fend off Dante?"

Mama waved her hand dismissively. "Harold Ashbourne's old, but he's not blind. He sees the writing on the wall."

My chest tightened. "The Ashbournes, the very people who'd love to see us fall. What's next, you want to make a deal with the devil himself?"

She shot me a cold glance, her lips curling into a tight smile. "Sometimes, Laurene, you've got to make the devil your ally. Harold's greed makes him territorial, but even he knows this is no longer a one-family game. If we fall, they fall next."

"Desperation doesn't look good on you, Mama."

What the hell had happened to Lush?

"Why can't Serena help you with this takeover plan? Are you —" Realization hit me. "You're asking me to—"

"You will honor the arrangement with Conrad."

Ice ran through my body. "He's *dead*."

"Yes," she said, "but the contract still stands."

"Who am I marrying?" I said slowly, the hairs on the back of my neck standing up. *Please, please no.*

"You'll marry the brother."

The brother.

The man I once loved, the man I trusted, the man who was

now my enemy. And she expected me to walk down the aisle with him?

"I can't marry him. You can't ask me to do this. Not with him. Not now. Not ever."

"You'll do it, Laurene," Mama said. "There's no 'can't.' You'll marry Reese. Blood and marriage makes us stronger. And Harold won't fuck us over if he can lose something too."

"I don't love him." I forced the lie out, and I felt my heart pulse in pain as I said it.

"Love is a *luxury*."

"There's other ways—"

"No."

"Then let's talk parameters. How long do I have to stay married to him?"

"We need to stick together long enough to make our alliances strong and show everyone how solid we are. And until I see if Dante is a friend or foe."

"One year?" I asked, trying to find some leverage. "Two?"

Her gaze remained icy. "Three years, minimum. I would prefer five. Any less, and it will look like a failure on both our parts. During this time, you are to live together publicly and privately. Separate lives are unacceptable."

"Five years?" I looked at her like she had fully lost it. "I'm not putting my life on hold for five years." I had plans. Things to accomplish. "Can we divorce after that?"

"Divorce and annulment will be a family decision."

I glared at her. "I'm forced into this marriage, and it's up to the *family* if I can divorce after? What if I'm miserable?"

"This family's needs come before your happiness. Remember, you have nothing in Paris anymore."

"And what about children?" I was scared to asked.

"Within the first two years," Mama stated. "You are to produce at least one heir. This is non-negotiable."

"You can't *force* me to have a child."

Her lips curled into a faint, humorless smile. "You misunderstand. I'm not forcing you, Laurene. I'm giving you a *choice*. You can have everything your grandfather intended for you, or you can walk away with nothing."

"This is my *life*."

"You don't have a pot to piss in or a window to throw it out. You will marry Reese, and you will fulfill your duty. Any concessions I grant are mere courtesies, not rights."

"And what about Reese? What if he refuses?" I asked, hoping that he might be the way out of this madness.

Her smile faded. "Reese will do as he's told. Harold made sure of it."

"And if he cheats?" That idea made me feel like someone punched me in the gut. Reese with another woman was not something I wanted to imagine.

Her eyes hardened. "Publicly, you will stand by him. There will be no scandals, no fractures in the alliance. Discretion is everything, or you'll both suffer."

"If I don't agree?" My voice faltered, but I steadied myself. "What if I just walk away? What will you do?"

Her smile turned predatory, the kind I'd seen before when she dismantled a competitor or crushed an opponent.

"That little life you built in Paris? It's already gone. Your apartment? Gone. Your bank account? Cleared. I've made sure of it. And as for your inheritance, the future you think you have waiting for you? You don't have one unless you play this game."

Mama snapped her fingers, and the staff quickly returned to their positions, their faces as neutral as stone.

"We all got a role to play in this family." Her voice dripped with condescension. "Time to step up. How you handle it? That's on you, but I know you'll figure it out. Stop all that whining. Toughen up."

She turned, her heels clicking sharply against the pavement, then paused and glanced back over her shoulder.

"Oh, before I forget."

Mama pulled a gold-embossed envelope from her purse, its

gleam almost mocking the harsh sunlight. With a sense of dread tightening in my chest, I took it from her hands, fingers trembling as I opened it.

Mr. and Mrs. Vincent King and Mr. and Mrs. Harold Ashbourne request the pleasure of your company at the marriage of their children:
Laurene Elizabeth King and Reese Christopher Ashbourne

A wedding invitation.
My wedding.
Scheduled for next month.
"We can't forget to invite the bride, can we?"

CHAPTER 2
Reese

"WE'VE GOT a potential game-changer with a ranch for sale in Fresno County."

"A ranch, huh?" I swirled my whiskey. Sunlight poured in, making the distillery grounds look golden and warm—a stark contrast to the business meeting in front of me.

Nathan dropped a file onto the table. "It's got the water rights we need. Plus, we could grow our own spices and botanicals quicker. Cuts down on supplier costs, gives us more control over the flavors."

"Water rights. That's something." I glanced at the file.

This business, this legacy, belonged to me now.

When Conrad first invited me into the business, I was suspicious. He never did anything without an angle, never offered something without expecting a bigger return. But against my better judgment, I said yes. And for a while, I actually liked it. Working at the distillery gave me purpose, something real. Something that wasn't just fighting to prove myself. Now it was the only thing I had control over in my life.

Six years. Six *goddamn* years since she'd walked away, and I still felt the loss like a punch to the gut.

Despite everyone in town hating me, Ashbourne Distilleries,

the west coast's largest liquor manufacturer, was mine. I had a few other ventures to my name—clubs in Las Vegas, Miami, and LA, each a testament to the Ashbourne flair for luxury and entertainment.

Bottles of rare whiskey shone on the glass shelf in front of me, representing our family's success. What I rebuilt in the rubble. Older members on the board had said I was reckless, too aggressive with expansion. But numbers didn't lie—production was up, profits were climbing, and every gamble I took paid off.

Still, my father and his cronies wanted to claw back control, drag things to how they used to be. Even with all my awards, I still couldn't outrun her.

"We're looking at a return immediately if we buy it."

My mind drifted. Fists flying, his grunts—he fought like hell, but so did I. Blood mixed with salt water in my mouth, the weight of Conrad's body as I dragged him onto the shore.

"Reese?" Nathan's voice yanked me back. "What's your take?"

I took a sip from the glass, feeling the burn. I'd just sunk a small fortune into importing a rare South American herb. I thought it would make or break our next release.

I needed more. More money. More success. More…*everything.*

"This ranch? They'll sell. Desperation breeds compliance."

Desperation had turned me into this—a man consumed by anger, hellbent on revenge, willing to destroy anything in my path to get back what was taken from me.

"Another win. That's what we need," I said, more to myself than anyone else. "Get me the ranch."

My mind was already whirling with what we could do with that property. After Conrad's death and our parents' retreat into their bubble of grief, my older sister, Jennie, and I took the reins, dragging the Ashbourne legacy kicking and screaming back to the top.

Jennie and I built beyond the bottle. Resorts and hotels, high-end fashion boutiques, a chain of gourmet restaurants. An empire so powerful it'd make the Kings *tremble*.

"We market the hell out of our sustainability angle on this new liquor line. Capitalize. More money for us."

The room buzzed with voices, but all I could hear was the thudding of my own thoughts, each one centered on getting back at the Kings, this town, my own damn family.

I fucking saved him. Pulled his lifeless body onto the shore, while everyone looked at me like I was a murderer.

"This isn't the way we do things. It's not tradition," Bernard, one of Dad's supporters, said, but I didn't care. My fingers fumbled in my suit jacket, searching for the case. I'd quit smoking years ago—for her—but that Reese was gone the moment Laurene deserted me.

If I had died that night instead of Conrad, would she have shed a single fucking tear? Would anyone have cared?

"Let's get one thing straight," I said. "I'm not running this company into the ground just so we can cling to the same product line that stopped working before Y2K."

I lit the cigarette, inhaling deeply, feeling the burn in my lungs like a small reprieve from the fury building inside me. First, I'd wipe out the Kings. Would Laurene regret it then?

I should've let her drown in her own lies. Instead, I took the fall, even when it'd been ruled an accident, the town didn't care while she walked away clean. But every now and then, the memory of her laugh crept in—the way we were before everything fell apart. I hope the guilt eats her alive. I hope it fucking rots her.

Bernard adjusted his tie. The man had been in this company longer than I'd been alive, and he wore his resistance like a badge of honor. "Reese, these old strategies sustained us for decades. Your father—"

"My father," I cut in, "also believed in fax machines and filing cabinets. Times change. So do strategies."

Bernard cleared his throat. "We need to show some loyalty, *some integrity.*"

That meant nothing. Not after all I'd lost.

"Loyalty and integrity?" I scoffed. "Money's what makes the world spin."

Laurene taught me that when she vanished. And Dad? He never gave a damn about integrity. Despite not being his first or second choice, I'm the one who picked up the pieces and turned this company around. But he'll never fucking admit it.

"Conrad had solid plans for this company—"

"But he's not here, is he?"

Bernard blinked and paled. "Conrad's strategies stand the test of time."

"I'm not sticking to a six-year-old plan." My ideas he had stolen. "Conrad's six feet in the fucking ground."

Laurene had thrown me under the fucking bus. I should've seen it coming. Should've known Laurene King would save her own ass before she ever thought about mine.

"Your time here is up, Bernard."

"Wait, what?" Bernard recoiled so hard he damn near snapped his neck.

"You're no longer working for Ashbourne Distilleries." I leaned back, watching the color drain from his face. "No room for people stuck in the past with a dead man. Pack your shit."

"I've been here for thirty years!"

"And that's exactly the problem." I exhaled smoke. "I'm running this company *my way.* Change is non-negotiable. Get out."

The room was deathly quiet, all eyes on Bernard.

"Get the fuck out!" I slammed my hand against the table. *Calm down. Don't fly off the handle, you're trying to change their opinions of you.*

Bernard's hands trembled as he struggled with his things. He stormed out, the door slamming.

"Everyone in this room needs to believe in me and in the vision. If you're here clinging to the past, don't bother staying. But if you're ready to work, we've got plenty to do. Now get me that ranch." I stared down the table.

They all rose. But then the office door swung open, and my father stood in the doorway.

"Well, well. Look who finally decided to show up. No one had to drag your sorry ass out of a bar?" I clenched my jaw as the staff filed out, leaving us to one of our typical yelling matches. "What do you want? I need to get to the airport for Germany," I said, putting out my cigarette.

"You're staying."

I raised an eyebrow. "Who's stopping me?"

"Don't test me, boy," Dad said, cool as ever, heading straight for the bar cart in the room.

"Where's Jennie to drop off this little message, like always?" I shot back. "Trying to play father of the year again?"

I communicated with my dad as little as possible. Fuck him. I ensured the success of this company for the past six years without his approval.

"I didn't spend decades building this company just to watch you burn it down because you're too proud to listen to advice of people like Bernard."

"Advice?" I let out a sharp, humorless laugh. "You mean sabotage. Don't think I don't see through your henchmen trying to pull strings."

"If I were pulling strings, you wouldn't be sitting in that chair."

"I took over because you bailed," I snapped. "Don't pretend you gave me control because you had some big plan. I'm cleaning up thirty-year-old messes."

Dad's fingers tightened around the liquor bottle.

"Think you can do better?" I continued. "Then do it. Take the title back. Hell, I'll clear out my desk today."

"You think I wanted to step down, boy?" His voice was dangerous. "Someone had to fall on the sword after what you *did*, and I took the hit so this family could keep its name and Yvonne King didn't swoop in on us!"

I barked a laugh, bitter and sharp. "Oh, you're a martyr now? Spare me the sob fucking story."

Dad walked over, two glasses in hand, sliding one across the table.

"There's a party tonight. You'll be there."

"Why?" I used to admire him—now I saw the monster beneath the mask. "I run the company, make us money. You stay out of my way. That's the deal."

"I've watched your absurd escapades for the last six years, Reese. Yes, you made us some money, but what about the other bullshit you've done?" He took a sip of his drink. "Aspen for the X Games, skydiving in Sydney, traipsing through the Amazon. For what?"

"Expanding our global presence," I shot back.

Dad sneered. "Did you know we have a hostile fucking takeover at our door?"

That made me pause.

"What are you talking about? We have more money than we can wipe our asses with."

"Your sister, chasing after deals she can't close, and you—" He paused. "You're no Conrad."

Conrad. Always fucking Conrad.

Conrad, the homecoming king, prom king, captain of the football team. Not like me. He could shake hands with investors, charm their wives, and still make it to Sunday dinner without a hair out of place.

He made it look so easy. Too easy.

"We can't afford another setback." Dad's tone was quieter but no less stern.

I reached for the cigarettes, giving in to the need.

"Those are bad for your health."

"You're bad for my health," I deadpanned, lighting the cigarette and taking another slow drag.

His scowl deepened. "Times are changing, Reese. The town's changing. We're being pushed out, and you don't even see it."

"Pushed out of what?" I leaned forward. "The country club newsletter? The charity circuit?"

"That's the kind of thinking that'll get us buried," he snapped, his voice low and venomous. "Dante Castillo. Yvonne won't tell me the truth, but that bastard... I saw him in LA talking to Jonathan Rhodes. And what happens months later? New developments, new money pouring in, renovations left and right. And we're not part of that deal? You don't find that suspicious?"

I shook my head. "Some celebrities, influencers, and a few techies move into town. It's nothing to lose your mind over."

"This town was built on *legacy*. And now it's being whored out to the highest bidder. These new types are flashy, crass, and reckless. They're parasites, feeding off what families like ours created. Soon Lush will be..." Dad's gaze fixed on the glass in his hand. "It'll be like Monte Carlo when the cruise ships dock. So, Yvonne and I agreed. The deal is reinstated."

"What deal?"

He smiled. "You're marrying Laurene King."

I blinked slowly and shook my head. "No."

"You are." He took a measured sip of his drink, savoring it. "You should be grateful. You don't see the way Yvonne's scrambling, how desperate she is. She's hiding something—something big. We're gonna find out what. The Kings have ruled over Lush for long enough. It's our turn now."

"Laurene left, remember? We don't even know where she is."

"She's back."

The room seemed to tilt.

The one woman I wasn't supposed to have. But still, I

remembered our secret moments: how she whispered my name, the sensation of her nails scratching down my spine, and the sight of her eyes rolling in ecstasy as I brought her to the edge.

"She was your brother's fiancée, but arranged marriages are simple. No emotions involved."

No emotions? I almost laughed. Her engagement to my brother had just been another chapter in the blood feud that defined this town. The Kings and Ashbournes didn't collaborate; we warred.

"After what she accused me of? You want me to marry her?"

He let the silence stretch just long enough for my pulse to throb in my ears.

Heat crawled up my spine. "You think I wanted that fight? That I wanted my brother"—my throat burned—"dead?"

"I think," Harold said, slow, deliberate, "you let your jealousy do the thinking for you. And that cost *my* son his life." He set his glass down with a sharp clink. "And what did it cost you, Reese? Nothing."

I forget the specifics, but the town was practically built on our family's feud—starting with Augustus King and Reginald Ashbourne, two ambitious men who turned from allies to enemies overnight. A broken deal and a bruised ego were all it took to light a fire that burned for generations of espionage, sabotage, and lies. Then Reginald killed Augustus during a brawl in a warehouse fire.

Accident or not, it didn't matter. There's been no love lost between our families since.

"This is my life!" I surged to my feet, the chair scraping loudly against the floor. "I can't marry her. How am I supposed to stand at the end of an aisle pretending like she didn't kill my brother?"

Dad shot up from his seat. "*You* killed your brother!"

Everything was always Conrad, Conrad, Conrad.

No one spotted the cracks. No one talked about the way Conrad always expected the world to bend to him, or how he'd tear anyone down who didn't worship him the same way everyone else did. He used his charm and smile to get his way, and anyone who didn't cooperate was simply removed.

"It's your duty," my father said. Cold. Final.

"I will never marry Laurene," I spat. "I'd rather die."

"You'll be there." He straightened his suit jacket. "You have no *choice*. Yvonne and I discussed it. Teaming up is the best way to ensure tradition survives."

I crushed the lit cigarette in my hand, the ember burning my skin. The thought of facing Laurene again—hearing her voice, breathing in her jasmine scent, feeling her soft touch—made my heart race. Had she changed her scent over the years?

"Be there tonight," Dad said, looking at his watch. "You'll be there, and you'll conduct yourself accordingly."

I got closer and glared at him.

"If you turn this marriage down. I won't just cut you off from the family business. I'll ruin you. Your name will mean *shit*, you hear me? I'll make sure you're blacklisted across this entire industry," Dad snarled.

My stomach twisted. My new liquor line was too close to being released to get nixed now. "You already did that, old man, when I was born into this fucked-up family."

That smile wasn't fatherly; it was predatory.

"Oh, I haven't even started yet. If you walk away from this marriage, I'll make sure you lose everything. Every connection, every deal, every partner you've ever worked with will turn their backs on you. Your new liquor lines? Gone. I'll make sure they're thrown off every distributor's shelf, pulled from every bar, and you'll be left begging for scraps."

He paused, letting the words hang in the air, savoring my discomfort.

"And I'll leverage every ounce of support I have in the company to make sure you're fired. You'll be a pariah in this industry, Reese."

He threw a gold-embossed envelope onto the table and headed for the door.

"Wear a damn tux."

I stared at the envelope, grabbed it, and ripped it open. Inside was an invitation to my own wedding.

Fuck.

CHAPTER 3

Laurene

THE SOFT HUM of the party below seeped through the bedroom walls.

The room felt suffocating. High ceilings, ornate walls painted in golds and creams, trapping me in memories I couldn't escape. The clutter from my teenage years still lingered—silk sheets, stuffed animals, curling band posters, an old life that seemed so far removed.

I opened the vanity drawer, my hand shaking. It creaked open, revealing old notes and keepsakes. Stuff I thought Mama would have gone through and thrown out.

But it was there…

Reese and me.

I was pressed against him in the photo, but it was the way he looked at me—intense and tender—that hit me.

What was I thinking? I wasn't thinking. I'd been in love with the town's bad boy. Defying my family by sleeping with the enemy had been thrilling then. But now Mama had me backed into a corner.

She always won. I checked. She'd been right.

I had no money. No apartment in Paris anymore. None of my old contacts were calling me back.

Fuck.

I was stuck.

I stormed down the hall, the heavy sound of Mama's shrill voice cutting through the walls. "Laurene!"

My heart pounded like a drumbeat, a cacophony of dread and anger as my heels clicked against the hardwood floors. Making us go to a charity event when Conrad was still in the hospital? The fake smiles, the condolences, the press.

I slammed my bedroom door shut behind me, rushing to my vanity. Oh God. What if Conrad died?

I gripped the edge of the vanity, staring at my reflection in the mirror. My eyes were red, mascara smeared. Reese.

We exchanged words earlier. Ugly words. Ones I couldn't take back. But he looked at me now like I was horseshit on the bottom of his shoe... And I deserved it. Maybe Mama was right. Reese was right. I was just like everyone else. Cold. A fucking heartless machine.

"Lu! Where the hell are you going?" Gigi stumbled in after. Tears welled up in her big brown eyes, and her lip trembled like she was about to cry again.

"Hold the door so she can't get in." I didn't have time for self-pity. Not now.

She hesitated, like she wanted to argue, but then she scrambled to the door.

I ripped open my closet and yanked out a suitcase. Only the essentials. I didn't even know where the hell I was going. All I knew was that I had to be light.

"You're leaving me?" Gigi's voice broke. It wasn't just about me. It was always about me. It was time for someone else to be the favorite.

"Yeah, I'm leaving you," Not caring how it sounded. "You'll be fine. You always are. I'm the one who has to figure this shit out." I slammed the suitcase closed.

"Please, Laurene..."

Everything's a disaster.

I took Gigi's hands. "I...I need to go. I can't be here right now but don't you worry. You are strong. You always have been. I sometimes wish I was more like you, G. Don't let anyone make you feel small. Not Mama. Not me. Not anyone. You've got everything you need inside you, and you can survive this. I'll be back before you know it."

And then I heard it—the sound of heavy footsteps thudding up the stairs.

I let her go.

"Don't go," she whimpered. "Mama—"

The door flew open, but I was already moving past her.

"What the hell do you think you're doing?" Mama's voice was cold, but underneath it was something else—something that made me want to cower and fight at the same time.

"Leaving," I said flatly without looking at her.

I hurried down the hall, her footsteps right behind mine, and I felt her grip my hand and spin me around.

"You think you can just walk away from this?" She shook me slightly. "I've spent years shaping you into something useful, and this is how you repay me? You made the family look weak."

I looked behind her to see Daddy coming up the stairs, frantic.

"I'm not your fucking puppet, Mama," I said through gritted teeth.

Her grip tightened, her nails digging into my skin. The look in her eyes—pure fury and disappointment stung more than I expected.

"We're living in your bullshit! You fucked up. You were supposed to marry Conrad, and the boy is in a fucking coma!"

"I didn't ask him to fight his brother!"

"I know you had something to do with it," Mama hissed. "Was that your plan all along? Make these brothers fight and you got out of this deal? Even when you know what—"

"You mean what it means for you! For the company!" I screamed back.

"You need to see this through," she spat. "You leave now, and there's no coming back. Do you hear me, Laurene? If I gotta fix this, you get nothing!"

I should've been afraid. For so long, she'd held everything over me —her approval, her money, the life she'd built like a gilded cage. But I felt nothing but exhaustion.

I wrenched free.

"Then clean it up," I said, my voice steady.

No. Panic was useless. I wasn't some fragile, wide-eyed girl anymore, and I wasn't here to beg. Mama thought she had me backed into a corner. She thought stripping me of my choices would make me obedient.

But she'd underestimated me.

I'd spent six years in Paris learning how to bend the world to *my* will.

This was just another game, and I was gonna play it.

I'd learned one thing from watching her all these years: people's fears made them weak.

And she feared Dante. I didn't know all the details, but I didn't need to.

She wanted me to get close to Dante? I would...but for myself.

I barely had time to shove the photograph into the drawer when a knock came. The door swung open, and there stood Noelle.

"I came as soon as I could," she said, her warmth filling the room. "Why is there a party going on?"

Erik's calls weren't my only lifeline. Noelle had been my best friend since we were kids and she sat next to me in elementary school, talking to me like we were old friends. She'd been the best friend I could have ever asked for. She called. She'd listen to me rant, cry, and lament. She gave me money when I first needed it. She never turned her back on me. She'd been more of a sister than my actual ones.

"I half expected to find you on a plane back to Paris by now."

Unsure of how to start, I deflected, glancing at her gown. "Is this a first for you?"

"What? This little old thing?" Noelle's rich, tawny-brown complexion deepened.

Noelle was biracial—Black and white—but that's all she knew. Adopted by the McKenzies, she'd grown from the scrawny kid struggling to find her place to the beautiful woman in front of me. The dress shimmered, iridescent green sequins catching the light as if they were made for a spotlight. The surplice neckline emphasized her shoulders, the fitted bodice hugged her curves perfectly, and that thigh-high slit? It was bold —seductive in a way.

"Erik must be losing his mind," I said.

"If he is, it's his problem, not mine."

I saw through their act. Erik's distance made sense to me. Mama had planned his future. He stayed away from Noelle to avoid the mess when Mama's arranged marriages happened.

"I'm staying out of it."

Noelle ran a hand over her gown. "Good call. So, good news, right? C'mon, tell me."

"Uh, well…" The scent of roses couldn't hide the tension hanging in the air. "The party downstairs is my engagement party."

"Engagement!"

"Yeah, can you believe it?" I tried to keep the edge out of my voice, but the bitterness slipped through.

"Who are you marrying?"

"Reese."

Her hand flew to her mouth to stop a gasp, and she stumbled back and sat on the edge of my bed. "You're marrying *Reese*? Um, this is, uh… Have you spoken with him since…"

"Not since that night." The night I'd let him take the fall without a second thought. "Mama made it clear that if I don't marry Reese, I won't get my inheritance. She sabotaged every-thing for me in Paris."

Noelle's face lit up, determined. "Alright then. We're going to fix this. This is just a problem to solve."

Her words helped, but also made things worse. A part of me wanted to say fuck it and walk away. But there was always that voice in my head, the one I've been trained to listen to. *Duty. Legacy.*

But if I was going to escape that voice, I needed ten million dollars. That was the price of freedom. That was what I needed to start my gallery.

A sharp knock shattered the silence, followed by the door opening.

My younger sister Serena. I hadn't expected her, but here she was, just like before—impossible to ignore, impossible to love or hate completely. She was twenty-eight now. Dark, velvety skin, flawless as ever, her bob sharp. Always so poised, so damn certain.

"Everyone's waiting for you downstairs."

I opened my mouth to respond, but the words never came. She never had to wrestle with herself when it came to Mama; she knew exactly what would please her, and she'd give it without hesitation.

"Are you coming downstairs or not? What should I tell Mama?"

Noelle shot a glance between us, her eyes flicking back and forth. "She needs a moment, Rena."

"A moment?" Serena pursed her lips. "Or are we going to have a repeat of the last time, when she made a grand escape?"

I exhaled slowly. "I'm here now."

"People are starting to ask questions. Mama doesn't like that."

She turned, her back straight, her exit a dismissal.

"Just follow your heart, alright? No need to stress. It'll all work out." Noelle pulled me into another tight hug. "We gotta have a girls' day. Café L'Amour for brunch. Just us four—you, me, Serena, and Gigi. Like old times?" she murmured.

I barely heard Noelle's voice as we left my room and walked toward the stairs. The hallway went on forever, and each step felt harder than the one before. The walls felt like they were closing in on me; the air was heavy and hard to breathe. After six years, I'd be seen again. Nausea hit me.

I gripped the polished railing, knuckles white, my breath

shallow. The chandelier overhead glittered too bright, its crystals catching the light in a way that made my vision spin.

The moment we reached the first floor, noise slammed into me—music, chatter, glasses clinking.

I cannot be having a panic attack right now. I don't have fear. I prepared for this, damn it, and I can get through it.

I tried to focus on the art adorning the walls, but everything around me pulsed.

"Noelle." A cold sweat broke out across my skin. "I...I need air."

She glanced at me. "What? Are you—"

"I need to get outside." Without another word, I yanked at the hem of my gown and darted down the hall toward the back patio.

The doors flew open, and the chilly night air hit me hard. I leaned against the wall, my fingers shaking as they pressed against my flushed cheeks, eyes closed tight, just trying to breathe. The noise faded away to nothing but rustling leaves and distant waves.

I pushed off the wall, my steps more deliberate. My old garden. The one Daddy planted for me.

I thought Mama would have gotten rid of everything that reminded her of me. I never expected it to remain intact. Sitting on the bench, I let the scent of the roses surround me, but it was smoke that hit—strong, pungent.

Reese.

I saw his cigarette brighten, then fade. A dark shape, shifting against the quiet night, came from the shadows.

I could feel his eyes on me, steady and intense.

"Laurene." The man who had once held my heart in his hands, like he knew he'd own it forever. "You're back."

CHAPTER 4

Laurene

"YEAH," I whispered, eyes locked on his. "I'm back."

He didn't just occupy the space; he *owned* it. His energy… *Fuck*. It was wild, untamed, like a storm brewing in the distance, ready to tear through everything.

"Didn't think I'd see you here again."

"Neither did I," I said.

God help me.

His eyes, blazing green, cut right through me. Pure rage, and something way worse that made my pulse jump.

Time had sculpted him into something raw and devastatingly destructive. His sun-kissed skin, richer and warmer than I remembered. Dark waves of hair, tousled and unruly. And those lips… The same lips that used to whisper my name like a prayer.

I hated him. But the ache between my legs didn't give a damn.

Reese started pacing slowly, hands in pockets, a cigarette dangling from his lips. I couldn't look at him, so I stared at everything else—the garden, the bench, the dirt, even the stars.

"You're smoking again?"

"I'm smoking."

I could almost taste that night before the engagement party.

The back seat of his Mustang, the scent of salt air mixing with the leather, the hum of his engine as his arm pulled me closer. My fingers traced circles on his bare chest.

"It's stopping me from wringing your fucking neck."

My heart skipped a beat, but there was no way in hell I was going to show any weakness. Instead, my eyes locked on his, and for a moment, I forgot everything else—everything we'd been through. All I saw was the man who had wrecked me, the man who had damn near destroyed me, the man who made me betray my family for his love, the man whose love I then betrayed for my family.

And still, I wanted him. Bad.

I wanted to drag him back to that fire we burned in before, back to the madness, the raw need. Rip him open with my mouth and tongue until we both bled from the inside out. I wanted to make him feel what he did to me—the way he burned me, the way he left me to rot.

And I had no fucking idea what to do with all of that.

"You haven't changed." I kept my face devoid of any emotion.

His lips twisted in a faint, almost mocking smile, as though he knew exactly what I was trying to do.

"I don't think I've ever been good at that," he muttered. Then, after a long moment, he added, "But you? You've changed."

"I know this isn't the...ideal circumstance to meet again." I straightened. "I didn't come back to play games."

"You fucked me over, and now, after six years, you just show up?" His voice shook, raw with something dark and dangerous. "You turned on me. We were supposed to leave together. Ran out on our plan like I was nothing—"

"It was *our* plan, Reese. You were in on it too."

"I know you, baby." His hand shot out, gripping my wrist—not hard, but enough to keep me there. "Six years is a long time to disappear, and I know you have something up your sleeve.

Come to finish the job? See your handiwork? Want to take the last fucking dime from me?"

"I didn't come here for *you*," I snapped, snatching my arm from wrist away. "Don't get flattered."

"Is that right?" He was getting too close, and damn it, my body was betraying me.

"Let's… I just… Before we go into that room full of people and pretend that we're both happy with this."

Four hours of staring at my bedroom ceiling hadn't been wasted. I'd come up with a plan.

"We're going to be married." My words tasted like ash, yet my voice remained cold. "Maybe we can make the best of it. Together—"

"No fucking way. I don't want a damn thing to do with you."

I didn't need his trust yet. Trust was earned, but belief? That could be engineered. If I turned his hate for this marriage into something useful, he'd go along with it. Clueless.

"Let's keep this professional. This is business."

The plan wasn't complicated, but it required finesse. Marry him—there was no getting out of that. Post-wedding, he was unnecessary. We'd have completely separate lives from day one— no shared bank accounts, no plans together. Reese had done well for himself over the years; I'd followed the news. I did need to stay with him for a certain length of time. California law would handle the rest. If I convinced him to agree to no prenup, then in the end, half of his wealth would be mine, along with my inheritance.

All money was good money, and I needed lots of it.

Then, when I had my inheritance and half from him, the first thing I'd do was get the hell out of this town. Disappear. Maybe fly to Switzerland and stash the money where Mama couldn't find it and Reese couldn't follow. It would be the biggest come up for me.

"We're just going to treat this as business?" Reese's voice cracked. "After everything between us?"

"We both know what's at stake now."

You don't love him anymore. Your emotions don't matter. All that matters is your money.

"Is that the same conversation you had with Conrad?" He flicked his cigarette into my roses.

"Let's keep it simple," I said. "You don't want to marry me, and I get it. There's a way for both of us to get what we want without turning this into a war."

Reese only stared at me. I didn't have money, but he didn't know that.

"When our parents check in, just say we're following the rules. We can lie. We've done it before. You don't want to live with me. I'll make it worth your while—monthly payments, upfront, no drama. You play along, and eventually you walk away with money you didn't expect."

"You think I'd just roll over for some cash?" Reese looked at me in disgust.

"I'm not asking you to love me." *Again. Love me again.* "I'm trying to find a solution that benefits both of us. We were *friends* once."

"I also fucked you in the back seat of my car once, but that means shit now, doesn't it?"

"Don't be petty." I shook my head. "We both know how this world can chew us up and spit us out. You think I'm asking you to play the good guy and sacrifice for my sake? Hell no. I'm asking you to do what's in your best interest."

I didn't have a leg to stand on, and I was praying he didn't bluff me out.

Reese flashed me a look of disdain. "Is that what you and Conrad secretly planned? Keep it strictly business? Marry the good son, but fuck the bad one? Did you not give a damn that the man who loved you would have had to watch from a distance while you married someone else? Never again able to touch you? Love you?"

My breath hitched. I forced myself to hold his gaze, but the cracks were already forming.

I was trying to protect both of us.

"Wow," he muttered, shaking his head. "How did I not see it before? You don't give a fuck. None of your family cares for anyone but themselves."

What if I had chosen differently? What if I had been brave enough to fight for us instead of running away?

"C'mon, Reese, it's not a hard choice."

Then, without warning, he was on me. At first, panic surged through my veins, but then—just as quickly—something else ignited. His fingers brushed my cheek, a soft touch, but the heat of it spread like fire, and for a second, I felt exposed in a way I couldn't explain.

"Every time I look at you, I'm torn," he murmured. "I hate you. But I can't shut off what I feel. I guess that's my flaw, huh?"

My heart pounded; it felt like hell not responding.

"I have a plan for *you*, Laurene."

I tensed, recoiling inwardly.

"You'll play the perfect little wife. I heard about our…terms and conditions. Let's not forget, we were always good in bed. We'll take care of the kid, and you'll stay with me. Here in town. Holidays, weddings, and funerals—we'll speak only then. I will get a cut of that money."

I pushed myself up to stand, taking a few steps back from him.

His smirk was sharp. "I'm not the same man you left behind. What if I expose you for who you really are?"

"I don't know what you're talking about."

"You know damn well what I mean." His smile widened, but it didn't reach his eyes. "We had a plan—our escape. You ditched me."

I shook my head. "Conrad was a happy accident."

Reese's eyes grew cold, and I knew I said the wrong thing.

"My brother's death was a 'happy accident'?"

"I didn't mean it like that—"

"I'll tell her. I'll tell your mom exactly what you're up to. You tried to bribe me in the garden. That's not a part of the rules, is it? Imagine what she'd do if she found out you were *using* her like that. That wouldn't be good for you, huh?"

"If you expose me, you're only exposing yourself."

He leaned closer, his breath warm against my ear. "And? You think I care now? There's nothing left for me to lose. But you? I'll make sure every second of your life is hell for you with me."

"Reese—"

"You'll feel every ounce of the pain you caused me." His grin was all teeth. "So smile, Princess. Cameras are watching."

CHAPTER 5

Reese

BEING near Laurene felt like standing on the edge of a cliff. One wrong move, and I'd fall.

I used to love her—*fucking love her*—but now? Now I just want to tear her apart, piece by piece.

The high-pitched tittering of a group of women grated on my nerves as I stepped back into the crowded party. I should've known better.

She looked the same. Beautiful. Untouchable. Like she never fucking suffered for what she did to me.

"Reese!" Nina, my mother's assistant, called. "Glad you could make it. Your mom and sister were worried you left."

I tried to give a fuck about what Nina said, but my mind kept drifting back to Laurene—those big brown eyes, her soft voice wrapped around me, her scent. I can still remember the taste of her on my tongue.

Laurene still smelled like jasmine.

All it took was one breath, and I was twenty-five again, drunk off her, chasing a future that was never mine to have.

I should hate her. I *did* hate her. So why did my fucking heart still recognize her?

I forced a smile. "How's Mom?"

"Hello, son-in-law," Yvonne interjected. Her gown swished as she moved in front of Nina. "Leaving already?"

Yvonne glared at Nina, who awkwardly bowed and quickly left.

"I'm not your mother, and I'm not here to coddle you. Look at these people." Yvonne swept her hands over the crowd. "They are here for you."

"So they know what's happening tonight?"

"I may have misled with an invitation to Laurene's home-coming party. We want to hold the surprise to the end, no?" Yvonne's mouth thinned.

Guests drifted past, their curious glances lingering. A hushed murmur spread like a ripple through the crowd, heads turning, eyes narrowing when they saw Ashbournes and Kings talking in a room. *In decades.*

"Reese." My father's arm slammed into my shoulder, yanking me forcefully into his side. "I know you aren't leaving, not before Yvonne can break the news to everyone."

"There he is!" Mom looked radiant in her bronze gown, the rich fabric highlighting her blue eyes and perfectly styled sandy blond updo. She opened her arms, pulling me into a tight embrace—then pushed me away just as quickly.

"Mom," I said, masking the sting of her sudden withdrawal.

"I told you he wouldn't try to sneak out," Jennie, my older sister, chimed in from beside Mom, waddling behind her.

Jennie was almost seven months pregnant, and getting closer to her leaving me with our father.

"Seems like everyone who matters is here." Yvonne tilted her head, her gaze sweeping over us.

Dad scoffed, sipping champagne as Vincent King, Yvonne's husband, joined.

The room tightened. Conversations died midsentence. No one had seen my father or Yvonne this close in years without a civil war breaking out. Laurene's siblings joined her parents. Erik stayed behind Yvonne, eyes narrowed, while Serena waited, arms crossed, tapping a finger. I did notice Gigi wasn't here.

"Oh, Laurene! We've been looking everywhere for you. Where have you been?" Yvonne said.

Guests stopped, parting like the Red Sea, revealing Laurene.

She floated through the crowd. Her gorgeous brown skin glowed in the light of the chandeliers. Her hair, once a wild cascade down her back, now lay tamed against her shoulders, the dark strands framing her face in a maddeningly perfect way, with the scent of jasmine still clinging to it.

She was utterly self-absorbed, demanding, and obnoxious. And she was all I longed for.

"Needed air, Mama."

I should ruin her. Walk right up, brush my thumb over that soft fucking mouth, and remind her just how dangerous I can be.

The crowd went silent, the kind of hush that sucked the air from the room. Then whispers, sharp and frantic, spread like wildfire.

"Is that…"

"It can't be."

"No one's seen her in years."

"And now she's back, just like that?"

I couldn't accept how much Laurene had changed. More fullness, more curves, more of everything. She wore a figure-hugging blue gown. It drove me crazy that she still had the power to effortlessly control me.

"I will only say this once. I expect everyone, but especially you two, to act like you got some sense tonight. Let me make the announcement before anyone says *anything*." Yvonne looked at me, then Laurene.

"Of course." Laurene nodded, her fingers casually tracing the single diamond pendant nestled between her breasts. I bit my lip so hard I drew blood.

I used to know every inch of her body. Now, she's just a stranger wearing the face I used to dream about.

"Yvonne's right," Dad said. "No fights. No arguments. We... like each other now."

Laurene looked at our parents, then touched my shoulder and gave it a squeeze. I remember that being her thing back then. My muscles ached from holding back, and it made me even madder that I wasn't even trying to get away from her.

With a final warning glance, Yvonne turned on her heel, her husband following her. Our siblings and Noelle gave us both looks that translated to "good fucking luck," and the air suddenly became awkward as they left us alone.

"Laurene! You're back! And Reese..." I didn't know the name of the woman who ran up, her voice bright and intrusive.

All eyes were on us. I hated this. That stiff air made me remember how out of place I always felt, especially after losing my brother. In their eyes, I was the killer, not the woman with me.

Laurene's fingers brushed against mine for the briefest second—a slip or a warning, I couldn't tell.

"I'm surprised to see both your families here," the nosy woman continued.

There was another collective gasp. Eyes widened. Conversations dropped.

In walked the mayor. *Fucking great.*

"Laurene," Dante Castillo said as he approached. I saw Yvonne's and Dad's glares as he strutted by, fake smile and all. "It's been too long."

The mayor of Lush wasn't an unexpected guest, but these days, I was hearing more rumors about him than his work for the town. He was tall, broad-shouldered, dressed in a sleek, dark suit. A snake oil salesman.

And Laurene—she was looking back. Interest flickered across her face, subtle but there. The slight tilt of her chin. The part of her lips.

Jealousy curled low in my gut.

"You've certainly moved up in the world, Dante. Last time I saw you, you were assistant to Mayor Johnson."

"Thanks to your mother's support," he said smoothly. "Hard work and persistence pay off. I never thought I'd see your two families not trying to kill one another."

His smile got wider, and I squinted at him.

"Quite the power move for our two oldest families. It's gonna be different in town moving forward, huh?" Dante grinned at Laurene and then glanced at me. "I wonder what's in store for Lush?"

"Don't get cute, Castillo," I said. "You're already pushing it just showing up here."

"Easy, Reese," he said smoothly. "I meant business only. I don't want to cause issues at Laurene's homecoming party. But I hope to see more of you two soon." Dante gave a final polite nod, that smile still glued to his face.

She looked thoughtful, her gaze following Dante as he disappeared into the crowd. My eyes caught on another man. Tobias Merrick. Laurene's ex. He was leaning casually against the wall, as if he had every right to be here, his eyes locked on Laurene with an intensity that made my blood run hot.

Laurene was back, and every asshole was already crawling out from under their rocks to see her.

"Excuse me, may I please have everyone's attention?"

Yvonne's sharp, clear voice cut through the low hum of conversation like a knife. A hush fell as everyone turned.

"I want to express my gratitude to everyone for warmly welcoming my daughter Laurene back home." The applause was polite, a ripple of sound that barely registered in the air.

Gone for six years. No explanations. No public statements. And now, just like that, Laurene King had returned.

"That's not the only reason we are here tonight. The Kings and the Ashbournes are putting the past behind us. Again."

Murmurs of disbelief rippled through the crowd.

"Tonight, we're not just welcoming Laurene back..."

A beat.

A pause long enough for anticipation.

"We're celebrating her engagement to Reese."

The room erupted.

Someone dropped a glass, shattering the stunned silence. Gasps. A woman audibly choked on her champagne. Some laughed, but it was the uncomfortable kind, like they weren't sure how to handle the situation. A man near the door sputtered, his voice a mix of disbelief and amusement, "Are you serious?"

I glanced at Laurene, but her expression was calm and unreadable.

"Is it possible for the happy couple to come up here?" Yvonne's gaze locked on to us, and I knew there was no backing out now.

"Shall we?" I muttered, holding out my hand to Laurene, every inch of me aching to pull away.

Laurene briefly hesitated, then took my hand. We walked to the center of the room as Yvonne started droning on about tradition, legacy, and all that bullshit.

I tuned it out till Yvonne turned back to us, and she glared at me. "*I said*, can we get a kiss?"

Laurene looked just as shocked.

Then she glanced at me, her eyes darting away, a flicker of defiance fading into something softer—resignation. It shouldn't have stung the way it did.

Without thinking, I leaned in, closing the space.

I gently raised her chin, buzzing with unspoken energy. I wish we weren't doing this here. All I could remember was when I watched her with Conrad do the same thing. Seeing him kiss Laurene so confidently, his smirk while he held her waist like it was meant to be.

And now? Now I was him.

We were a breath away now, our faces so close I could feel the soft flutter of her breath on my lips.

I kissed her.

CHAPTER 6

Laurene

MY BEDROOM DOOR slammed open with a loud bang.

"Honestly, Laurene." Serena chucked letters at me, the papers strewing everywhere. "When did I become your personal assistant? I have a company to run."

I lifted my chin, smoothed the sheets, and schooled my expression into ice on Serena. "And yet, here you are. Personally assisting."

If Serena's eyes were lasers, there would be a hole straight through me.

The door slammed open again, and I hear a loud squeal before a burst of colors flew past and onto my bed.

"Holy shit, Mama wasn't lying. You're home!" Gigi burst out.

Serena frowned. "And I see Sint Maarten got tired of your bullshit early."

"What can I say? It wasn't worth missing my big sister coming back home!"

At twenty-three, the youngest in the family, Gigi was a knockout. Her gorgeous deep brown skin shone. Her skirt was short, ass cheeks out, and her cropped shirt revealed a pierced belly button. Today, a long ombre blond wig flowed down her back.

"By the way, if we're talking bachelorette parties? How about we go back to Sint Maarten? The men there are *foooine* as hell. I wanted to ask one if he had his passport and his shots."

I heard a yelp as she plopped down her bag, and her miniature schnauzer, Walter, peeked his head out.

That made me gasp. "That dog is still alive?"

"Unfortunately, evil doesn't die," Serena muttered.

Walter's fur used to be salt and pepper, but now it was mostly salt. He was half-blind and half-deaf at nearly twenty years old, his face framed by the classic schnauzer beard, though scruffier these days, adding to his old man charm.

"You're just mad because he's cuter than you," Gigi said.

"Cute?" Serena gave Walter a wide berth as she crossed my room and leaned against my dresser. "That dog don't even know where he at."

"You're such a fucking hater, Rena. Honestly." Gigi narrowed her gaze. "Don't be mad just because somebody loves Walter more than they'll ever love you."

I snorted, despite myself. Serena and Gigi glared at one another.

"Spill, Lulu!" Gigi demanded. "Mama is seriously forcing you to marry Reese Ashbourne? First of all, *scandalous*. You a freak, girl. Brothers? Eiffel Tower, huh? I'm sorry, that's disrespectful. Rest in power, Conrad. But this is some reality TV shit!"

I shouldn't have kissed him. I told myself it was because we had no choice, because appearances had to be kept. But deep down, I wanted to know if that spark still existed—if he still burned for me the way I sometimes, shamefully, burned for him.

"You sure you wanna know how I feel?" I asked, fingering my unraveling headscarf.

"Ooh, yes!" Gigi snapped her fingers at Serena. "Take notes, babe."

"Hold up." Serena folded her arms, her gaze slicing toward me. "I'm not doing a damn thing. Let's not sit up here pretending everything's fine. We need to address the fact Laurene is here like she didn't fuck everything up."

"Seriously?" Gigi muttered. "Why you gotta bring that up right now? She's home. Our *sister* is back."

Serena turned to me. "How is it that *you* get to waltz back in, like nothing happened?"

"I didn't exactly disappear for fun." I frowned at her. "Nor do I really wanna be back."

"What's stopping you? The door is right there." Serena pointed at it. "It's always been about you, hasn't it? You're back and everything has to come to a halt since you've graced us with your presence again. Now I gotta make sure you get mail? We gotta make sure *Laurene* is comfortable."

"Don't be a hater 'cause Mama ain't pick you to marry Conrad first, Rena," Gigi said.

"Rena, be real. You're not angry about me coming back. What is it?"

Gigi sighed. "Can we please just keep the conversation vibin' and not do this?"

"You're *you*—just blink, and people fall over themselves to do what you want. I've been here! Mama's been relying on me, but she's asking me to bring your fucking mail?"

"You know Mama likes to start stuff," Gigi said.

"How long did you know you were coming back? Hmm? You planned this, right when I was about to make the biggest announcement of my career." Serena glared at me.

I frowned. "Mama called me."

"Really? I think you went broke or got tired being alone. Or you wanted more? What's gonna be enough for you, Laurene?"

"I'm sorry I interrupted your plans, but this blindsided me like everyone else. Being here doesn't evoke happy memories."

"You mean the part where she told you to get out of her house and never come back? That you were a disappointment? I don't get it, you're back and her favorite again? That's bullshit." Serena's eyes narrowed.

I ignored her. "You think I *wanted* that life?"

My fairy tale had once been to marry Reese, but from his reaction last night, that dream was dead, along with the girl I used to be.

"Oh, poor Laurene. I've been working my ass off here, and nobody gives a fuck! Gigi, can you back me up here?" Serena glanced at her.

"You're on ten, and Imma need you to come down to a two." Gigi lowered her hands.

We *all* had to bend to Mama's will, and we handled that pressure in different ways. I had tried to please Mama. Erik knew how to placate her. Gigi...she just did whatever the hell she wanted. But for Serena, she desperately clung to Mama's approval.

"No offense, Rena, but you always been a bit of a kiss ass for Mama—"

"Shut the hell up!" Serena snapped at Gigi, who frowned.

"She's right," I said. "You've spent your whole life trying to be Mama's favorite, and for what? You want my position that bad, have it. Newsflash, though: it's not gonna make anything in your life any easier. In fact, you'll fucking hate yourself for it."

Serena's chest rose and fell rapidly.

"Wake up, Serena. Stand up to her now, before it's too late like it was for me. You're yelling at me, but I think you need to be having a conversation with Mama."

"Look, just don't, okay? You left your family—*us*—when we needed you. You try to act like Mama's so bad, but she's not. You're just jealous you're not the favorite anymore, and I did what you couldn't."

I sighed. "We all know Mama needed help after Grandpa died." I pushed the comforter back, standing. "That's why Mama started spiralling. But nobody in this family wants to admit that. She needs help. Her behavior now is coping."

Our grandma died years ago, so Grandpa was Mama's only parent. Grandpa Ben had been the glue of the family. Mama hadn't always been this way. She had been caring—she was always strict, but not like this. Not so…manic. Mean.

Grandpa had been handling a deal, but his condition challenged his abilities, and we lost a lot of money. The moment he wasn't that strong man anymore, Mama decided that appearances were more important. She had to fill in the holes of the sinking boat that was our family. His death broke her, and we all failed her by assuming she could handle it by herself.

I had some pity for her, but that wouldn't stop me from sabotaging her.

Serena's face hardened. "That's not true."

"He had dementia, not the plague!" I snapped. "She locked him away. I'm the only one that said something, and then suddenly I have to marry Conrad Ashbourne, and she's taking over companies? That's part of the reason she kicked me out, because I called her out."

"Can we just stop?" Gigi's voice was soft as her eyes darted between the two of us. "Why are we doing this? Why can't we just *talk*?"

I wanted Serena to hurt now.

"I saw you, you know."

Serena blinked. "Saw me what?"

"I saw you and Miles sneaking away at my engagement party back then."

Gigi gasped, and for a split second, Serena's face cracked.

"Oh shit!" Gigi said. "You and Miles? *Miles*, Miles? Does Erik know?"

I hummed, tilting my head. "Erik's gonna be mad you're sleeping with his ex–best friend. And Mama—*whew*. Mama explicitly said we don't speak to the Whitmores anymore. That's not favorite daughter behavior, is it?"

"Serena, please tell me you're not…" Gigi looked at her. "After everything that happened? How can you risk this?"

Serena's throat bobbed. "I wasn't— It wasn't like…"

"What would Mama think if she knew?"

The silence that followed was thick, suffocating.

There was a knock at the door, and Mama walked in. "What's going on in here?"

I straightened, crossing my arms tightly over my chest. Serena's face was flushed, her jaw tight, and she turned away.

Gigi, still sitting on the bed, looked between us. "We're discussing world peace?"

Mama stood there, waiting. Her eyes flicked between the three of us, and I knew she didn't believe us. Serena sucked her teeth loudly, looking at Mama only.

"Excuse me, I'm late for a meeting." Without another word, Serena spun on her heel and stormed out.

Gigi and I exchanged looks, and Mama watched Serena go before she glanced back at us. "Why are you still in bed, Laurene? You've got a job interview to get ready for."

I blinked. "What? Where?"

"If you are gonna live in my house again, you work. I got you an interview at the art gallery downtown. Be thankful."

Just then, Gigi jumped into action.

"I'll help you get ready, Lulu. We can pick out an outfit together," she offered, and she hopped up from the bed heading to the door. "Lemme go get my stuff."

"You know, Gigi," Mama said, her voice dripping with disdain, "you really should be looking for a real job."

"I do have a job, Mama."

"Oh really?" Mama arched a brow. "And what, exactly, is your job? Posting online for your followers?"

"There's money that can be made online. People wanna hear what I got to say. I have, like, two million followers." Gigi's smile faltered. "I'm building something. It might not be what you want, but—"

"You'll never be taken seriously. You need to finish that college degree. You keep starting and stopping. C'mon, Georgiana, how long are we gonna do this?"

Gigi's shoulders tensed, then deflated. There was no point in fighting it.

"Fine, just go." Mama waved Gigi off, and she basically bolted from the room. Then Mama turned to me. "Remember what I said last night."

"I wouldn't dare forget." My smile was dry.

She nodded curtly before leaving, the door clicking shut behind her.

I'd often thought about Grandpa when I was away. I sometimes wondered if he hadn't ruined that deal, if we hadn't lost millions of dollars, maybe Mama wouldn't have partnered with Harold. Maybe I wouldn't have been sold off to him, and maybe one day Reese and I could have been together for real.

I had to run my new plan by Noelle.

I had to get the hell out of this house.

Heading to my ensuite bathroom, I noticed the letters Serena brought earlier on the floor. Sighing, I bent to pick them up. I flipped through them again, getting ready to put them in the trash, but I noticed one with no return address, just my own name stamped on.

I hesitated, my thumb grazing the edge of the envelope before I ripped it open. Inside was a single sheet of paper, plain and simple, but when I read it, I felt the room shrink around me.

You know what you did. I spent six years miserable. Now it's your turn. This time, there's no escape, Murderer.

Photos fell from the paper. I stared, pulse racing, at the grainy but clear image.

Reese and me, stumbling out of the bathroom, disheveled, tangled in the aftershocks of a moment that should have never happened. His hand was on my arm, but the way he was looking at me—hungry, daring—made my pulse spike all over again.

And then, in the next photo, my engagement ring caught the light as Reese's body pressed me against the wall, his lips just inches from mine.

Someone in Lush knew.

CHAPTER 7

Laurene

THE BLACK LIMO skidded to a halt on the gravel drive.

"Leave the engine on," I said to my driver and jumped out before the car fully stopped.

Reese's place. His home was a cold, towering villa on the edge of town, its sharp lines slicing through the fog rolling in from the cliffs.

Isolated. Defiant.

Just like him.

My palms were clammy, but the letter burned in my purse as I approached Reese's door. The gossip mill in town was quick to tell me he bought this home right after the *accident*. Nearly on the edge of town, up in the cliffs.

My fist slammed into the door—once, twice, over and over, until the sting in my knuckles matched the one burning in my gut.

No answer.

"Reese!"

I banged harder, my palm flat this time. He *had* to be here.

I knocked firmer on the door again.

"Reese, I swear to God, open this damn door!" My voice cracked; I hated that. I hated needing him so much right now.

I needed to keep calm. I needed to think clearly. Panic wouldn't get us out of this.

Moments passed, then I heard the click of the dead bolt and the door swung open.

"What the hell do you want?"

His chest was bare, damp from a shower. I exhaled slowly, my eyes tracing the thick lines of his tattoos, some new and some familiar. The low light of the hallway hit him just right, casting shadows that danced and twisted, making him seem less like a man and more like something darker, like an incubus.

I didn't say anything. His eyes burned into me with anger; he was waiting for me to say something.

"Get the fuck out of here, Laurene. I'm busy."

He started to slam the door, and I shot my hand out. The sharp metal of the doorknob bit into my palm, but I didn't flinch.

"It's an emergency."

"You've got five minutes," he muttered, stepping aside just barely enough to let me in.

The faint scent of cedar and old leather hung in the space, mixed with something rawer, more...*Reese*—a touch of sweat, salt, wood, and whiskey.

His smell was still the same.

"What's the emergency?"

I swallowed hard as I took in his space.

The walls were lined with books, but none of them looked pristine. Some books had edges curled and pages dog-eared. A guitar rested against the wall. A stark black-and-white photograph of a barren landscape, with a cracked earth and twisted trees, hung above the fireplace. The place felt lived-in, but in a way that made it clear Reese was the only one allowed to really exist here.

"Working on a weekend?" I muttered, looking down at the coffee table, where a cigarette was burning in an ashtray, surrounded by scattered business papers. "That's unlike you."

The thud of his bare steps vibrated through the space, and I had to remind myself how to breathe. I wasn't twenty-six anymore, lost in his bad boy charm. So reckless, so perfect for a girl like me who didn't break the rules.

"Don't come here pretending like you give a shit now, princess."

I'd dated other men since Reese, knew how to make them want me, how to stay in control. And yet, two minutes in, and I was twiddling my hair and trying to find the right words to say. I sank into the cushions, crossing my legs as I scanned the room.

"Did somebody die?"

I fought the urge to roll my eyes. "I've been calling you."

"I don't answer unknown numbers, and I blocked your old number years ago."

He grinned as he said the last part, and I clenched my fists. The man in front of me wasn't *him*—wasn't even close to the guy I used to know.

"I got a photo this morning."

Reese raised a brow. "What photo?"

I tossed the photo onto the coffee table between us. He glared at me, then squinted at the photo, before looking back at me.

"What the hell is this?"

I pulled the letter from my bag and slid it across the table to him, my fingers brushing his hand as he reached for it. "Blackmail."

His jaw clenched, and he snatched the letter from me with more force than necessary.

"Is that why I got those?" He pointed over to the mantel.

A vase of lilies.

I jumped to my feet and slowly walked toward them. I'd seen the news photos from Conrad's funeral, and lilies had been everywhere. I pulled out the unopened envelope nestled in the flowers to find a newspaper page.

Mama already had us on the front page of the society paper.

The headline read "Wedding of the Century," but it was crossed out, replaced by jagged, angry strokes of red ink—

"Death of the Century." The photo of me and Reese, on stage at our engagement party, had ink scribbled over our faces, holes where our eyes used to be.

I gasped, dropping the paper.

"Did you plan this? Is this how low you'll go?" Reese's voice was calm.

I whirled around on him.

"You think I set this up?"

I was raised to be perfect. But loving him was the first thing I ever did for myself.

"I'm supposed to believe this? After what you pulled in the garden? Your big plan? This is too damn convenient, don't you think?"

"Does it look like I'm joking? Someone's blackmailing us, Reese."

If he thought it was me, why couldn't it be him? An old part of me didn't want to believe it. But with Reese, I couldn't be sure. He was unpredictable, volatile.

"Is it you?"

Reese squinted at me. "What the hell are you talking about?"

I crossed my arms, ignoring the heat creeping up my neck. "Cryptic threats. Anonymous photos. Your threats of revenge. Did you send me that note? You have motive. How do I know this isn't part of your revenge plot?"

A laugh burst out of him, sharp and bitter, slicing through the room like a knife. "Cute. But that's *your* family's MO, not mine. After what you did, I would want you to know if I'm the one hurting you."

I sighed. "You were hell-bent on getting me out of that marriage. We had a plan, Reese. You and Conrad—"

"You sat there and told them I was *jealous*. That I caused the fight. Did you tell them what you did? No. Princess had to stay protected. I was just the bastard younger brother, hm? For months people were petitioning the sheriff to throw me in jail, even though Conrad's death was ruled an accident. No one would come near me. I still can't fucking wrap my head around the concept that you left me to rot, Laurene. You didn't even have the fucking gall to look me in my eye after what you did."

Guilt hit me, forcing me to stare at the ground.

"Conrad died because—"

"Because he was an asshole, just like my father and your parents!" Reese's voice thundered, silencing me. "You encouraged the fight. You *liked* it, didn't you? You didn't tell anybody how you—"

"What are you talking about?" I whispered, not wanting to hear it, not wanting to admit it.

Reese's eyes were wild, burning with the betrayal.

"You were playing both sides. Smiling in Conrad's face, and then kissing me? Did you tell him I couldn't handle the pressure? You fed his damn ego."

"I pulled Conrad away from you! He was my fiancé. What would I have looked like not intervening? We didn't even get to talk to him until you both snapped. *Be cool.* That's what I told you. But nooo, you flew off the handle like you always do, and Conrad took that as an opening."

Reese let out a breath. "You think I'd fucking stoop this low to blackmail, when I would be just as affected?"

"Then who?" I demanded.

Too many enemies over time, too many secrets and things done for me to remember.

"I don't know." He crossed his arms. "But don't you fucking forget who saved you when we crashed, who was willing to risk everything for you. I lost more than you ever have."

"Someone's out there, Reese. Watching us. Waiting. They saw us back then, so that means our relationship wasn't a secret. And that is a problem."

His jaw tightened, his eyes narrowing as he stared at the photo. "If this is real—"

"It's *real.* We need to come up with a plan to deal with this." I stepped forward until we were nearly chest to chest, and I tried to keep my eyes on his face and not his abs. "Let's start planning damage control. We cover this up. Push it aside till we find the truth."

His lips parted, a sharp retort hovering, but he stayed silent, his gaze drifting back to the photo.

"Let me guess," Reese finally said, his voice cold and laced with mockery. "You've already got the narrative lined up for when this shit hits the fan? This time will you tell me before you fuck me over?"

I bristled, refusing to take the bait. "Save the drama, and let's focus on what the fuck's at stake. Either way, we both won't come out of this spotless. It's about sticking with the fact that Conrad's death was an accident. Which it *was*. We need to work together. I need you in this."

"We fucked in the bathroom, Laurene." Reese scratched his five-o'clock shadow, and I hated how my eyes trailed down his chest to the happy trail that disappeared into his jeans. "Can't change the optics on that."

"We kissed," I shot back, my voice rising in defense. "It was a moment of weakness. That's all. That's all the photo shows."

Reese only glared at me.

"No matter what, our families can't pay for what we did."

"They're the reason we're in this mess!" He walked over, inhaling his cigarette. "And you want to tiptoe around our parents? Fuck that. Whoever's doing this, we need to find them and end it."

I looked at the photo over his mantel, counting back from ten.

"We don't know if it's one person or more. What else do they know? If we make a move without thinking, we could make things worse. Because whoever this is, they've already got the upper hand."

"Let's sit here and *think* while they burn our lives to the ground. Maybe we can send them a thank-you card while we're at it."

I watched him get the bottle of whiskey from the cabinet and set it down on the coffee table. I crossed the room, sitting across from him, and when he poured his drink, I snatched it from him, downing it.

"Let's think… We pool our resources together, find everyone who was on the boat. Cover up. Buy people out. Share any clues we find. Keep this only between us, and keep our parents happy. Figure out who's sending these notes."

"I don't trust you."

"Do you really want to watch Ashbourne Distilleries fall into someone else's hands? After everything you've built? All the money you've earned? You're not the kind of man who just gives up."

That made him pause, and he raised an eyebrow. "What else?"

"Mutual protection," I said. "If we're going through with this arranged marriage, we need to present a united front. We do this together, always. We keep each other safe and alive."

Reese's posture shifted from defensive to focused. "Fine."

I stood, setting the glass down, and this time, I picked up the bottle and drank from it.

"First, we need to figure out who might have seen us that night. We start with everyone on that boat and at the engagement party. Your family, my family, Blair, Hollie, Tobias—everyone who was there is a suspect."

"And what's stopping you from turning on me when it suits you?" Reese said quietly.

"Nothing. But there's nothing stopping you from doing the same either."

Without a word, he reached for the bottle. He tipped the rim to his lips, his gaze still on mine, and drank deeply, finishing the last of the whiskey.

"Talk to your mom, I'll talk to mine." I was ready to go.

Be strong, Laurene.

He set the bottle down on the table with a deliberate clink, then slowly licked his lips, wiping the back of his mouth with his hand.

"It's a truce, then?" I asked, taking a step back from him.

"I'm still going to ruin you and your family. Just give me time in between saving my ass."

The finality in his voice sent a chill through me. "Reese—"

"Shut the door behind you when you leave."

CHAPTER 8

Reese

I HISSED as the hot water hit my body, the heat biting into my sore muscles.

All night I tossed and turned after Laurene left. Couldn't sleep, couldn't think straight, couldn't shut it off. I hadn't felt like this in years—restless, raw, like every wound I'd convinced myself had healed was splitting open all over again.

I'd gotten up at four in the morning and run.

Lush had stretched before me—the tall cypress trees on the cliffs were swaying in the breeze, their dark branches standing out against the light sky as the sun came up and covered everything in a silver mist.

Even a grueling ten-mile run didn't exhaust me.

Why couldn't I get her out of my head?

This place, for all its charm, carried ghosts. Every street, every view of the water, every sound of the waves felt like a punch to the gut. Laurene was everywhere here. For years, I'd wondered where she'd gone, what corner of the earth had swallowed her up.

We were never supposed to love each other. But tell me—when has fate ever cared about the rules?

How many times had I been to Paris? How many flights, how

many hotels, how many goddamn conferences? I'd probably walked down the same streets, been blocks away from her without even knowing it. She'd probably been sitting in some café, laughing, sipping wine, living her perfect little life, while I was drowning.

I stayed and picked up the pieces after Conrad's accident. His time in the hospital had been short. A coma. Then seizures. And then the stroke that took him for good.

God, I *needed* to hate her. But emotions, memories, and all the other bullshit were twisted in a mess.

I couldn't forget her in my living room. Her legs crossed, the curve of her calf catching the light. That brown skin, warm and shimmering golden like sunlight, filtered through whiskey. Her presence bled into every corner of my damn place.

College was one of the few neutral territories for our families. No business deals or simmering tensions, just teenage chaos that made everything else fade into the background.

I'd been arguing with Conrad—he'd said some fucked-up shit, something sharp enough to cut deep. I didn't even remember the words, but my fists curled at my sides, ready to swing.

And then I looked over his shoulder and saw her.

She'd been surrounded by her usual entourage, all of them laughing, talking too loud, like they owned the place. But she wasn't looking at them. She was looking at me.

She smiled.

Not the kind of smile that came with an agenda, or one of those polished, pretty ones she used on everyone else. It was simpler than that. Softer. Like she didn't see the mess. Like I wasn't just the fuck-up everyone else saw.

I froze. For a second, I forgot where I was, forgot the sting of Conrad's words, forgot everything except that damn smile.

And then, before I could stop myself, I smiled back.

I let my mind bring me back to the present. My head fall forward, the water streaming down my face as I exhaled deeply.

Laurene was too damn easy to want, too damn hard to forget.

I slammed my fist against the shower wall, the pain grounding me, but it didn't stop the ache in my chest.

It was like every part of her was designed to drive me insane. The sharp, teasing smirk that tugged at the corners of her lips. The way her voice lingered in the air, low and warm, wrapping around me. Even the silence after she left felt heavy, like she'd stripped something vital from me on her way out the door.

I picked up my washcloth and soap, and as I lathered up, my mind flickered like a slide show of recollections. Since she left, I'd barely given any other woman a second look. Not for lack of options—a couple of nights here, a few drinks there, but nothing ever felt real. I didn't let myself get close.

It was safer that way. Easier.

Those full, dangerous lips, the way her dark eyes could pin me down without a word. Damn, I felt myself hardening.

Reaching down, I grabbed my dick and stroked slowly, envisioning her on her knees in front of me, her pretty mouth wrapped around me, looking up with those big brown eyes watering.

Closing my eyes, I remembered her body had shifted the way her hips swayed just a little too much as if she *knew* how much it messed with my head.

I still remembered those nights in my car. She didn't hold back then, she took control, every move bold, reckless, just like her. Sex with her wasn't soft or easy; it was like a wildfire, something I could lose myself in, something that scorched and stayed with me.

Money, power, reputation—I lost everything. Except the way she still looked at me like I could be more.

I could feel the heat creeping up my neck. I stroked myself faster, imagining her bent over and spread, her pussy stretched around my cock. I used to count how many rounds it would take for her to take me to the base without crying.

Even now, I could still feel her, the way she moved, her

breath against my neck. But she was always a trouper, and I'd always make it up to her by holding her thighs apart, her pussy on display for me only.

I still wanted her. *Badly.* I wanted to fuck her hard and fast, make her scream with pleasure and pain, my nose buried deep in the crook of her neck. Just to get the anger out. Rid my body of the final frustrations.

My hand moved faster as I thought about corrupting the town's perfect princess. I'd make every thrust count. Until she was slathering my dick with her slippery essence.

"Fuck!" I grunted as I felt the tingling surge up my legs.

I braced one hand against the wall, feeling the rush hit me hard, relentless. My head dropped, breaths coming fast. Her image burned behind my eyes and left me raw and unsteady as my release swirled down the drain.

The day had started shit and, hours later, was going to shit *again*. It always did when I had to step into my parents' house.

"Reese," Nina greeted me, stepping aside to let me in. "Your mother's in the kitchen."

I nodded at her and walked in without a second thought, the familiar smell of the house hitting me like it always did—wood polish, fresh flowers, and something faintly sweet coming from the kitchen.

"How's she doing?" I asked, glancing back at Nina. Nina had been with the family for years. Conrad had hired her a few years before the accident, and she'd stayed with us after. Loyalty. One of the rarest things in our world, and she had it in spades.

"She had a session today, which seemed to have gone well. You know how she is. Keeps herself busy. The medication helps."

"Good. She needs that."

"So, how's it going with Laurene?" Nina asked, switching the conversation with professional ease as she motioned me to follow her to the kitchen. "You and her adjusting to things?"

"It's going." I didn't want to think about the engagement now. "Hey, Mom."

Mom popped up from behind the enormous center island. Her brow briefly furrowed. "Reese? What are you doing here?" She gestured toward a can on the counter. "Stick the peaches up top, will you? And oh, what do you think about this centerpiece arrangement? I'm going to show it to Yvonne later."

I grabbed the can, placing it carefully on the top shelf of the cabinet. The kitchen was an explosion of grocery bags and vases upon vases of flowers as if a florist threw up in here. I looked at the flowers on the kitchen island as Nina took over unloading the groceries onto the counter.

"I just came to talk," I said.

"You could at least pretend to care. It's your wedding, Reese."

I sighed. "No one's going to care."

Mom sucked her teeth. "Fine. Don't worry about it, I'll handle it." She paused. "You don't have to come over here to talk. Just call."

"I felt like talking in person, is that so bad?"

She moved around the island, and her hand brushed my back as she headed for the cabinet, and I forced myself not to react. Her touch was barely there, but it felt intentional, like the same way she used to straighten my tie or brush lint off my jacket before a big event.

"It's just… Well, you're always…" She made a gesture with her hands, her blue eyes squinting.

Busy.

It's what she always says when she didn't want me to stay, didn't want me lingering around too long. It was easier for her, for us both really, to think I had somewhere else to be, rather than face the fact that I didn't come around as much because I didn't know *how* to be around her anymore.

But if things were going under, I needed somebody on my side.

"I'm here. Always. Whenever you need me." Because no matter how much I wanted to be there for her, I knew I couldn't undo the past.

I noticed how the skin on her hands had thinned, the veins more pronounced. I remembered those same hands pointing at me years ago, trembling with anger. When she screamed at me that it was my fault. That *I* should've been the one in the hospital bed instead of Conrad, that I should've been the one who—

"It's about Conrad."

Her hand froze, a can suspended in the air, and for a second, the only sound was the soft hum of the refrigerator.

"We need to talk about him."

She glanced down, biting her lip before she nodded slowly. "Conrad? What about him?"

"I'll get started on those calls, Mrs. Ashbourne," Nina said, gathering her things and leaving the room.

Mom turned to face the thick cream-colored curtains that hung on either side of the windows. "Let's head to the living room to talk."

Mom had tried to stop time after Conrad's death.

Inside the living room, on the left wall was a massive fireplace carved from Italian marble that stood like a shrine, lined with photographs. Conrad dominated the space. His pictures were everywhere, all facing forward, as if the house itself couldn't let him go. There were other things too—some old letters Conrad had written half hidden behind the frames, a trophy he'd won in middle school, an old baseball glove he'd worn when we were kids. There were a few photos of Jennie and me as kids, just afterthoughts.

"Do you still blame me?"

Mom froze. Blinking, she looked away, easing herself down into the chair gently.

"You killed him. You killed my baby!"

The hospital room had been suffocating, sterile, the hum of machines blending with the harsh overhead lights. Conrad had lain there, still, as if he was already gone.

I'd stood frozen, Jennie gripping my side, while Mom's words hit me like a knife to the gut.

"You killed him. You killed my baby," she whispered, her voice trembling with venom. "You were jealous of your brother, weren't you? You couldn't just behave? He would never do this to you!"

"It was an accident," I'd pleaded, trying to make her understand. "We lost control—Mom... Please. He lost control too—"

"No! You hurt him! You took him away from me!"

"I didn't mean for the fight to happen." The words slipped out, softer than I intended, almost like a confession I'd never spoken aloud before. "Conrad... We just starting arguing like before."

I hadn't wanted any of it. Not the fight, not the damage, and damn sure I never wanted a plan to begin with. Things were supposed to be simple. I didn't want to hurt Conrad. But somewhere along the way, he had become hell-bent on hurting me, and I didn't know how to stop it.

"Reese," she said, tears forming in her blue eyes. "I...I...I don't know."

"You don't know?" The words came out sharper than intended. "You don't know how you feel about me? Your own son?"

"Some days...some days the anger just bubbles up. It's hard to separate it from the pain. I want to blame something, someone." Her nails, painted a soft pink, were perfectly manicured as always, but now she picked at her cuticle I saw blood. "Losing a child is a pain no parent should endure."

"Yeah," I muttered, the words feeling jagged, "I get it."

Her shoulders slumped slightly. "I know it's been hard for you. I should have been stronger. I'm sorry for how I reacted that night. I shouldn't have blamed you."

I didn't know what hit me first—the tightness in my chest or the way her voice cracked, the rawness in it, the apology. For a second, I couldn't move, couldn't breathe.

"Why?" Mom whispered, looking at the mantel and the shrine to Conrad there. "Why did Conrad have to die? What did I do to deserve this? Should I have stopped him when he wanted to take the yacht out?"

"Mom." I struggled to find the right words. "It's not your fault. None of this is your fault."

Part of me had always wondered what if I had just given up and let him have Laurene?

You would never do that.

"I couldn't protect him." She shook her head. "I couldn't save him. What kind of mother does that make me?"

"You've always been the strongest person I know. None of this was your fault. None of it." My throat tightened. "You did everything you could. We all did."

I squeezed her hand gently, hoped she could feel the love and reassurance I was desperately trying to convey. I watched her face, the exhaustion and guilt in her eyes, and something inside me broke, just a little.

"I know you tried to save him. You loved your brother." Tears fells down her face, and she quickly wiped them away.

"I'm going to do better. You and Jennie shouldn't have to look after me anymore. I won't break again. We have your wedding and a grandchild on the way!"

She cupped my cheek tenderly, and instinctively I leaned into her.

"I love you, Reese. I need you to know that."

I felt my heart swell, and it was as if a dam had broken inside me, and all the years of pain and misunderstanding rushed out.

"I love you too, Mom."

We both leaned back, overwhelmed by what just happened. I hadn't expected that. I expected screaming, yelling, accusations.

"I've been thinking about the after-party, and the hospital," I said, returning to the plan Laurene and I had concocted. "When Conrad was in the hospital, did anyone unexpected drop by?"

Mom snapped her fingers, and a maid immediately entered with a glass of water.

"Why?" she asked.

"Just curious," I said, trying to smooth over the tension in my voice.

Mom's gaze didn't leave mine, but her fingers brushed against the rim of her glass, like she was calculating her answer. "No. It was mainly family and doctors. Nina was there too, of course." I watched her think. "Blair. Noelle McKenzie, and her parents. Mayor Castillo, of course he wasn't mayor then. And Hollie was there as well—"

Hollie being there wasn't a surprise; she was Jennie's best friend.

"Anyone else? Maybe someone surprising who asked a lot of questions about the accident or sent flowers?" I pressed.

Mom paused again, deep in thought. "Well, there was Tobias Merrick," she finally said. "He and Conrad were friends. He came to the hospital and sent flowers. I remember he shared a little about what happened on the boat."

Tobias? The fucking weasel. He had damn near pushed all the women out the way to be the first one on the boat.

"What kind of flowers?" I asked, the question slipping out before I realized how strange it sounded. But the details mattered.

Mom seemed confused by the question, blinking a few times before she answered. "I don't know. White. Peonies? Gardenias? Lillies? It's been so long."

I leaned back. *This asshole.*

"Did Conrad ever mention him? Anything about their friendship? I don't remember them hanging out."

"After you had that argument with your father and he, um, cut you out the business, Conrad took over everything. Jennie was getting her MBA at the time. But, um, they were working together on something. A business deal, I think?" Mom's gaze drifted momentarily. "Conrad put Tobias's restaurant in the resort. Your brother didn't really discuss his work with me."

Conrad could partner with Toby, but not his own damn brother?

"No one thought to tell me that he was making deals with Tobias? Or after when I took over?"

"Jennie has always been better at handling the resort." Mom sent me a look. "Let's be real, Reese. You didn't care about the business at all until these last few years."

I nodded. That was true. "Anyone else?"

"Miles Whitmore came. That was lovely of him." My mother's fingers tapped the edge of her glass. "He was just concerned, wanted to know how we were handling things. Sweet boy, especially after everything with his father."

"What else do you remember?"

She sighed. "It's hard for me to remember those days. They're all jumbled together in my mind."

"Mom, please." I leaned forward farther, my hands reaching out instinctively to clasp hers.

"It's not that simple. I don't—" She shook her head, biting down on her lip. "I don't want to remember those things. They hurt too much." She tried to pull her hands free, but I tightened my grip.

"This is important."

"I don't want to remember!" she snapped back, her voice trembling as her hands jerked against mine. "All I remember is pain and his body and how cold it was and I—I can't..."

She snatched her hands from me and sank into the couch, her fingers kneading at her temples.

"Mom, take a breath," I said, reaching out to touch her arm.

Her chest heaved as she clutched at the fabric of her sweater, her fingers clawing at the neckline like it was suffocating her. "I can't—I can't do this. It's too much."

"Mom." I slid off the couch and onto my knees in front of her, my heart pounding. "Mom, you're okay. You're safe. Just breathe, okay? Look at me."

But her eyes stayed fixed on something distant, and her trembling turned violent. Her breaths came in rapid, shallow bursts now, like she couldn't get enough air.

I had pushed too hard, too fast.

"I'm sorry," I whispered, "I'm so sorry, Mom."

She shook her head, tears spilling down her cheeks as her body shuddered. "I can't… I can't stop seeing him."

"Listen to me," I said firmly, gripping her hands tighter. "You're here with me, not there. You're not alone. Just focus on my voice."

"G-get my medicine, now!"

In a panic of my own, I dashed up the stairs to my parents' bedroom, my footsteps echoing loudly in the silent house. I hurriedly rifled through the medicine cabinet, searching until I found the small bottle of pills.

Maybe I was being biased. Or maybe not. But Laurene's ex-boyfriend being friends with my brother was an issue. *Tobias.*

Did Laurene know anything?

I shook off the nagging thoughts and brought my mother her medication.

"Here." I kneeled beside her. "Take these. It will help."

Tearfully, she accepted the pills with trembling hands. "Thank you."

I sat beside her, rubbing her shoulders and feeling utterly helpless as she calmed, the medication gradually taking effect.

"I'm sorry," she whispered, her eyes filled with regret. "I'm so sorry—"

"Shh." I brought her to my side, gently rocking her as I felt the tension melt away. "Don't worry. Just calm down."

I think I had our first suspect.

CHAPTER 9

Laurene

"GREAT JOB TODAY," said Arthur, my new boss, as he entered my new office.

The Lush Art Gallery needed an art curator after the previous one left town under circumstances Arthur vaguely described as "a difference of vision." Convenient timing, really, but then again, Mama had a knack for convenient timing.

It'd only been a few days since I'd returned, and I'd already climbed the corporate ladder.

The moment I stepped into the gallery, heads turned. The hushed whispers, the polite-but-too-long stares, and the not-so-subtle glances over their shoulders

"Is that Laurene King?"

"Didn't she leave?"

"Why is she back?"

"Did you hear she's engaged to Reese Ashbourne now?"

My phone buzzed—twice in quick succession.

"Thank you," I replied. I kept my voice measured, pleasant, just warm enough to hide my irritation. Reese hadn't been answering me.

Arthur rested against the door. "Must be overwhelming, stepping into this role so quickly."

"It's exhilarating, actually. Stepping back into a gallery… It feels like coming home."

I hadn't been here since Grandpa died. The two of us used to stroll the gallery halls for hours when I was a kid. And he loved it here; his eyes would light up, especially after the dementia hit.

My phone buzzed again.

"Popular tonight?" Arthur joked.

"Something like that," I muttered, pulling the drawer open just enough to grab the phone. I thumbed the screen, my breath hitching as I read the notification.

New Message from Unknown Number

I tapped it open. The image loaded slowly, pixel by pixel. My stomach lurched. It was a photograph of me in this very office, taken from outside the window. The room suddenly felt too small, too hot, like the walls were pressing in on me.

It said:

Don't get too comfortable

Do I respond? Delete it? Pretend I never saw it?

"Everything alright?"

A slow, creeping fear slides down my spine.

This person was playing with me. This person had to want money. I curled my fingers into fists, my nails pressing hard into my palms.

"Is that for me?" I eyed the folder under his arm.

I had bigger problems than that text.

Reese.

Not a text. Not an email. Nothing.

What was he doing? Was he even bothering to read the stuff I'd sent him? It was easy enough to pick Mama's and Daddy's brains without tipping them off. But it was just like him to ignore orders and do whatever he felt like.

Isn't that what attracted you to him in the first place?

Arthur handed me the folder, and I skimmed it—donor lists, upcoming exhibits, dry notes from the previous curator. I snapped the folder shut and forced a smile. "Thanks. I'll make sure to get on this tomorrow."

"The meeting today…"

"Yes?"

Arthur's first task for me was to come up with the spring exhibit. Instead of getting people excited, my exhibition proposal was a complete flop.

"You sparked an actual conversation in there."

He was lying. The meeting had been brutal. Who knew suggesting a change would cause such a mess? The reaction was explosive; it was as if I had proposed tearing all the art off the walls and burning it.

"It felt like I was talking to a brick wall," I muttered, leaning back in my chair. The meeting was filled with skeptical comments, fake nods, and complaints.

"Change is hard for some people. You're new here, and it'll take time for them to warm up to you again."

"I'm here to do the job you hired me for. I'm not doing that by simply existing and hoping people like me at some point."

"I trust you, Laurene," Arthur said. "Let's just focus for now on our auction coming up. Getting the most money we can is the priority."

I reached for my phone again, scrolling through to the settings, hovering over "block number." There was a knock on the door, and then it opened a second later.

"Wassup, stranger?"

I stiffened, frozen in place as my other ex-boyfriend walked in and wrapped his arms around me. Arthur's brows rose, his expression carefully neutral, though his lips twitched.

"Toby." I pushed my chair back from him. "What are you doing here?"

He looked just as I remembered: light-skinned with a buzz

cut that highlighted the sharp angles of his face, his gray eyes catching the light like polished steel. His smile was too big, too bright, all teeth and audacity.

"Thought I'd check in on an old friend. That was some shit your mama pulled. Tricking the town to come to your engagement party?"

"Sad it wasn't you?" I shot back.

His grin widened. "You missed me when you were gone, don't lie."

"I, uh, guess I'll leave you two to catch up." Arthur cleared his throat. Before I could respond, he disappeared through the door.

"Sit."

"You're not happy to see me." He dropped into the seat. "That sucks, babe."

How simple life would have been if I'd been in love with Toby and not Reese?

"What are you doing here?"

"That engagement party? I thought it was a big joke, but you're marrying Reese for real?" The way Toby said it was like stepping into a pile of dog shit.

"Toby…"

"Relax, babe. I'm just saying, damn, this town got more men. Your mama coulda hit me back up. You, slumming it with a guy like Ashbourne? He killed your last fiancé, shit." He scoffed, sitting up straighter.

I swallowed hard, keeping my face unreadable. "That's not what happened."

"People say Reese got lucky. That if it weren't for your family, he'd be sitting in a cell."

Jail? Mama and Daddy never said anything about jail. Reese was an Ashbourne, and their family had been here just as long. If anything, he would have gotten a slap on the wrist.

"Wasn't that long ago people wouldn't even let Reese in their stores. You know the old guy who used to run Fillmore's Hardware? He used to close early if he saw Reese coming. What if he was coming for an axe to kill Harold and Pauline next?"

I swallowed.

"And the diner?" Toby went on, eyes sharp with amusement. "They used to 'forget' his orders. Man would sit there for an hour, just waiting for a plate that was never coming." He laughed, shaking his head. "Shoulda seen the look on his face the first time it happened. After that, he stopped going out much. Stopped talking to people too."

Would he have stayed for me? The thought cuts deep. I know the answer. Yes. He would have burned the whole town down for me. But I wasn't that brave. "After that...he got real angry. Got into it with a couple of guys down at Murphy's. Some out-of-towners running their mouths, and next thing you know, Reese is knocking teeth out." He let out a low whistle. "Every week, he was kicking somebody's ass. His sister got him out a few times. But it was actually your brother who bailed him out last, pulled him off a guy damn near covered in blood. Harold was gonna leave him to rot."

Erik never mentioned this to me.

At all.

I felt something heavy settle in my stomach. "Why are you telling me this?"

Toby shrugged. "I dunno. Maybe I figured you'd wanna know what you're getting into. Or maybe I just wanted you to see how good we were together. I always thought we'd end up back together again, at least professionally."

"That was college, and not a chance in hell again. You crossed a line when you hid the fact that you *have a child*."

He scoffed. "I got a paternity test. The kid isn't mine."

Toby and I had been the perfect couple in everyone's eyes. Till that little scandal, and Mama was quick to make me cut ties, which I was more than glad to do.

Then Reese happened.

Then Conrad a few years later.

"C'mon, Laurie. I'm the only one that has your back. You heard what they been saying lately?"

I shook my head.

"Some say Harold Ashbourne is about to cut Reese out of the will. But the company's been bleeding money. I'd think twice before you marry Reese."

I felt the blood drain from my face.

"But *my* company's been growing, and I need someone with real expertise to crunch numbers. See the patterns. And you? You're the best at that. Everyone knows that."

"So, that's why you're here?" I finally said, coolly meeting his gaze. "Insult my fiancé, and then ask me to work for you?"

"Let's get lunch. *Just as friends.* Think about it."

Could Toby be the one behind the blackmail?

"No thanks, Toby."

He chuckled, then he stood heading for the door. "Holler at me. This town is small, right? I can fill you in on some more details."

Once Toby was gone I closed my eyes, leaning back in my chair. I had too much on my plate already. My family. The wedding. The note.

Reese's family doesn't have money? Mama said Dante was the reason we had to join forces with the Ashbournes, but was it bigger than I thought?

Was something going on in the company that Reese didn't mention?

I barely had a chance to process my thoughts when a knock echoed through the office door. I didn't even bother hiding the annoyance in my voice as I called out, "I told you to go—"

The door swung open, and I froze.

Reese.

His charcoal suit fit his broad shoulders perfectly, but his white shirt was wrinkled like he'd just rolled out of bed. His shirt was unbuttoned at the top, and his dark hair was a mess, like he'd been running his fingers through it.

"Hey." His voice was raspy. "Got a minute?"

I should not still be affected by this man. He was not a friend. He was a very reluctant partner at best, and a full-blown enemy at worst.

"Take a seat," I replied, motioning to the seat Toby had occupied.

Reese shook his head. "Mind if we step outside?"

"Hang on, I'll grab my stuff." I rose and gathered my belongings. As I left, Reese grabbed my arm.

"What's wrong?" he asked.

"Nothing. I'm fine."

"You're a terrible liar."

The truth slipped out before I could stop it. "I got a text. From the blackmailer."

Reese's expression dropped.

I hesitated for only a second before reaching for my phone, and unlocking it with a quick swipe. I hesitated before showing him the text.

He grabbed my phone, his fingers brushing mine. The contact sent a shiver down my spine, but I forced myself to stay still, even as something hot coiled low in my stomach.

"They're just trying to get in my head."

"Tell me what you need." His voice was lower and rougher, and I couldn't stand my reaction to it.

"I've got it under control."

"You don't," he murmured. "But lucky for you, we're in this together."

Taking my phone back, I headed out of the office. I made myself ignore how warm he was and his cologne as he caught up next to me. We were nearly out of the gallery when people rushed in. I instinctively grabbed his hand.

His skin was so incredibly hot, it sent shivers down my spine. Everything faded when I touched it—the noise, the crowd, the air.

I glanced up, meeting his gaze—darker now, intense, probing, searching.

I wanted to escape, but my body wouldn't let me. His thumb brushed the back of my hand, just barely, and the air in my lungs turned heavy. He wordlessly pulled me close, his arm around my shoulders.

Did you forget you don't love him anymore?

I held my breath as we passed a group of onlookers, some whispering, some nodding in approval, others clearly trying to sneak a picture.

Reese leaned in as if to kiss my temple, but his lips stopped a breath away, his voice just loud enough for only me to hear.

"Good enough?"

I forced the rise of my emotions down. "Yeah."

Reese's hands ran up and down my sides, his gaze lingering on me in a way that was almost tender—too tender for two people who were nothing more than a sham of a couple.

We slipped outside, the cool breeze offering a brief respite from the gallery's intensity and *him*. And then I spotted it. His red Ford Mustang Boss.

"You still have that?"

He released me abruptly, putting space between us. "Some things I can't let go of."

I slid into the passenger seat of his car. The last time I was in here was before Conrad and I got engaged. Reese started the car, and we sped off.

"I thought you wanted to talk." I glanced at him, his eyes fixed on the road ahead.

"You remember these drives? When we used to disappear like this?"

I remembered how I loved being the one in this spot, the girl who got bad boy Reese Ashbourne. He's the boy they warned me about. The man I could never resist.

But that girl didn't exist anymore.

Back then, it felt like being with him was a rebellion of my own, a chance to step outside the pristine lines I'd been groomed to follow.

Away from it all, I had time to think. Mama demanded perfection from us all. Years chasing her approval, making sure the King name endured, thinking if I just did more—smiled brighter, stood taller, won more—maybe I'd finally feel like I contributed enough.

But one day, I realized there wasn't enough makeup, enough trophies, enough anything to fill the gap between what I was and what she wanted me to be. That realization had been like stepping off a cliff into nothingness.

The awakening was terrifying. I traded impulsive daydreams for sharp edges, naïve rebellion for clarity.

"I doubt we're here to just reminisce, so where are we going?" I pressed again.

"It's Tobias Merrick."

I twisted in my seat to look at him. "What?"

"He's the one blackmailing us."

"*Toby?*"

I knew Toby better than Reese did. The two of them never liked each other for some male bravado reason I couldn't care less about. Sure, he'd made questionable investments, and his taste in cologne was, frankly, an assault. But Toby? Calculated? Manipulative?

"That's what my gut is telling me."

"What about the brief I sent? There's the Sterlings, Annabelle Asher, that weird guy from our art class in high school—"

"It's Toby."

"Why?" I demanded.

"Didn't you say that's our deal? Report everything we know. Protect each other. Or was that a lie?" Reese's voice went icy.

"I'm just saying if this is because he stole your toy—"

"It wasn't just a toy, Laurene." His voice dropped. "It was a limited-edition collectible worth seventy-five thousand dollars. *That* he stole from me."

"I know Toby," I shot back. "If you said he was trying to get you to invest in a BBQ joint inside a strip club, I'd believe you. He's not that smart."

"You're too dismissive of him. Guy's a clown, but he's not dumb."

"What could he possibly gain from this?"

"Money, revenge, sex?" Reese glanced over at me, his green eyes full of conviction. "Maybe he's mad about how you broke up with him. He's a sleazy bastard."

"It seems far-fetched and convenient. Let's explore other options."

"I spoke with my mother," Reese began. "She mentioned that Tobias had been asking around about our family business and poking into Conrad. He showed up at the hospital when Conrad was in the coma. Sent flowers. Didn't I get flowers?"

"You make him seem like a supervillain."

Reese glanced at me before returning to the road. "Desperate people can do desperate things. Did he tell you that over half of his restaurants got shut down in the last year? Salmonella and lawsuits. I decided any partnerships Jennie didn't end with him before were done."

So, he just came to me and lied?

Who was telling the truth?

"You think he stumbled onto our affair? Held on to it for six years, not knowing if I'd ever come back?" Reese subtly flinched. "And now that I've returned, he can put his nefarious plan into motion?"

"Exactly."

I frowned at him.

"I don't want to be around you. If this keeps on, I'll never be free of this, and I want to be free of you. I just want to live my life without this fucking cloud of bullshit hanging over me!"

His words hit me like a slap, and I fought not to let the hurt show. *Focus on the goal, your inheritance*, I reminded myself.

"I don't want this," I whispered, trembling. "I loved my life in Paris. It was *mine*. I just want to open my own art gallery. Being here? It's a fucking inconvenience, but I'm doing what needs to be done. I don't want anyone after me, and I sure as hell don't want to be married to you. I just need us to be safe."

"For how long?" I couldn't ignore the pain in his sharp tone. "Until things get uncomfortable again? Until you decide it's easier to pack your bags? Somebody else dies?"

The anger just left, leaving me all wobbly and raw; I slumped in my seat.

"Stay. Go. I don't care what you do," Reese said, parking in the lot of the yacht club, the marina close, and he stepped out of the car. "But I'm not going to sit here and debate when there's a knife to our fucking throats."

The car door slammed, the noise booming in the stillness.

You might be wrong in all of this, Laurene.

CHAPTER 10

Reese

I DESCENDED INTO THE MARINA, the sounds of creaking and smells of salt and diesel heavy in the air. Sleek yachts filled each slip, gleaming in the sun. I could still see Conrad out on the water, the rhythmic splash of oars echoing across the lake as he rowed with his team, his face set in fierce concentration. I followed the path to our slip.

It was still empty.

Conrad had a sleek, powerful boat. The way he'd handle that damn thing, like it was alive. He loved it more than anything. Hell, he cared for it more than me.

"Everyone on board!" Conrad called as he stood at the dock's edge.

Music and laughter spilled from the raging engagement party; half the guests were up in the yacht club, and the other were giggling excitedly, coming down the wooden dock to the boat. Conrad smirked, his hand resting on the railing.

I watched him closely. I just wanted this night to be fucking over and done with. "You really think they're gonna just let us go wild out there?"

"Relax. No one's looking for trouble—unless you are." Grinning, he turned his head toward me. "Dad may have an issue with you if you want to start a fight tonight of all nights."

I clenched my jaw, fighting the urge to snap. Just then Laurene came down the dock. I inhaled sharply, and the wind picked up, lifting her hair over her shoulders. We had a plan. I just had to do it.

"Damn, look at you," he drawled, reaching for Laurene's waist as soon as she was close enough. He tugged her in, his grip too casual, too possessive. "Did you wear this for me, baby?"

I froze.

Laurene stiffened before forcing a smile, but I caught it. The split-second hesitation. The way her eyes flickered toward me.

"You look tense, Reese. Maybe you should loosen up a little with one of these young ladies out here." He tugged Laurene closer before he released her, shoving her toward the boat.

I moved before I could think, stepping into Conrad's space.

"Put your hands on her like that again," I murmured, "and I'll break your fucking fingers."

Conrad's smirk wavered briefly.

Then it was back, wider, amused, like he wanted me to snap.

"Chill out," he said, throwing up his hands. "When you get a fiancée, or someone to actually love you, then you tell me what to do."

I didn't blink, feeling the tension in my muscles.

Conrad clapped his hands, calling out to the group, "We getting on this boat or what?"

"You alright?" Laurene's voice startled me.

I turned sharply, not realizing how close she'd gotten. She stood just a few feet away. The breeze tugged a strand of hair across her face, but she didn't brush it away.

"I'm fine," I mumbled.

"You don't look fine." Laurene hugged herself. "God, I thought...I thought I could handle this. But seeing it again..." She shook her head, blinking fast as she looked around. "What are we doing here?"

"You don't have to be here, you know." I didn't want to be here but this was where everything started. "No one's making you stay."

Her jaw clenched, a muscle twitching in her cheek as she bit her lip. Then she let out a slow breath. "And leave you to face this alone? I've done enough."

My hand moved before I could stop it, brushing against her temple as I reached to tuck a strand of hair behind her ear. *What the hell was I doing?* My fingers only grazed her skin, just the barest touch, but it was enough.

What does she want me to say? That I forgive her? That I don't still feel it?

She shifted, her lips parting like she wanted to speak, but nothing came out. She tilted her head just slightly, as though daring me to do it again. It would only take the smallest move to close the distance, to cross the line we both knew existed but neither wanted to acknowledge.

"We'll get through this. Together."

Last time she said that, she left town for six years.

I remember diving in, over and over again. The alcohol had burned away, leaving my mind sharp.

"Together," I echoed. "I just… I don't know if I can trust that yet. Why couldn't you have told the truth about what happened that night?"

Her eyes searched mine, and my resolve slipped. The curve of her face pulled me in first, soft and sharp all at once, but it was her lips that unraveled me. Painted a red so vivid it burned.

I swallowed hard.

"You don't get it, Reese. It wasn't just about us. My mother… My family. Everything I've done, everything I've been…" She exhaled, her breath shaky. "I was going to lose it all. And I couldn't. You were…you were the wrong choice. And I had to do what they told me. I had to play the part," Laurene said.

"I loved you," I said, the words slipping out before I could stop them. "I was ready to give up everything for you."

My fingers twitched at my sides, an urge blooming there—raw, reckless. I wanted to reach for her, to feel the heat of her skin beneath me again. I couldn't tell if she leaned in or if I was imagining it. She was close, her hands on my chest, staring up.

"You make it so easy to forget why I shouldn't want you," I blurted out.

"I'm sorry, Reese. I should have spoken up."

Do it. Do it. Do it. Get it out of your system.

"I can't..." I desperately attempted to keep my grip on reality. "That apology... It's not what I envisioned."

She had been the only softness in my world of sharp edges.

"Do you want me on my knees? I'm sorry. I fucked up, and I was wrong, and it's haunted me every day. I'm just...*so, so sorry.*"

I leaned in, her lips tilting up toward me, soft and inviting, as if daring me to cross the line we'd declared. The world seemed to hold its breath, every sound and sensation fading until there was only her.

My hand hovered near her waist. Her eyes fluttered, her lips parting ever so slightly.

But at the last second, my resolve buckled.

Her hair brushed against my cheek as I shifted in, leaning past her lips and into her neck. Her skin was impossibly warm, impossibly soft, carrying that faint intoxicating scent that was hers alone. It clouded my senses, drowning out logic, reason —everything.

But I couldn't trust her.

I felt her hesitate; I thought she might pull away. She should've. I should've.

Her fingers curled into the fabric of my shirt with an almost desperate grip. Her breath tickled my ear as she let out a small, shaky exhale, and I wondered if she was disappointed—or relieved.

I closed my eyes, pressing my face deeper into her neck, feeling her pulse quicken beneath my cheek.

It was too much—too familiar, too raw.

"I don't know how to do this," I said, my voice barely audible.

"Neither do I," she whispered. Her hand rose slowly, brushing a loose strand of hair from my forehead.

The urge to drown in her, to be *home* again, to replace the ache of the past with the taste of something pure, something that felt like hope was strong. I built an empire out of my own ruin. But none of it mattered if she won't stand beside me, if I can't look at her the same.

"I know I've made mistakes," she said, "but this is where we are now, and there's no way out except forward. Together."

My hands tightened around her waist.

"But I need you to trust me now."

Her warm palm found my cheek, her thumb tracing gentle, deliberate circles that sent shivers down my spine.

"Why can't you just let me hate you?" I pulled back slightly. "It would be so much easier."

Laurene opened her mouth to respond, but then we heard—

"Hey, y'all can't be down there! This area is off-limits."

I slowly backed away, as if wading through mud. I needed the anger to surge back, to be a protective barrier against whatever I had just let slip through.

"Wait…is that you, Lulu?"

Laurene frowned, and she turned and gasped.

"Miles!"

I was scared, scared to let her in again, scared of what that might mean. And yet, a part of me craved the connection, the warmth of her understanding that I missed for so long. But I needed to remember the betrayal, to stay strong. Letting her in would only open old wounds I fought too damn hard to sew shut.

"Girl, it is you! Where the hell you been?" Miles Whitmore's voice carried across the dock. I caught sight of his tailored outfit, his hair braided back in cornrows and his light brown skin tanned.

The Whitmores, for as long as anyone could remember, had been the Kings' best friends. They went as far back to Miles's great-grandparents, who had been friends with Augustus King and followed him here and helped found the town. Until six years ago, right around the time of Conrad's accident, when the Whitmores and Kings severed all ties.

"Damn, it's been too long." Miles's arms opened wide for a hug. "When did you get back?"

"Not too long ago."

Miles glanced over at me with a hint of suspicion in his eyes. "What I read about was true, then?"

"It's true," I said flatly, holding his gaze.

Laurene stepped back to me, and I felt a bit of pride when she pressed closer and nodded at Miles.

"Damn." Miles's eyes narrowed slightly as he glanced between us. "Well, congratulations to both of you then. Tell me where to send a wedding gift."

I snorted.

"I wish you could have been at the party," Laurene murmured, her hand brushing against mine as she gently wrapped her fingers around it.

"Yeah, well." Miles's expression tightened, his hands slipping into his pockets. "What brings you two to my yacht club? Last I checked, trespassing wasn't your style."

Laurene and I exchanged surprised looks. "You own the club now?"

I hadn't heard of any deals lately, but with the way secrets ruled this town, who the hell knows.

"It kinda went downhill after…well, you know." He gestured between us and the ocean. "But you're not here to talk about that, are you?"

We were here to return to the scene of the crime—see if anything was left behind or if someone had seen something. I looked down at Laurene to explain.

"We're here because…" Laurene began, glancing at me, and I shrugged. "We wanted to discuss some arrangements for the wedding. Thought this would be a good place to start."

Miles gawked. "Wedding? Same plans as before?"

I locked eyes with him. "Just exploring options. Nothing to worry about."

A brief silence settled before Miles cleared his throat.

"Actually, Reese, it's good you're here. Conrad's memorial is still up. The last owners kept it up all these years because he was captain of the row team. No disrespect, but we wanna do something new for the place. I was planning to reach out to your family about it, but since you're here..."

I nodded, balling my fists at my sides. "Yeah, I can take care of that."

"Let's hit it, folks."

Following him, I glanced back at the empty pier before entering. The water lapped against the posts, sluggish, almost too still, like it was holding its breath.

The yacht club's interior was magazine-worthy. The polished marble floors gleamed under the soft glow of ornate chandeliers and framed photographs of the row teams and sailors. Passing the bathroom, Laurene and I glanced at each other. There was a tiny spot not too far away—perhaps that's where the photo was taken.

"Here you are."

Conrad's locker, adorned with flowers and a photo, stood against the wall. I inhaled sharply, my throat tightening with emotion.

Laurene took my hand.

"I don't wanna give you another boring speech about what Conrad meant to this club. We all know he meant a lot to all of us." Miles eyed our clasped hands, eyebrow raised. "I have a box for his things."

Laurene's voice was steady beside me. "We won't be long."

"Well, if you need anything—"

"Thanks," I interrupted.

"Alrighty then," Miles said. "Laurene, hit me up. We have a lot to talk about."

Conrad's rowing coach mentioned the memorial after the funeral, but none of us in the family had the guts to go.

"I dream about the accident all the time," Laurene said quietly. "I keep thinking, what if you hadn't pulled me out of the current? What if I could have stopped you both from fighting? You didn't have to do what you did that night. But you did."

"I loved you," I admitted. "I wouldn't have let anything happen to you."

"We should start packing these away." Laurene reached for a framed photo, her fingers lingering over Conrad's smiling face. "Maybe we might find something for our...situation?"

We moved in near silence, the weight of the moment thick in the air. Flowers, wilted and brittle, released a faint sickly sweet scent as I brushed them aside. Beneath the bouquet, my fingers grazed something cold and metallic.

A small silver pendant. Its sailboat shape was delicate, almost innocent. My breath hitched as I held it up, the faint gleam catching the dim light. For a moment, I hesitated, the chill of the metal biting into my skin.

How long had this been here?

I opened the locker door, revealing his belongings neatly arranged—a snapshot of his life, frozen in time. It was the usual junk at first, but I found small wooden box at the bottom of the locker. I picked it up, its weight heavier than I expected. Laurene paused and glanced up. Neither of us spoke, our breaths held as I eased the lid open.

Inside was a set of keys, a worn leather wallet, a journal with frayed edges, and a folded piece of paper.

I unfolded the paper, studying the contents—a faded map of Lush marked with notes and symbols. My heart quickened as I recognized Conrad's meticulous handwriting, detailing places and times for a new resort.

"This is Conrad's blueprint," I murmured, my mind racing as the pieces started to fall into place. The sketches, the annotations

—expansion plans for a new resort. Tobias pissed over us ending our deal.

And then it hit me.

"Tobias."

The bastard. Mom was right. Tobias always had his eye on this shit. Six years, and he still couldn't get over the idea of trying to pull something from my family's grasp. But why the hell would he want this now? Conrad was dead; the world had moved on.

"He's been after Conrad's plans all along."

Laurene's brow furrowed in disbelief. "Reese—"

"It could explain everything—why he'd been so interested in Conrad's work back then, why he was lurking around, pretending to be concerned. Why he's back now."

"Reese, calm down." She stepped in front of me, blocking my path. "He didn't say that earlier—"

I stopped pacing, narrowing my eyes at her. "What do you mean, *earlier*?"

Laurene froze. Box in hand, I stormed toward the exit, seething. I couldn't get to the car quick enough. I ripped the door open and dropped the stuff in.

"Reese!"

Laurene was rushing toward me.

"We need a plan."

"What's there to plan?" My patience was worn thin. "We need answers, and we need them now. Let's go confront Tobias about this bullshit."

"You're letting your emotions take over." She took a step closer, eyes cold but focused. "We don't go charging in blind. We gather what we need, then we make him answer for it."

I began to protest, but Laurene interrupted me.

"You never think about the fallout." She shook her head. "You haven't even said what that paper is for! What will Toby do with that now? If at all? Are you just picking him to be guilty?"

"Now it's my fault?" I scoffed. "Just like it was back then, right? I was always the one to blame for wanting more, for wanting us to be something."

"You're impossible!" she shot back. "You never listen. You're always making everything about *you*."

"You're damn right it's about me!" I retorted, stepping closer to her, trying not to be entranced by that damn perfume. "Because you never gave a damn about us. About what I wanted. At what point do I stop hoping that you'll do right, Laurene? At what point do I stop only wanting to meet in hotels and sneaking to other towns to be with you like I wanted? I was honest from the beginning."

"You were *reckless*, just like now! It was fun when we first started dating, but we weren't in a vacuum, Reese! We had families, reputations. I just said I'm sorry—"

"You care so much about duty? That's rich coming from you." Anger flooded my veins. "Do you really love your family that damn much? Huh? The same people you cried on my shoulder about? The mother that arranged this bullshit? I wanted a life with you, not a series of stolen moments!"

Her eyes glimmered with unshed tears. "Do you think I didn't want a life with you?"

"Then why didn't you do something?" I pressed, my frustration boiling over. "Why didn't you stop the damn arranged marriage if you cared so much? *You* had the power to change everything! Maybe Conrad would be alive if you had."

Laurene's face went white.

"You were too busy playing the martyr because that's what you're used to, Laurene. People coming to save you. Everyone loves the girl who looks good while suffering."

Her expression hardened. "And what about you, Reese? You think you're some kind of hero? You were too busy pretending you didn't care what people thought, but you did. You always thought Conrad was better than you, and you use him as an excuse to be an asshole. You're judging me about giving in? You let this town and their opinions, their judgments, get in your head too."

I opened my mouth to argue, but she wasn't done.

"You don't get to act like your pain is bigger than anyone else's."

The breeze stirred, lifting strands of Laurene's hair in a gentle dance around her face. Despite our argument, she looked stunning, a haunting reminder that Laurene King was my greatest love and my worst mistake.

"We should go," I murmured finally. "There's nothing more to say."

Her jaw tightened. "Trust goes both ways, Reese. And right now, I don't know if I can trust you."

"You don't trust me?" I bristled, my hands clenching into fists at my sides.

Silence. The words she didn't say stung.

"I can't do this right now," she finally said, her tone weary as she held herself. "I need some space."

"Laurene..." I started, but the words got tangled in my throat.

She shook her head, her expression hardening.

"Fine." I forced myself forward, but my heart was screaming. I reached my car, and I stole a glance back at her. "I'll talk to you later."

Slamming the door, I started the engine and peeled out, leaving Laurene shrinking in my rearview mirror.

CHAPTER 11

Laurene

ERIK'S sleek sedan purred quietly as he drove through the gates of the Ashbournes' resort, up a gorgeous driveway with perfect hedges and bright flowers.

I checked the rearview mirror again, but my own wide eyes stared back.

Erik glanced at me, then behind us. "What do you keep looking for?"

"Nothing."

I forced my hands to still in my lap, but the feeling crawled up my spine anyway, cold and certain—like I was being watched.

With the wedding three weeks out at this point, almost everything should have been sorted already. Coming here was taking up time to follow leads about our blackmailer. Maybe Mama was trying to twist the knife further and shove this in my face? Let me know how little choice I had?

"What the hell was that asshole thinking?" Erik muttered, but I shook my head. "He had no right to leave you like that."

I sighed. "It's complicated. He's just…stubborn."

"Don't excuse stranding you like that." His voice rose. "Do you want me to talk to him? Set his ass straight?"

I chuckled despite myself. "No need to get violent, E. I'm a big girl."

He sighed, rubbing his face. Mama had been running him ragged lately.

"Yeah, you've got your moments, but I still remember having to be the one to sneak out and pick you and Noelle up from Monterrey 'cause y'all got busted with those fake IDs from China."

I rolled my eyes. "Why you bringing up old news? They worked for a while until our faces got scratched up."

Erik laughed, but luckily, I remembered the old guest list for the engagement party. Mama still had it tucked away in the basement. Something told me it was worth another look.

Blair's name had been there, front and center.

How could I have forgotten *her*?

"It's between us. I'll handle it."

Blair Sterling had a way of making herself a problem. Six years later, and just her name still pissed me off. Over the years, we butted heads over everything—pageants, school elections, even whose family threw the better charity gala.

I mostly won, but Blair kept trying.

I didn't agree with Mama on much, but when it came to the Sterlings, we were on the same damn page. There was always something *opportunistic* about them, and gossip from Gigi had revealed that Blair and Reese had apparently become close friends since I left.

Reese had befriended my fucking nemesis—and didn't tell me.

Erik's eyes narrowed. "You sure? I can handle him. Hell, I *wanna* handle him."

"I'm sure." I injected as much calm into my voice as I could muster. "Why didn't you tell me you bailed him out of jail a few times?"

Erik gripped the wheel, then shrugged. "'Cause it wasn't about you."

That threw me.

"What?"

"Look, I don't even *like* dude like that. But he reminded me of —" He stopped, drumming his fingers on the wheel. "I don't know, Lu. You was gone. Reese was… You ever see somebody and just know they on the edge?"

I shifted uncomfortably, pressing against the door.

"He was out there fuckin' up, gettin' locked up, actin' like shit didn't matter. Everybody was acting like they didn't care. Not his people, not the cops, sure as hell not our folks. And I—" He hesitated, then shook his head. "I thought if someone gave a shit, he wouldn't end up another name we only say in past tense."

A lump formed in my throat.

I hadn't expected that.

"You could've told me."

He snorted. "Yeah? And what, have you run back here tryna save him? You were in Paris, tryna hold yourself together, and I was here holdin' everything else down. I didn't need you worrying about the family that already fucked everything up."

I stared at him. "So you did it because you actually care?"

"Look, don't read too much into it. That fool still dumb as hell."

The car went quiet, the only sound the hum of the tires against the road.

You fucked up so bad, Laurene…

I should have just told the truth. Maybe I would have been disowned, but now I understood why Reese was so angry. What if I were him? Could I even look at myself and not feel that rage? Regret? Disappointment?

I could survive anything—except the weight of knowing I failed him.

But he still didn't tell me about being friends with Blair. He knew how I felt about her. Was that him getting back at me?

Had something gone down between them while I was gone? Or worse, was it happening now?

Was she using him? Prying her way into our mess for her own damn benefit? The thought made me sick. Did she see us that night? Could she have known what was really going on?

I watched as the resort got closer. "Miles was able to drive me back home."

"Don't bring that shit up. I'm not in the mood."

"He used to be your best friend. Why won't you talk to him?"

"It's not that simple."

"I get it, what Omar did to Mama and Daddy was..." I exhaled, searching for the right words. "It was bad. But now we *know* he wasn't in his right mind. He was using. Can we blame Miles for choosing to defend his father?"

Erik's silence was more telling than any words.

As we drove up, the grand entryway was framed by imposing white marble pillars. Impeccably uniformed valets stood ready. Erik parked, and a valet was right there to open the doors.

Erik turned, sighing sadly. "Some things are beyond forgiveness."

Reese's words were on my mind. All these years, I had told myself that I'd done what I *had* to do.

I slowly exhaled, fingers curling in my lap. If I had told the truth back then—if I had stood my ground, instead of letting the weight of my family and this town hold me in place—what would my life have looked like now?

Conrad would still be alive. Reese wouldn't have suffered. I wouldn't have lost those years.

"Do you think they intentionally chose this place for the wedding?" I asked as the valet opened my door.

Years ago, my grandfather had fought tooth and nail to keep this property, but in the end, it slipped through our fingers and landed in the Ashbournes' lap. They never let us forget it, and now, to use it as the venue for my wedding?

Erik gave me a look. "Hell yeah."

Instrumental music played as I looked around. A woman in a sleek black dress walked by, her phone tilted slightly—was she taking a picture? My stomach did a flip. I scanned the parking lot and driveway.

Chill out. The Ashbournes own this. It's safe.

"You're free to go," I said, seeing Erik near the car.

I was partially scared of what Erik would do to Reese, but it still felt weird to interact with Reese in front of my family, and not in secret.

Erik raised a brow. "I'm not gonna swing on him."

"You have a company to run. You don't need to babysit me."

"And catch hell from Mama for not showing up and making sure the Ashbournes ain't fuck shit up? Nah, Mama would have my head."

"I'm thirty-three years old." My chest felt tight. "If I can survive Paris on my own, I'll manage here."

Erik studied me for a long moment, jaw tight.

I held his stare, unflinching.

Finally, he sighed, shaking his head. "Stubborn as hell."

"I learned from the best."

A motorcycle roared up, cutting me off before I could say anything. My heart skipped as Reese sped in on his Harley Davidson Fat Boy.

Erik's expression darkened. "Speak of the devil."

The bike grumbled, then growled to a halt. I felt annoyance, excitement, and longing all at once.

Control yourself, Laurene. Focus.

Shit, I might have to let Gigi hook me up with her friend who sold vibrators.

Reese swung off the bike smoothly. Sunlight glinted on the chrome; his jacket clung to his shoulders. He removed his helmet, his tousled hair tumbling free, and his piercing green eyes locked on to mine.

Memories slipped in, uninvited—the countless times I'd ridden with him late into the night. Lying to Mom and Dad about seeing Noelle or attending a charity meeting. The rush of breaking the rules. The wind was blowing through my hair, and his body felt warm against mine.

"You got some fucking nerve," Erik snapped, blocking Reese from me. "You just gonna show up like nothin' happened? That ain't cool, man."

I placed a hand on Erik's shoulder. "It's okay."

"She knew her way home," Reese said flatly.

I was proud he held Erik's gaze. Erik had a scary side.

Erik chuckled, and wiped his nose. "You're a cocky bastard."

"Just realizing that?"

I sighed.

Erik slapped Reese's shoulder lightly, the gesture friendly at first, but I saw the way his fingers dug into Reese's shoulder blade.

"Got some nerve, I'll give you that," Erik said, his tone still playful, but then his expression hardened. "But if you do that again and leave my sister stranded"—he stepped in closer, his voice dropping an octave—"I'll whoop yo' ass like you stole something."

For a brief second, I saw Reese go pale.

I had to hold back my laugh. A tiny part of me enjoyed seeing this. I doubted anybody had ever talked to Reese this way before.

"Even God wouldn't get me up off you if you do some dumb shit like this again." Erik's threat was clear. "Remember, you're about to be family. Act like it. I'm only sayin' this once. I would hate for you to have a black eye at the wedding and mess the photos and shit up."

I laughed. "I think we're good."

"Nah, if we gon' be brothers-in-law, he needs to know the

rules." Erik let go of Reese, giving him one last intense look. "So, let's keep things smooth, alright? Govern yourself accordingly."

Though less brash, Reese didn't look away.

"Holler if you need anything." Erik glared at Reese.

He left, and when Reese looked my way, his scowl was even deeper.

I quickly turned toward the resort. Staff stood ready, offering crystal glasses of water, their trays gleaming with lemon slices. Above us hung a huge glass-and-gold chandelier.

"Laurene!" Jennie appeared.

Conrad was the eldest Ashbourne; Jennie was a year younger. Like Gigi, Reese's older siblings were five or six years older.

With a big smile, she rushed over for a hug. We chatted at the party, and she was always sweet.

"I told Reese to swing by my mom's with you so we could catch up faster." Jennie shot Reese a dirty look.

She was Conrad's double. Those piercing blue eyes held an intensity that made me momentarily uncomfortable. While hers were warm, Conrad's had been colder. He never looked at me with any real feeling. Jennie inherited her mother's tawny-gold hair; Conrad's was black.

I used to joke that Conrad was an ice-cold Clark Kent.

He had the looks, the charm, the easy way of making people want to believe in him. But where Superman was all heart, Conrad was… There was nothing. No heart, no soul, no real care. Just a guy who knew how to play the part and make everyone believe it.

I saw it at the gala that night. We'd just taken a photo; his arm was around me, and he had this easy, charming smile. He seemed delightful, gracious, and perfect. But the second the camera flashed and the photographer turned away, his expression dropped like a mask slipping off.

The warmth drained from his face, and all that was left was…nothing. I knew it then. Conrad didn't feel—he performed.

Reese remained silent as Jennie chattered. "Let's not keep the wedding planner waiting. Yvonne wants you to do a walk-through of the venue. Just one last glance to make sure nothing's missing."

I walked with Jennie, dreading another wedding. Would I make it to three, four weddings in this life?

"How's running the place, especially now?" I gestured to her stomach.

"It's a whirlwind, honestly. But seeing everything come together, especially with this little one on the way, it's like every-thing makes sense now." Jennie's face brightened.

"What are you having?"

"It's a surprise," she said. "Everyone hates not knowing. But David and I like it this way."

"Just like you. Always keeping everyone guessing," Reese chimed in.

"You're invited to the baby shower, Laurene!" Jennie told me. "Hopefully baby won't be at the party with us yet, though."

We stepped through the grand door of the terrace, and it unveiled a breathtaking ocean view, and a stone pathway lined with seashells and lanterns led to an enchanting gazebo. It was draped in flowing white chiffon, adorned with vibrant bougainvillea, filling the air with the sweet scent of jasmine.

"You like it?" Jennie asked, breaking the spell.

I was speechless.

Rows of elegant white chairs and delicate white silk bows fluttered gently in the breeze. It was far beyond my expectations. Memories of my previous wedding planning flashed through my mind, just stifled conversations and hurried directions.

"Here's your guide for the tour. I need to catch up on some business," Jennie said as a staff member approached.

Jennie squeezed Reese's shoulder as she passed him. "Are you coming to the mansion party next week?"

My brow furrowed in surprise. "Mansion party?"

Jennie glared at Reese. "You haven't told Laurene about the party? She has to come."

"We've been busy," Reese said.

To avoid upsetting Jennie, I smiled. "I'll gladly come."

Grinning, Jennie playfully punched Reese then left. "Good. You better make sure she's there, Reese! Black tie!"

The staff gestured toward the far end of the terrace. "Should we keep going?"

We were led through the resort, and at certain moments they pointed out details for our ceremony. My heart did a little flip when she led us to the bridal suite. The room's muted tones unsettled me, especially the empty space for the bridal gown.

Will this all be over before the wedding?

I noticed something strange on the dressing table, and I stepped closer to investigate. A hairpin and a bracelet scattered near the edge—and a vase of white lilies.

I stared, transfixed by a sudden chill.

I looked back at Reese. When he recognized the flowers, his face lightened.

The *bracelet* was Conrad's wedding gift to me. The first thing I'd tossed into the trash at the airport after everything fell apart. How was it here? How could it be here?

"Are these from the last bride?" I asked, trying not to let my panic show.

I lifted the hairpin, another gift from Conrad I'd thrown away.

My heart pounded in my chest, a sharp rhythm, like a countdown.

"Sometimes they leave personal things behind, but I wouldn't worry."

I didn't love Conrad. Our engagement was just a show, a way for the family to stay in control.

"This way."

The ornate double doors swung open, revealing a private

room. Cakes were on a table in the middle. Reese bristled as the planner told us we would be cake tasting for our wedding cake.

"Do we really need to decide on this right now?"

"I know wedding planning can be overwhelming, but this is one of the fun parts!" They looked between us. "Mrs. King insisted you two choose the cake."

Reluctantly, Reese and I sat at the table, facing the food. My stomach started growling as the planner stepped out in the hallway. Reese immediately noticed.

"Did you eat anything today?"

How could I eat with everything going on? "Honestly, it didn't cross my mind."

He sighed, shaking his head. "Skipping meals like this is bad for you."

This was an old argument we'd had a hundred times. Reese reached over, grabbed a fork, and swiped a piece of cake from a nearby platter and held it up to my mouth. "Eat."

My eyebrow rose. "Are you serious?"

The cake and frosting looked delicious. But I'd gotten back into Pilates and yoga, and that couldn't be disrupted.

"C'mon, don't act like I haven't fed you before," he said, a playful smirk tugging at his lips.

There had been countless late nights, me curled up in his lap, sharing bites of takeout while the glow of the television flickered across our faces. We'd laugh until our sides hurt, the world outside forgotten.

"You know you love it when I take charge."

My heart pounded; I inched closer, watching him.

Reese's eyes glinted dangerously as he offered me cake. He fed me, his fingers brushing my lips. The sweetness of the cake exploded on my tongue, with the tingle of his touch left behind.

"See? Not so bad, right?" he murmured, his voice smooth and rich, almost a purr. I felt challenged by his words, my pulse racing.

"Not bad at all."

It was actually fun tasting cakes. I reached for another cake, vanilla this time, and cautiously took a bite, trying to get rid of butterflies in my belly. It wasn't the same as when he fed me.

"It's good," I murmured.

He nodded, his lips twisting. "Yeah, not bad."

I caught the look on his face and shook my head, a small laugh slipping out before I could stop it.

"You hate vanilla."

Reese paused. "I didn't think you'd remembered that."

"I didn't forget. Don't just settle for the first one." I pulled the plate away from him.

He couldn't hide the smile. "I figure if we settle on the first one, we can avoid trying all the flavors and get the hell out of here."

"And what? Have this cake stuck in our freezer forever?"

I almost forgot we wouldn't have a real marriage.

We weren't gonna spend *years* together. I was focused on getting my money. And leaving Reese behind. But it was nice to have a light moment, forget about life or death, or that blackmailer maybe watching.

"Now that you put it like that...this shit is awful." Reese chuckled warmly and genuinely.

We moved on to the next cake—a rich chocolate ganache. He gave me another bite, and his fingers lingered on my face a bit too long. We tried a few more flavors—lemon chiffon with blueberry compote, red velvet with cream cheese frosting—each one delicious, and slowly I found myself relaxing as conversation between us flowed.

The planner returned with her clipboard. "So, which was your fav?"

Reese was lost in thought, slowly licking the lingering cake off his spoon. That sight gave me goosebumps in a good way.

"Can you give us a moment?" I waited till she left, but Reese spoke before I could.

"I need to apologize for everything I said at the yacht club," he began. "You were right. It's not something to just rush into without a plan. I'm sorry."

"You must be really terrified Erik's gonna kick your ass."

Reese snorted. "I think he's the only one in town who could."

"I'm sorry too," I said softly, my fingers tracing the edge of my glass. The words felt strange in my mouth, foreign. "I shouldn't have said…what I said before. It wasn't fair."

I peeked at him. For a second, Reese didn't say a word; his face gave nothing away. The silence stretched between us, and I almost wished he'd interrupt, save me from the rawness of the moment.

But he didn't.

I had to say this.

"I know we used to talk about leaving it all behind, but I lied to you. I lied about wanting to start over. Deep down, I liked how safe I was, how everything made sense. I thought it would be easy—letting you handle telling Mama I wouldn't marry Conrad." Though my voice shook, I continued. This was the truth. I'd avoided it too long.

"It wasn't easy. I didn't want to give all that up. When she stared me down in that room, I caved. I gave in so fucking easy. I wasn't as brave as you." I swallowed hard, the weight of it pressing down. "I didn't realize until Paris what it truly means to stand on your own. I thought leaving was easier, but it wasn't. Not for me. And certainly not for you."

I breathed shakily. "You deserved so much more and someone who stayed. I'm sorry I caused you to suffer because I only cared about saving myself. I know we have to do this arranged marriage, but I hope you find someone who helps you carry the weight. I'll make sure you're vindicated after. I'll tell the truth."

His expression surprised and silenced me.

"My family… We all went to therapy right after Conrad died," he said finally, almost like he was confessing a secret.

"They said it helped. My mom, my sister—even my dad went. And I tried, I did. For a while."

I blinked in surprise. "Therapy?"

"Went, yeah. Sat there, mostly. Never really talked." He shrugged, but his tension showed. "I didn't want to dig all that up. Figured if I ignored it, maybe it'd just go away."

"Did it?" I asked gently.

Reese's jaw tightened, and he shook his head. "It just sits there, like this damn weight that never leaves. I was angry. I felt like if I talked about it, all the anger, the guilt, it would just swallow me whole."

That really broke my heart. "Shutting it out doesn't make it disappear. It just makes it hurt longer."

"I know. But when I was there, I couldn't stand the idea—I felt like something broken that needed fixing, but I knew I couldn't be."

I placed my hand over his.

"It felt like…if I admitted I was messed up, that maybe I couldn't come back from that," he went on. "I felt like I'd just end up proving everyone right. That I was the screw-up they thought I was. And so I quit."

I didn't know what to say. His words unraveled something inside me, something raw and unsteady.

"I don't know why I'm even telling you this," he muttered, a trace of his old defensiveness creeping back. "Guess I figured… I dunno. It doesn't matter."

But it did matter.

Reese wasn't soft. He was all bravado and reckless decisions. Back then, what got me was how he lived life on his own terms, ignoring all the rules. It was the opposite of everything I was, of everything I'd been taught to be. I told myself I came back for business. But deep down, I think I was always coming back for him.

Back then, in the shadow of family feuds and public scrutiny, he'd made me feel alive in ways I hadn't known I needed. The stolen moments, the whispered arguments that turned into heated make-outs, the secret we shared.

With Reese, I wasn't the carefully controlled version of myself that the world expected. I was just Laurene.

And he was the only one who saw *her*—my rawest form.

I should've said something cold, something to push him back into that safe distance. I wasn't staying in Lush. We were under threat.

Instead, something in me faltered.

My old self was coming back. The sweet and kind Laurene. I hated how much I noticed the subtle hitch in his voice, the way he ran a hand through his hair like he didn't know what to do with himself. He survived without me. And I hate that I can't say the same.

"I have to tell you something too. I've been thinking…what if Blair Sterling could be behind the blackmail?"

Reese raised an eyebrow, clearly taken aback. "Blair?"

"Why not? She was at the engagement party that night, and I've been combing through old photos. She's in almost every single one of them."

Reese pursed his lips. "Blair's more the type to stab you in the chest than stab you in the back."

"When were you gonna tell me you were friends with her?" My voice came out sharp, a lot sharper than I intended. "Or were you just waiting for the right moment to rub it in my face?"

Reese's expression hardened. "It's not like that, Laurene. She's not even—"

"Did you fuck her while I was gone?"

I needed to know. If he'd done it, everything would've changed. It'd all be different.

"You think I'd do that?" Reese's voice had a sharp edge now.

"Yes or no?"

He opened his mouth to speak but then closed it, visibly fighting with himself. His eyes shifted, and for a split second, I saw it—the crack. But then he shut it down. "You don't get to ask me that."

"I'm going to be your wife—"

"This is not a real marriage. Whoever I may or may not have fucked is not your business, and whoever you were with is not mine." His gaze locked on to mine, intense. "Let's focus on what's coming for us, Laurene. We've got bigger problems."

I took a breath. I guessed it was time to finally confess.

"She confronted me at the engagement party."

Reese raised an eyebrow. "Confronted you? About what?"

I paused, thinking it over. It had been years, but the memory still stirred something in me that felt like mild shame mixed with justification.

"She wanted to talk about the pills I caught her taking."

Reese's eyes widened in surprise.

I never wanted to be that person—*the manipulator*. Like Mama who turned every moment of weakness into an opportunity. Blair left me no choice then. I mean, she'd do the same to me if we were in each other's shoes.

"Right before my last pageant, a few months before the engagement party, I saw her in the bathroom. She was popping pills like they were candy. God knows what they were. For her to lose weight, maybe?" I swallowed, the bitterness rising in my throat. "I took a photo of it."

Reese blinked, his expression now a mixture of disbelief and judgment. "That got leaked online. Everyone saw."

"There's a consequence for every action." I shrugged.

I did not leak the photos. I just gave someone else the opportunity to.

"Holy shit, Laurene. You really think that makes it okay?" He pushed his plate slightly away.

"Blair isn't some innocent victim. She don't get to pick and choose when karma's a problem."

He wasn't convinced, not fully.

"She had sent me a couple of threats after that, leading up to the engagement party, but I just brushed them off."

Reese leaned back in his seat.

"If there's someone who dislikes me more than anyone in town, it's Blair. If we're gonna accuse Toby, let's put her on the list too."

"What exactly did she threaten you with?"

"She threatened me with some photos." I swallowed, not even wanting to think anything of it. "Blair had gotten her hands on photos of my father. They were taken during a trip he'd made to Miami."

"Photos of your father doing what?"

That was my father's business and his alone. "Partying. Daddy doesn't do it often. But if the photos got out it would be bad press."

Reese's brow furrowed. "So, what did you do?"

"I paid her off," I said flatly, my gaze shifting as I remembered it. "It was everything she asked for, and then some."

Reese's eyebrows lifted. "So you just…gave in?"

"Not exactly." I didn't look at him. "I hired a photographer to be there when I paid her. I mean, what would the town think if they caught photos of Blair extorting *me*? Well, gosh, if those photos got out it would be terrible for her family, wouldn't it?"

"This is too much. Blair blackmailed you. You blackmailed her right back. Now she could have blackmailed you again? I mean…" Reese ran a hand through his hair. "You know what? I need to go."

"Wait," I said.

"I used to think you weren't like this town, Laurene. You didn't do the bullshit lying, manipulating, and cheating, like everyone else here does. But now I see you're the same. You *are* this town." He paused, then added, almost to himself, "I need time."

Shit, why did I tell him?

Reese walked out, and I gathered my things in a daze, ready

to get the hell out. I told the staff to pick a cake as I brushed past them. When I stepped into the lobby, I paused, taking a deep breath.

I thought we were in this together.

I felt a rush of uncertainty and anger coursing through me. Blair was playing a dangerous game, and now it was clear I had to be ready to fight back.

The lilies in the bridal suite.

I didn't get to bring them up with Reese. Without thinking, I turned on my heel and headed back toward the bridal suite. Each step amplified my frustration. I entered the suite, the familiar scent of the lilies hitting me.

My gaze flicked around the room.

The hairpin and the bracelet—they were gone.

I moved toward the couch, flipping the cushions up. Nothing. I opened drawers, sifting through the contents. Nothing but tissues, cotton pads, and thank-you notes. The neatness of the room was almost unsettling.

Frustration bubbled inside me. I crouched down and yanked at the edge of the plush rug, pulling it back. Nothing but polished wood. I tossed the rug back as I stared at the vase of lilies on the table. I stepped back and immediately lost my balance, my foot caught in the overturned rug. I reached for the table, but my elbow slammed against it instead.

Pain shot through my arm, and the vase teetered.

Shattering glass echoed through the room, and lilies scattered across the floor.

"Damn," I muttered. I knelt down to collect the broken shards when I noticed something—something small and metallic nestled among the remains of the lilies. My heart thudded louder as I pulled out a lens with wires.

Wires?

I turned it over in my hand. It was a spy camera.

CHAPTER 12

Reese

THE AIR still smelled like oak and citrus from the test last night. What did I miss?

Apparently quite a fucking lot. Blackmail for blackmail? What else were the women in town doing—plotting murder?

Sighing, I reviewed my whiteboard notes. Blackmail or not, business went on. But Blair? She'd been right there the whole time. This town prized dishonesty. Laurene and Blair disliked each other more than I thought.

All the years Blair and I had been friends, all the parties and business deals, and she hadn't said a word.

Blair unexpectedly became a friend. When you're the black sheep, the group of people who'll stick by you is small, and most of them don't exactly invite you in. Despite what others thought, she was loyal—and more than once she'd helped my business out with contacts she met in her modeling.

She was one of my few supporters after the accident. At least, I thought she was. And now? I wasn't sure.

"Clean, modern, but not pretentious. Something that feels like a damn good time." I mumbled, tapping my marker against my palm.

The board was empty where my new liquor name should be. Ideas swirled around it—tequila with lime and basil, whiskey with smoked honey, vodka with wildflowers. The taste was perfect, but now I had to sell it.

I quickly grabbed my phone and started recording a voice memo. "Target market: rooftop parties, music festivals, late-night bonfires. The kind of bottle you reach for to bring to a party."

My phone buzzed, cutting me off midsentence. An email from the board. I knew what it was about without even opening it. The subject line: Production cost concerns.

I frowned, deleting it without even reading it. The same damn thing every week. I'd been making all the right decisions, or so I thought—risky, sure, but this was how you grew the brand. But the numbers weren't lining up. The balance sheets were off. Production costs were high, but they weren't supposed to be this high. I'd have to deal with it later, maybe after the wedding, when things calmed down.

When Dad found out, he would have a fucking fit, but he didn't need a big reason to come down hard on me. It's how it's always been.

Under the chandelier, the table gleamed—all polished and cold as ice.

Dad sat at the head, and Conrad sat across from him, relaxed, cool. They looked like they belonged, like this was all perfectly natural. Me? I felt like an intruder.

Jennie cleared her throat, looking a little unsure. "I'm almost done with my MBA, and Truman Capitals offered me a job running their business. But I got them to team up with us instead—we're opening a new resort in Vancouver."

"Good," Dad said quickly.

Jen slumped back, relieved, and gave me a "good luck" look.

I started to speak, but was cut off.

"Asia's our next market," Dad stated. "Conrad, you really knocked it out of the park with that Shanghai deal."

Conrad leaned back, a little smirk playing on his lips. "It's a done deal, but did you really doubt me? I'm thinking Japan next? There's a really niche market for whiskey there."

Dad wasn't just interested in the deal; he was interested in Conrad. It was always Conrad. Dad gave him his blessing like a king.

"So, Reese," Dad said, looking over his glasses at me. "Now that you've finally come to your senses, Conrad told me he gave you something to do. What was it?"

"Yes, it's—"

Conrad cut me off. "He's working on revamping our whiskey line. Not too big of a deal if he screws up."

They chuckled, and I narrowed my eyes on Conrad. Jennie gave me a sympathetic look.

Dad said, "What are your thoughts on the new product line? Anything we need to tweak before we finalize the plan?"

I wasn't only doing whiskey. I was the one who'd spent sleepless nights brainstorming new branding concepts, researching the market, tweaking the formulas. Conrad minimized it, saying it was "no biggie."

I swallowed, my jaw tight, and said, "I've—I've actually been working on a few new angles. The packaging needs to stand out more—"

"Yeah, sure, but honestly, Reese," Conrad said, leaning back in his chair, hands folded casually in front of him, "you know the branding stuff doesn't really matter until we finalize the price points. Don't waste time on packaging details if we don't even have the margins right and you can't keep costs down."

I made fists, stopping myself from snapping back.

"This is a money-making business, son." Dad scowled at me. "What do you think pays for that motorcycle of yours?"

"Product design matters, Dad," I said, my voice tense. "If the bottle looks like shit, the product won't sell. That's—"

Conrad just shook his head. "Language, Reese, Jesus. Dad is trying to school you on the right thing to do. Thank God I'm running this company because where would we be with you? Don't worry, Dad, I'm keeping an eye on him. I won't let him screw things up."

My pulse roared in my ears, and I felt a heat rise in my face, but I bit back the words that screamed inside my head. Where would we be without me, Conrad? Where would we be if I hadn't been the one to come up with half of this shit, the ideas you stole from me? That are making us money?

Dad was staring at Conrad now, nodding like he was the one with all the answers.

"See? Now this is the kind of vision we need. A good head on his shoulders. You could learn a thing or two from your brother."

"Dad—"

"Your brother is in charge, you listen to him. You can only dream of being half the man he is."

I was frozen. My throat felt tight, my heart pounding so hard it hurt.

"Enough for today," Dad said, dismissing me with a wave of his hand. He didn't even look up as he gathered his papers.

Conrad flashed me another one of those perfect smiles, the ones that made me feel like a fucking joke. "You'll figure it out," he said. "Just try not to fuck it up too much, okay?"

Conrad had stolen plenty from me over the years—ideas, credit, opportunities—but back then, I let it slide. That was just how it was with him. You fought him, or you accepted it. How stupid I'd been thinking that something would change between us. That Conrad would be my brother.

CEO of the company I never planned to run, cleaning up a mess I never made. Some days, it felt like justice. Other days, it felt like a curse.

Snatching my phone, I pulled up Blair's contact, my thumb hovering over the call button. I wanted to yell at her and demand answers, but another part of me, the part that trusted her for years, hesitated.

I tossed my phone down and glanced at the lineup of sample

bottles on my desk. I grabbed the lime-basil tequila and poured myself a shot. The aroma hit first—bright and fresh—and then the taste followed, smooth with a subtle kick of herbs.

"Damn," I muttered, setting down the glass. "That's it."

Blair could explain herself if she wanted; she knew how to reach me.

I looked at my whiteboard; I needed to finalize the marketing.

Influencers? Nah, overplayed. Celebrities? Maybe, but it depends on if they're a good fit. Someone real. Someone raw. Someone who could sell a dream without making it feel like a pitch.

A knock snapped me out of it.

"Yeah?"

The door creaked open, and my assistant peeked in. "Erik King, sir."

Erik? What the hell was he doing here? I got nervous, and I really tried not to show it. Laurene's brother didn't just pop in unexpectedly. Especially not after the argument she and I had last night.

No doubt she'd told him everything.

"Send him in."

My assistant nodded and disappeared, leaving the door ajar. A moment later, Erik walked in.

"King," I said, leaning against my desk. "Laurene sent you to do the dirty work?"

Ignoring the jab, he stepped in. "This is where you think, huh? Didn't know you did that."

"I try to keep thinking down to once every quarter. Grab a drink. This one's basil-lime tequila—smooth as hell." I pointed to the sample bottles.

He walked over, hands in pockets. He eyed the liquor before pouring a shot, giving it a slow swirl before taking a sniff. "What if it sucks?"

"Then you can brag about surviving."

Erik flipped me the bird just before he slammed the shot. His expression didn't change as he set the glass down, rolling his shoulders like it was just water.

"Not bad," he admitted. "Still waiting on the kick, though."

I couldn't help but laugh. "What do you need?"

Erik started walking around my office, looking at my notes. "You smoke?"

"Sure."

Erik tossed me a cigar, sat down, and took out his lighter. He lit it, still eyeing my office while giving me the lighter. "How do you feel about this arranged marriage?"

"Is that what you want to discuss?"

I lit my cigar, inhaling its oaky flavor as Erik stared. "It wasn't in my plans."

"But you're real comfortable, aren't you? With Laurene, this whole marriage thing—no tension, no hesitation, not a lot of fighting on your part."

I shot him a dirty look. "What are you getting at?"

"When we were kids, Laurene used to scrape her knees climbing the old maple tree in the backyard. Mama told her not to do it. Laurene's stubborn, so she did it anyway, and Mama expected it. She told me, 'You're the oldest. You take care of your sisters, no matter what.'"

Erik leaned forward, taking the tequila bottle and pouring himself another shot. I didn't bother hiding my shit-eating grin.

"One day she fell, busted her shit up quite nastily." He shook his head as if reliving it. "I patched her up before Mama got home."

"Heartwarming story," I said, confused about where this was going.

"Laurene and I figured out our roles early. I was the heir, and she was the chess piece Mama could move to make deals. We had to be perfect—no room for mistakes. Mama called it responsibility, but all it really did was teach us how to endure pain. Laurene's a fighter, just like her. It's why they clash. It's why she runs. But no matter what, she's my sister. My job has always been to protect her, even from Mama, even from herself. And maybe that's why I pulled you out of that gutter, Reese. If this was a perfect world, I wish Mama would have picked you for her first."

I didn't expect Erik King to be the one to drag me out of the fire. Hell, I didn't expect anyone to.

But Erik? He saw something worth saving. I still don't know why.

I edged the ashtray nearer for his cigar. I understood. Conrad was the heir, Jennie the spare, and I was an accident.

It's not like we talk about it. Men like us, we fight, we drink, we endure. That's how we say "I got you." But I remember what he did. And I don't forget my debts.

"Laurene was fighting too hard for you the other day. I get the arrangement, the business angle, but you didn't seem uncomfortable. Not like I'd expect."

I leaned back in my chair, trying to play it cool as Erik watched me closely. "We've both got our parts to play. Doesn't matter how it looks."

"But I know my sister. I've seen how she looks at you. How you look at her."

My stomach twisted, but I didn't flinch. Not outwardly, at least.

"What are you trying to ask me?"

"Were you and my sister in contact when she was in Paris?"

"My condolences," a woman murmurs, her voice soft and distant as she passed me by.

I nodded, watching the casket descend. My mother's cries pierced the air. She was holding on to Jennie for dear life. Dad wouldn't even give me a glance. Near the back, Nina's blotchy skin and red tear-filled eyes spoke volumes.

The hushed murmurs of prayers and the weight of silent judgments hung heavy in the air around me. I know it's awful, but a twist part of me was glad it's over. Like a pressure I didn't realize I had is finally gone.

My big fight with Conrad was finally here—I'd been planning this since day one at the distillery. For years, he'd stolen my ideas, passed them off as his own, and I let it slide because fighting back wasn't an option. Not until Laurene and I were ready.

I'd gathered proof, lined up allies on the board, and set the perfect trap. All we needed was for Conrad to take the bait. If we exposed him in front of the board, he'd have no way out. He'd lose their trust, and for the first time, our father would have to concede. I'd finally win.

I told him the whole story, and he didn't even blink. His laughter was cold and cruel, like he'd been waiting for this moment.

They buried Conrad, and I felt every pound of that dirt. No more decisions, no more fights. Just...done.

"Reese."

I looked and there was Noelle, a gentle pity in her eyes, but she looked remorseful. I looked past her at the space where Laurene should've been, where all the Kings should have sat, but instead a bereavement bouquet was sent in their place.

Noelle fidgeted, glancing around nervously. "Reese, I—"

"What?" I snapped, not bothering to hide my irritation.

"I... She's gone."

"What do you mean, gone?"

She looked down. "Yvonne kicked her out. Laurene's at the airport, Reese. She's leaving. For good."

For a second, the words didn't register. They couldn't. Laurie—my Laurie? The one I'd been through hell and back with? The one I thought would be there, no matter what?

"No." I shook her head. "She wouldn't...she wouldn't do that."

But Noelle's face was tight. She wasn't lying. It was true. The raw, ugly truth that Laurene had made her decision, and I was standing here like a fool, blindsided.

"Why didn't she tell me?"

Noelle swallowed. "I wanted you to know because...because I thought you'd want a chance to stop her. You both are meant to be together, and I know y'all didn't do this on purpose. But I can't change her mind."

Laurene was leaving, and if I didn't do something now, I'd lose her forever.

"Where is she going?"

"I'm already telling you too much that she's leaving."

I turned and walked away, then I started running—fast—my feet pounding on the dirt and gravel of the cemetery. I righted my bike, the engine roared as I twisted the throttle, ignoring all the stares.

"Reese!" Jennie yelled.

I sped, breaking every speed limit, the wind like a thousand tiny knives. My mind was consumed with Laurene. She claimed I was the only one for her. Yet, when things hit the fan, she betrayed me.

I gripped the handlebars tighter, teeth gritted, as memories flashed before my eyes. Late nights under the ink-black sky, her fingers tangled with mine, her breath warm against my ear as she whispered, "I love you."

Damn it, I'd believed her. And I let myself love her.

The private airstrip came into view, its lights cutting through the evening fog.

I tore across the tarmac, skidding to a halt. I saw it—her plane, rolling forward, about to lift off. I jumped off my bike and ran.

Her face appeared in the window of the plane. She was staring right at me. For a flash, I hoped she'd stop the plane, come back for one more shot. To make things right.

But she didn't.

She pulled down the shade, and then she was gone. Leaving me standing in the bright lights.

"No," I said, quick and firm. "We weren't."

That was the truth. Noelle never told me where she went, and I never bothered to chase it down. The rumors floated around that Laurene went to Dubai, New York, or São Paulo, but the Kings didn't talk. And Laurene disappeared from online without a trace.

Erik nodded and leaned back. "She's lying to me."

My grip on the cigar tightened.

"She's got something up her sleeve now. Something's off with her. She's not telling me anything straight anymore." Erik tsked. "I don't need to tell you Dante's changing this town. I'm watching him and I'm not as scared as Mama, but we're vulnerable right now. *Your* family is vulnerable."

He leaned in.

"If you can figure out what she's up to, tell me," Erik said, his voice low and firm. "You protect Laurene, but she's got something brewing—big, and I don't know what it is. Whatever it is, it's gonna shake things up, and not necessarily in a good way. She needs to stay focused on the company, not whatever rebellion she thinks she's pulling against Mama."

I swallowed, considering our predicament.

"Do you love her?" Erik demanded, but then cleared his voice at my shocked facial reaction. "Better yet, do you think you can love her?"

The question was loaded. I used to love the way Laurene looked at me when we were together. I loved how she felt against me riding on my bike. I loved the way she danced on the dance floor. I loved the way she commanded attention and respect. I loved that she chose me out of everybody in town.

But I also remembered the way things fell apart, the way I felt when she was with Conrad.

I spent years convincing myself she didn't matter. And now? I'm one wrong move away from proving myself a liar.

"I—" I didn't know what my feelings for her were now, but it couldn't be love. Not yet.

"I can care about her," I said instead. "I'll protect her."

Erik offered me his fist. I dapped it back, watching as he stood. He paused at the whiteboard before my office, tapping it.

"If you can help me figure this out, maybe we can be friends." His flat tone made it hard to tell if he was serious. "Have some more of that weird drink you made."

I leaned back, raising an eyebrow. "Is this Erik King trying to bond with me? Guess hell froze over."

"Hell's still hot, trust me. Just don't make me regret this." He smirked, turning to my whiteboard. "Rebel Spirits?"

He gave me the deuces and left.

I just sat there, staring at the board, letting it all sink in. Finally, I stood, gathering my things and shoving them into my bag. I needed to get out of here.

Outside the glow of the streetlights cast an eerie halo around my motorcycle, its chrome gleaming in the dark. I mounted the bike and revved the engine, and the deep rumble vibrated through my body. How the fuck was I gonna survive this?

But then, a movement caught my eye. A dark sedan loomed near the entrance of my parking lot, parked at an awkward angle, half in the shadows, the other half positioned to see the gym's entrance.

My heart skipped a beat, instinct kicking in.

I squinted, my pulse quickening as I tried to make out the figure inside. The tinted windows reflected nothing. I killed the engine and climbed off the bike, the silence around me amplifying the rustle of leaves and the distant hum of the town.

Think, Reese, think.

I stepped closer. Through the windshield, I saw a silhouette. The figure was hunched over the steering wheel, and I couldn't tell if it was a man or woman.

I couldn't afford to make a mistake. The shadow inside was still, too still. I kept walking toward the car. Then the unmistakable sound of an engine starting, breaking the silence like a shot.

The headlights flared on, spilling harsh white light across the pavement, blinding me.

Before I could react, the tires squealed, rubber-on-asphalt sound as the sedan shot forward. I flinched, stumbling back as it sped out of the lot, the taillights a streak of red against the night as the tires screeched.

But just before it disappeared, something caught my eye—a

decal on the rear windshield. Faint, barely visible in the dark, but I knew I'd seen it before. A crest. A seal. My phone blared suddenly, a shrill sound that cut through the air. The shock of what just happened made me fumbled for it.

Laurene's name flashed on the screen. I barely managed to speak before her voice shattered through the line.

"Reese. Please. Help me."

CHAPTER 13

Laurene

I SHOULDN'T HAVE TOLD *him about Blair.*

No. Mistakes meant you weren't cut out for it. I was. This house taught me survival was not about trust. It was about getting the most out of things. However…

Remembering Reese's reaction to Blair hurt. If I wanted his trust…*if* I dared to hope for that, then I had to be someone worthy of it. Was that even really me?

With Gigi in Chicago, the mansion was unsettlingly still. But I wasn't gonna let fear keep me cooped up. I heard hushed voices from downstairs.

I promised myself I'd be tougher when I returned to Lush. Hardened. The woman I'd become in Paris didn't bow, didn't falter. She learned to make it in a sink-or-swim world. And I'd swum. Fiercely.

But here, in this house, it was so much harder to keep my head above water.

Now I felt…*ashamed.* Lost. I felt like I was looking at the girl I used to be. Dutiful. Refined.

But Lush wasn't Paris.

Things were tougher here, the stakes higher, and the consequences more brutal. And I wasn't sure the woman I'd become there could survive this world without fracturing into pieces of the girl I used to be.

I paused, considering interrupting my parents.

You have to talk to them at some point.

I opened the doors and went in.

Mama and Daddy sat at the dining table; Daddy's expression was sharp, focused.

When Daddy married Mama over thirty years ago, he did something rare. He took *her* last name. Daddy came from the prominent Callaway family. They made a killing in the export business in Miami. He was the younger son; it was hard to think he'd been wild like Gigi, till he met Mama.

Mama never asked him to take her name. She would've married him regardless.

Grandpa Ben made one thing clear: if he wanted to be part of the King family, he had to do more than marry into it. He had to *become* it.

So, he became a King. But I sometimes think it's for the worse.

"Where should we place the Chen family?"

"Grace proved herself in that litigation she handled. Saved us millions." Daddy flipped through a stack of cards. "Don't want to lose her by sitting her near the Warricks. Andrew drinks."

"Hmm, right, and if they talk politics all hell will break loose," she agreed. "We'll put Andrew with the Johnsons. Robert likes to party, so that should keep things lively. And Lian—"

"She should sit with Serena," I said, cutting in.

Their heads turned toward me, Mama's gaze sharp.

"Grace's daughter is an amazing investor," I continued. "Serena can introduce her to the Martinezes. They'll respect Lian's credentials, and the Martinezes are already warming to us after Serena's last project."

Mama leaned back, her fingers steepled under her chin. "Interesting."

"Good evening, sweetheart." Daddy broke into a warm smile. "Going for a jog?"

"Something like that." I fixed my hoodie and took a seat. The dining table was covered in organized chaos—photos of guests, seating charts, and Mama's tidy but aggressive handwriting. "We're still discussing the guest list? We only have a few weeks till the wedding."

"Laurene," Mama said, "if you're going to contribute to this discussion, make it meaningful. Otherwise, go on about your business."

I tried to remind myself that she didn't choose this. It was forced upon her. Taking over the company wasn't her first choice, but it was necessary. But if that was true, why did it feel like she never fought to hold on to the woman she was before?

"Lulu's right about Lian, Yvonne." Dad's nod felt more like consolation than approval.

"But the woman wears stripes and dots."

"I didn't know my wedding was a fashion show," I muttered, picking up one of the pictures and shifting it toward the edge of the table. "What about the Andersons?"

"The Andersons? Really?" Mama rolled her eyes. "We need firepower against Dante."

Power. Influence. Money.

I missed her. God, I missed her. It was annoying that all I saw of her now was the one who put me down with a look, who treated me like a pawn in her game. I wanted to ask her if she remembered what it felt like to love without conditions. But I knew the answer already. She didn't.

My grip tightened as I moved another photo. Mama slapped my hand.

"Really?" I snapped. "Was that necessary?"

She gently put the photos back where they belonged. I felt a surge of anger when a staff member came in with a tray of martinis and biscotti. "You see I'm working here."

I told myself that underneath all the layers of ice and steel, she's still there. The mother who used to braid my hair. The mother who used to bring me my favorite chocolates after a long day. The mother who once loved without rules or restrictions.

"I'm the one getting married. I should have a say."

Mama raised a brow. "I won't have you sabotaging my wedding."

"*Your* wedding?" I scoffed. "I'm just the broodmare?"

"Don't start with me, Laurene."

"Lu, baby, let's not go there tonight," Daddy said.

"No. We're not gonna pretend like usual, Daddy," I bit out, my voice raw. "It was about Mama. She doesn't give a damn about me. Never did. And you know it."

Her lips pressed into a thin line. "You think you'd have the life you do if I didn't protect it at all costs?"

"Protect it from what?" I shot back. "From people finding out we're human? That *Grandpa* made mistakes? Daddy, are you gonna sit here and let her keep doing this?"

"I wish you would stop bringing up your grandfather—"

"And I wish you would get help."

"Your grandfather almost ruined our foundation," Mama said. "I had to step in and make sure it didn't all fall apart."

"You're crazy!" I said. "Grandpa was eighty-three, Mama. He ran King Enterprises for nearly sixty years. What happened before he died wasn't him—it was the sickness. He deserved better than being forced into that home that killed him. You didn't know how to handle your grief, and you went from our mother to our drill sergeant."

She never grieved him. Not really. She channeled her grief for him into becoming stronger and more demanding. But grief doesn't disappear just because you ignore it. It festered. It twisted. And I saw it in her—in the sharpness of her voice, in the way she worked herself to the bone, in the way she wouldn't let herself rest. She thought if she stopped, even for a second, it'd all catch up to her.

"Laurene," Dad warned me, but I ignored it.

"I'm the one keeping this family afloat!" Mama snapped. "I had to rebuild everything from the ground up while the rest of you were too busy mourning or, in your case, running away."

"I didn't run off," I mumbled, still bitter. "I left because I couldn't breathe here. *Because of you.*"

"Do you think I enjoy making these decisions? Forcing you into situations that hurt? It's called sacrifice, Laurene."

She thought she was honoring Grandpa. Carrying on his legacy. But legacies shouldn't cost you your soul. I thought if Grandpa Ben were here, if he could see what she'd become, he'd tell her to stop. To breathe.

Daddy shifted uncomfortably, but he didn't intervene this time. His silence made my anxiety worse.

"I'll be damned if I let this family fall apart. The world doesn't care anymore about what we've built, about the power we've held for so long. And whether you like it or not, this is what the family needs."

I let out a bitter laugh, shaking my head. "No, you need that."

"I've given my fucking all to this family, and you're not grateful!"

I loved her. Even after everything, I loved her. And that's why it hurt so much. Because I didn't just want her to be power-ful. I wanted her to be okay.

"At what point do I stop being an asset and become your daughter? When Erik puts *you* in a home?"

"Laurene, cut it out," Dad finally said.

"The way you've been since Grandpa passed…"

"What the hell do you even know?" Mama stood, her chair falling. "The nights I spent wiping my own father's ass, watching him not remember who I was, begging people to keep quiet, praying that our empire wouldn't crumble before our eyes. Don't you dare stand there and judge me."

"You won't admit it, will you? That maybe—just maybe— you could've saved him. That if you'd tried harder, if you'd kept him home instead of locking him away in that cold, sterile facility, he might've had more time. But you saw your chance and took it. You signed the papers, handed him over, and never looked back. You threw your own father away, and now this family is your guilt."

Mama's angry hand shot up; I braced myself.

"Yvonne!" Daddy's voice cut through the room like a whip as he grabbed her wrist.

She was frozen stiff, breathing hard, her eyes wild with anger and pain.

"No," he said firmly, voice quiet. "This is our daughter, and she's hurting, just like you are."

The room fell silent. Mama freed her arm, glaring in disbelief and betrayal.

"Her over me?" she fumed, turning back to me. "I won't let you speak to me like that. Not in this house."

"Yeah, whatever," I replied, keeping my voice even, despite feeling like a volcano about to blow. "Let's sweep this under the rug too."

"Laurene!" Daddy's voice boomed.

I walked away, legs wobbling, but I didn't stop. Outside, the night air hit me like a slap of its own, sharp and bracing against my skin. My chest hurt, my throat was tight, but no tears came.

I ran.

My shoes crunched on gravel. I fumbled for my phone, jammed in my earbuds, and cranked up the music to block her out. I hit the end of the driveway, onto the narrow street, and I went faster.

She didn't care, and never would.

The trees were all a blur, with their shadows stretching out long and dark. I ran till my lungs burned more than my heart ached, till the music was louder than her words.

She was set in her ways. Why the fuck did I think she would?

She couldn't. And maybe that was what hurt the most—not just that she wouldn't, but that I still wanted her to. Even after everything, I still secretly hoped she'd change her mind and see me for who I was.

Tears blurred my vision, and I fucking hated I was breaking, but I let the tears fall for once. They were mine—hot, angry, and painfully real. The years of isolation, the betrayal, the choices made for me that I never wanted. The blackmail. Reese.

The street ended at the park, stretching out ahead, quiet and empty. I quickened my pace, the music in my ears a shield against the silence.

Then came the blow.

A sharp push to my side sent me crashing to the ground, the air knocked from my lungs. My head struck something hard—a rock, maybe—and a jolt of pain exploded behind my eyes.

The world blurred into dizzying chaos. Erykah Badu's voice was still playing in my ears, a sharp contrast to the pounding in my skull. Dazed, I groaned, touching my forehead. My fingers came away slick with blood, the pain searing behind my eyes as my body fought to catch up with what had just happened.

Before I could even register it, something cold and rough clamped on to my ankle. I gasped. I was yanked hard, sliding across the ground, scraping my skin.

Panic overwhelmed me.

I twisted, clawing at the ground, but the grip tightened. My leg shot out, and my heel whacked something hard. A grunt. The hands on me faltered for half a second—just long enough for me to see them.

Dressed in black, a hoodie pulled low over their head, obscuring their face. The only clear thing was the glint of metal at their wrist, flashing against the dim light.

Another yank, a harder one this time. I gasped, my fingernails digging into the dirt as I was dragged deeper into the bushes.

No. *No.*

With all my strength, I heaved my knee upward, then drove my foot forward, the impact echoing as my foot connected with something—stomach, ribs—I didn't care which. A guttural curse ripped from the figure's lips, their grip loosening ever so slightly.

I acted quickly.

I freed myself with a kick. Adrenaline masked the pain as I pushed myself up.

The figure recovered quickly, lunging for me again—but I was faster this time. I kicked them again, hitting their wrist. The metallic glint vanished as their arm jerked back.

And then, just as quickly as they'd grabbed me, they bolted. Disappearing into the thicket.

But whoever that was?

They had tried to take me.

And they would try again.

My head throbbed; the world spun, but I stood. I fumbled for my phone with blood-slick fingers, my vision doubling as I unlocked the screen.

His name calmed my racing thoughts.

Reese.

I hit the call button. Seconds later when the call connected, I didn't give him a chance to speak, "Reese. Please. Help."

I dragged myself back up the path. Every step hurt like crazy. Reese's voice cut out on me. "Laurene? What's going on? Where are you?"

"P-Park."

I just kept moving, one step at a time, until I reached the edge of the park. My legs buckled, and I collapsed onto the curb, clutching my head. I don't know how long I sat there, it felt like forever, and no time at all.

I smelled burning rubber and heard tires screech, then saw a car skidding to a stop. Reese appeared before me instantly.

"Laurene!" He cupped my face, tilting it up, his thumb brushing my cheek. He touched my head and the pressure made me wince.

"What the hell happened? Are you okay?"

"I'm fine," I croaked. "Someone pushed me and tried to drag me."

"Shit, let's get you to the hospital—"

"No hospital," I muttered, shaking my head, though the motion made the world spin all over again.

"You're bleeding and barely standing," I felt him push my hair back, and he touched a bump forming. "Don't argue with me right now."

"I swear I'm fine. They didn't hurt me, just pushed me from behind to scare me."

Before I could protest further, his hands slid under my knees and around my back, lifting me off the ground.

"Reese—"

"Shut up," he said gruffly.

He carried me as if I weighed nothing, his long, purposeful strides a blur as he headed toward the gleaming chrome of his car. He opened the door and let me down gently.

"You scared the hell out of me," he muttered, more to himself than me, before slamming the door shut and rounding the car to get behind the wheel.

I rested my head on the cool window; it felt good on my burning skin. I took a breather, the pain was muted, knowing Reese was close by. When the car's engine finally cut out thirty minutes later, he didn't waste any time.

He picked me up from the car again; I felt his body heat through my clothes as he sprinted to the door with me. Inside, he carefully settled me on the living room couch.

"Stay with me."

He went to remove my hoodie, muttering under his breath, and seconds later, his hand went to the hem of his shirt. Before I could process what was happening, he yanked it over his head, revealing the toned muscles of his chest, the light from the dim lamps catching on the tattoos that snaked down his arms.

He dabbed at the blood on my head with his shirt. The shirt

was soft and warm, still holding his body heat. His touch was pure concern, no fear or hesitation.

"Shit," he murmured, his thumb gently tracing the bloodied gash along my temple. His touch felt good. His hand was large, rough around the edges, but the way he handled me felt like he was trying to do everything right.

I should push him away, but I couldn't. Not when my head was pounding. Not when the only thing keeping me upright was him.

"You should've let me take you to the hospital," he said quietly, voice almost like a growl.

"I'm fine," I replied, my voice hoarse, though I was far from fine.

"Let's pray you don't have a concussion," he said quietly, then stood watching me for a moment before walking away down the hall and turning on the lights. Seconds later, he was back with a first aid kit.

"You didn't have to do this," I whisper, my voice too soft, too vulnerable. I hated myself for it.

"No," he said, voice thick with something I couldn't name. "I didn't."

He came back, dabbed my forehead with a wet cloth to clean the blood, but I liked his shirt better. He was busy cleaning and adding the antibiotic. I closed my eyes, just for a second. Big mistake. Because suddenly, I was twenty-one again, tangled in his sheets, whispering his name into the dark.

No. Stop it. That girl was dead. I buried her the night I left him.

But my body betrayed me—leaning into his warmth, into his hands, into the only place I've ever felt safe. Even when I shouldn't.

"Reese," I said softly. "I'm sorry."

He just stared at me, like he was trying to memorize my face. He put his thumb under my chin and tilted my face up. Then he reached for a Band-Aid.

"Why are you apologizing? You know when I find who did this," he murmured, his voice low, rough, full of a promise I didn't doubt, "I'm gonna fuck them up. No questions asked."

I let out a shaky but genuine laugh. Hearing old Reese—the one who never gave up—was strangely comforting. My unwavering protector, even if it meant destroying the world.

A momentary shift occurred. My number-crunching, inheritance-securing mind paused. Only then did I see how I'd been clinging to that one goal. But right here, between us, I couldn't ignore the question that crept in.

What did I *really* want?

I spent years convincing myself that love was a distraction, that Reese was a mistake, that my ambition was enough.

But the truth is—it's cold at the top. And I am so, so alone.

I got that old craving again—the way he moved, so reckless, so bold. I saw a changed Reese.

My hand grazed his chest. He got stiff.

"Reese."

I could feel the searing heat of his touch, a burning brand against my skin, and I couldn't pull away, lost in the raw, aching need that pulsed through me like a wildfire.

He wasn't pulling away. He inched closer, his presence overwhelming.

Every part of me was screaming for him. No time to think, no time to hesitate. I just wanted to feel him, that's all. I was desperate to connect, to break down my walls, and find something real and unconditional.

I leaned in and kissed him.

The kiss was slow and unsure, like I was asking permission. And I did, letting the warmth of his touch melt the coldness inside me.

For the first time in ages, the anger, pain, and confusion were gone, replaced by something soft and fragile. I didn't care about the blood, bruises, or the past hanging over us. So, it was all about that quiet connection, that tender moment—something I'd avoided for so long.

He pulled me closer, his hands on my back. Our hearts beat as one.

Reese pulled back, blinking slowly. I was lost for words. I was still all tingly from the kiss, but the headache was killer.

"You need to rest," he said quietly.

Every brush of his hand against my skin felt electric, and he quickly finished patching me up.

"You're not sleeping on that couch," he said. "C'mon, let's get you to bed."

He hauled me up, his hands keeping me steady as I wobbled. My legs were like noodles, but he wouldn't let go.

We walked down a dim hallway, my nerves bubbling up as I followed him into his room. It was a simple space, but it was clearly his, down to the leather chairs, the piles of records, and his scent of leather and wood.

He opened a drawer and pulled out a shirt for me. "You can wear this."

I took the shirt, and he left.

I quickly threw on the shirt and hopped into bed. His scent was faint on the sheets, and the mattress felt so comfy. I was almost asleep when I heard a soft knock.

Reese stepped in before I could say anything, carrying an ice pack, a bottle of water, and a couple of aspirin.

"Here," he said, putting everything on the nightstand next to me. "You need to take these. Help with the swelling."

I sat up, grabbed the aspirin and water, and showed him I took it.

"Are you alright?" he asked, leaning in.

I just nodded. I was too tired to fight, but I still really wanted him to stay.

"Reese…stay," I breathed, the words lingering between us.

He looked at me, his expression unreadable, hesitation flickering across his face. But he said nothing. He got in bed next to me and pulled the covers over both of us.

The warmth of his body radiated against mine as I nestled my head on his shoulder, the soft hairs on his chest tickling my cheek. His heart beat beneath my ear, a slow, powerful rhythm.

"This wasn't random," I murmured.

Reese exhaled sharply. "I know."

The blackmailer had gotten violent. *Fast.*

I hated the way fear curled inside me, the way my chest tightened at the memory of the attack. I had always been untouchable—too rich, too powerful, too carefully guarded. Until now.

"I don't know what they want," I admitted. "I thought it was just money, but this—this was personal."

Reese's grip tightened, his thumb pressing into my side like he was holding himself back. "There was a car in front of my office…with an official seal."

That made me look up. "Seal? Like—"

"Yeah…"

Hmm… An official seal could belong to the yacht club? The resort? *The mayor's office.*

"If they were willing to hurt me, they won't stop here."

"You're right." Reese's voice was tight, but there was something in it—a promise. "If they're willing to cross that line, they're not backing off. And neither are we. Now sleep. I'm here."

I closed my eyes, leaning into him again, my head resting on his chest. My breath slowed. My chest eased. That awful loneliness alleviated for a bit.

For the first time in ages, I slept.

CHAPTER 14
Reese

"REESE! Where the hell have you been? Mom's been looking for you." Jennie walked out of our family's mansion. The open windows let out music as people laughed and came and went.

I barely heard any of it. My jaw was tight as I checked my phone—messages from the security firm, updates on the new patrol schedule.

Not enough. It still wasn't enough.

All I could think about was her.

How the fuck did they get to her? She was hurt. Hurt, and I couldn't do a damn thing about it. Whoever the fucking coward was who laid a hand on her, they were gonna pay. Nobody's gonna get away with hurting Laurene.

Sudden change of heart?

"Something held me up," I grumbled, and Jennie hooked her arm in mine as we walked in.

Her expression softened, but I could tell she wasn't happy. She lifted the hem of her gown with one hand and held a champagne glass in the other that she held it out to me.

"Drink. You're going to need it," she said.

I snatched the glass without thinking. Everyone loved

Ashbourne parties; they were legendary. With my surprise engagement, I knew the gossip mill would go crazy.

"What's wrong?"

I looked at Jennie. "Hm?"

"Mrs. Haddington just pinched your butt, and you didn't react."

I turned, looking over my shoulder to see the older woman grinning at me and giving a little wave.

"I can't believe we still do this every year." I scanned the familiar faces.

"It's what Conrad loved," she replied softly. "He always looked forward to these parties."

He had been the life of the party, the one who loved being in the spotlight. I could almost hear his laughter mingling with the clinking glasses and soft jazz playing in the background.

"This is how we keep his memory alive. We have to celebrate the good times."

I turned to her. "You think he'd want us to do this? To pretend everything's fine?"

"I think he'd want us to be together. To remember him."

"Reese!" Mom called out.

I instinctively straightened and looked to see her approaching with Nina close on her heels. "Shouldn't you be with your fiancée, Reese?" she asked. "Why have I been chatting with her by myself for the past thirty minutes?"

Laurene walked in as I was about to respond. The crystal chandeliers lit up her sequined red dress, which shimmered as she walked.

Makeup and hairspray covered the bump on her head. I knew it was hidden, just like everything else she kept secret. I wondered if she was still hung up on our kiss last night—a kiss we shouldn't have had.

The moment I climbed into that bed next to her, I knew I was making a mistake. I shouldn't have been there. Shouldn't have let myself get so close to her again. But I couldn't walk away.

My life was all black and white, no in between. It felt like a switch had flipped so quickly with a phone call, and now I wasn't sure how to act around her.

"You made it." Laurene looked from Mom to Nina to Jennie, then at me. She smiled, a little unsure but sincere.

For so long, thoughts of revenge, of confronting her had fueled me, but here we were. No flare of anger, no bitter words. Just a strange feeling of acceptance.

I reached out my hand and Laurene took it, and I felt something within me slide back into place.

"You look incredible," I murmured. "Absolutely stunning."

She smiled softly. I stared at her, trying to find the girl I used to know, the one who broke my heart so beautifully.

Was she really a monster?

"You two look great together!" Mom said. "The guests are quite eager to see the two of you. I've had twenty people inviting me to afternoon tea this week."

Jennie chimed in, "I'm so excited for the bridal shower! You're gonna love it, Laurene. We have it planned for this weekend at the resort."

Right after she finished, I felt someone behind me.

"Harold," Mom greeted him. "Where have you been?"

"Just got back from Vegas." He nodded, glancing between Laurene and me. "Reese. Laurene. You're both standing and no blood spilled, so everything is going great, hm?"

Hearing "blood," Laurene squeezed my hand, drawing closer.

I began to reply, but a loud *clank* stopped me.

We turned toward the noise. Laurene gripped my arm tightly, her eyes wide as she looked around us. Near the entrance, a tray of crystal glasses lay shattered on the floor. A server stood frozen in front the wreckage, his eyes wide with shock.

"For God's sake," Dad muttered, his face twisted in disgust. "Maybe we need to start firing the invalids. The tax break from hiring them isn't enough."

I felt Laurene stiffen beside me.

"Dad," I said. "You don't have to be an ass."

He looked at me, his face unreadable. "If those *people* can't handle the job, they shouldn't be here."

"I'll go take care of it," Jennie said, and gave me a look before she hurried over to the server.

Without missing a beat, Dad turned to Laurene. "I trust you find the evening to your liking, Laurene?"

"Yes, everything is lovely."

"Lovely? I expect more than 'lovely' for an event on this scale. We spent good money on this for you. Or has your taste declined slumming it around in Germany?"

I clenched my jaw, and Laurene's hand tightened in warning. Dad's eyes flicked toward me then, a faint smirk playing on his lips.

"Paris, Mr. Ashbourne, I was living in Paris," Laurene said slowly, and I bit my tongue for her.

"Ms. King, I trust you understand the importance of our partnership here." His tone oozed with false congeniality. "Your family's connections and resources are invaluable assets to us. We're not just here to piss around on hors d'oeuvres."

"Harold," Mom hissed.

"Are you fucking drunk?" I snapped.

Dad's eyes flickered, narrowing into slits. He straightened, adjusting his jacket like the accusation slid right off him. "Watch yourself, boy."

"You're pathetic."

His jaw tightened. "Excuse me?"

"You're talking to my *fiancée*. Stop making an ass of yourself while ruining my mother's party. Watch your mouth."

"How dare—"

"Respect her, or I'll make damn sure you regret it."

The room seemed to still for a moment, the air thick with tension. Dad stared at me, his expression icy, but I didn't back down.

Mom shifted awkwardly. "Reese, let's not—"

"Mr. Ashbourne, I am not oblivious to the context surrounding us being here tonight," Laurene said. "*We know what our job is.*"

"I hope so. Maybe you'll be useful, unlike my foul-mouthed son here."

Laurene's grip on my shoulder tightened, but it was too late. That barb hit its mark.

"You're gonna continue to be a dick here?"

Dad looked at Mom. "Pauline, this boy of yours. This is why he shouldn't be CEO—"

"I've told you several times I don't want this fucking company. But you never actually wanted to do the work, did you? You just want to stand on the sidelines and throw your criticism at everything I do. That's your style, isn't it, Dad? Nitpick and *bullshit*?"

I hated that I still cared. That I still wanted to prove myself to a father who could never see me for who I really am. But I was done fighting for his approval.

"You think standing here spouting off makes you a man? You think it earns you a seat at the table?" Dad glared. "Let me remind you, Reese, you've done *nothing* to earn the respect you're demanding. You've coasted on this family's name your entire life. And now, suddenly, you want to act like you're a man of importance because of this...*arrangement* with Laurene?"

I felt my fists clench at my sides, the blood pounding in my ears. "You don't know shit about me."

"Those military schools did nothing for you." He scoffed, stepping closer, his frame towering over mine. "You're a liability, Reese. Nothing can fix you. What have you contributed? What have you ever done that actually mattered?"

"I think both of you should cool down." Laurene tugged my shoulder back. "This isn't a conversation for now."

"Exactly," Mom added, hands wringing. Nina put a hand on Mom's shoulder.

"What have I contributed?" I repeated. "How about the fact that I'm still standing here, even after you tried to get rid of me at every damn turn? After you shoved me aside for Conrad and Jennie for years? After you undermined me for with employees? Talking to investors behind my back?"

Harold scoffed, stepping closer. "You were a useless kid. You never listened, and frankly, I'm tired of trying to make you into something acceptable. You think because you've managed to stay out of the tabloids for a few months, suddenly we forget the hell you put us through—especially after your brother?"

"Yeah, I was reckless," I shot back, my voice rising. "But maybe if you'd given a shit about what I wanted—about *me*—things would've been different."

He shook his head. "All your life, I've waited for you to prove me wrong, to show me you were worth the sacrifices, the name I gave you. You just never amounted to the man I needed you to be. I knew from the second your mother gave birth to you that you wouldn't be useful."

"You miserable piece of shit." I took a step toward him. "You act like I was some burden you had to deal with, but you *made* me this way. Can you even fucking acknowledge that?"

"You should've been the one to die, not Conrad. Conrad was ten times the man you'll ever be. He understood what it meant to be an Ashbourne."

Something inside me broke at that. The last fragile piece of hope I'd held on to—some sliver of belief that maybe, deep down, he gave a damn about me—was shattered.

"If I'm so worthless, why don't you go dig up Conrad? I bet the worms haven't gotten through all of him yet."

Dad grabbed my jacket, yanking me forward. People were yelling—some scared, some shocked.

"You can't talk about your brother like that!" he yelled, his face close, reeking of booze and anger.

"Or what?" I felt the adrenaline coursing through my veins.

"Harold!" Mom's voice was a desperate cry. "Don't you dare!"

"You little bastard," Harold growled, his face inches from mine.

"You better get your hands off me before I forget you're my father and beat the shit out of you like you deserve," I said calmly.

"Harold, let him go," Mom pleaded.

"This isn't helping anyone," Laurene told me.

The guests at the party turned their heads, their murmurs growing loud. I could feel the weight of their stares, a hundred eyes burning into the back of my skull. My heart raced, and the room felt like it was closing in.

"Look who's causing a scandal now?" I taunted her.

Laurene's hand cupped my face, turning my attention toward her, blocking Harold out of my line of sight.

"Is this worth fighting for?"

Harold hesitated, his eyes narrowing as he looked at Laurene. "This is none of your business, girl. Stay out of this."

"It is now," she said firmly. "Let him go."

She was the only one who saw me—not just the disappointment I'd become, but something else.

Harold's hand still gripped my collar, his face still twisted in that mask of pure fury. But then, he shoved me back, hard enough that I stumbled, barely catching myself. Laurene was immediately by my side.

"You're nothing," he spat, his voice shaking with barely controlled rage. "You'll always be nothing."

I stood there, breathless, and for the first time in ages, I wasn't angry.

"Get out of my sight," he muttered. "Before I do something we both regret."

With a final, disgusted look, Harold turned on his heel, shoving his way through the crowd. As if he couldn't get away from me fast enough. The people around us parted, murmurs filling the air as his back became smaller and smaller.

"We need to salvage this," Mom said, her voice urgent as she motioned between Laurene and me. "Dance. Start dancing."

Nina snapped her fingers at the band. Music played, and without another word, Mom hurried after Harold, Nina rushing behind her.

Laurene stopped me as I was leaving. "Reese, wait."

"Please—"

"*Dance.*" Laurene didn't look away, her gaze locked on mine. I felt like an animal at a circus. "Dance with me."

"Why?" I shot back, my anger flaring again. "What's the point?"

"Just…be with me for a minute."

The sincerity in her gaze chipped away at me. I hesitated, my anger warring with the pull I felt toward her.

"Just focus on me."

CHAPTER 15

Laurene

WE WERE DANCING CLOSE, but even though he seemed relaxed, I could feel the tension in Reese, like he was about to snap.

"You see?" I murmured. "Not so bad, right?"

He didn't look at me. His eyes stayed glued to the spot where his father was a second ago.

You were a mistake.

Mama could be harsh, even manipulative, but Harold…

I was unprepared for what I saw tonight. The way he looked at Reese, like he was nothing—nobody deserves that.

But Reese did. His entire life.

I studied his expression. He held me steadily, eyes stormy but jaw firm. It wasn't the grip of a broken man; it was the grip of someone who refused to be broken, no matter how much the world weighed him down.

That's what I had loved about him.

"Reese," I said softly, my voice trembling. "Talk to me."

His eyes met mine, and for a flash, the act dropped. There was a glimpse of something real and fragile in his eyes.

"What's there to say?" His voice was low and bitter. "It's nothing new."

"You didn't deserve that. No one does."

I expected him to push me away. But instead, his grip tightened slightly, just enough for me to feel it.

"You don't have to do this, Laurene," he said, his tone quieter now. "Pretend you care."

"I care," I said, meaning it. "I always have."

He stared into my eyes, and I wondered if he could read the truth—that I'd never stopped loving him.

The music changed to a slower beat, and we automatically drew closer. I rested my hand on his shoulder, my head on his chest.

"Just focus on me." I tightened my hold on Reese, hoping that my presence could offer some solace and my what? Love?

Stay focused, Laurene.

I was here for one purpose only—get my money, then leave. Love had no place in my carefully constructed plans. Love didn't exist between us anymore.

But for once, I wasn't stressing about the inheritance, blackmail, or what came next. I was thinking about Reese—his pain, his resilience, the fire that had always drawn me to him. Maybe it was selfish, but seeing his pain, I felt the urge to be the one to soothe the storm raging inside him. To show him he wasn't alone.

And maybe, just maybe, I wanted to let him back into the parts of me I'd tried so hard to lock away.

"What's going on in that head of yours, Laurene?"

"Nothing," I lied, a reflex I hated but couldn't seem to shake. "Just thinking about everything that's happened tonight."

His lips twitched in something that wasn't quite a smile. "You're a terrible liar."

Be honest.

"I always wanted this," I admitted softly. "To be able to stand beside you, to hold your hand without fear, to be public about us. But I couldn't, not with my family."

Reese didn't speak.

"It was horrible pretending," I continued, not sure why I was telling him this. "Each time I saw you at a party or an event, my heart would race, and all I wanted was to run to you, kiss you, be with you. Instead, I had to pretend you didn't exist. It was easier to pretend than face judgment."

To them, I'm a King—a legacy, a prize. To him, I was just Laurene. And maybe that's why I fell.

"You chose yourself, your family," he said, and there was no anger in his tone—just a resigned acceptance that hurt more than any accusation ever could.

"I chose wrong," I whispered, the confession tasting bitter on my tongue.

Reese was silent for a moment. The music changed again, something softer.

"You always were good at picking the practical option," he said, his voice low. "Even when it broke your own heart."

We figured it'd be easy: Reese would threaten to expose all the ideas Conrad had taken from him to the board, Conrad would back out, and we'd all be free. But Conrad didn't just back out. He turned on us.

I should've been in charge, making sure everything worked for us. Instead, I watched it all crumble.

I took a deep breath. "I didn't think about the damage it would cause. I wasn't thinking about the fallout for you or our relationship. I never thought it would break you. And I didn't care enough to stop it."

Could we go back?

He stared, eyes dark and inscrutable. "You don't get it, Laurene. I didn't just miss you. I missed the parts of myself I lost when you left."

I forced myself to breathe. His words twisted something in my chest. I hadn't let myself think about him, not like this, not about how he'd been after I left. Why did I think he'd moved on? That he'd been fine without me?

"I didn't...I didn't really cope at first," I said, my voice low, unsure of how much I should admit. "At first, I just existed. I wasn't *living*—I was just going through the motions. And for months, I didn't do a damn thing. I didn't even know how to start again, so I just froze. I thought if I didn't move, if I didn't feel anything, it would be easier."

"So why did you stay?" he asked, his voice rough, laced with a vulnerability that echoed my own. "Why didn't you call me?"

"Because I was embarrassed."

The touch of his hand on my cheek, warm and firm, grounded me; his thumb gently stroked my skin. "I would have wanted to be there for you, no matter what. I spent so long feeling like I wasn't enough. Not for you, not for anyone."

"You were more than enough," I said softly. "Fuck what you dad said. You matter, Reese. You're more than just this screwup you think you are. You matter."

He lifted my chin. "You didn't trust me."

"I trust you now," I whispered.

Without thinking, I leaned closer, my breath mingling with his, the anticipation hanging heavy in the air. Reese didn't hesitate; he closed the distance between us, his lips crashing onto mine in a kiss.

The warmth of his lips met mine, and his hands cupped my back, pulling me near as if to devour the space that had separated us for so long. The scent of his cologne filled my nostrils.

The world around us seemed to fade away, leaving just the two of us connected in a way that felt both familiar and new. The taste of his lips, the feel of his breath against my skin—it was intoxicating.

I missed this. I missed him.

I sighed into his kiss. He tasted like whiskey and those damn cigarettes he needed to stop smoking. When we finally pulled away, breathless and flushed, I looked into his eyes and saw the same desperation, relief, and possession reflected back at me.

I started to talk, but then I saw Blair Sterling behind Reese—

smirking. Our eyes met, her smile faded, and she practically ran for the door.

Reese's firm grip stopped me.

"Laurene, hold on."

Pulling away, I said, "I need to talk to Blair."

I brushed past him before he could say anything else.

The air outside the main hall was cooler. People milled about in small clusters, and *there*—I spotted Blair's distinct red hair. She headed toward the staircase leading upstairs.

I followed her.

Upstairs was quieter, the ambient noise of the party fading into the background.

She turned a corner, disappearing from view momentarily. I quickened my pace.

Rounding the corner, I ducked against the wall when I spotted her by a door. She knocked, then the door opened.

I counted five seconds. The door was slightly ajar, letting light spill into the hall. I zoomed to the door, hoping they didn't spot my shadow. I craned my neck to peek through the crack.

Candlelight cast shadows on the table, but Blair was nowhere in sight. The room, with its bookshelves and trophies, looked like a study.

"Did anyone see you?" I heard a voice.

"No."

Blair stepped into my view.

She wasn't alone.

Harold.

I sucked in a breath. No. Not him.

He stood close to her—too close—his face shadowed by the dim light. His fingers brushed her wrist before trailing down her arm. I stiffened.

"I don't like this," he said, his voice lower than I'd ever heard it.

Blair's tilted head caught the candlelight, highlighting her smirk. "You never do. And yet..." She stopped talking, gently smoothing his jacket collar. A soft, loving touch. "Here we are."

Harold let out a sharp breath, his shoulders tightening up. His wedding ring sparkled in the firelight as his hands rested near her waist.

"This is the last time."

Blair hummed, unconvinced.

I pressed a hand over my mouth, nausea rolling in my stomach. Holy shit.

I swallowed the bile rising in my throat.

This was an affair.

Blair let out a quiet laugh. "Don't look so guilty," she teased, her fingers brushing his chest.

I spun around and raced down the hall. *How do I tell Reese?* I was heading downstairs when I heard shouting below.

Suddenly the hall door burst open, startling everyone in the vicinity. Toby came hurtling out, his face flushed with panic.

When did Toby get here?

He glanced back, eyes wide, like something—or someone—was on his tail. Then Reese ran out of the hall.

"Reese!"

Guests followed hoping to catch more drama. I had to weave through the clusters of people. Toby darted into a waiting car, his movements sharp and urgent. He slammed the door shut just as Reese reached him.

"Damn it!" Reese shouted, pounding his fists on the car's window as it sped away.

I stumbled to a halt beside him, breathless and wide-eyed. "What just happened?" I gasped, the chill of the night seeping into my bones.

Reese turned to me, jaw clenched, frustration almost palpable.

"I almost had his ass!" he seethed, eyes glimmering with anger. "He knows something."

I took a step closer, feeling the tension crackling between us. "What do you mean?"

Reese ran a hand through his hair. "Toby said—" He cut himself off. "He said, 'You're looking in the wrong places.'"

Wrong places—but what the hell did that mean?

CHAPTER 16

Laurene

"IF IT WERE ME, I'd have just beat her ass right there," Gigi called from the fitting room. "Party was already ruined after what you said about Reese and his daddy. What's one more fight?"

We'd been at it for hours. Next to me, Noelle was just scrolling through work emails on her phone.

"I can have some of my boys run up on her. I know where she likes to shop too. Couple quick shanks to the gut, twist it so the wound doesn't close. *No one* would know," Gigi continued.

Why was Toby even there? He doesn't just *happen* to be places —he *places* himself there. Was it a warning? A taunt? Or just Toby playing his little games again?

"We're not killing Blair." I pinched the bridge of my nose. "And for the last time, *what* boys? The ones you know who drive Teslas and buy craft kombucha in bulk?"

Gigi huffed. "I know people. Movers and shakers who are not afraid to get dirty."

"You know gangsters?" wide-eyed, Noelle asked incredulously.

"Noelle, that's outdated. 'Street consultants,' babe. Keeps it classy," Gigi quipped from behind the curtain. "Am I sexy?"

She dramatically yanked open the curtain, showing off a sparkly dress that was way too tight. Walter let out a little "arff" from my lap, his old body wiggling when he saw her.

"I think Walter's already given his answer."

Gigi blew Walter a kiss. "You're such a good boy, hyping up your mama."

Harold is sleeping with Blair. The epiphany was jarring and unexpected. I had no clue how to tell Reese. He'd lose it, and that would be the end of his already fragile relationship with his father.

Gigi twirled, admiring her reflection.

"Sexy." Noelle nodded. "Very, very sexy. But this is what you want to wear for church?"

"It's not for church." Gigi giggled. "I lied to get you here."

"What is this for, then?" Noelle asked.

"Court."

Not court again.

"Don't tell me you're still stealing?" I asked while Noelle's eyes widened.

"First of all, that was *one time.*" Gigi glared at me. "It was a *dare.* But no, I'm not the one in trouble. Thanks for that vote of confidence, big sis."

I sighed. If Toby knew something, I was going to find out.

"Since y'all so damn nosy, I'm supporting my homegirl. She was doing a hundred in a thirty-five zone, but only because she knew my IBS was acting up. How can I not support?"

Walter let out a small bark.

"That's right, Walter baby. Anyway, I'll change. I didn't love the look on y'all's faces."

"We've been here for hours, Gigi!" I called angrily as she shut the curtains.

My mind wandered. I had to talk to Blair. The idea felt suffocating. Maybe Reese was right. But what if it wasn't her, and I tipped my hand? The lilies and hidden camera felt too deliberate to ignore. Was this payback? Was I overthinking again?

No, I wasn't overreacting. I had to trust my instincts. They'd never failed me before—at least, not when it mattered.

Noelle pushed a piece of hair behind her ear. "You alright, Laurene?"

I scanned the boutique. Nobody looked out of place.

"Noelle, I—" A heavy feeling constricted my throat. I took a deep breath to center myself. "I need to talk to you about something important."

"What's up?"

I counted back from ten as I petted Walter. "Someone's trying to blackmail me."

For a moment, her face froze in disbelief. Then, to my horror, she let out a bright, incredulous laugh. "No way. You're messing with me, right? Who blackmails someone these days? Isn't that, like, old-school villain stuff?"

Her reaction was so Noelle—earnest, a little naïve, but with just enough edge to keep me from rolling my eyes.

"I wasn't honest about everything that happened on the boat with Conrad…"

"You're serious." Noelle sat up straighter, her usual lightness replaced by sharp focus.

"Absolutely."

"Oh my God." Noelle paled, and her hazel eyes dulled. "Are you safe? I mean, this sounds dangerous. What are they—"

"The day after I got back, I got a threatening note. Someone shoved and dragged me while I was jogging. Toby's acting weirdly friendly. And then there's the camera I found in the bridal suite last week. Blair. Oh, Reese got sent lilies—just like the ones at Conrad's funeral. It's all too much. I feel like I'm losing it—"

"Slow down." Noelle leaned in, her tone calm but firm, her practicality now cutting through my spiraling thoughts. "What's their angle? Are they looking for money? Stocks? What exactly are they holding over you?"

I hesitated. "It's…complicated."

"Complicated." Noelle's eyes narrowed. "Have you called the police? Does Reese know? Your mom—"

"He knows. I haven't told anyone yet but you."

Noelle shook her head, a crease forming between her brows. "If someone is watching you—"

"I know!" I interrupted, frustrated. "But you know as well as I do that the whole town would know about it in less than an hour if I went to the police."

Noelle clutched her phone. "You can't just handle this on your own. Keeping secrets got us here in the first place."

I moved Walter, then reached into my bag. I held up the camera for her.

"Shoot, you were serious." Noelle took the camera, and her face hardened, her fingers trembling. "This camera could be from anywhere. Do we know if it's for sure related?"

"Are you kidding me? It doesn't just coincidentally show up where I am." I felt my pulse quicken, my voice rising. "After everything that's happened, you really think this isn't related?"

She paused, eyeing the camera.

"Can you help me figure out what's on this? Maybe where it came from?"

I hated to bring Noelle into this, but she was my only hope. She had all the resources and connections I didn't, thanks to her tech company. And I trusted her to keep it quiet.

She studied the camera in her hands. "So, what really happened that night?"

The memory tightened my chest.

"Conrad and I got into it. He…grabbed me. I never told you that."

Her eyes snapped up, catching the hesitation in my voice. "He what? When?"

"I went downstairs. Conrad was there. We exchanged words," I exhaled sharply, my voice clipped with frustration. "Reese came down. That's what started the argument."

Noelle's brows furrowed. "Okay, but why would that set him off like that?"

"Conrad had been taking Reese's ideas—stealing them—and passing them off as his own. And Reese just had to sit there and take it."

Noelle nodded, but I pressed on. "We were planning to expose him. That was the plan. But…Conrad found out about us. He was gonna tell on us." I swallowed hard. "And Reese lost it."

Noelle exhaled. "Shit."

I nodded.

I watched Noelle look down at the camera before sliding it into her purse. Gigi stepped out of the dressing room, her arms full of clothes.

"What's the vibe, ladies?" she asked, glancing between us, completely oblivious. "I couldn't decide on one dress, so I'm getting all seven."

Noelle and I changed the subject. I didn't want Gigi involved. We stepped outside, and Gigi was still blabbing away. Then, I saw them across the street. I saw Blair talking to Mayor Castillo near the curb.

They were so close, faces almost touching…

Gigi held up Walter's leash in my face. "Oh! Before I forget, Lu, do you mind taking him home with you?" Giving the small dog a quick kiss on the head, she headed in the other direction. "I've got this party up in the Bay, and I'm already running late."

I looked down at Walter.

"Thanks, babe!" she called over her shoulder, hopping into her convertible. "Love ya! I'll be back in three days! Make sure he takes his joint supplements."

I glanced back across the street, where Blair had just stepped toward her car, still deep in conversation with the mayor.

Noelle stepped beside me, her gaze darting across the street. "What's going on over there?"

"It's Blair. I think she could be the one doing the blackmailing."

Her eyes shot wide open, and she turned to me, face full of shock. "You think it's *her*? Why didn't you tell me that part?"

"I'm not sure, but I need to find out before—"

Blair fumbled with her car door, oblivious to us watching.

"I can't just stand here," I muttered.

Noelle's voice dropped to a sharp whisper. "Are you *out of your mind*? Don't! You don't know what could happen if you do this."

Dante walked to his car, peeling out quickly, and as he passed, I saw a seal on the back of his car.

I couldn't react because Blair swung the door open. I started to turn.

Noelle grabbed my arm. "Wait! What if she sees you? What if this turns into something *way worse*?"

"I can't just let her walk away." I couldn't shake the feeling that Blair could help figure this out.

"Laurene!"

I quickly turned, scooping Walter up as we headed toward Erik's car. I hoped he wouldn't mind if I took his car on a little joyride. I needed to buy my own car but I refused to use my parents. I buckled Walter into the passenger seat to keep him safe.

Blair's headlights flashed on, and I held my breath, watching her car pass. I waited a beat before starting mine, doing a quick U-turn to follow.

What am I doing?

I gripped the wheel, focusing on keeping a safe distance. If I hadn't taken that photo of Blair all those years ago, maybe none of this would be happening. Maybe she wouldn't be unraveling, and I wouldn't be chasing her, not knowing what comes next.

What was the plan when she parked? Pretend to be the police and yell "Freeze"?

Reese should be here.

The headlights cut through the winding road as Blair's car swerved up the hill.

The road narrowed, hugging the coastline like a jagged ribbon. A few cars sped by, their lights flashing across my windshield, blinding me for a moment, but I stayed focused. Blair's taillights flickered ahead, weaving through the dark curves.

I glanced at Walter. "We got this, don't we?"

His ears twitched, and he gave a sharp bark. Good boy.

I shifted, still tracking her car, but something felt off. Where the hell was she going?

This was my neighborhood. Beyond our house, there were Noelle's parents, Reese's family, the Whitmores, and a few others. The Sterlings lived near the wharf.

Her brake lights flickered again. I caught a glimpse of her head down. Was she texting?

I closed the gap. A deer darted out from the woods, its body a blur against the road. Blair's car swerved, tires screeching, barely missing the animal.

I slammed on the brakes.

"I'm so sorry, Walter, are you okay?"

I quickly glanced at Walter, looking for any injuries, but he seemed more surprised than hurt.

Blair's car jerked back onto the road, speeding up. She must have realized I was following. She was trying to lose me.

As I rounded the bend, a sharp thud sent my car lurching. I gasped, white-knuckling the wheel, but it was too late. The car veered right, grinding to a halt.

Heart racing, I realized what had happened.

"No, no, no." I slammed my hand on the wheel.

Turning on the hazards, I threw the car into park and stepped out. The right front tire was completely blown.

"Damn." I'd hit a pothole, and Blair was long gone.

Walter poked his head out, eyes watching me as if waiting for instructions.

"You're a man. Fix the tire."

Walter barked in protest.

I took out my phone. I only had eight percent battery left.

The signal flickered between one bar and nothing. Barely. I looked around—no traffic, no lights, just the silence of the cliffs and the distant sound of waves crashing far below.

Walter growled, low and guttural. I spun toward him. His small body was rigid, hackles raised, eyes locked on the trees.

"Walter?"

His growl deepened, then he started barking, sharp and urgent.

I stared into the inky blackness of the woods. Nothing. Just shadows. But I still felt like something was out there.

For a split second, I thought I saw movement—quick, fleeting between the trees. My throat dried up. I held my breath, watching to see if something—or someone—was there.

I was stuck. That empty road felt creepy; the silence was heavy.

I pulled out my phone—5% left. I lingered over Reese's name on my screen. My pride swelled. I really didn't want to ask him for help again so soon. But I promised we'd do this together.

I hit the button, holding my breath as it rang.

He picked up after two rings. "Laurene?"

"Hey," I said, forcing my voice to sound casual. "Don't freak out or anything, but I need a little help again."

There was a brief pause on his end. Then I could hear sheets shifting. "Tobias?"

"I blew a tire. I'm fine," I added quickly, but the words felt hollow. "But I'm kind of stranded out here in the middle of nowhere."

"You're gonna give me a heart attack with these calls, Laurene. Where are you this time?"

I told him where I was, but that creepy feeling from the park came back.

"I'm on my way," he said, and I could hear him getting out of bed. "Get in the car and lock your doors. Don't go anywhere."

"Reese, you don't have to—"

Walter growled again, making me look back at the trees. Then, Walter jumped out the window and into the bushes.

"Walter!" I yelled. "Walter, no!"

"What's going on?" Reese shouted.

"Walter just jumped out the window!" I scrambled to chase after him, the phone still pressed to my ear. "I've got to get him!"

"Laurene, don't go in there alone."

I fought my way through those bushes, branches tearing at me, calling for Walter. His barks echoed in the distance, guiding me, but I could barely keep up.

"Walter!" I sprinted through the trees, the ground uneven beneath my feet. The dog was a blur in the shadows, moving impossibly fast—nothing like the senior dog I knew.

"Laurene! Laurene!" Reese's voice boomed from the phone, but I couldn't stop.

"Walter, come on!" I shouted, my breath ragged, lungs burning as I fought through the thick underbrush. The sharp branches scraped my skin, and the sound of my pulse pounded in my ears, the rhythm of my frantic steps matching the frantic beat of my heart.

I tried hard, but Walter still outpaced me.

How the hell was this old dog moving like this?

I tripped over a root, the rough bark scraping against my ankle, and then the world turned upside down. A gasp escaped my lips as I hit the ground hard, arms flailing, my body tumbling down the steep incline, the sounds of rocks and dirt crunching under my weight filling my ears. My phone clattered to the ground.

The impact knocked the air from my lungs. It all went black and silent for a bit, my head throbbing and my ears buzzing.

I flipped over, short of breath, muscles killing me. I couldn't lose Walter.

Dirt and leaves flew out of my mouth. I made a face, and struggled to my feet, grabbing my phone.

Gigi would owe me big-time.

Walter barked again, closer. I used the trees and roots to pull myself out of the small alcove. Annoyance gave way to fear; I had to reach him.

"Walter!" I shouted again, my voice hoarse.

He barked in response, and I pressed forward, swiping at the leaves stuck in my hair, ignoring the sting of the branches that scratched at my skin. I burst from the trees, a wreck.

Bristling, Walter barked wildly at a nearby tree. Stiff and growling, he glared at the branches.

"Walter, I know you didn't—" Following his gaze, I saw the cause of his frenzy.

On a branch, a fat raccoon stared.

"You've got to be kidding me," I muttered, wiping a hand over my face, half laughing, half furious. "A fucking raccoon? *Really?*"

Walter continued barked, his whole body trembling, oblivious to the fact that our terrifying intruder was just a glorified trash panda. Fuming, I scooped him up.

"You scared the hell out of me for *this*?"

Walter squirmed for a moment, still focused on the raccoon. I glared up at the animal that had sent us both into this ridiculous chase.

"You better stop, Walter. That thing can take you. You're out of your weight class here."

The raccoon gave us one more bored glance before turning and scurrying higher up the tree.

"You and your mama owe me a new Diamante skirt! You hear me? Five hundred dollars!"

I turned and started making my way back through the trees, my legs aching with every step.

"You're lucky I love you," I muttered under my breath. Walter finally settled down in my arms, his little head resting on my shoulder, tuckered out.

The farther we walked, the more my relief of it *not* being a person began to sink in.

I imagined worst-case scenarios and a lurking stranger. Frustrated and breathless, I saw the car.

"Finally," I breathed, dumping Walter in the passenger seat. He wagged his tail, unfazed.

"You're a menace, you know that?" I grumbled, scratching his head.

Reaching for my phone, I glanced at the screen—1%. Of course. I tapped the screen, but the phone went black, dead.

"Great. Perfect," I sighed, slumping against the side of the car. Alone, no phone, covered in mud, stranded. It couldn't get worse.

Walter was out like a light, snoring away while I waited, grumbling. Soon after, I saw Reese's headlights cutting through the dark. I stood up straight.

He got out of the car; he looked concerned and frustrated. Furrowing his brows, he scanned the area, slammed the door, and walked toward me.

"If I get another call from you out alone at night—"

He stormed toward me, then stopped, surprised by my state and Walter's snoring.

"Don't you dare," I warned, flipping him off as I wiped the mud from my cheek. "It's not funny."

Reese snorted again, his shoulders shaking as he fought to contain his laughter.

"I mean it, Reese, shut up. Just fix this tire."

Reese let out a hearty laugh then got to work. He walked around the car, checking out the damage. I saw him kneeling, focused on the tire.

It reminded me of the times I used to watch him work on his bike. The way his brow furrowed, his tongue poking out, deep in concentration as I knew his brain was running a mile a minute. He crouched, his jacket straining across his back.

It was unfair, the way I remembered those shoulders—how they'd easily pushed my legs over his shoulders.

He leaned in, tracing the tire with his fingers.

Why was it so hot to watch him touch a tire?

A flood of memories hit me—those same fingers trailing fire down my skin, slipping beneath my panties, pulling them off with a quiet, deliberate tug. And worse, those fingers thrusting slowly inside me, each movement sending a shockwave of heat through my body.

Shit. Get a grip.

At the nape of his neck, sweat glistened under the dim light, a few stray curls sticking to his skin. I could still feel the way I'd clenched around him when he had me on the bed, my legs wrapped tight around his waist, every thrust of his hips making me forget about everything else.

He looked solid. Capable.

"Yeah, you fucked this up," Reese muttered as he stood, and I swallowed hard. The heat flooded low in my belly, and I forced my gaze back up to his face, praying he hadn't caught me staring.

He knew, his eyes showed it.

"Seriously, are you okay?" he asked, gentler now. "It wasn't anybody out there this time?"

"Yeah," I mumbled, totally wiped out. "I'm fine. Just embarrassed."

Reese paused, then softened, his warmth returning. "Wait here."

He went back to his car. He popped the trunk, rifling through a bag.

He returned with a towel and water. He opened it, pouring some onto a towel before stepping closer. He silently wiped my face with the towel. I shuddered at the touch.

He whispered, "I'm getting the hang of caring for you again."

As he kept talking, he gently held my face, his fingers almost touching me, and suddenly all the tension disappeared, leaving me breathless.

"C'mon, you and..." Reese paused. "When did you get a dog?"

"He's Gigi's," I muttered. "Both of them stress me the hell out."

Reese called a tow truck for Erik's car, and we hopped in his car and drove to my house.

"Why were you out here alone?" Reese asked. I shouldn't be jealous of the way he lazily petted Walter or how Walter leaned into his rubs, nearly crawling into his lap. "The truth."

"I was following Blair."

Reese's jaw tightened. "You what?"

"I had to," I defended. "Something's off with her, Reese."

"You couldn't just—" He shook his head. "What if something had happened? You were out there alone, Laurene. Somebody already attacked you. What were you gonna do if it was worse this time?"

I didn't have an answer for that.

"I can't have you running off like that," he said, his voice dropping lower. "I need to know you're safe. I can't—"

I saw fear in his eyes.

"When I heard you screaming," he began again, "it brought me back to the yacht."

The words came out in a rush, like he'd been holding them in for too long.

"I couldn't find you then, and I thought—" His voice cracked, just slightly, before he composed himself. "I can't go through that again."

Reese's hand brushed mine; I eagerly held it.

"Look, if you think it's Blair, then let's go in that direction, but you cannot be doing shit like this alone. I *will* tell Erik."

"Oh, so now y'all friends?"

He gave me a look. "Actually yes. He brought me a cigar."

I didn't have time to figure out of he was lying or not.

"What about what you said before…in the garden?" He'd promised me hell, and I hadn't forgotten.

Reese's hand still held mine but his eyes darkened, as if every hurt, every bit of anger between us was running through his mind in this moment.

"I thought I needed to even the score."

With just one hand, he effortlessly steered the car too smooth and sexy.

"I haven't forgiven you," he said. The look in his eyes was intense. "Hell, I don't know if I ever will."

He squeezed my hand, then let it go gently.

"But I can't keep holding on to that. Not with everything going on. We've got bigger problems than our past."

My heart clenched at his words.

"So maybe we calling a real truce for now."

I nodded slowly, feeling a little hopeful. "A truce sounds good."

Reese smiled.

"I think we need to add Dante to the list of suspects."

"Dante? But—"

"I saw him with Blair. And my mother, she's terrified of him."

Reese cursed. "Okay."

At my house, Reese parked, his hands lingering on the wheel. We were both quiet. I could only hear Walter's soft breaths, all snuggled up in my arms, fast asleep.

"Crazy, isn't it? I used to drop you off way back there, right at that gate." He gestured toward the dark iron gate farther down the drive. "Didn't even think I'd get this close to the house without your family calling the cops."

"We don't have to sneak around anymore," I said, my voice dropping as I leaned in slightly, eyes locked on his. "We're getting married."

Reese watched me settle Walter gently in the back seat, his eyes following every movement. I leaned over toward him, the space between us shrinking, and reached for his seat belt. My body pressed closer to his, my breath warm against his skin as I unbuckled the strap, feeling the faint tension in the air.

I let my lips brush near his ear, my voice a teasing whisper. "Is this part of the truce?"

"I guess it is," he muttered, his eyes briefly meeting mine with a flicker of something unreadable.

Reese swallowed hard. But then something shifted inside me, a boldness I couldn't ignore. I reached for him, my hand sliding to the back of his neck, fingers threading through his hair with a possessive pull, drawing him to me.

His breath hitched, just a beat before his lips pressed against mine—slow, deliberate, like he was savoring the moment. I melted into him. Reese's hand slid from my neck down to my waist, pulling me closer until I was almost in his lap, our bodies pressed together in the confined space of the car.

"Laurene…" he breathed against my lips, and I could hear the strain in his voice. "We shouldn't do this."

"Do you want to stop?"

Reese blinked slowly, and for a moment, I saw that familiar glint in his eyes—the lively, mischievous one. It was like seeing the old him.

"I need you."

He pulled me fully onto his lap, and I gasped, my knees sinking into the leather seat on either side of him. He dragged his thumb over my bottom lip; I let his thumb slip inside my mouth, and I sucked.

A low growl escaped his throat as he felt my lips close around his thumb. I ground my hips down, feeling him growing hard beneath me, his fingers digging into the fat of my hips.

Yes.

The outline of his cock between my thighs was enough to make my mouth water and remind me how long it had been since someone had touched me. I pick up my movements. He urged me to move faster, his breath coming out in hot, soft pants.

His lips and teeth grazed my skin, a soft groan rumbling in his chest, a desperate need in his touch, as if he couldn't get enough. I let out a soft moan as I shifted my body, feeling the seam of my jeans brushing against my clit with the perfect amount of friction.

Suddenly, the car door flew open, and a gust of cold air blew in—along with a voice.

"Miss Laurene." The calm, unflinching tone of my mother's butler sliced through the haze.

I froze, flushed, my heart hammering in my chest. Reese held on to my waist just a beat longer than he should have, then sat up straight, letting out a breathy sigh of frustration.

"Your mother wants to know if you're coming inside."

I searched Reese's face one last time. His smirk sent shivers down my spine and made my heart race. He stayed silent, leaned back, eyes twinkling mischievously.

"Yeah." I hauled myself out of the car and grabbed Walter. Reese's gaze followed me. At the doorway, I took one last look.

Reese remained motionless, his dark silhouette a stark contrast against the car window, his intense gaze fixed on me, an unnerving intensity that had consumed me.

It was like a promise and a threat all in one.

CHAPTER 17
Reese

I WAS STILL BUZZING after my workout. A good, thorough workout that kicked my ass was exactly what I needed. But I was already thinking about Laurene, my family, and that huge mess I couldn't seem to fix.

I had a woman waiting by my car.

"Blair," I said flatly, walking closer.

"Hey, Reese!" She cocked her head. "You look tense. Rough day?"

I just unlocked the car and ignored her comment.

"Really? That's it? No 'Hey, Blair, good to see you'? No catching up with an old friend?" she asked, stepping into my path.

"Friend?" I stopped and looked her in the eyes. "Were we that?"

She blinked, and her smirk vanished. "You're mad. But I come bearing good news. Remember that VP I was dating? Well, he knows a friend that owns a luxury car brand and wants to collaborate with you. Your liquor with their cars? Big win."

"What's your cut, Blair?"

She narrowed her eyes. "Excuse me?"

Blair was there for me after Conrad passed. Quirky as she

was, she understood how I felt. Apparently, the experience of being the town's pariah was universal. Especially after her dad's company got dragged into a scandal because of those leaked photos.

"I don't get why you're so mad."

"Seriously? You don't know?" My voice became sharper. "Why didn't you tell me about Laurene? That she paid you off? You didn't say a goddamn thing. Just sat there, playing pretend."

"What was the right thing to do?"

"Be real for once! Act like you gave a shit about me. You wanna call yourself my friend? Then fucking prove it."

I remained unmoved as Blair blinked back tears.

"That's not right," she said sharply. "I was trying to be a friend, Reese, not stir up more shit when you were already going through hell. If I wanted to ruin your fucking life, I could have."

I shot her a glare. "Yeah? So what were you doing then? Plotting something? Hell, maybe you still are."

"Plotting?" She scoffed. "You think I spend my days scheming? Gossiping and swiping my credit cards?"

I just stared her down.

Blair shook her head. "You're so wrapped up in Laurene, you can't see what's right in front of you. What is it about her that every fucking man in this town goes crazy over her?"

I searched my bag for my cigarettes.

"You know, I've wondered. For years. Why you never tried. Not once. Never looked at me the way you do her—even when she wasn't around." She let out a dry laugh, a bitter smile tugging at her lips. "And now I get it. It was her. It was always her, wasn't it?"

I froze, the cigarette halfway to my lips.

Her gaze didn't waver. She tilted her head, that bitter smile still in place. "You were with her back then, weren't you?"

I turned to face her, her accusation heavy on my chest. "You don't know what the hell you're talking about."

"I saw the way you looked at her. How you *always* looked at her, like she was the center of your fucking world. *Always.* And I never understood why. Now I do. You both were *together* from the very beginning."

"You're reaching," I shot back.

"Reaching?" Her voice dropped into something softer, more dangerous. "I was *there*. On the yacht. Laurene was standing at the rail, and then you showed up. I didn't think anything of it. But something told me to *watch*. You didn't say anything at first. Just stood there next to her. Then you touched her."

My stomach twisted, but I kept my expression neutral. "That's not what happened."

Blair's smile widened, venomous now. "Wasn't it? Because I remember her turning to you, and the way you leaned in. Like you wanted to *kiss* your brother's fiancée. Oh God, did Conrad find out? Is that why you fought?"

"That's enough," I said.

"I could have told *everybody*. But I didn't, because you were my friend, Reese. I thought, hm. I'm so stupid, and I'm still helping you! I held that secret for *you*."

"You didn't gossip about me? So I should be grateful?"

"Yes!" Blair shouted.

I swallowed, but something felt stuck in my throat. I'd always known Blair had been there for me, but I hadn't realized how much of it had been conditional.

"You couldn't be bothered to see what was right in front of you. You couldn't even see how much I gave you. How much I *kept* giving. You took and took! Don't act like I didn't give everything I had to you, just to watch you screw it up over and over again for *her*. Now I have to watch you two get married?"

The air crackled with years of unspoken things.

"I thought you were different. But now, I see it. I see it all. You and her in her perfect little fucking world, and I'm nothing. But that's what she does, right? She wins. She always fucking wins."

Her words hit me harder than I cared to admit.

"Did she seduce you? Convince you to kill your brother?"

My instincts urged me to lash out. But then I heard Laurene's voice in my head.

You don't need to fight every fight, Reese. Sometimes you just gotta walk away.

I relaxed. Maybe Laurene was right. Maybe Blair was the blackmailer, and if she was, I couldn't lose my head. The anger was still there, burning in my chest, but I refused to let it consume me. Not this time.

"You're bitter," I said finally. "Bitter because you know we can't be. You've only been and will only be my friend, Blair. My heart is branded by Laurene. I'm sorry."

Blair blinked, and I saw her eyes get watery and she shook her head.

"Don't ever bring my brother into this again. Not if you want to keep what's left of my patience and our friendship."

Blair scoffed, shaking her head. "What are you gonna do when she leaves again?"

"She won't."

"Laurene used you back then, and she's using you now. She was with Conrad at the yacht club that night. Before we boarded."

I narrowed my eyes. "What are you trying to say?"

Blair shrugged. "They were in the hallway, and let's just say it didn't look like your perfect little princess was playing nice. He was furious. Kept saying he couldn't trust her. And Laurene? She didn't deny it."

"You're making this up."

"You think so?" Blair let out a sharp, cruel laugh. "She grabbed his arm. She kissed him."

She lied. Again. *You don't know that; you don't,* I told myself.

"Just ask Noelle."

"Noelle?"

"Oh, you didn't know? Noelle saw the whole thing—she told me later that night, but by then..." She gestured vaguely, as if the wreck was just an inconvenient punctuation mark in the middle of her story.

"Noelle is Laurene's best friend. She wouldn't tell you shit."

"She might be her best friend, but she was a little drunk, a little emotional, started talking to me and I just listened. I figured it'll be useful at some point. Guess it is now."

I felt a knot tighten in my chest.

Was Noelle even a friend?

"Is there anything else you need to tell me, Blair?" My voice came out hoarse, as if I wasn't sure if I really wanted to know the answer.

"Yes…" She exhaled, and this time I saw the tears fall down her face and I turned my head. "Dante's been asking about Laurene, Reese."

I went still. I clenched my fists, nails digging into my palms. *Why?*

Blair swallowed hard, her mascara smudged beneath her eyes. "He asked about the wedding, about her family, about what Laurene might know… what she might do."

My pulse raced. "What she might do?"

"He wanted to know how loyal she is to you. If she'd ever turn against you." Blair shrugged. "And if you'd ever turn against her."

"Why the hell would he care about that?" A chill crawled up my spine.

"Don't worry about it. I handled it for you."

My teeth clenched. "Handled it how?"

"I gave him something else." Her voice dropped. "He's looking to expand; the Whitmores are trying to get back their footing in town. I heard some things about Miles, he's sleeping with Gwyn Miller and she's still with Eli… He seemed more interested in that. Doesn't hurt they hate the Kings."

The Kings had enemies everywhere—rich and richer, and those who just plain resented them. But Dante didn't ask about them. He asked about Laurene.

"He smiled. Like he already knew that. Like he was testing me just to see what I'd say."

Dante... He just keeps coming back.

"I know how to deal with guys like Dante, and I'm interested in making a deal for *my* family. I let him know he was barking up the wrong tree."

"Then...thank you."

"Save it." Her eyes, still damp from earlier, hardened. "That's the last favor you'll ever get from me."

I watched her hesitate and turn.

"No." She shook her head. "I just hope this information doesn't get out before your wedding."

I opened the door before she could knock again. Laurene stood breathless, wide-eyed. "I got here as soon as I could. Something happen? Did you get hurt?"

She looked me over, and I shook my head no.

The truth. I just wanted the truth, damn it.

She stepped forward, my hands itched to touch her, but I stayed put.

"Reese." She wrapped her arms around me, her hands coming to my face. "What's going on?"

"Did you know Dante is asking around town about you?"

"What?" She recoiled.

I nodded, and Laurene's eyes flickered to me.

"How do you know this? Did you speak to him?"

Now it was my turn to look away. "We need to keep a closer eye on him. I saw that seal on that car, now he's asking about you..." I shook my head. No coincidence.

"You're right. We should be careful."

"You're full of surprises, aren't you?" I muttered in frustration. "Every time I think I've got you figured out, there's more. There's always more."

Recoiling slightly, she met my gaze, eyes wide.

I stepped back, and ran a hand through my hair, clearing my head. "Did you kiss my brother before we got on that yacht?"

Silence.

Laurene's eyes flashed; I couldn't decipher the emotion. "And why would you ask that, Reese?"

"Did you kiss him?"

The quiet got heavier. "Where'd you hear that?"

"Is it true?" I moved closer, invading her space, and she backed up, but I kept going.

Her lips parted, but she said nothing. "What does that change?"

"It changes how I see you. How I see *us*." I crowded her, forcing her to look at me until there was barely any space between us. "Kissing him wasn't the plan."

Fear. It was clear in her eyes.

"Did you?"

"Yes," she admitted.

I released her instantly, my head shaking, a whirlwind of emotions and questions flooding my mind.

"Wait! It's not what you think—"

I spun around. "You kissed my brother!"

Her eyes darted, guilty, but she didn't speak.

"Why?" I growled. "Why the hell did you do it? Still keeping secrets after everything. And you expect me to trust you?"

"I was protecting us," she said quickly, eyes wide, but I wasn't buying it. "Protecting you, protecting what we have. That's why I did it."

My head shook in anger.

"He dared me to do it."

I froze. "He *dared* you?"

Laurene nodded, and this time she pushed past me, heading toward my kitchen.

"He was…*testing* me, Reese. I was about to leave to get on the yacht, and Mrs. Fontaine caught us. She started talking, and then she wanted to get a picture of the new couple kissing for the *Lush Chronicle*."

I watched, frowning, as she searched my cabinets.

"I thought he was just going to kiss me on the cheek, but he pulled me in too fast, and I couldn't turn my head in time. He kissed me on the lips."

She avoided my eyes, sighed, and pulled out the emergency cookies. Sweets soothed her stress.

"If I hadn't done it, he would've gone to my parents, to your family. He would've exposed everything, and the whole plan would've fallen apart. I couldn't risk it, Reese. Not after everything we'd done. I had to keep the act up."

Her words felt raw and real.

"What about the argument you two had?" I pushed.

"He wanted to pretend for everybody. I didn't." Laurene scoffed. "And he was pissed because I slapped the shit outta him after for what he did."

"You slapped him?"

"When I told you it was me and you," she started, her words slow and deliberate, "I meant it, Reese. I meant it in a way I've never meant anything in my life."

She stepped closer, her eyes locking on to mine.

"I never touched Conrad willingly. Not once. I never kissed him willingly. When I told you I loved you, when I said that you were the only one I wanted, I wasn't lying. I've never wanted anyone the way I wanted you. Not him, not anyone else—just you."

I felt my pulse pound at the truth in her words.

"I…I just thought—"

"Oh, so you stuck now?" Laurene side-eyed me. "Hey, we're a team, I didn't mention it because I knew it'd upset you."

I grimaced. Laurene chuckled, then got serious. She looked a bit gentler, but her eyes still blazed. "Who told you?"

I pursed my lips, and she narrowed her gaze at me.

"We're being honest, right?"

I swallowed, the words feeling like stones in my throat. I didn't want to bring Noelle into this—still, I couldn't make myself say it. Noelle needed to tell Laurene. "Yeah. Honest."

Her eyes held mine.

"Blair."

She nodded slowly, wound up like a spring, ready to snap. She fought to hide her emotions. Then her face blanked; she walked past, cold and silent.

"Wait. Hey, *hey, hey, hold up*—" The words were out of my mouth before I could stop them, my hand instinctively reaching for her arm. I expected her to pull away, but she didn't. She stiffened, letting me hold her.

She didn't look at me, even as she spoke. "Did you sleep with Blair?"

I saw the anger in her eyes, but something else was there too. Vulnerability. Pain. Betrayal.

This was the actual Laurie.

No mask. No manipulation. No games. Just the woman underneath it all. I was shocked. I never thought I'd see her like that; she's usually so guarded, especially with her return.

I had spent so long believing the version of her that played the game. I'd convinced myself her distance and coldness were her true self. But in that instant, I saw everything I'd missed.

"Say it, Reese," she bit out, her voice trembling, though she was trying to hide it. "Tell me if you were with her."

"No." The word came out like a growl, sharp and unshakable. "Never."

I stepped closer, close enough to feel the heat of her body, close enough that she couldn't look anywhere but at me. My heart pounded, but my voice remained steady.

"It's always been you, Laurene." My chest ached with it, the weight of every year, every moment, every time I'd wanted her and no one else. "Only you. My first choice. My last choice. The only one who's ever mattered."

I reached for her, fingers brushing her jaw, tilting her face up until I could see the doubt flickering in her eyes—the doubt I needed to destroy.

"No one else has ever owned me the way you do." She held my gaze. "No one else ever will." Laurene's lips were on mine— quick, desperate. The kiss was hard, demanding, but it wasn't just anger. It wasn't just pain. It was need.

It was all about finding her again, getting to the real her, the part she'd hidden away. I could almost sense her just below.

Next thing I knew, she was in my arms, and we were heading to my bedroom.

Her movements were so warm and alive, it felt like my head was spinning. I gently laid her on the bed, but she immediately began to undress me. Every little touch and move made me realize how much I missed her.

I watched her, the way she touched me—like she needed to convince herself I was real, that this was real, that after everything, we'd finally found our way back. I could feel the old wounds bleeding through.

All that time apart, the silence, the anger…it just melted away when she touched me.

She had me. She'd always had me.

I loved her. Maybe I never stopped.

It had always been so easy to fall into her, to let her pull me under.

And as her fingers traced over me, like she was memorizing every inch, I stopped fighting it. Despite everything, I was still hers. I'd always be hers. I knelt down before she could unzip my pants, and that made her lean back. Her breath hitched when I caressed her smooth curves.

"Reese," she murmured. My trembling hands unbuttoned her jeans, igniting a fire within me.

Just one taste.

Her pants were tossed on the floor. I gently bit into her belly. She tasted amazing, and her moans kept me going.

It was a point of no return. No more secrets, no more walls. Just this intense longing to be one. Going lower, she ground against the bed. I wanted now to taste her pussy. Just taste it. Enjoy her.

After *so, so* long.

I ran my fingers along her hip and felt her body tense up, like she was resisting at first, but then she relaxed. She nudged me with her knees. I grunted and my hand went to her inner thigh, pressing down to make sure she stayed put.

"Don't fight me," I breathed.

Her moan hit me hard. Though small, it felt immense. "Quit playing games with me."

Her hips swayed, and her clothed cunt brushed my face, the delicate contact sending a fire through me. I breathed her in, the scent intoxicating, consuming. I only got a tiny taste of her —just a quick taste—and it made me lose it. I was desperate as I pulled down her panties and dove in with my tongue.

She was so sweet, it just made me want more of her.

"Oh my God." She shivered; her voice was rough and unfiltered.

I really took my time rediscovering her body. I used my tongue on her clit and my thumb on her slit, and she moaned before falling back on the bed with her legs spread. It didn't take long before my chin glistened with her essence. I tried my best to ignore the growing ache in my pants.

"Still so damn sweet, baby."

Her breath hitched, stomach rising and falling in sharp, uneven waves as I ate, licked, sucked. Consumed.

"Reese, damn," she whimpered, and I slipped a thick finger inside, slow, deep, searching—until I found it. The spot that made her break.

"Can I still get you to come?" My voice was low, hoarse; I was desperate to know. To own that answer.

Her moan shattered in her throat as I moved my fingers in slow, deep strokes, working her open, making her feel every inch. Could I still do this to her? I had to see it, hear it—watch her unravel because of me.

Her desperate cries set a rhythm as I teased her with my finger and tongue. I looked into her eyes while licking her slowly and deeply.

I wasn't done.

"Whose pussy is this?"

I watched her fall apart—her lips parting, eyes fluttering shut —and God, it wrecked me. I loved her. I had always loved her. No matter the distance, the silence, the wreckage between us, she was it. My gravity. My ruin. My salvation.

Some things in life don't need an explanation. Some things are just written.

Us? We were inevitable. We were war and passion, fire and fate. From the moment I met her, I knew—whether we burned together or burned each other, there was no ending where she wasn't my purpose.

"Yours," she whispered, breathless, her voice a sharp, aching truth.

I wanted to make her feel this. I wanted her to understand, with every touch, every kiss, that despite everything, there was still something here—something worth fighting for, worth holding on to, even if it was broken.

I knew her body like a prayer—the rhythm that unraveled her, the way her breath hitched, the way her thighs trembled before she lost herself to me. I let my eyes close, drinking in the sound of her, the scent of her, the way she opened up for me, eager, desperate, perfect. I wanted more. All of her. I wanted to lift her onto me, arms locked under her legs, and let her ride me until she forgot her own name.

I wanted to feel her—hot, wet, mine—wrapped around me, clenching, pulling me deeper, until there was no space left between us. Until we were tangled together, inseparable.

Her voice broke into a cry, a melody of need echoing off the walls.

"Louder," I growled against her. Her grip tightened in my hair, but I didn't let up. Didn't let her hide from me.

"I want to hear you," I murmured, my voice thick with hunger, with intent, with possession. My lips brushed against her trembling skin, and I smirked before giving her another long, slow lick.

"I want you to scream for me, baby. Let me hear how much you've missed this."

There was a dull rumble in my chest when I pressed on her clit. My eyes were glued to her. This wasn't the composed Laurene the world saw. This was my Laurene. Solely mine.

"Reese!"

The moment she reached her climax, a potent bawl ripped out of her throat. She was shaking, panting. Then air released from her lungs before she fell back. Overly sensitive, she tried pushing away, but my grip kept her put.

Her mouth formed into a circular shape, while she tried to make an attempt at catching her breath, and whatever spilled from her pussy, I simply licked up again, savoring the taste.

She opened her eyes, and the moment her gaze met mine, the air between us tightened. Still. Heavy. Charged.

Then, she reached for me. Her fingers—soft, trembling, desperate—traced my jaw, pulling me closer, her touch an unspoken demand. A plea. A promise.

"Don't stop," she whispered, her voice raw, breathless, aching.

"I need to feel you."

My fingers curled around her neck—careful, gentle—but there was a pressure there before pulling her bottom lip down with my thumb. I leaned into her, capturing her lips in a kiss, letting her taste herself on my tongue.

She began pulling off my shirt, the cool air tickling my skin for a second before she snuggled up to me, her warmth pushing it away. I got my pants down to my knees and then scrambled for a condom.

"Hurry up," she whispered in my ear, grinding against me.

"Are you sure?"

"Now, Reese!" Her nails dragged over the muscles of my upper back, edging me on.

I grabbed my shaft, running it along her wet folds. With a final brush over her clit, my dick slid into her pussy, causing her walls to clench around me.

"Damn." I counted back from ten. Her grip was just as tight and strong as I remembered. I knew she could handle it all. I only had three inches left to go. "Relax, baby."

A tremor ran through Laurene's thighs, and I carefully leaned forward, feeling the warmth of her body beneath mine, careful not to overwhelm her.

"Here you go." I kissed her neck, the scent of her perfume intoxicating. Beneath me, she breathed in deep, then out slow, trying to control the sharp, staggered inhales as I pushed deeper, stretching her inch by inch. Welcoming me. Taking me in. She hugged me tight, her breath warm in my ear.

"Don't let me go." She let out a soft, helpless sound, her body melting into mine, her arms winding around my neck. Pulling me closer. The heat of her skin, the way her breath shivered against my ear—it was too much, and not enough all at once.

"I won't," I promised, my voice steady, even as everything inside me churned. My strokes were slow yet forceful as I paced myself. With her legs draped across my shoulders, we watched, mesmerized by the connection, a silent understanding passing between us.

With each thrust, my desire for her only grew stronger. The sensation of wet flesh hitting each other sent shivers down my spine. The pace was limitless, measureless, a desperate, gnawing need. There was no point in holding back any longer.

I thrust my hips faster. I felt her hands trace down my back to my ass, pulling me closer. I gazed downward, my eyes half-closed as I lifted her top up, exposing her breast to me as I leaned in to suck on her dark nipple.

"Shit! You're gonna make me come again!" she whimpered.

"Yeah?" I rubbed her clit faster, and a rich, creamy mess coated every inch of my shaft. I felt my thighs tremble. "Cover this cock with your cum, darling."

With each passing second, her walls tightened, the pressure building, sweat trickling down my forehead, my heart pounding in my ears. She shook uncontrollably, cursing and screaming as she released a torrent of liquid that soaked the blankets beneath us.

"Messy fucking slut."

"Yes, yes!" Her furrowed brows were a mix of pleasure and intensity. "It's too much, Reese!" She moved my hand from her clit, gripping my wrist tight. I groaned, my back muscles tightening with each slow, deep, aching thrust, my Adam's apple bobbing as I threw my head back, the pleasure unbearable.

Laurene lay beneath me, dazed—wrecked, undone, fucking beautiful. The final waves of release crashed over me, hollowing me out, leaving me raw. Spent, but not empty. Never empty with her. I collapsed against her, careful, but needing to feel her. All of her. My lips found the curve of her neck, the taste of her skin, damp and flushed. My hand traced her stomach, slow, reverent, inching higher until I cupped her breast, my fingers spreading over her like I could claim her, keep her.

"I love you," I whispered, the words slipping out before I could stop them. But I meant them. I meant them like I meant every breath in my lungs.

She stilled beneath me.

I didn't move—I couldn't. My lips hovered near her ear, my next words a confession, a surrender, a truth I could never take back.

"I never stopped."

CHAPTER 18

Laurene

TWO WEEKS BEFORE THE WEDDING...

"ISN'T THIS JUST HEAVENLY?" Noelle murmured beside me as the masseuse worked on her shoulders.

The tension in my shoulders had nothing to do with the day. It was Reese.

I'd only wanted my inheritance, but instead I felt something new and undeniable. And now, he was asking me to dismantle everything I'd been prioritizing, all with three simple words.

I love you.

"Laurene?" Noelle's voice broke through my thoughts.

"Hmm?" I managed, lifting my head up from the massage table.

My chest ached with...something. Maybe it wasn't love, maybe it's just caring, or maybe I never stopped loving him. *Duty, legacy, perfection.* That was the King family mantra. Love was a luxury for other people.

But Reese had always been the exception.

I couldn't afford feelings, though. Feelings got in the way. They distracted you, made you vulnerable. Vulnerability could kill you. For fuck's sake, someone was taunting us.

But I was changing. I was letting myself feel all over again.

I didn't think I was that naïve Laurene anymore. Who used to believe she could be the exception, change our past, and end up with Reese happily ever after.

And now, he'd gone and said it.

Damn him. Damn me for the way my heart leaped at his words.

It brought up things I wasn't ready to deal with. Like how opening the gallery wouldn't mean a damn thing if he wasn't there to see it now. He was in my dreams almost daily. Or how no amount of money could make up for the way his touch made me feel so safe and secure.

It was the way he made me laugh when I was on the verge of breaking. The way he worked with me, alongside me, piecing together this mess we were tangled in; he carried some of the weight for me without me even asking.

Reese had always gotten under my skin, into my heart, whether I wanted him there or not.

I remembered the first time I realized I loved him—really loved him. Not some silly crush, not just lust, but real, deep love that lodged itself into your bones. We had snuck away to LA, and he took me to a gallery opening for my favorite artist.

His fingers had traced lazy circles on my wrist, his voice teasing, coaxing, making me laugh so hard I forgot to guard myself. He stayed by my side all night; then, I saw us in the mirror. We looked like a real couple. Comfortable, at ease. I wasn't worried about my image, or presentability politics.

He looked at me and it had hit me all at once—like a crash, like a fall.

And now…now he was doing it again.

I felt it all.

Even if I wouldn't admit it.

Even if I knew better.

I put my finger to my lips, hoping to squash that thought. Reese didn't fit in with my carefully planned life. But the truth was, I didn't want to survive anymore.

I wanted to *live*.

And that terrified me.

For so long, I had convinced myself that my purpose was to rise above—to be untouchable, undeniable, untamed by anything that could hurt me. I had mapped out every move, every play, determined to build a life so grand, so opulent, that no one—not Mama, not this town, not Reese—could ever touch it.

And I loved it. The glitz, the glamour, the power of walking into a room and knowing I belonged there. The way diamonds looked against my skin.

Reese unraveled parts of me I thought I'd buried, and I realized—maybe for the first time—that I wanted something else too.

Something deeper. Something real. Something that had nothing to do with revenge or proving a point.

It meant trusting someone with the parts of me I'd hidden for so long, the parts that felt too fragile to expose. It meant loving Reese—and letting him love me back.

With a sigh, I sat up.

Noelle looked over at me. "You okay?"

"I can't relax," I admitted, watching the candles flicker.

"One moment, please," Noelle requested to the masseuses. Once we were alone, she turned, eyes sharp. "This isn't about the wedding, is it?"

It was dangerous. Because loving him, trusting him again, meant taking the kind of risk I swore I'd never take again. I'd lost last time to Mama.

"No. It's… What did you find on the camera?"

She sat up, clutching the blanket.

"It wasn't just some cheap, throwaway device," she said, her voice low. "This thing was custom."

"And?" I cleared my throat.

"I reviewed the footage. Most of it's pretty uneventful—staff coming and going. Nothing that stands out." She paused. "But the camera's footage goes back three days."

I sat up fully now. "You're saying someone knew I'd be in that suite *three days* before I got there?"

"Did anyone else know you were coming?"

The soft hum of the massage table's heating element filled the room. Someone had been watching, listening, before I even set foot in that place.

Who the fuck were we dealing with?

"The footage isn't clear," she said. "I did get a glimpse of somebody, but they weren't there long."

I'd gone through the engagement party's guest list a hundred times. Every name was crossed off except for a few that I couldn't track down. Too many unknowns. Too many gaps. My chest tightened with frustration.

"I saw a silver bracelet. Maybe Cartier?"

Finally, we knew something. A bracelet. My mind raced, sorting through every person in town with Cartier. That didn't narrow it down by much. It wasn't much to go on, but it was more than we'd had before.

Someone had been watching, waiting, and now they were steps ahead.

"You're sure it wasn't Jennie?" I asked, though I already knew the answer.

Noelle tilted her head, considering. "Why would she do that? Jennie would've gotten caught with her pregnant belly. And what motive does she have? This was careful."

Careful. My stomach twisted. She always had jewelry on but I could be biased.

Blair.

"Blair fits," I muttered.

"Blair fits *too* well," Noelle countered gently. She adjusted her towel. "She's an obvious suspect, but don't you think that makes it…convenient? Men can wear Cartier too."

"Convenient or not, she has motive," I shot back. "She told Reese about me kissing Conrad. She's already tried to sabotage me once. Why not keep going?"

"She *told* Reese?" Noelle's eyes widened.

I snorted bitterly, my anger bubbling just beneath the surface. "How did she even find out? I thought she left earlier. Unless someone else saw us and told her. Which means someone else in this town hates me. It seems like we can't get the suspect list down at all."

Noelle's mouth parted slightly, and she sighed. "I have to tell you something."

I looked at her expectantly, and she looked down at the ground.

"Blair found out because I told her."

"You did what?" My voice was sharp, disbelief curling around each word.

Noelle winced. "I was drunk. I was blabbing. I didn't mean to." Her hands twisted together in front of her. "I wish I could take it back. I *swear* I do."

She met my eyes then, her own wide, pleading.

"Laurene, I'm so, so sorry."

My stomach twisted. A hot, nauseating rush of emotions churned inside me—betrayal, anger, embarrassment. Noelle? Of all people?

I swallowed. "I can't believe you would do this."

I let out a long breath, hoping to get rid of the betrayal. But it clung to me. She was supposed to be my friend. My safe place. The one person I thought I could trust.

"You're my best friend."

"I know. And I hate that I hurt you." Her voice was thick, pleading. "But I wasn't trying to be malicious, Laur. I was drunk, and I wasn't thinking, and before I knew it, it just—" She exhaled sharply, shaking her head. "I wish I could take it back. I would in a second. I didn't say anything but I was afraid, but it was stupid of me."

I pressed my lips together, my fingers digging into my arms. I wanted to hold on to my anger, but hadn't I done that by not telling Reese I kissed Conrad?

Noelle was my best friend. And despite everything, I believed her.

"We don't have time for this." My voice was quieter now, controlled. "Let's just... Let's move on. It's okay."

Noelle blinked, thrown by the shift, but she nodded quickly. It was awkward for a few moments, then she spoke.

"You need to tell Erik then."

My stomach twisted at the thought. "No. Absolutely not."

Erik would go crazy. He'd instantly switch to protective mode without hesitation, and that anger, that strong urge to defend me, was exactly what I was worried about. It could get him hurt.

"Laurie—"

"I said no."

She shook her head, disbelief flickering across her face. "Laurene, do you hear yourself? If they're planting bugs? Assaulting you? What's next, bombs? You need protection."

I winced at the word. *Protection.* I wouldn't let it get that far. Reese wouldn't either.

Noelle sighed, her voice soft but firm. "I hate to say it, but you need someone with power—someone like your mom. Someone who can actually handle this quietly and won't run their mouth."

I opened my mouth to answer, but the words didn't come. No one came to mind, not at first. But then, it hit me.

I'd seen him with Blair. And shit, he'd wanted to meet when I came home. Reese told me he asked about me. All signs were pointing toward him.

"You thought of someone, didn't you?"

"I don't know if it's a good idea."

"You don't have a choice."

I inhaled. "Mayor Castillo."

"Dante? Are you sure about that?" Noelle's lips parted, her eyes widening in recognition.

Was I? Not entirely. But I didn't need certainty to make it

work. Mama had let him keep his seat for a reason, and if he was tangled up with Blair somehow, that gave me leverage—leverage I could twist in my favor. Whether he liked it or not.

"We saw him with Blair. He already wants to 'talk business' with me. If she's mixed up in this, keeping him close makes sense. And the enemy of my enemy…"

Noelle arched a brow. "Is a friend?"

"Exactly," I said, a cold smile curling my lips.

"You'd really use that? Blackmail the mayor? Laurene, that's" —Noelle hesitated, searching my face—"bold."

"If I have to, I will." My voice was flat, matter-of-fact.

Noelle stared at me like she didn't recognize the person sitting across from her.

"You've changed," she murmured. "You could be making *another* enemy."

"I'll make sure I'm not wrong, and Blair gets put down."

The door swung open.

"I need this *every* day…" Gigi strolled in with a small entourage of staff behind her draped in a plush robe.

"I'm glad someone is enjoying this day," I said, watching as she tossed her new red hair over her shoulder and plopped into the chair across from us. Cucumber slices were immediately placed on her eyes, and within moments, one person was massaging her feet, another working her shoulders.

Gigi leaned forward, the cucumbers slipping slightly. "What's wrong, boo? Reese? Is he acting up? Don't tell me I gotta choke up my new best friend already."

I didn't even wanna know what was going on there. "Yeah, it's just the wedding stress. You know how it is."

"Speaking of stress, have you talked to Serena? I thought she'd join us. Or are y'all still fighting?" Noelle said.

The mention of Serena twisted something in my gut. I missed my sister, but when she got like this, it was no use.

"I invited her," Gigi admitted. "Against my better judgment.

I thought she would pull her head out of her ass and come. But I see the evil heifer chose the dark side."

"She must've decided she wasn't ready," I said evenly, keeping my tone measured. "And we can't really be mad at her for that."

"Serena is just an asshole." Gigi lifted a cucumber and bit into it. "You said nothing wrong. She just mad 'cause it's true."

"Gigi," I said.

"Ain't nobody gonna beg her to talk to us," Gigi said. "It'll be a cold day in hell before I do that, and if you do, Lu, Imma punch you in the throat."

Noelle glanced between us. "You don't think she'll come to the wedding?"

"She'll be there, otherwise Mama will be on her ass like white on rice, and Lord, let's not upset Mama," Gigi huffed.

Jennie, Pauline, and Nina walked in, all smiles, chatting away.

"Hey, Laurene, I was just thinking about the wedding presents!" Jennie said with a bright, cheerful voice. She gently settled onto the comfy chaise longue, one hand resting on her baby bump. "Should we set up a registry at that home store downtown?"

Pauline clapped her hands together. "Oh, that place has everything! We can make it a fun day to browse. Nina, call the store. Have them shut it down for us for a day next week."

"Yes, Mrs. Ashbourne," Nina said.

I forced a smile. Home décor was the least of my worries. Spa staff entered, carrying a large garment bag and a small ornate box.

"We have a surprise for you," Jennie said. "Your mom sent a gift."

I was curious, but the moment they unzipped the garment bag, my stomach knotted. Fabric tumbled out, and as the bag fell away, there it was—*the dress*.

"Oh my God."

It was a dress that belonged to a different life of mine. A different me. The same wedding dress I was supposed to wear to marry Conrad. Every eye in the room was on me, waiting for my reaction, but I was frozen.

"What…what is this?" I finally managed.

Pauline looked from me to the dress. "We thought you might want to try it on again. For old time's sake, plus it saves us time."

It wasn't just a dress. It was a message, a sharp reminder of the life Mama expected me to live—to do what she wanted.

"Are you serious?" I snapped. "Why would I want to do that?"

"Because it's beautiful!" Jennie insisted, clearly trying to be kind. "I mean, you never got the chance to wear it before, and… well, it's just such a gorgeous dress. You deserve to have that moment."

"It's not just a dress," I said, slowly standing. "It's…" It carried pain, a reminder of a life filled with broken promises and forced decisions. "I—no," I choked out, I staggered back, nearly tripping over my own feet. "I can't…I can't wear that."

"You need to calm down, honey," Pauline said. "It's just a dress."

I swallowed hard. I couldn't do this today, *again*—not in front of them. "Excuse me."

"Laurene, wait—" Jennie began, but I was already turning toward the rack of plush robes, reaching for one and slipping it over my shoulders.

"Lu!" Gigi and Noelle called my name.

I hurried down the quiet hall, my footsteps echoing sharply in the stillness. I turned a few corners when I finally reached the sauna. Pushing open the door, I stepped inside, the thick heat wrapping around me instantly.

The only sound inside was the gentle hiss of steam as I sat on one of the warm wooden benches, letting my head fall back.

The door of the sauna opened.

"Blair," I said flatly, not even bothering to hide my surprise. "What the hell are you doing here?"

"Surprised to see me?" Blair asked, a smirk tugging at her lips.

"Actually, no. You always show up like a damn cockroach."

"I'm here for the sauna, queenie. It's the best in town." She shrugged, settling on the bench across from me. "You look like hell. Rough day?"

"I saw you with Harold."

Her expression faltered for just a second, shock flashing before she buried it under that fake-ass indifference. "What?"

"Don't play dumb with me, I don't have the patience." I leaned back, staring her down, my voice low and cold. "You don't have any shame, do you?"

Her laughter bounced around the sauna. "Shame? Me? I think you've confused me with yourself. Fucking two brothers? Shame on you."

I opened then closed my mouth before a smile curled on my lips. "No, but I do have the guy you always wanted but could never get."

Blair's eyes widened.

"I know Reese doesn't know about you and Harold yet, or you wouldn't be breathing."

"You don't know what you're talking about, Laurene." Her voice was steady, but there was something sharp in her tone. "Maybe you should stick to your own mess before you start worrying about mine."

She stood up, adjusting her towel.

"I also saw you with Dante down by the boutiques."

Blair snarled at me. "What are you trying to imply?"

I leaned forward. "You know damn well what I'm implying. You're getting cozy with the mayor, just like you got cozy with Harold. How's that working for you? It must be nice to have all those powerful men wrapped around your finger."

Blair opened her mouth, but I didn't give her a chance to speak.

"Tell me, Blair, do you ever stop and think about the damage you're doing?" I couldn't hold back the smirk. "I should slap the shit out of you for telling Reese about Conrad. But I think I'd rather see you squirm."

Blair's face turned a shade paler, but she quickly recovered, throwing me a cold look. "You're making a lot of accusations. None of them are true."

"Are you Harold's sugar baby? Dante your pimp? Your daddy low on money? Tell me when to stop listing reasons."

"You're out of your mind, Laurene. Harold and I are business associates. And as for Dante, we're friends. Nothing more."

"Is that so?" I said. "Funny how that 'friendship' seemed to look a little…personal."

She stepped closer to me. "You don't even *deserve* Reese. How do you just get him because you're a *King*? You have no idea how to love him." Blair narrowed her gaze at me. "Everybody talked about you when you were gone. They all said they'd never met someone so hollow, so cheap and desperate. This town hates you and your family. You fucking bi—"

I felt something snap inside me.

My hand moved before I could stop it. The crack of my palm against her cheek rang through the sauna. Her head whipped to the side, her red hair fanning out, and for a split second, the venom drained from her face, replaced by pure, stunned shock.

"You think you can talk to me like that?" I said. "Let me remind you who the fuck you're dealing with, Blair. My family built this town while yours was still struggling to wipe their asses. I don't need to prove a damn thing to anyone, especially not you."

Her eyes narrowed, and I leaned in, letting each word sink in deep, making sure she understood how much she fucked up.

"And Reese? He's *mine*. No matter how much you want it, cry about it, or pray for him. He's coming home to me. *Every single night.* Now and forever. And yes, because I'm a *King*, I get whatever the hell I want. And I get him."

I paused, savoring the power shift between us.

"You know, he doesn't just kiss me—*he devours me.* He always did. The way he holds me, like he can't get close enough. That rough, almost desperate way he takes his time, like he's trying to memorize the taste of my lips, the scent of my skin. And when he starts kissing right on my neck—he'll nibble there. That's where he loves to leave a mark."

Blair's eyes darkened.

"And as for what you told him about me and Conrad? You knew damn well it would hurt him. But don't you worry about it at all. Here's what's going to happen. I'm going to make sure your little affair with Harold comes to light. That's the least of it, though. The King family's untouchable, but you? You've got no real friends, no allies."

I wanted this to hurt her. I wanted her to cry.

"I'm going to ruin you in front of everyone you care about. Your mom won't get another society invitation. Your dad won't be able to get fucking *bus* money. And when I'm done, when everyone sees you for the cheap, desperate bitch that you are, I'll make sure you'll never get close to someone like Reese again."

Blair shot me a final, disdainful look before striding out, leaving me alone.

I sat back down, my heart still beating from the exhilaration of defeating Blair. I closed my eyes and relaxed for a few more minutes.

A bang hit the sauna door.

My heart leaped into my throat. I exhaled sharply. A figure loomed on the other side of the glass door, indistinct in the fog.

"Hello? Is someone there?"

I waited for a few seconds, the silence stretching uncomfortably. My chest tightened as the scent of cedar, once calming, now seemed too strong, filling my lungs with every inhale.

I waited.

Seconds stretched like hours.

Nothing.

Suddenly, the lights flickered.

I froze, eyes darting to the ceiling. The light sputtered, casting quick flashes of shadow across the sauna.

The soft hum of the lights buzzed in my ears. Then with a final flicker, the lights went out.

Total darkness.

The steam grew heavier, swirling thicker, drowning me in the inky black. It had to be temporary. Just a malfunction.

When the lights didn't turn on right away, I stood up fast, trying not to panic. A weak hallway light glowed through the tiny sauna window. I could barely see through the fog, but I made it to the door.

My hand reached for the wood handle, slick beneath my fingers. I pressed against it, gently at first. Then harder.

Nothing.

I pushed again. The door wouldn't move.

No.

No, no, no.

A wave of panic surged through me. My hands trembled as I tried again, harder this time. The steam was thickening with each second, making the room feel smaller, tighter. Was it getting hotter? My vision blurred as droplets slid into my eyes.

"Hello! Can anyone hear me?" I shouted, the slick sheen of sweat sticking to every inch of me.

I shoved my shoulder against the door. The door groaned and creaked, but wouldn't budge.

Stepping back, I turned to the small window. Maybe I could see outside, get someone's attention. I wiped the glass with the back of my hand, but the steam clung stubbornly. Finally, the glass cleared and I could see in the mirror's reflection across the hall something had been placed on the door. A sign taped to the door that read "Out of Order."

Holy shit.

I pressed my forehead against the cool glass, desperately scanning the area for any sign of life. The hallway was empty.

"I'm locked in here!"

My mind raced. I couldn't just stand here. The door wouldn't open, and yelling for help would do no good if no one was around to hear me. I needed to think.

There had to be another way out.

I pounded my fist against the wood. The sweat dripped down my temples, and my breath quickened, growing shallow. But then I felt it—a ripple of heat, sharper than before. It was getting hotter. The sauna was becoming a hot box, and I was trapped inside.

"Someone! Please!"

The idea of passing out, of succumbing to the heat, clawed at my mind. *Get it together, Laurene.*

I stepped back, taking stock of my surroundings. There had to be another way out.

I looked around for anything that could help me—something to climb, something to break the door down. *There.* A small vent high up on the wall.

I needed to climb. I took a step back, my heart racing. The heat was stifling, but I steeled myself and ran at the wall, using all my weight to jump up. I barely grazed the edge of the vent with my fingertips.

I took a breath, wiped my sweaty palms on my towel, and tried again. This time, I focused on using my legs more. I launched myself up, fingers grasping for the edge of the vent.

Praying it would come loose, with a grunt, I yanked. The cover rattled, but held firm.

I drew in a sharp breath, summoning every ounce of strength left in me. I pulled again, the metal groaning in protest. Finally, with one last desperate tug, the vent cover broke free, crashing to the floor with a loud *clang*.

The opening was small—too small. I couldn't crawl out.

What if there was no way out?

Hell no. I didn't come back from halfway across the world to die in a sauna.

Picking up the metal cover, I ignored the pain from the heat on my fingers, and I turned to the glass window.

I swung the metal cover at the glass. A thud sounded, but cracks formed on the glass. I didn't stop to think. I swung again.

Crack!

The window broke open, sending shards cascading to the floor.

"Please, someone help me!" My heart raced as I pressed my face against the jagged edge, trying not to cut myself, but to see in the hall. "Help! Someone! Please!"

Then I heard it—a soft humming, melodic and eerily cheerful.

Where was everyone?

I caught a fleeting glimpse of movement from the corner of my eye near the fall—a shadow flitting, but I couldn't turn my head to see clearly. Suddenly, I heard rushed footsteps approaching. Nina's eyes widened at the sight of me.

"Laurene! Oh my God!"

"I'm trapped!" I rasped, my voice cracking. "I can't get out!"

"Hang on! I'll get you out!"

The heat bore down on me, oppressive and stifling. I felt light-headed, my breath quickening as I leaned against the door. "Hurry! Get me outta here."

To my surprise, the door swung open with little effort, almost as if it had been waiting for her.

"Are you okay?"

"What the—" I stammered, confusion flooding my senses. "I —I couldn't get the door open. It was locked, it was…"

"Just breathe," Nina said. "You're okay now. Pauline and the others were worried about you."

Noelle was right. This whole situation was spiraling, and I

couldn't shake the feeling that I was being watched, manipulated. Someone had locked me in that sauna.

I wasn't crazy.

CHAPTER 19

Reese

"MORE TO THE LEFT."

I dropped the crib on the hardwood floor with a thud. The fan was going full blast, but the air was still stuffy with paint and baby powder, and sweat ran down my back.

"Well?" Jennie rocked in her chair, ice cream in hand. "Get to it."

The nursery was painted in pastel stripes, baby clothes were stacked to the ceiling, and a corner was full of stuffed animals with shiny eyes.

I only came to borrow her drill.

"Careful," she warned. "It's antique Norwegian wood."

With a glare, I shifted the crib nearer to the bookshelf. I glanced over the shelf and saw kids' books and family photos, but one picture really hit me hard.

Jennie, Conrad, and me as kids, all huddled together.

"Thank you," Jennie said. "I'll be so glad when this kid gets off my bladder."

The crib creaked as I adjusted it. "There. Happy now?"

"Actually, yes." She glanced around. "Oh, could you scoot the changing table a little to the left? It's driving me crazy."

I moved the table. "How's that?"

"Perfect," Jennie said. "You always know how to make things right."

I was glad somebody thought so.

"Good. Are you gonna give me some of that ice cream as payment?"

Jennie gave me the pint, grabbing another spoon from the diaper drawer. I eyed her skeptically.

"Pregnancy cravings," she explained. "I need to keep snacks in here when I cry."

I chuckled, taking the spoon. Jennie was wrong: I always made things worse. Every single time. With Laurene, it was like I couldn't stop myself.

"Reese?" Jennie's voice snapped me back.

"Yeah." I cleared my throat. "Just thinking."

"Remember building forts with Mom's blankets?" Jennie laughed. "We'd spend hours setting them up and then refuse to take them down for days."

"How could I forget?" I said. "You said I was your puppy and had to do what you said. Then Dad would barge in and order the staff to rip them down just so he could watch the news in peace. Like we were nothing but a fucking inconvenience."

"He wasn't a total monster," she said quietly.

I ate more ice cream. "Yeah? Name one good thing."

She didn't answer. She didn't have to.

Dad's voice echoed in my head, that cold, clipped tone he used whenever he addressed me. *You'll never be anything but a disappointment.*

I stared at the spoon in my hand, at the way my knuckles had gone white from holding it too tight. Maybe he was right. Maybe that's why Laurene couldn't look me in the eye when I told her I loved her. The way she rolled out from underneath me, like I was the fucking plague. The way her lips had pressed into that thin line.

I'd laid my heart bare, and she hadn't said a damn thing.

Maybe she thought I was too reckless, too much like my

father. That thought burned more than anything. I wasn't him. I'd spent my whole life trying to prove I wasn't him. But the longer I stayed here, stuck in the same cycle of anger and failure, the harder it was to believe it.

"Have you looked at the quarterly reports for the clubs yet?"

I glanced at her, surprised by the shift in tone. "Not yet. Why?"

"I've been combing through the resort accounts, and something's…off. There's a discrepancy in the numbers. Not huge, but noticeable." She chewed on her bottom lip.

My stomach tightened. "How much are we talking?"

"About fifty thousand, give or take." She swallowed.

I needed to step up investigating this missing money. "You're not imagining it. I noticed something similar with the distilleries last month. I'll get Nathan to speed up his audit."

Jennie nodded and I handed her back the pint. "You notice anything strange about Dad lately?"

"Strange how?"

"Just, you know. He's been acting different." She hesitated. "He took the jet last minute without telling anyone where he was going. I had a meeting in Arizona planned, and suddenly it was gone."

I raised an eyebrow. "The more he's gone, the better it is for all of us."

"I'm serious, Reese. I called him, and after ten times he finally answered. When I asked where he was, he hung up on me."

I scraped the empty ice cream container, my mind wandering. "What do you want me to say? That he's a selfish bastard? That he doesn't give a damn about anyone but himself? You already know that."

"This is different," she insisted. "Mom told me he's been leaving the house for hours and days sometimes. I called the investors in Phoenix, and he never showed for the meeting."

"Your primary concern should be having a safe pregnancy, not worrying over that asshole."

"Forget it. I shouldn't have brought it up." Jennie's eyes searched mine. "Did Laurene tell you what happened?"

That made me look at her.

"I feel so guilty, but the bridal shower, it didn't go as planned. Nothing awful, just...not well. We gave her the wedding dress."

I frowned. "Wedding dress?"

"I guess it just unsettled her," Jennie said. "I mean, now that I've thought about it, it was wrong."

"*What* wedding dress, Jennie?"

She finally met my eyes, guilt flickering across her face. "The one she was supposed to wear when she was going to marry Conrad."

A sharp, angry heat flared up inside me. "You gave her *that* dress?"

That dress would have painfully reminded me of the past. A sick, aching reminder I was always second place, second choice, never the one who was supposed to matter.

"Yvonne suggested it. She thought it might give her some closure."

"Closure?" I scoffed. "It's not 'closure'—it's a damn slap in the face to her, and to me. Did you even think about how I'd feel?" I snapped, my voice rising. "That was a hell of a thoughtless move, Jen."

No words came from her.

"I shouldn't be surprised," I muttered. "Why would anyone think about me?"

"It wasn't about...replacing anyone, or making you feel less than," Jennie mumbled.

"She was supposed to marry Conrad in that dress," I said. "And now you want her to wear it again for me? Like I'm just picking up where he left off? Like it's supposed to fit my life the same way it fit his?"

"That's not how anyone sees it, Reese," she said, her tone almost pleading.

"It's how *I* see it," I shot back. "It fucking hurts. Why the hell am I still living in his shadow? Nothing I ever do will be enough to be seen as more than his replacement."

"I didn't mean it like that," she said. "I know you and Conrad never got along—"

"I'm just supposed to grin and bear it, right? Play the role? Pretend like it doesn't fucking kill me? You're the only person in this family that gets me. You out of everybody in this family should have stood up and said *no.*"

"Reese—"

"I've spent my life trying to be different from him," I went on. "But the truth is, it doesn't matter what I do, does it? I'll always just be the one who wasn't *Conrad.* I bet you wish I was dead instead, just like Dad does."

Jennie's face fell, but I didn't let myself feel sorry for her.

"I'm not Conrad, and this wedding isn't his memorial service. It's *my* day."

I took a deep breath.

"I need to go." I leaned down, planting a kiss on the top of Jennie's head, but she wouldn't look at me. "Tell David he owes me a drink for hauling that crib up here."

"Reese, wait—"

I was already heading for the door, my mind racing with thoughts of Laurene.

I reached my car, slid in, and put my head back. My grip on the wheel tightened, and before I knew it, I was turning the key.

What the hell was I thinking? A cake? A fucking cake? I ran a hand through my hair, staring at it. I parked outside the Kings' place, my heart racing.

I stopped off at Café L'Amour on the way. I knew Laurene loved that place—they served her favorite dessert.

I grabbed the box. Whatever, who cares. I slammed the car door and went to the front door.

Sighing, I rang doorbell. The door opened, and there he was: the butler who saw us in my car.

Great.

"Good afternoon, Mr. Ashbourne," he said. "Can I help you?"

I played it cool. "Um, is Laurene in?"

"Miss Laurene's in her studio near the garden, sir. Shall I fetch her for you?"

The cake box felt heavy. "Uh, no. That's okay. I'll go to her."

"Very well, Mr. Ashbourne. I trust you know where it is?" He smoothly stepped aside, and I swore he was smirking.

The grand mansion loomed, its high ceilings echoing faintly, marble floors cold beneath my feet. I stepped onto the warm patio, surrounded by lush greenery.

I found the little guest house way at the back of the garden; it was painted a pale green. The last time I was there was before she got engaged to Conrad. I pushed the cracked door open.

"Reese? What are you doing here?" Laurene turned to me in paint-covered jeans and a too-small T-shirt.

I felt ridiculous holding the cake box. "Got you something."

"From Café L'Amour?" She blinked, a hint of something vulnerable in her expression. "You didn't have to do that."

"Yeah." I rubbed the back of my neck and handed her the box. "Figured you could use a pick-me-up. Jennie told me what happened."

Laurene gave me a look and nodded. "I can't believe they still make this. You remembered." She broke off a piece of cake, and her eyes fluttered shut as she licked the frosting off her fingers.

I was captivated watching her expression soften, and I felt my dick harden in my pants.

"It's still so good." Her eyes met mine, and I wondered if my face was a billboard for my feelings: total admiration, guilt, fear, and lust.

I cleared my throat. "I only came by because I wanted to check on you after the whole shower thing. I'll get you whatever dress you want."

"I'd never wear that dress. I know what it means—to both of us."

The relief that swept over me was sharp, almost startling.

"Good," I murmured. "Just pick another dress you like."

"Gigi's already on the case."

I watched as she quickly devoured the cake and suddenly the decision didn't seem stupid. Her eyes met mine for a brief second, but she quickly looked away, focusing on something in the distance.

"Something else happened at the spa," she told me. "I got trapped in the sauna."

"What? What the hell happened? You should have called me immediately. We're going to need to hire more—"

"I tried to get the door open, but I couldn't," she cut me off. "It's been playing in my head… I think it's personal. Of course it's *personal,* but I'm being targeted more than you." Her nails tapped against the table in an erratic rhythm. "I've been going over everything in my mind, and what if you're just collateral? I've done so much shit—or maybe it's somebody after Mama but…" She trailed off, jaw tightening.

"Laurene."

She exhaled sharply and turned to face me, something unreadable flickering in her eyes. "Maybe you should go."

The words came so suddenly that for a second, I wasn't sure I heard her right.

"I'll tell my parents I called off the wedding," she went on. "I'll take the heat. You don't have to be dragged into this. You don't have to stay."

"Are you serious right now?"

Her eyes flashed. "Reese—"

"No." I shut that down immediately. "I'm not going anywhere."

She swallowed. "I mean it, Reese. If this is about some mistake I made, there's no reason for you to be—"

"This isn't just about you." I said. "You think I'm fine because they haven't locked me in a sauna yet?"

I shook my head.

"I know what this is. I know what it means when someone wants to break you down, make you paranoid, get inside your fucking head. Who is to say after they hurt you, they won't come after me? I've done things I'm not proud of either."

Something flickered across her face.

"I'm in this with you, Laurene," I said. "You don't get to push me out. I don't care how much you try."

Soft, moody music played from her open laptop. I glanced at it, then back at her.

"Let's go back to the beginning."

She glanced at me, brow furrowing. "The beginning?"

"We've been reacting this whole time. Every new threat, every new message—we're just chasing whatever comes next. But if we really want to figure this out, we need to go back. To the first sign something was wrong."

She exhaled, nodding. "The first thing was the letter."

For the next hour, we worked in sync, piecing things together, ruling things out. Laurene's fingers moved fast as she searched names, scrolled through old news articles, and pulled up grainy photos from gossip blogs and social media.

"Here." She turned the screen toward me. A blog post from a couple of years ago, half speculation, half scandal. The photo was small, slightly blurred, but it was someone we both recognized.

"That's Dante," I muttered, narrowing my eyes. "And he's with..."

"Toby."

The headline was bait for clicks: "Lush Foundation Welcomes Unlikely Benefactor."

"This was for the Lush Initiative," she murmured.

"I remember this—it was some scholarship fund for kids. Dante started it after he got elected." I frowned. "Toby was never the 'give back to the community' type."

She scrolled down. The article was mostly fluff—mentions of wealthy patrons, the night's entertainment, and a few named donors.

Then she stopped.

"'A generous contribution from local businessman Tobias Merrick helped launch the second phase of the program.'"

I scoffed. "What money? Most of his fast-food chains shut down after that salmonella outbreak."

"But this was before all that. Back when his businesses were still standing." Laurene tapped a nail against the laptop. A thought clicked into place.

"I've just never seen them together, even now. Maybe they're hiding their relationship?" I asked.

She exhaled sharply. "Or they were in business together all along. Toby didn't just donate—he was the biggest contributor. If you said you ended all your partnerships that Conrad made with Toby, maybe he went to Dante for a bailout? Dante's expanding this city, so he has money…or access to it. And this was required of Toby to fulfill the deal, help with Dante's plan?"

I leaned in, studying the photo again. It was subtle, but Dante's posture, the way he leaned in close, the way Toby looked tense despite the forced smile—it didn't look like a friendly conversation.

It looked like business. Messy business.

She sighed, rubbing her temples. "I need a break before my head explodes."

"Okay. That's enough for now. So… Still avoiding the whole 'I love you' thing, huh?"

Her eyes snapped to mine, and her expression tightened.

"Reese, I—" She stopped herself, like she'd been about to say something she wasn't ready to say. The walls were back up, higher than before. "Would you like to see some of my paintings from Paris?"

Paris? What the hell did Paris have to do with this? With me baring my soul and her sidestepping it like it was nothing? My chest tightened, frustration and something I couldn't quite name clawing at me.

"Sure."

A blink, and suddenly her face looked soft, almost fragile. Like she was surprised I said yes. Now that I had, she was lost.

Laurene moved slowly to the canvas, handling it as if it would break. She brought it into the light, then stepped back. Suddenly, the room felt smaller, the air heavy as I moved closer.

Paris at dusk. Long shadows stretched across the cobblestone streets, the streetlights glowing softly in the windows. It was so peaceful, like the city was waiting for nightfall.

I stared at it, my heart beating too loud in my chest.

"It's beautiful," I said, my voice quieter than I intended.

She shifted beside me, her arms crossing over her chest. "It's just something I worked on while I was there. Nothing special."

"Don't," I said, sharper than I meant. "Don't act like it's nothing."

Her eyes met mine, wide and uncertain. "Paris was smelly, dirty, rats everywhere, but there's a raw beauty there too."

I could see her in each shade of blue, green, and gold.

"This…this is how you felt, isn't it?" I gestured at the canvas. "This is you."

Her breath hitched, and for a second, I thought she might deny it. Shut me out. But she didn't.

"It's easier to paint it," she said softly. "Than to say it."

She lifted another canvas. This one was simple: a woman hunched over, her back arched, with a small furry dog trailing behind her on a leash.

"Every day I saw this woman buy a baguette and an espresso

from the café near my apartment." Laurene ran her fingers over the painting. "She was always in such a rush but couldn't move than two miles an hour, and the dog probably moved at half of that. I got brave enough to say hello one day."

"What happened?"

She laughed. "Cursed me out in French. Called me out for being American."

"Damn." I grinned. "Did she also steal your lunch money?"

"Practically." She nodded. "Next day she gave me her baguette because I looked 'too skinny to live.'"

"She insulted you *and* fed you?"

"It became our thing after that. She'd insult me, then slide me an extra croissant. She actually became one of the few friends I had." Her smile softened. "I admired her, in a way. She didn't care about being liked. She just *was*."

But just as she moved to pass one painting, a quick flash of movement caught my eye.

"Wait. Go back," I said, already stepping closer.

She froze, then slowly lifted the canvas.

It was a portrait of *me*.

The brushstrokes were raw, intense. My eyes in the painting were sharp, focused, like I was looking at you.

"Why didn't you finish it?"

"I—" Her gaze dropped to the floor. "I didn't know how to finish it. Or if I should."

"Why?"

"Every time I tried to complete it, I kept thinking about us. It was like finishing it would mean we were really done. That everything was over."

"And now? Do you still think about us?"

Her eyes met mine, a storm of emotions swirling within them. "Every day. But I'm scared. Scared that finishing this painting means accepting that we're over. Or maybe now that we're not."

"Finish it."

Her brows furrowed, but she turned back to the canvas and grabbed her palette and brush. I stepped back, and she shook her head. "Sit there, near the light."

I moved to the chair she'd pointed to.

"Take off your shirt."

I raised an eyebrow. "Is that necessary?"

"The lighting on your shoulders will help capture the contrast better."

"Just looking for an excuse to see me shirtless again?"

Her cheeks flushed. "Just take it off and shut up."

"Anything for the art." I tugged my shirt over my head and tossed it onto my jacket. "I know I'm sexy, but show restraint, okay?"

"Hush, fool."

Her brushstrokes were precise. Her lips parted slightly as she concentrated, and her hand paused before each stroke and her eyes darted between me and the canvas.

"What's going on in your head right now?" My voice was low, breaking the silence.

She paused, her brush hovering midair. "I'm trying to get this right."

"That's not what I meant."

Her eyes flicked up to meet mine. "You make it hard to stay focused."

"Hard to focus, huh? I'll take that as a compliment."

She shook her head, biting her lip. "You're impossible."

I inched closer, almost touching, but still keeping some distance.

"I think you're the one making this impossible," I murmured.

Her brush stilled in her hand, her gaze darting to the canvas like it held all the answers. "It's not that simple."

"What's not simple? Finishing a painting, or us?" I tilted my head, studying her.

"Both," she finally said, her voice barely above a whisper.

"Then tell me how to make it simple."

She set the brush down, her hands trembling for a moment before she hid them behind her back. "That's the thing. You can't make it simple, Reese. You just…make it harder to ignore. I have to make a decision."

"And what do you want?"

She stepped closer, closing the space between us, her hand pressed over my heart.

"I've spent my whole life being what everyone needed me to be. What my family needed me to be. When I tried to stand up, I failed. Choosing something for myself… It still feels selfish, even though I have every right."

"It's not selfish to want something for yourself, Laurene. It's human."

She shook her head. "I need to finish this."

I didn't know if she meant me, the blackmail, or the painting.

"You always have a choice. You just have to decide if it's worth it."

Her jaw clenched, but she didn't back away. "And what if it's too late?"

I reached out, brushing a stray strand of hair from her face. "Then finish it. The painting, us—whatever you're so afraid of. Just don't leave it undone."

Not being able to resist, my lips found hers, and I didn't even try to deny it.

I broke the kiss for a moment, my forehead resting against hers, breath coming in short gasps. "I'm not leaving."

She pulled me in and kissed me deeply—exactly what I needed. I just wanted to touch her, any excuse to close the gap that always felt too wide.

My hands moved on instinct, drawn to her like gravity. One traced the curve of her waist, the other dipping lower, grazing the edge of her jeans. Her breath hitched, her stomach tensing beneath my touch, but she didn't stop me. She pulled me closer.

I slipped my hand beneath the waistband, finding her.

Heat. Wet. My pulse slammed in response.

Her body trembled, and when my fingers teased, parting her, she gasped—soft, breathy, so fucking sweet I nearly lost control.

"Tell me," I rasped against her skin. My lips brushed her jaw, her throat, tasting the warmth of her. "Is it good when I touch you here?" My fingers stroked, slow, deliberate, pressing into her in a way that had her thighs tightening, her hips rocking forward. "Or maybe here?"

I pushed deeper, drinking in the way she clenched around me, the way her breath came in short, uneven pants. She was burning up, her body practically begging for more, for me to lose control right along with her.

Fuck, I wanted to.

A choked moan escaped her lips as she leaned into me, her breath warm against my neck, sending a shiver down my spine. I moaned as I hear the ridiculously wet sounds of her cunt. I watched the slickness build on my knuckles.

"Reese."

"You're so wet," I murmured, my voice rough even to my own ears. It wasn't just desire that thickened my tone—it was everything else. The years of waiting, of wanting, of never being able to forget her, no matter how hard I tried.

She trembled. I was making her give me everything she had. She said my name again while I increased the pressure on her clit with my thumb. Her beautiful lips, smooth thighs, and dark skin all seemed perfect to me, and the best part was that she was all mine.

She was *my* wife.

Not Conrad's. Not anyone else's.

My woman, forever. Everyone would know. Her face was a whirlwind of emotions. I pressed a kiss to her temple as her thighs clamped around my hand, trying to slow me down.

"Stop—I'm about to—"

"You don't want me to stop." I knew her terribly well. "Baby, pay attention and look at me."

My fingers found her sweet spot. Her shocked gasp echoed as I pressed on the fleshy pad, causing her to writhe in my grasp.

"Don't you get it? We were always supposed to be together. Just me and you against the world, princess. That's what you told me years ago, right?"

A beat of silence hung in the air before I rapidly increased the speed of my fingers, compelling her to meet my gaze.

"Isn't that right?"

"Yes!" Her eyes rolled back, and with a small growl, she buried her face in my arm, her teeth sinking into my flesh.

"Are you watching me?"

I leaned in closer, sucking firmly on her neck and teasingly nibbling on the delicate skin. My fingers moved in and out of her, exploring every inch. Hotter. Faster. Her hand gripped my wrist, digging her nails in. And then—she shouted.

It wasn't just a cry of release. It was a breaking point.

Her body went rigid, her pussy clamping down on my fingers. When she opened her eyes again, they weren't just full of the pleasure of the moment, they were full of something more.

I withdrew my fingers from her, a sticky string of her wetness stretched between them, making us both gasp. Slowly and deliberately, I tasted her on my fingers, never once looking away from her eyes. I moved closer and kissed her slowly, letting her taste herself on my tongue.

"Laurene," I whispered, my voice steady even as my chest burned. "If you don't want this, if you don't want me, tell me now. But if you do, don't make me fight for you alone."

I couldn't help but admire the way she fought to steady herself, the way she tried so damn hard to control the things that were breaking inside her.

A sharp knock on the door followed.

"Miss Laurene, a gift has arrived for you," her butler said through the door.

I didn't want to move, didn't want to break the fragile moment. Quickly fixing herself, she let me put my shirt back on, then called for him to enter. The butler placed a small black box on the table beside her.

He quietly exited, leaving us alone again. Laurene didn't immediately reach for the box.

"Who is it from?" I asked.

"No name."

I swallowed, and our eyes connected.

"You think it's from—" I started as she picked up the box. The lid clicked open, and there was silence, except for the faint sound of her breath catching.

There was no note, no letter. Just a small tattered piece of rope, stained dark brown, almost black.

I felt my blood run cold.

The rope was thick, jagged at the ends, frayed like it had been ripped away from something—or someone. It looked familiar. Too familiar. It was the same kind of rope used to tie down boats, the kind I'd seen on the docks before.

And worse, it looked as though it had been cut loose from the wreckage of the boat where Conrad had died.

CHAPTER 20

Laurene

THREE DAYS BEFORE THE WEDDING...

"BIIITCH!" Gigi came in, her sequined jumpsuit shining, heels clicking with every step. She dramatically threw out her arms. "Stop what you're doing. This is an *emergency intervention!*"

"Not quite the entrance we'd planned," Noelle mumbled, following behind Gigi. "But here we are."

I squinted at them. "You both are dressed nice. Should I be worried?"

"Worried? Since when have I made you worry?" Gigi jumped on my bed, grinning, and sending pillows flying. "Never mind. Don't answer that."

Gigi flipped her hair.

"Fine, fine. It's your bachelorette party!"

"Bachelorette party?" I said.

"Duh! I know this owner of a club in Vegas. Generous donor. Gonna fly us out on a private jet, limo service from the tarmac, give us a section. Basically we're gonna be bad bitches tonight."

I raised a brow. "Did you sleep with him? Don't tell me this is one of your shady connects."

"No, it's not. But I low-key feel like I should be the maid of honor and not Noelle because not only have I planned a kickass bachelorette party, I'm looking for the wedding dress. I need to tell Mama to put me on the payroll."

Noelle sucked her teeth. "You stole all of that from me!"

"Hush! You know I'm *better* at this kind of thing. And wait, wait, hold up, you're on an IUD, right?" Gigi squinted at me.

I stared at her for a long moment.

"I'm just looking out for you, girl. 'Cause when I say shit's gonna be poppin' off tonight? *Shhiiittt.* We're doing this right. No accidental nieces or nephews on my watch."

"I mean…" Noelle shrugged. "Statistically speaking, Gigi's right. Unexpected pregnancies do happen at bachelorette parties."

I looked at the both of them like they were batshit crazy.

"Shaking some ass at the bachelorette party is mandatory." Gigi rolled her eyes. "You're not getting out of this."

"It's tradition," Noelle chirped. She brandished a sash that read "Bride to Be" and draped it across my shoulders.

I touched the cheap sash. "Did you pick this up from the dollar store?"

Gigi hopped up and went straight for my clothes. "Jesus, your closet's bland as hell."

I sucked my teeth as she muttered, tossing a pair of black boots over her shoulder. "I may just call down to Celeste's boutique and have her send us some clothes…"

"Those boots are Rene Caovilla."

Gigi shot me a look. "You'll thank me later."

"You deserve this." Noelle smiled.

"And trust me, Lu, if I'm planning it, it'll be epic. None of that bullshit." Gigi walked out of my closet, holding up a gold sequined dress like she was planning to wear it herself.

"Fine," I said, standing. "But let's keep it reasonable, alright? No leopard print or feathers."

A sharp rap echoed through the quiet room, making her jump. The door flew open, and Serena was there.

"You finally decide to crawl out of your hole?" Gigi asked.

Serena turned to me, her expression unreadable. "I came to talk to you."

A month of silence. A whole damn month where not a word came from her. My stomach churned as I stared at her, trying to decipher whatever hidden agenda she had.

"Why don't you go back under your rock? 'Cause we got plans, and you're *definitely* not invited." Gigi snapped her fingers, pointing to the door. "Step, homie."

"Since when are you Lu's lap dog?" Serena glared at Gigi.

"Jealous?"

Serena's gaze remained steady. "Don't test me, G. You don't want to go down that road."

"No, you don't want to go down that road with me."

"Enough, you two," I interjected. "Can y'all give us a minute?" I glanced at Gigi and Noelle.

Gigi narrowed her eyes, clearly offended. "Wrap this up. I have a stylist coming in fifteen."

She strutted out, shooting Serena one last over-the-shoulder glare. Noelle followed, albeit less dramatically, her hazel eyes flicking between me and Serena. The door shut, and we were alone. I wanted to say something, but I waited to see what she'd do.

"I wanted to apologize," she said finally.

I blinked, surprised. Apologies weren't Serena's usual thing. "For what?"

"I'm not going to give you some grand emotional speech."

"I wouldn't dream of it."

Her eyes flickered to the right, and she sighed, her shoulders drooping.

"For before," she said. "For the things I said."

"You're going to have to be more specific. We've had a lot of befores."

Serena's mask slipped for a moment.

My little sister, always so strong, so calculated, now looked out of place, as if she'd walked into the wrong room.

"I've been thinking. About the fight and what you said. You're not wrong," she admitted. "I do let Mama use me or whatever you want to call it."

"I didn't mean—"

"You did," she interrupted, her tone sharp but not cruel. "But you don't understand what it's like being the one who stayed."

What could I say to that? She was right.

"You were the perfect daughter. Gigi and I grew up hearing it, feeling it." She paused, her lips curling into a bitter smile. "Mama used to say, 'Why can't you be more like Laurene?' every time I made a mistake or when Gigi got in trouble. Even when you were gone, that didn't stop."

"I didn't leave to hurt you. You know that, right?"

"I know. But it felt like abandonment all the same. *You and Erik*, Mama made it clear she had plans for y'all. Gigi and I were afterthoughts. And then you weren't there. Suddenly, all the things you were supposed to do, they were dumped on me."

A sharp pang of guilt hit me.

"When Mama turned to me. It felt good, Lu. To actually be needed for once."

No matter how horrible I felt staying here, I never wanted Erik or my sisters to suffer.

Serena crossed her arms, her gaze distant now. "I got good at reading Mama. I thought I made her happy. I'm good at helping the business. I'm actually fucking great at my job."

Her voice wavered slightly, and it felt like the room held its breath.

"I hate that Mama treats me like a tool. I hate that Gigi thinks I'm boring. I hate that no matter how much I do, it's never enough. Because I'll never be you."

"Serena…"

"And the worst part?" she continued. "I hate that I still look up to you. After everything. After you left. I still look at you and think, 'That's the kind of person I wish I could be.'" She let out a bitter laugh, shaking her head. "How pathetic is that?"

I stepped closer. "It's not pathetic."

"Don't," she warned, raising a hand to ward off any hug. "Don't try to fix this. You can't. I don't need you to."

This was the first time in years I'd seen Serena hurt and trying to keep herself together.

"I'm sorry," I said, stepping back to give her space. "For everything. For leaving, for not seeing what you were going through. For making you feel like you had to be me, like you couldn't just be you."

Serena didn't say anything at first, her eyes flickering with something I couldn't quite place. Finally, she nodded, just once. "Thanks. I needed to hear that."

"You know I love you, right?" I said. "Even when I left, even when we fought. I always have."

She looked away. "Don't."

"I mean it." My heart ached for her. "You're you, and that's valuable. You're my sister. My brilliant, complicated, impossible little sister. And I love you. Always. And I'll spend the rest of my life making it up to you."

"Ew." Her lips pressed into a tight line, and then she looked at me, smiling.

And then, cautiously, like she wasn't sure she could let herself, she leaned forward. Her arms wrapped around me in a stiff, almost mechanical hug. I froze for a moment. But it was real. I wrapped my arms around her, slow, giving her time to pull back if she needed to.

She didn't. Serena just stood there, holding on—when she finally pulled away, her movements were abrupt, her expression already hardening back into something more familiar.

"Don't make this a thing," she muttered, brushing an invisible wrinkle from her sleeve. "I should go."

"Hang out with us."

Serena shook her head and already she was back on her phone, rapidly typing. "I'll leave the fun to Gigi."

"Stay. I want to celebrate with my girls."

For a moment, she hesitated, her eyes scanning my face like she was searching for something. Then, with a sharp breath, she nodded. "Alright."

As soon as the words left her mouth, the sound of muffled voices on the other side of the door broke the moment.

"Ugh, why'd you invite her?" The door swung open and Gigi's arms were crossed, her glare aimed directly at Serena. "I've got three hours to make everyone in this room look presentable and make a flight. And that's including *her*."

"We're all back together!" Noelle grinned, looking like she wanted to cry.

"Shake ass first, cry later," Gigi snapped.

And for once, I was happy to obey.

The bass was thumping so hard, you could feel it in your chest. The strobe lights, a dizzying kaleidoscope of color, bounced off the bar's sleek surface, illuminating the crowd's rhythmic swaying, the air thick with the smell of sweat and alcohol. A chilled bottle of champagne sat before us, and I was surprisingly enjoying myself.

"This place is poppin', right?" Gigi stated.

Noelle grinned while filling our glasses. "Let's make a toast! To Laurene and her last night of freedom? Or let's cheers to the men I'm adding to my roster?"

"Don't you have a harem already?" Serena arched a brow.

"Don't be jealous. It gives you crow's feet."

Was Reese having a bachelor party? The thought of him being surrounded by women made my stomach curl. I could still feel him, on me, within me, but his final profession to me still rang in my ears.

"I'll give the toast," I said. "Here's to letting go and, in G's own words, *shaking ass*."

Gigi raised her glass with a loud laugh. "Shaking ass!"

I clinked my glass against theirs, and we downed the drinks before Gigi clapped her hands.

"Let's dance!"

She grabbed Noelle's hand and pulled her onto the dance floor. Serena and I exchanged a look, and I was surprised when she just shrugged off her jacket and followed.

Secrets and guilt kept me in survival mode for too long. Tonight, I decided to forget it all. I went with the flow, not recklessly, but gently. Maybe trust. Or hope.

The bass shook me to my bones as I hit the dance floor. Gigi whirled around, her hair sparkling. Serena went with Noelle, their arms raised, howling with laughter over the music. The four of us moved together in a tight circle, the rhythm pulling us in.

I let my head tilt back and felt the heat of the moment press against my skin. Lights flashed above us—neon pinks and greens strobing through the smoky haze.

Everyone was packed in tight, moving together like one big wave. But then, the space around me shrank. There was another brush of skin, shoulders jostling mine, strangers' voices too close, too loud in my ears. The lights that had dazzled now seemed to blur, their colors bleeding into a disorienting kaleidoscope. My breath caught, shallow and quick, as the warmth of the crowd became stifling.

All of a sudden, the memory of the spa slipped into my mind. My chest tightened.

I scanned the sea of faces, searching for Gigi, Serena, or Noelle.

The press of bodies seemed less accidental now, less friendly. The air buzzed with something more than music. Something heavier.

I couldn't shake the feeling I was being watched.

I focused, trying to stay calm, but the loud noise and moving crowd made me stumble.

"Gigi?" I yelled, but my voice was swallowed by the music. "Noelle! Serena!"

No answer. Just the crowd, the heat rising. I tried to push through the sea of bodies, the sweat on my skin turning cold.

I needed to find them. I needed to get out.

I spun wildly, bumping into people. Each hit jolted me; I flailed, grabbing for something to hold on to, but the crowd was merciless. I was pushed back harder and harder each time I tried to get through.

My legs grew heavy, and the music shifted abruptly, the familiar beat replaced by a thunderous bass drop that slammed into the speakers and reverberated through my skull. My breath came in short, shallow bursts, my chest tightening as the crowd surged again.

It felt deliberate now, like I was being swallowed whole.

My hand shot to my pocket, frantic, only to remember Gigi's insistence on this tight dress. No pockets for a phone; purses abandoned in the limo. I panicked. A hand brushed against my back, firm, deliberate. I whirled around, my heart racing, but they'd vanished into the crowd.

"Laurene!" I heard a distant shout.

I pushed past everyone, their yelling and dirty looks just noise. A hand, cold and firm, grabbed mine. I fought against it, heart racing, until I looked up.

Noelle.

I trailed behind, wobbly and gasping, the crowd opening up for her unlike me.

I finally got out of the crowd, gasping for air and feeling like I'd been underwater. Noelle's grip on my hand was firm as we weaved through the last stragglers until we reached the booth. The bass still rattled my bones but I was calming down.

"Are you okay?"

I nodded, still shaken up.

"You're not okay," she said, giving me the once-over. "Wanna go?"

I shook my head. I didn't want to let this blackmailer win. "No. We're here to dance."

She hesitated, her lips parting like she was about to argue.

"Can you get me some water, please?"

She let out a small sigh. "Of course."

Noelle squeezed my hand before turning, weaving her way back into the crowd.

I sagged against the booth, my fingers digging into the vinyl. I closed my eyes as I tried to calm my racing heart.

"Laurene."

My eyes snapped open, and there he was, standing just a few feet away. Reese. His broad shoulders framed by the dim, smoky light, his presence commanding even in the haze of the club.

I let out a shaky breath; relief washed over me, almost making me weak-kneed. I hadn't realized how desperately I needed him, a physical ache in my bones and a hollowness in my chest, until he stood before me.

"Reese. What are you doing here?"

Reese's lips curved into a slow, devastating smirk. "My club."

I blinked, the pieces started to fall into place, one after another, too fast to catch. "You're the generous owner?"

It hit me then—the private jet, the limo, Gigi had insisted on this night, the effortless way everything had fallen into place. And there he was, the man behind it all.

He stepped closer, head tilted. The tailored fit of his dark suit molded to his body like it had been made for him—sharp, sleek, dangerous. The open collar of his shirt teased a sliver of tanned skin, the kind that made my pulse flutter.

"Is that what Gigi called me? That's better than 'Pimp of Vegas,' huh?" Reese teased, but his eyes held something more when he looked at me. His hand brushed over my arm, check-ing, as if he were silently making sure I was still whole, still *here*.

"But with your track record..." He trailed off, his brow furrowing slightly, his voice softening into concern. "I needed to know you were going to be safe tonight."

I could practically feel him radiating protectiveness.

"Guess I'll have to be good," I said.

Reese chuckled, completely blocking my view of the club. "Laurie, you've never behaved a day in your life."

I stiffened at the sound of my old nickname.

"You called me Laurie," I whispered, almost unsure if I had heard him right.

Reese blushed slightly. He quickly rolled his eyes, dismissing it. "Habit."

"You're not the type to slip into old habits after a month."

He smirked, but his eyes held something real. "You're special, princess."

"So, you're babysitting me?"

"Keeping you safe." His tone had shifted. "You deserved a night off, a real one. But I wasn't gonna sit back and hope nothing happened."

"Dance with me," I heard myself say.

Reese's brows furrowed, like he wasn't sure he'd heard me right.

"Remember when we used to sneak into those clubs in LA?" Those nights had been ours—reckless, intoxicating, free. I wanted that again. "Dance with me, Reese."

His jaw tightened. I thought he might turn away, leave me standing there, wanting.

His hand, warm and strong, slipped into mine. He silently pulled me onto the dance floor. When he turned to face me, his other hand brushed the small of my back, pulling me toward him.

"Laurie," he murmured, his voice rough, the words like a caress against my ear, barely audible over the pulsing beat of the music.

I shivered, tilting my head back, letting the feel of him consume me. "Don't," I whispered, my lips barely brushing his. "Don't say anything. Just…dance."

His hand slid from my back to the base of my neck, his

thumb grazing my skin, sending a shiver down my spine. My hips rolled with the beat, slow and deliberate, and I saw his eyes drop, the heat in his gaze making my insides tighten.

I arched my back slightly, letting the rhythm take over, turning, so he was flush against my back. His breath was warm and unsteady against the back of my neck, his hands settling on my hips, steadying me. I let my hips wind, my body undulating to the music, and my head fell back, hair brushing against his jaw. His fingers dug into my hips, syncing with every movement, pulling me closer, tighter.

"Why do you do this to me?" he finally said, his voice a ragged whisper against my ear.

I swallowed hard, my fingers tightening on his shoulders. "Do what?"

"Make me want something I can't have."

I took a shaky breath, eyes closed. I had been running from this—*him*—for so long. From the promise he made, our plan, our families, from the fear of what it meant to give myself fully only to lose him, to surrender completely. But here, with his arms around me and his heart on the line, I realized I decided.

"You already have me, Reese. You always have."

I gently detangled myself from him and turned to him.

"I love you too," I finally said, the words trembling on my lips.

In saying them, something shifted. Something inside me broke open, and I was both terrified and *alive*.

For a moment, he was still, his hands frozen on my back, his breath hitching in his throat as if the words had stolen the air from his lungs. I felt his heart pounding like crazy against my own. His voice, when it came, was hoarse, almost unrecognizable. "Laurene…"

"I love you."

Everything inside me shifted, unraveling the tightly wound knot of fear and regret. My heart hammered in my chest, but this time, it wasn't fear. It was the pure, exhilarating freedom of finally letting go.

There was nothing but this raw, aching connection between us, and I knew I couldn't walk away from this. Not anymore. Not ever again.

"I thought you'd never say it again," he murmured, his lips brushing against mine as if he needed to taste the words, to make sure they were real. And then, without a word, he reached for me, pulling me into his chest, crushing me against him like he never wanted to let go. His lips, fierce and desperate, crashed against mine.

There was nothing controlled about it. It wasn't a kiss of calmness or restraint; it was a kiss of *need*—the kind that tore at you from the inside out, raw and passionate. His hands slid into my hair, pulling me deeper into him, and I melted into it. My heart raced, a frenzy of emotions tangled with desire, as his lips left mine only to trace the line of my jaw, the sweet heat of his breath dancing over my skin.

"You have no idea how long I've waited to hear you say that," he murmured against my ear, his voice dark and thick with longing. "I've been waiting for you to stop running. For you to come back to me. And now that you've said it, I swear I'm never letting you go again, Laurene."

Every slow roll of my hips pulled a low growl from his throat as we continued to dance.

"You're playing a dangerous game."

"I'm sorry it took me so long," I whispered, my voice breaking, my hands tracing his jaw. "But I can't choose anything but you. I can't live without you, Reese."

He was the one who held me when I was broken—physically, emotionally—without hesitation, without question. The one who refused to leave, even when I doubted I deserved his love. He saw something I didn't. And despite every reason to walk away, he stayed.

For so long, I ran from this—ran from him, from the undeniable truth of what we were, what we could be because of fear of Mama and the King legacy.

He was still *him*, still going after his liquor line. Supporting his sister. Dealing with the fallout of Conrad and our new lives. Reese never let me fall into doubt or fear. But most of all, it was how he loved me without conditions—he loved me when I wasn't ready to love myself. How he loved me enough to let me find my own way back to him.

I couldn't ignore it anymore. I had to stop lying to myself and him. I loved him—because he saw me. It wasn't my legacy or duties, it was me. Reese loved who I was, even when I didn't. Loving me, he showed me I could do it. I was bigger than my past mistakes. And suddenly, running didn't feel like freedom anymore. It felt like losing. I wasn't going anywhere. Not without him. Not without fighting. Inheritance or not.

"Follow me." He grabbed my hand, and we started weaving through the crowd.

I completely forgot about my sisters, Noelle, and the bachelorette party.

He led me through a discreet door tucked behind the bar, and we climbed some steps before we entered a room filled with sleek black furniture and floor-to-ceiling windows, offering a perfect view of the pulsing crowd below.

"Do you always take girls back here?" I asked, my voice light, though the pounding of my heart betrayed my composure.

He smirked, his dimples flashing in the dim light. "You're not just any girl, are you?"

Reese strode forward towards a sleek, low-backed chair and sat. The way he leaned back, legs spread and arms draped lazily over the armrests, was a challenge all its own.

"Say it," he whispered, his voice a low, rough demand that made my knees weak.

"Say what?"

"That you've never wanted anyone the way you want me."

"You know it's true," I said.

He chuckled. "You just can't let me win, can you?"

I tilted my head, giving him a mock pout. "Win? What, are we playing a game now?"

"Oh, we've been playing for a while," he said, his voice dripping with that unmistakable confidence. "And you're losing, Laurene."

I rolled my eyes, but the heat building between us made my stomach flutter. "I wouldn't be so sure about that."

He leaned in, eyes never leaving mine.

"Dance for me."

I should have felt shy, but instead, excitement thrummed through me. "What if I say no?"

"You won't," he said simply.

The bass beat matched my heartbeat. He watched as I approached, my heels clicking on the floor.

The music moved me. His eyes locked on mine, pupils dilated. I turned, my hands gliding smoothly over my sides, to my ass, feeling the silk of my dress against my skin as my hips swayed.

"You're taking your time," he growled.

I glanced back, the heat of his gaze quickening my pulse. "Good things come to those who wait."

Reese shifted in his seat, his legs spreading as he settled deeper, his fingers gripping the armrests, a slight smirk curling on his lips. The power in his stare, the way he was so comfortably at ease, watching me—it sent a thrill through me, making me feel every inch of his attention.

"Slower," he murmured, his voice low and rough.

I let my fingers slide slowly along the curve of my neck, head tilting slightly, feeling his eyes follow every movement. He leaned forward slightly, lifting his hands just enough to let the hem of my dress rise, exposing my thighs. The way he looked at me almost possessively made my heart race, but it only fueled me more.

"Like this?"

Reese's tongue darted out, catching the corner of his lip—a quick, slick movement that sent a tremble of power down my spine, the taste of anticipation thick in the air. I approached him, leaning forward, hands on his knees.

"You're making it real hard to stay in this chair." His eyes locked on to mine, a dark fire burning within them, daring, warning, promising all at once. But I stayed put.

"Strip."

I froze, a gasp caught in my throat.

"You heard me."

Not wanting back down, I reached for the straps of my dress. I slid one strap off my shoulder, then the other, the cool silk slipping down inch by inch.

His green eyes got darker, his smirk disappearing, replaced by a serious, almost animalistic look. "Keep going."

The quiet command, husky and low, sent a wave of heat through me, and I obeyed, pushing the dress lower, letting the silk pool at my feet. The air kissed my bare skin, cool against the heat radiating off me, and I resisted the urge to cover myself.

"You're stunning," he murmured, his voice almost reverent. "Now, dance for me."

My heart raced, but there was a strange, intoxicating sense of power in the vulnerability. I could do this. I could own this.

"Take the bra off."

My stomach twisted, doubt flickering briefly before I exhaled sharply and unclasped my bra. The fabric, smooth and cool, parted, revealing my skin, which prickled under Reese's unwavering gaze; the silence hummed with unspoken tension.

"God, they're still so beautiful, just like the rest of you," he muttered, his voice thick with desire. "So fucking pretty."

My breath quickened. He wasn't judging, wasn't pulling back. He was consumed by me, by how I moved, by how my body responded to him.

"On your knees."

I didn't hesitate. I sank to the floor, the cold surface against my skin only adding to the heat coursing through me. Our eyes locked, the tension between us palpable, silent but deafening.

"You still remember how this goes?"

I nodded and crawled slowly over to him, and he leaned back, watching as I placed my hands on his knees. Without a word, he allowed me to pull him out of his pants.

I let myself feel him, without the rush and frenzy of emotion. My hand ran from the base of his dick to his tip, his throbbing veins standing at attention. I wanted this, wanted to give him every ounce of pleasure he'd ever craved, to feel him unravel beneath my touch.

He didn't speak, but the way his jaw tightened and his chest rose and fell told me everything I needed to know. My eyes stayed trained on his face, memorizing every twitch and parting of his lips.

Reese's hand cupped the back of my head, his fingers threading gently through my hair as he guided me closer. The warmth of his touch sent a ripple of heat down my spine, igniting every nerve ending. I let my tongue roll over the seam of my lips, teasing him, savoring the way his body tensed beneath my hand as I continued to stroke him with deliberate, unhurried movements.

I glanced up, meeting his eyes—dark, hooded, and filled with an unspoken need that mirrored my own. His grip tightened, not demanding, but urging, and the quiet groan that escaped his lips sent a thrill through me.

Slowly, I leaned forward, my lips brushing over his sensitive tip as my hand slid to steady him. I let my tongue flick out, tasting him, reveling in the low, guttural sound he made in response.

"Fuck," he murmured, his voice rough, his control slipping with every passing second. The power of it, the way I could unravel him so completely, filled me with a heady mix of pride and desire.

I took him deeper, letting the weight of him rest heavy on my tongue. My lips stretched around his length, and his taste, warm and musky, spread across my palate.

Another deep moan of his bounced off the walls. "You look so damn pretty with my dick in your mouth."

My fingers gripped his thighs, anchoring me as I found a rhythm, slowly taking him into my mouth before he hit the back of my throat.

"Eyes up here, baby. Look at me with my cock down your throat."

Reese's hand tightened in my hair, the slight pull making heat pool low in my belly. His hips rolled forward, matching my pace. The control I had over him was intoxicating.

"Shit," he hissed through gritted teeth, his head falling back. The muscles in his thighs tensed beneath my touch as I hollowed my cheeks, taking him deeper. "You're gonna ruin me."

The flicker of a smirk curved my lips even as I kept him in my mouth. My gaze lifted to his face—eyes squeezed shut, jaw clenched, his brow furrowed with the kind of pleasure that bordered on pain.

I slid my tongue along the pulsing vein running up his length, feeling his grip falter and his body jerk involuntarily. He was so close, every tremor, every shudder telling me he was losing himself in me.

"Don't stop," he growled, his voice hoarse, a command wrapped in desperation.

I relaxed my throat and took him in deeper, trying to express what words couldn't. I relaxed, trying to breathe through my nose, but something about this moment felt so *right*.

I released him with a pop, letting him see my tongue before I slowly licked over his balls and back up. "I want you to cum for me so badly, Reese. Can you do that?"

Reese's groan was guttural, his head tipping back as his hand tightened in my hair. "You keep talking like that, and I won't have a choice," he rasped, his voice thick with need.

I smiled, slow and wicked, letting my lips brush over the

sensitive head of his cock before taking him back in, inch by inch. His body jerked at the sensation, a sharp inhale betraying his attempts to hold on to any semblance of control.

"That's it," I murmured between strokes, my voice soft but firm, coaxing him closer to the edge. "Let go, Reese. I want to feel it. I want to know it's because of me."

His hips bucked involuntarily, a shudder running through him as he cursed under his breath. The tension coiled in his body, every muscle taut, his breaths coming faster and rougher.

I hummed around him, letting the vibration push him further. My hands worked in tandem with my mouth, teasing and stroking, giving him no escape, no room to think, just the pure sensation of my touch.

When he finally shattered, his release hot and heavy against my tongue, I swallowed him down, savoring every second of his unraveling. Reese's body trembled as the last waves of his orgasm rolled through him, and I let him rest against my lips, the intimacy of the moment filling the space between us.

When I pulled back, wiping my lips with the back of my hand, I looked up at him. His gaze was dark and hooded, his chest heaving as he stared at me with an intensity that sent a shiver through me.

"Six years," he murmured, his voice rough and raw. "And you still fucking wreck me."

CHAPTER 21

Laurene

WEDDING DAY...

"THIS IS IT," Noelle announced as she stepped into the room. The heavy oak door closed behind her, muffling the faint strains of a string quartet drifting up from the courtyard below.

I turned from the floor-to-ceiling windows to a suite that was a masterpiece of gilded mirrors, cream silk drapes, and fresh peonies spilling out of crystal vases did little to calm me.

I smoothed the lace of my gown, the intricate beadwork catching the soft light like tiny stars. Gigi had come through with the best wedding gown possible, and finally, it was time to complete my contract with Mama.

Reese.

Every step of this journey had led me here, and yet, standing in this moment, I felt untethered, like I was floating between two worlds.

"How are you feeling?" Noelle's hand on mine broke my thoughts.

I hesitated. The answer sat heavy in my chest, too tangled to express. "I don't know, Noelle. I really don't."

She sank onto the plush velvet chaise beside me, lacing her fingers through mine. The diamonds on her wrist caught the light, sparkling like the chandeliers above.

"It's okay not to know," she said softly. "This is your day, but it doesn't mean you have to have all the answers right now."

The hum of voices and laughter beyond the door seemed to grow louder, a reminder of the hundreds of eyes waiting for me downstairs.

"But one thing I do know"—Noelle tilted her head, studying me—"is that Reese looks at you like you're the only thing that matters. He always has."

I glanced back out the window. The terrace stretched endlessly, and somewhere down there, Reese was waiting.

"I told him I love him."

She gasped. "What?"

"I know I shouldn't have. I came back home just get through *this*—"

Noelle leaned forward. "You love him again. Isn't that enough? Or are you really still doing this for the inheritance and planning to leave again?"

"Yes, I *love* him. But I still want my gallery and my inheritance."

"Why can't you have both?"

"You know how Mama works. Even after I marry Reese, she could find a way to twist things, to delay the inheritance, to make me jump through hoops I haven't even seen yet. Loving Reese doesn't protect me from her games."

Noelle's expression darkened. "That's bullshit, Laurene. Outsmart her! You're still making excuses because you love him."

I flinched. "Don't."

"Lu, you've changed. You're not alone in Paris anymore. Haven't you learned from these last six years?" Noelle shot back.

I turned away.

"Power isn't enough. *Love is.* Or maybe you *are* your mother."

I recoiled at her words. "I'm nothing like her."

"You're making decisions out of fear, out of obligation, just like her. The difference is, Laurene, you *know* better. You've seen what that kind of life does to people. Let the old you that had to survive *rest*. Return to the Lu we love. No sabotaging your mother. No revenge. Be better."

I swallowed hard.

"Money fades, businesses crumble, but love? The kind you and Reese have? That's something people spend their whole lives looking for. Some of us can't be with the one we want. Don't throw him away."

I blinked, a tear slipping down my cheek, and the door to the bridal suite swung open, and Mama stepped in.

"Am I interrupting something?"

"No, Ms. King. I'm actually gonna join Serena and Gigi down by the terrace." Noelle released my hand, giving me a sharp look, and left, leaving me alone.

"How do you feel?"

That made me scoff.

Noelle was right. No more cold feet. This time, I was going to fight for what I wanted.

"This wedding is exactly what we need. King Enterprises has just secured a deal with Devereux International. All thanks to you. Did you get the information I need on Dante? I would like to end him sooner than later. At least so he can see other companies are practically begging for our partnership again. We may even bring back the investment company if you would like—"

"No."

Mama blinked, and frowned. "You had one job."

"I don't care about any of that." I cut her off. "I don't care about your damn deal or King Enterprises."

If I was marrying Reese, it had to be done my way.

"I love Reese."

"Love?" She looked visibly ill.

"Yes, *love*. He's the man I've always wanted to marry. When we went into the interrogation room back then, I lied. I'd been having an affair with Reese. For about two years when you wanted me to marry his brother. He's always been the one for me. Never Conrad."

"You can't be serious."

"The boating accident… You don't know the whole story."

Mama's brows furrowed, her focus sharpening.

"There was a mess, a lot of things I should've told you. But I couldn't. I couldn't let you know that I'd been living a lie just to please you. That you were selling me off to a man who cared about titles just like you. Conrad grabbed me. Who knows what else he would have done to me? I couldn't even tell my own parents about my fiancé because you would have told me to suck it up. What if things had escalated?"

"You're telling me this now? Before one of the biggest moments of our lives?"

"This may have orchestrated this, but you don't win. What I've been missing… It's not the money and diamonds. I'm marrying someone who loves me, and I'm finally standing and choosing him. I can appreciate my legacy, but not being a slave to it."

"I gave you everything. I made you who you are. And this is how you repay me?" Mama was visibly shaking, like a rabid dog.

"Love isn't fleeting. It's something that endures, Mama. Not business deals, not feuds, not the rules you keep trying to force. Love is Reese. Love is Erik helping me and bearing the brunt of *you* for years without complaint. It's me understanding my sisters, *listening* to them. It's Daddy, quietly helping me behind your back because he understood that I needed a choice, not an ultimatum."

Her face tightened, her eyes narrowing as the words hit their mark.

"Love is Noelle calling me out that I was slowly letting myself turn into you, and I'll be damned if I do that," I added, my voice steady. "Look, Mama… Grandpa got sick, and I know that hurt. But you need to grieve, *honestly*. Not planning business expansions, horsewhipping us, or escaping to Bali. Sit with someone and talk about why you think and feel the way you do. I'm not here to be praised when I'm doing what you want and discarded when I don't fit into your plan. I'm done being the obedient daughter, and I'm done being the one you mold into your perfect image out of fear."

I saw her lips purse, chest heaving.

"You can have the theatrics of today. The gown, the guests, the media coverage, everything you want. But I'm marrying the man I've loved forever and your manipulations couldn't destroy us. If you don't change, Mama, you're gonna lose your family. Then what's the point of all your hard work?"

Her lips twitched into a scowl.

I turned toward the door, pausing before I left, my voice sharp as I looked over my shoulder. "If you must be in my wedding photos, Mama, smile or move to the back."

Her gaze burned into my back, but I didn't turn. Slamming the door felt good, and I made my way down the hall. I found my sisters waiting for me—Noelle, Gigi, Serena—and I realized something in that moment. I was *choosing* this life.

I smiled, my chest light, and walked forward. I could see Reese through the glass door, standing at the end of the aisle.

Gigi started the procession, followed by Serena and Noelle. I stood waiting for my cue when I heard, "I can't believe my little girl is getting married."

Daddy stood, waiting for me, looking handsome though his tie was slightly askew, as if he'd tugged at it one too many times.

"Daddy."

He smiled, a mixture of pride and sadness. "Seems like just yesterday you were running around the backyard making me put up that garden for you." He reached out, brushing a stray curl from my face. "And now, look at you."

The warm, salty breeze tinged with the faint scent of coconut oil and sun-warmed orchids blew past us.

"You have nothing to worry about. You'll fulfill your obligation, and all will be well."

"Mama still doesn't care, after all this time, you know."

He didn't deny it, but his eyes softened as he searched my face. "Your mother is…complicated."

I crossed my arms. "Was this like it was when you both got married?"

"I thought I understood her when we first got married. But your mother is driven by something different. I'm not saying what she did was right. But it's not as simple as you think it is."

I shook my head, the frustration building again. "You're okay with this, with everything being about her plan, her game?"

Daddy hesitated, looking down for a moment before meeting my eyes again. "Laurene, I love your mother. I've always loved her. I'll tell you that like I told your grandfather when I asked him for her hand. She's your mother, but she's my Yvonne, and our relationship isn't your business to understand."

"It is when we're affected. Daddy, for years we've watched you adhere to Mama's plans. All the times you could have stood up for us, you didn't."

He swallowed and blinked. "Loving someone doesn't mean agreeing with everything they do. Sometimes you have to accept the parts of them you don't understand. And sometimes, to survive, you have to make sacrifices."

"You're telling me you sacrificed your happiness to survive with her?" My voice shook, the bitterness cutting through.

"Never. I saw her goal. I always hoped she'd see things my way when it came to y'all, and sometimes she did. But not always, and I accepted that."

Daddy's face held a rawness I hadn't seen from him in years. "Your mother has been scared for a long time. You gotta understand, baby, we're the exception. I should have said something, I see that now. But you don't see her like I do."

The music began to swell faintly beyond the terrace doors, pulling me back to the moment. Daddy offered me his arm.

"That's not enough." I looked at his arm. "You've been standing by her side, but where's the support for me? Where's the support for Erik and Serena and Gigi? Why didn't you ever fight harder for us against her?"

He let out a soft, regretful sigh. "You're right. I haven't been the best father—"

"You've been the worst. A sorry isn't going to fix this." I shook my head. "I deserve a full apology. As well as Erik, Serena, and Gigi. You need to state *why* and you need to make a change. Starting today."

Daddy's eyes widened and I kept going.

"I refuse to have anyone in my life not serving me well. That includes you. So what's your decision?"

They were waiting for us, but I didn't care. I focused on Daddy and I felt the beating of my own heart.

"I apologize, Laurene. For everything I didn't do. For letting your mom run things instead of this marriage being a partnership. I know my words aren't enough, but I vow to you, baby. I'll fix things. For all of us moving forward."

I swallowed, and Daddy placed a kiss on my cheek and smiled at me.

"Don't mention this to your siblings—especially Gigi—but you're the brightest of my kids, Laurene. You're a leader." He paused, his gaze steady on mine. "But what I hope you'll learn—and maybe even do better than me—is how to balance that vision with what's in here."

He tapped a finger lightly against my chest.

"I don't feel like a leader," I muttered.

"Leaders don't always feel like leaders, Laurene. They just lead and sometimes they do it scared. Do what's in your heart." He offered me his arm. "Let's focus on you, sweetheart. The rest, we'll figure out in time."

I nodded, gripping his arm.

This is it.

The doors open. Together, we stepped forward. A sea of faces turning toward me.

Daddy's arm was my anchor, the only thing keeping me tethered to anything real. But it wasn't the music that filled my mind. It was *him*.

Reese.

There he was, standing at the end of the aisle. My first love. My past. My unfinished story. My future.

The one person in the world meant for me.

Every step felt like a reckoning, like I was moving toward a choice that I couldn't take back. This was it. I finally chose *Laurene*. We were finally getting what we deserved. I stopped in front of Reese, and for a split second, everything else disappeared.

The crowd. The noise. The world itself seemed to hold its breath.

My father placed my trembling hand into Reese's.

"You take my breath away, Laurie." Reese's voice was almost a whisper, and I smiled at him, brighter than sun, and tightened my grip.

Mama won't win this. The blackmailer won't either.

The officiant's voice was calm and practiced. I could hardly make out what he was saying, until finally, he signaled for the rings. Reese slipped one onto my finger.

"You may now kiss the bride."

When his lips finally touched mine, it was an explosion of heat. The taste of him, sharp and familiar, filled my mouth, and my fingers curled into his jacket, pulling him closer.

"I love you," I said, breaking the kiss.

A light shone in Reese's eyes.

In his arms, I was home.

CHAPTER 22
Reese

I WAS MARRIED.

In the reception hall, the air crackled with energy; the glittering chandeliers reflected the movement of the crowd, a perfect blend of luxurious, vibrant chaos. In the corner, the string quartet flawlessly transitioned into a high-energy jazz number, causing guests to get up and dance.

"Congratulations!" a voice chimed nearby, and I turned, shaking hands with someone I barely recognized.

I scanned the room and found Laurene.

She was laughing, her head thrown back on the dance floor. She twirled, her ivory gown billowing with every spin. Gigi had her arm slung around Laurene's shoulder, pressing a shot glass into her hand.

"Bottoms up, bride!" I could hear Gigi yell over the music.

She tipped the glass back, her sisters cheering her on. Even Serena cracked a rare, genuine smile before joining them on the dance floor, and the three of them fell into an impromptu routine, their movements fluid and perfectly in sync.

Laurene looked happy.

A waiter passed by with a tray of champagne, and I grabbed

a flute. The sweetness hit my tongue, but it didn't come close to the warmth blooming in my chest as I watched her.

I let my eyes drift over the crowd, and felt coldness run down my spine.

Yvonne and Harold stood together, heads bent. They weren't laughing or sipping champagne like everyone else. Their conversation was quiet, hurried, with Yvonne gesturing sharply as Harold frowned and then she walked away.

Laurene caught my eye then, her cheeks flushed and her smile so wide it was almost too much to look at. She raised her glass to me, her movements loose and carefree.

My phone buzzed in my pocket. A quick glance at the screen revealed a message from my accountant: *We need to talk about the accounts — urgent.*

I slid the phone back.

"What's up, brother-in-law?"

I turned to see Erik striding over, his grin easy, his hand extended for a dap. I met him halfway, the clap of our hands followed by a quick pull into a half hug.

"Erik," I said with a nod. "You enjoying the party?"

"This is nicer than expected," he said, taking a moment to scan the room. "Champagne flowin', good food, good music. Gigi over there got Laurene takin' shots like we at the club."

"Yeah," I murmured, watching her. "Everyone's having a good time."

"And you? You good?" Erik leaned on the back of a nearby chair, crossing his arms.

"I'm good."

He raised an eyebrow. "So did you do what I asked?"

I knew this was coming.

"Yeah," I said, keeping my tone even. "I did."

"And?" His voice dropped, his jaw tightening.

"And there's no plan."

There had been a plan six years ago. Our plan now was to finally live for ourselves. That's all he needed to know.

Erik straightened, his brows pulling together in disbelief. "Bullshit."

"Listen," I said. "She's not plotting against your mom, or whatever you think is going on."

"You don't know her like I do," he snapped. "Laurene doesn't just come home for no reason. She's got something up her sleeve, and if you can't see that, maybe you're not looking hard enough."

"I know her better than you think, Erik. And I'm telling you, there's no secret plan. She's here because she wants to be. She's staying because she wants to stay. And maybe it's not about your mom, or business, or anything else you've got going on in your head."

His eyes narrowed. "Then what is it about?"

"I love her." I looked him in the eye. "I'm in love with her. And she loves me. That's why she's here. That's why she's not leaving Lush. She's staying because we're building something. Together."

For the first time all night, Erik was silent.

"You lied to me, you two *were* together before then."

"I did what you asked. She's not plotting."

Erik stared at me, his jaw working like he was fighting back words. Finally, he took a slow breath, his eyes still locked on mine. "So that's a yes."

I just shrugged and let him think what he wanted.

He let out a low curse, turning away for a moment before spinning back to face me. "You better not fuck this up, Reese. If you do—"

"I won't. Because I love her."

"Shit," he muttered, shaking his head. "You *really* love her, huh?"

"Yeah." No hesitation in my voice. "I do."

"I guess I got what I wanted in the end, huh?" Erik didn't respond right away, and for a moment, the tension hung between us, thick and heavy. Finally, he nodded once, almost to himself. "Alright," he said gruffly. "Guess that's that."

"Yeah," I said, a small smile tugging at the corner of my mouth. "Guess it is."

"Excuse me, gentlemen, are you gonna dance or just stare all night?" Noelle's voice came beside us.

I saw Erik staring, totally dumbfounded, as Noelle spun in her pale pink bridesmaid dress and grinned brightly at us.

"Don't all ask me at once," she teased as she smoothed the skirt of her dress.

"Both of you go dance," I told him. "Have fun."

Erik gave me a hard look but offered his fist. I grinned and dapped him back.

"Don't hold up the wall too long."

He took Noelle's hand, and they both headed to the dance floor.

But the gnawing feeling in my gut wouldn't let up.

I looked across the room and saw Dante at the bar. He lifted his glass to me with a subtle nod. A chill ran through me.

The more I thought about it, the more I realized how little I truly knew. I needed to dig deeper. Trust no one.

Because everyone here was hiding something.

CHAPTER 23

Laurene

MY FUN ENDED when I spotted Harold talking to Mayor Castillo.

The music's beat matched my fast heartbeat. I left Gigi and Serena dancing and made my way over to them.

Harold and Dante. Blair's men, standing side by side.

My eyes locked on Harold, and something tight and uncomfortable coiled in my chest.

"Mr. Ashbourne." I tried to keep my voice steady. "Mayor Castillo."

Dante grinned. *"Mrs. Ashbourne."*

I glared, focusing on Harold. "Laurene. Lovely reception, isn't it?"

"Harold. We need to talk."

"I'm in the middle of business here. Surely my son can entertain you, or you can fix that pretty makeup of yours."

"It's urgent," I pressed.

He sighed and gestured to Dante. "Excuse us, would you?"

Dante glanced at us before leaving. I'd handle him at another time.

Harold eyed me irritably. "Ruining my night, Laurene?"

"It's about Blair." I met his gaze, keeping a poker face.

"Remember your hidden meeting at your house? Your mistress?"

Harold's expression shifted in an instant. The color drained from his face, his eyes flickering with panic before they hardened. He glanced around quickly, his gaze landing on Pauline, laughing next to Jennie. "You don't know what you're talking about."

"Don't I?"

He led me to a quiet room off the main hall.

"Blair's been helping me with business. Nothing more."

"Business?" I repeated. "I'm not buying it."

"You should tread carefully. I've played this game longer than you've been alive."

"What if I tell Pauline what I saw?"

His eyes snapped to mine, sharp and cold. "I'm not sleeping with Blair."

"What are you hiding?"

He paused, but didn't turn around. "I'm not answering any more of your questions."

"Would you blackmail your own son?"

I had to ask. I'd watched Harold all night. He didn't look like the happy parent with a new partnership. He looked agitated. Constantly checking his phone. A drink always in his hand.

He spun around. "What?"

"Reese has spent his entire life trying to live up to a standard you made impossibly high for him. I know you don't like him."

"He's lazy. Undisciplined. Weak," Harold snapped. "He had every opportunity handed to him, and he squandered them all. Do you know what that's like? To give someone everything, and they spit in your face?"

"Everything?" I laughed bitterly, shaking my head. "You gave him *nothing*. But that's not the problem, is it?"

Harold's nostrils flared, the muscles in his jaw tightening. He was visibly seething now. "It's about what I've invested. In him. My company, *your town*."

"Invested?" I echoed. "What are you trying to protect, Harold? Paranoid too?"

He stiffened, the walls going up again. "I'm done talking about this."

My hand shot out, grabbing his arm. Somebody better give me an answer. "What the hell are you hiding?"

Harold spun, his grip on my wrist tightening with surprising ferocity; I gasped. He sent me hard against the wall.

His face was inches from mine, his eyes wild with rage. "You don't know who you're messing with, Laurene."

"Let go of me," I said, though a small part of me was afraid. But I refused to give in. I would not let him scare me.

"Your mother she thinks she's controlling everything. But she's blind to what's really happening."

I stared at him, confused. "What do you mean?"

"Dante," he said. "You don't think I see them both plotting against me? I know your mother had a plan with this arranged sham."

I blinked, feeling a shiver crawl down my spine. "What is Dante planning?"

"Worry about him instead of me."

He released me, and I immediately pressed my wrist against my chest.

A sudden knock on the door shattered the silence, sharp and unexpected, and Reese stormed in. Immediately his eyes were on me and my arm, and I immediately forced it down by my side.

"What the hell is going on in here?" Reese demanded, his gaze darting between me and Harold. "Laurene? Is everything okay?"

I opened my mouth, ready to respond, but before I could get a word out, Harold said calmly, his voice cold, "Nothing to worry about. Just a discussion about family matters."

"Really?" Reese's jaw tightened, his eyes narrowing on his father.

"I was just leaving," he muttered, brushing past Reese without even sparing him a second glance.

The door clicked shut behind him, and Reese turned to me, concern flooding his features. "Laurene. What did he say to you?"

I didn't trust myself to speak about it yet without breaking. "Can we go?"

"Let's get the hell out of here."

What do I say to him?

We pulled up to his house, and Reese killed the engine and got out first, circling to open my door. "Come on."

I pulled up my dress; the rough stone steps were scratching at the delicate fabric. The image of the send-off at the resort kept haunting me—confetti in my hair, car packed with wedding gifts. But now, it all felt so far away and suffocating.

I grew more exhausted with each step.

"Want a drink?" he asked once we were inside, while loosening his tie.

I nodded.

Reese headed into the kitchen. I replayed my conversation with Harold.

What the hell was going on? One answer just led to another question. It felt like one of those never-ending handkerchief magic tricks.

The blackmailer hadn't made a move in the past week.

So far, we'd looked into Miles. Tobias. Blair. Harold. *Dante.*

It all kept coming back to the *mayor.*

He had always been ambitious—too ambitious, maybe. But to play us all like this? He and Mama had a deal. A deal I didn't know shit about. But to align himself with my family, to cozy up to my mother, and then turn on her? That didn't add up either. What was his endgame?

Reese's voice broke through my thoughts. "You okay?" he called from the kitchen.

"Yeah," I muttered, strolling to the windows, fingers brushing the smooth leather couch. Dark cliffs met a black, endless ocean.

The more I thought about it, the less sense it made. So Dante was involved in the blackmail, right? Then why the delay?

A quiet click, then smooth music started playing.

Harold, Toby, Blair, Mama—round and round we went.

I found the latch to the patio and stepped outside.

All of this needed to be over. Done.

My hands clutched the wrought-iron railing as I looked out.

I felt this huge sense of dread; it was like we were waiting for the other shoe to drop. I turned to see Reese, clearing his throat, holding two glasses, sleeves rolled up, showing off his arms.

"You seem thoughtful."

I paused, our fingers brushing as I took a drink. That whiskey was strong, but it felt good going down. "We're married."

"We are."

My wedding ring was proof that we had made it through everything. We were married now. He was my husband.

"I'm all yours, Laurene."

My heart skipped a beat, and I grinned.

"What happens next?" I finally managed.

"We handle whatever comes," he said. "Together."

There were so many layers to this. So many things still hidden.

"Reese—"

"Whatever it was with Harold," he said, "let's leave that for another day."

He swallowed hard, gently putting his glass down.

Reese was on me before I could say anything. The warmth of his hands on my waist sent a pleasant shiver down my spine.

"You're overthinking," he murmured, his warm breath ghosting my temple as his fingers, long and slender, traced the curve of my back. "I can practically hear it."

I swallowed hard, my hands trembling slightly before I finally rested them on his chest; I could feel the steady beat of his heart beneath my fingertips.

"Reese—"

He leaned closer, his lips brushing the edge of my ear as he whispered, "Whatever's going on in that head of yours, let it go for just one night."

I tilted my head up, and the intensity in his eyes, a mixture of sadness and understanding, stopped me cold.

His mouth was on mine, a demanding, hot kiss that stole my breath. His hand, warm and strong, caressed my neck, sending jolts of electricity through me. His fingers threaded through my hair, pulling me into him until my legs gave way.

My mind went completely blank for the first time all night. No Harold, no blackmail, no secrets—just Reese and the way he touched me, tasted me, and whispered my name on my lips like it was the most important thing ever.

"I'm never letting you go again." The words hung in the air, heavy with unspoken promises.

"You're mine," I whispered.

"Damn right I am."

Reese's hands went down to my waist, tracing the delicate lace on my dress. Leaning in close, his warm breath a whisper against my neck, he pressed a slow, deliberate kiss to the sensitive skin below my ear.

"Take it off," he rasped, igniting a fire within me.

He carefully loosened the bodice strap by strap. He stepped back, looking me up and down.

"I need you. Here. Now."

The silk gown slid to the floor.

"Out here?"

Reese's lips curved into a slow, devilish grin. "Why not?"

He reached for his shirt, his fingers working one button at a time, and I couldn't tear my eyes away. The faint moonlight caught on the hard lines of his chest as he revealed it inch by inch. My breath hitched as the intricate tattoos decorating his skin came into view—sharp, bold, unapologetically him.

God, I wanted to trace every line with my lips.

I took a step toward him, my pulse hammering in my ears, but he held up a hand, halting me in my tracks. "Not yet."

The words were a soft command, a low rumble vibrating in his chest. "Don't touch me."

Without a word, Reese sprawled on the chaise longue by the patio, legs out, one arm resting on the back.

Frustration and longing overwhelmed me. "Are you teasing me?"

"I like it," he replied. "Or maybe I just want to watch you crawl to me."

"You like me on my knees too much." I moved forward, only in black lacy panties, no bra.

"I'm happy with you in whatever way I can have you." He sat up a bit as I reached him, and his hand brushed my hip. I settled onto his lap, and his warm hand found my back, rubbing slow circles.

I slowly began to grind against his thigh, each movement pulling a low hum from deep in his throat, and Reese took my chin, tilting my face so I was forced to meet his gaze. Then he kissed me.

A sigh escaped my lips as our mouths met, soft at first, then a deeper, more passionate kiss. He brushed my hair behind my ear. His tongue coaxed me open. Our tongues met, slow and unhurried.

I was on the chaise longue, flat on my back, before I knew it. My whole body shook as heat pulsed between my thighs. I tilted my head back, letting him kiss me all the way down. When his fingers grazed under the swells of my breasts, I shuddered. He gently touched my nipples.

I gasped as his lips drew a hard nipple into his mouth. His tongue ran small circles over me, and he grunted softly against my skin.

"Damn, you so fucking wet."

He moved my panties and slipped a finger in, making me moan. I almost screamed when his tongue wrapped around my clit.

"Reese!"

My hand landed on top of his head, I made eye contact as he ate my pussy. I couldn't stop my body from twisting and turning as he released my clit with a loud smack.

"I don't want to hurt you," I said softly.

Reese paused, and it was the closest I could come to admitting the truth: that I was afraid of losing him more than I was afraid of loving him.

He added another finger, then tugged me closer, burying his face between my thighs.

"Oh God." Making eye contact with him again, I succumbed to the pleasure. Letting out a strangled noise as he pushed my thighs to my chest, I struggled to breathe, and within seconds I felt my pussy clamp down on his fingers.

"Reese!" My heart was pounding in my ears, and I lay looking up at the night sky.

Before he could respond, I moved, flipping us with a burst of urgency that left him momentarily stunned. His hands were on my hips as I shifted forward and pushed his cock into me. I gritted my teeth; the first few inches were always a stretch, but after that the pleasure began to take over.

My toes curled as I sunk into his lap, every rise and fall measured, teasing.

Reese's hands grasped my ass possessively, bringing us close. My thighs began to tremble as I tried to close them, but he shook his head, and I felt his breath, hot and ragged, pushing me over the edge.

"Nope, spread 'em." He used his free hand to move my thighs apart, and I threw my head back.

"Oh God… Reese, I'm…" I could barely get the words out; I was so overwhelmed. The heat from him, that salty, woodsy, ocean smell—it filled my senses.

I wasn't embarrassed by the way my body responded, the slick sound of us echoing between gasps and moans as I rode him harder, each thrust drawing me deeper into the moment. I was wet, the friction felt good, the wet noise gave me chills. My ass met his thighs with a force that jolted me forward.

"Fuck, you're so fuckin' tight." I loved how he looked falling apart.

He was panting, sweat slicking his skin as his hands explored my body, tracing the map of my stretch marks, dips, and scars, making me feel breathtakingly beautiful. I felt my stomach clench and burn as an orgasm built.

"I can never seem to get enough of you." He sat up, forcing me to make eye contact before he mercilessly drilled up into me. "Wanna come?"

"Yes, Reese, fuuuck yes," I cried, my voice breaking as my nails dug into his shoulder, leaving crescent-shaped marks. He slowed, just slightly, and the drag of his cock sent a sharp jolt through my body. Each thrust was deep, purposeful, as if he were imprinting himself into every inch of me.

I didn't care about tomorrow, or the chaos waiting for us. This moment was ours. Just ours. Perfect.

I quickly moved from my knees to my feet, bracing myself against his chest. Each movement made him press deeper inside me, and the new angle sent a cry tumbling from my lips.

Reese's hands shot to my hips, guiding me with bruising force as I rode him, each thrust harder and faster than the last, until the world blurred, and all that mattered was the tightening coil threatening to snap inside me.

I watched, mesmerized, as his Adam's apple bobbed, his ragged breaths catching in his throat, each gasp a desperate, uneven struggle against some unseen force. The rhythm of his movements shattered, replaced by frantic, instinctive reactions.

"Shit," he said, taking my hands and intertwining our fingers. "Look at me, Laurene. I love you."

I dropped and raised my hips even faster. *He loves me.*

No matter how far Reese's cock pulled out of me, my hips chased his. I hugged him tight.

"You're taking me so well, baby. Hold on, I'm almost there."

He was going to make me cum. My legs were trembling, and I just couldn't stop myself from clinging to him and eagerly accepting all that he gave me.

"You're so deep." I reached down to push at his thigh, and he smacked my hand away.

"So hardheaded," he growled, his pace slowing but not losing any of its punishing precision. Every thrust still found my spot, sending shockwaves through me. "Quit pushing me away and take this fuckin' dick."

"That's my spot," I gasped, my voice breaking.

"Right here?" His smirk was downright devious, his hips angling to hit that spot over and over. Each slow stroke had moans spilling from my mouth like a broken record.

"Fuck!" we shouted in unison, our voices tangling in the heated air.

Pleasure hit me so hard, I nearly fell back. He held on to my hips tight while he went deeper and harder, making sure I remembered every moment.

I could feel myself getting him all wet, slippery and wild, dripping down from his cock. Reese's cock pulsed inside me, his release driving me higher, my walls clenching around him in one final desperate grip before I collapsed against his chest, trembling, spent, and entirely his.

I took a few moments, letting my heartbeat come down and

listening to the steady beat of his as he softly stroked my back. I faced him, and his smile was gentle, almost goofy.

"I'm scared," I choked out.

"I know," he murmured, the scent of his cologne filling my nostrils, pulling me closer until his arms wrapped around me completely. "Me too."

CHAPTER 24

Laurene

THIS WEEKEND WITH REESE? Perfect. Just us, uninterrupted. It was like time stopped—we just talked, made love, and enjoyed each other's company. I didn't want to get out of bed from under him when Monday came and reality hit.

At my desk, I went through every sketch and plan for my art exhibit. My team wasn't exactly on board, but oh well. I was gonna make that exhibition happen, no matter what they thought.

A voice crackled over the intercom.

"Mrs. Ashbourne." The way my new name sounded—so unfamiliar, yet so right—made me smile. I hadn't expected it to feel like this, and a quiet, unexpected joy settled over me. "You have a visitor."

"Who is it?"

"It's the mayor."

A wave of nausea washed over me. *Dante. Here. Why now?*

"Send him in," I managed to say.

After all this time, after everything, this was how we finally came face-to-face.

He walked in, cool and commanding. Dante Castillo was a

man you couldn't quite pin down. His charm was disarming, his smile as polished as a mirror. "Laurene. As beautiful as ever."

I stood, extending my hand with practiced grace. *God, I wish Reese were here.*

"As charming as ever," I said, concealing my emotions. His lips brushed my knuckles; his hand was warm against mine. A performance, like everything else about him.

Because no one—least of all Dante Castillo—showed up without a motive.

"Being a newlywed doesn't stop work, does it?" He gestured to the papers on my desk. "I've heard about your upcoming exhibit. It's creating quite a buzz."

"You already know about that?" I feigned shock. "It's not public knowledge."

His harsh features softened in a knowing smile. A neat beard framed his strong jaw. Long, dark hair added a touch of untamed elegance to his otherwise meticulously tailored suit.

"Information travels fast when people are eager to impress."

I sat, raising an eyebrow. *"Impress?* I didn't know you had so much clout?"

"Don't underestimate me, your family isn't the only one that makes people jump." His eyes challenged mine.

"I don't remember you being into art. You liked to steal cars."

He smirked like he was enjoying the memory. No one could forget the wild, reckless boy who once ran these streets like they owed him something. Before he "reformed" into the mayor.

Not that I bought the reformation.

His aunt, Isabel Castillo, was the town's and all of California's most influential theater director. Her productions were legendary. All anyone really knew was that one day Dante showed up on her doorstep in town. Whether he was related to her by blood or something else, no one was sure.

"I've broadened my horizons since those days. I appreciate the finer things in life now."

I studied him for a moment, my gaze steady. "What do you want, Dante?"

He reached in his pocket and pulled out a picture. He stared at the photo, his lips pursed, then he shoved it across the desk to me.

I sat up and flipped the photo over.

Conrad was lying unconscious, his face pale, eyes closed. There—*shit*—there we were. Reese and me. Standing beside Conrad's hospital bed. His hands were on my face, cupping my cheeks, and mine on his chest. We were kissing...over Conrad.

A cold, hard lump formed in my throat as I turned my gaze back to Dante.

"This?" he said, lightly tapping the photo. "This will never see the light of day."

A jolt of pure terror shot through me, freezing me in place.

"What do you want for it, Dante?" I repeated, trying to keep my voice steady.

"Nothing." Dante shrugged. "Not yet, at least. Just a small favor." His voice was smooth, almost indulgent, but there was an edge beneath it. "But I'm curious," he went on, watching me too closely. "What little mess has Laurene King gotten herself into that I managed to get my hands on a blackmail note about her? How lucky for you that it ended up with me—and that I'm willing to protect you and your family."

I wanted to lash out, a surge of anger coursing through me, but a strange calmness settled over me. *Be cool. You know about him, and he knows about you.*

"I don't do favors, you should know my family by now," I said.

Dante chuckled. "Believe me, I know your family probably better than you."

His eyes locked on mine, and I could see the satisfaction in them. He was enjoying this.

"You really expect me to buy this whole 'protection' spiel?" I raised an eyebrow.

"I didn't come here to start a war. I meant what I said at your engagement party. I want to be allies. I'm sorry I've been busy and we haven't been able to speak till now."

"You seem a little too desperate to be friends with me."

"It's not desperation, Laurene. There is no one like you." His voice softened, like he was trying to make me believe him. "You're unique. I'm not interested in what's happening behind closed doors in your marriage. I *am* interested in what you can offer this town. You could be a key piece in my plans."

I smirked, tilting my head.

"That's funny because my mother asked me to spy on you. Get close. Become your friend." I let the words hang there, watching for his reaction. "What went wrong between you two?"

"Your mother and the rest of them want to keep this town locked in the past. That's not how the real world works." He frowned. "I wanted to modernize things, bring in outside investors, shift the balance. Make Lush more than just old money and backroom deals. Your mother saw that as a betrayal."

"Erik told me she helped you get elected," I reminded him. "You benefited off those backroom deals."

"And she expected me to be her puppet," Dante shot back. "I'm not dumb, I know her support was conditional. I just thought she could be reasonable. Your mother asked me to do something...I couldn't. So, she turned on me."

I searched his face, trying to find the lie in his words. Because there had to be one.

"You become mayor of a town like Lush and then complain about how we do things is like going to a burger joint and complaining there's no pizza," I said. "So why run? What's your real angle?"

Dante's smirk flickered, just for a second, before he smoothed it over. "You think I hate old money? No, Laurene. I just hate *some* of the people who decide who gets to sit at the table. I envy you, Reese, the rest of this town—you survive off your name alone. You could burn everything down and they'd still hand you the keys to the city. People like me? We have to fight for every inch."

I narrowed my eyes. "So what did my mother ask you to do?"

His gaze darkened slightly. "She wanted me to push through a zoning law that would give King Enterprises control over half the commercial properties downtown. It would've driven out smaller businesses, cut off other families, and locked in your family's control for another generation. I refused."

"And that was it?" I asked, because it was never that simple.

Dante let out a quiet laugh, something sharp and knowing. "Of course not. She didn't just walk away. She started sabotaging me—backroom deals, under-the-table payoffs, making sure any investor who backed me suddenly had a reason to back out." He tilted his head. "You really didn't know?"

I pressed my lips together. No, I hadn't known. But I also wasn't surprised.

"She plays the game better than you," I said.

Dante exhaled through his nose, shaking his head. Then he leaned in slightly, his voice low and almost amused. "I'm the one with blackmail on you, Laurene. It's smart to be nice to me."

I leaned forward just a little, eyes narrowing. "And if I don't want to play your game?"

"I'll find another way," he replied easily, as if the whole thing was inevitable. "But I'm hoping we can work together. For both our sakes."

I didn't respond immediately. Instead, I sat back in my chair, studying him.

"So what exactly is your vision for Lush, Dante?"

"Lush has been a closed system for too long. Same families. Same power. Same cycle." He gestured vaguely. "But I don't want to destroy the old system completely. We just need to modernize it—bring in new investments, new ideas, and new opportunities. Not just for me, but for the whole town. It can work if somebody would just listen."

"You're being stonewalled then?"

"Bingo." He nodded. "It's only so much I can do. I need friends."

"Why me? I just got back."

"Because I've been watching you, Laurene. For the past six years, while you were in Paris, I saw how you worked your way up—by yourself. You didn't need anyone's help. You left everything behind, even your family, and you built something from scratch. You earned respect. That wasn't the same Laurene we used to see here. The way you think, the way you see things differently than your mother—you prove the old families can change."

I blinked, caught off guard by his words. "You've been following me?"

"See? I could have told everyone where you were. I didn't. Doesn't that mean you can trust me?"

"Obviously, you know my help is not free."

"I know your upcoming exhibit is important to you, Laurene. I also know how costly these things can get. I'm prepared to make a substantial donation to the gallery in your favor. And when the time comes, you'll support me. No questions asked."

I'd been pushing the limits of the gallery's budget, and the financial strain was beginning to show. A donation could give me the leverage I needed my exhibit to the next level, even if I had to do some dancing to make sure it didn't come with strings I didn't want.

But I had connections. I could get donations for the gallery another way. And I could get Dante's substantial donation to replace my inheritance, in case my mother didn't come through on our deal.

If he was offering money, why not ask for more? Enough to cover my gallery, let me build a safety net for myself, and finally free me from my mother's grip. With that kind of cash, I wouldn't have to accept my inheritance and could walk away from her control entirely. No need to play by her rules anymore.

Dante clearly had some sort of power, and now he was at a stalemate. I just had to know.

"Tell me about your relationship with Toby."

Dante laughed. "Toby? You care about him? What does your husband say about that?"

"Just answer the question. You're trying to convince me, remember?"

"He owes me."

I crossed my arms. *"For what?"*

"For keeping his secrets. For keeping him standing when he should have drowned. Shall I go on?"

Exhaling slowly, I didn't even know where to start with this one.

"You want specifics, Laurene? Fine." He leaned forward. "He was desperate. Drowning in debt, bad investments, bad choices."

I was right. Dante had given him money. "And you bailed him out."

"I gave him a chance to fix it," Dante corrected me smoothly. "But a man like Toby? He doesn't know how to stay clean. So he made more bad choices."

"Like what?"

Dante smirked. "Like sleeping with Blair."

The words hit like a slap across the face.

"You're lying."

"Am I?" Dante's eyes flickered with something sharp, predatory. "Come on, Laurene. You know Toby. You know Blair. Him being sloppy gave me more opportunities to…work with him. Reese knew about it. I heard he confronted them. *Your husband* didn't tell you?"

Reese knew? Reese knew, and he hadn't said a word? A hollow, nauseating sensation curled in my stomach, like the ground had tilted beneath me. I clenched my fists before he could see the tremor in my hands.

"What does that have to do with you?" My voice was steadier now, even as my nails dug into my palm.

"Everything." Dante's gaze darkened, the amusement slipping just slightly. "Because Toby made a deal. With me. With Blair. And now he can't get out of it."

A cold shiver ran down my spine.

"What kind of deal?"

"Sorry, that's all you get from me. Now about our business?" Dante leaned back looking like the Cheshire Cat.

It was time to get Dante out of my office.

"Ten million dollars, *to me*."

He blinked, surprised.

"You're asking for a lot," he said. "I can give you a substantial donation, but ten million? That's pushing it, they'll notice it in the books."

I smiled, leaning forward slightly. "You came to me because you needed something I can provide. So I'm asking for what my trust and loyalty is worth. Ten million, no strings attached. It's a fair deal, considering you're essentially asking me to betray my mother. Work with you and not her?"

His eyes narrowed.

"Unless you don't have the money, of course." I dug the knife in further.

"My money is good. You don't have to worry about that." Dante sniffed. "Ten million, huh? You're a hard negotiator. But I'll consider it."

"No." I straightened up. "My way, or no deal. Obviously you've been stepping on toes and you want my help to get you back on some good sides."

Dante's frown deepened, and now it was my turn to shrug.

"I mean, it was nice of you to hold this picture for me. I can continue to not say anything about you sleeping with Blair Sterling."

His face stiffened, but only for a split second, and that was enough to know I had him.

"Blair?" His voice was too smooth, too casual, trying to brush it off.

"You don't have to lie to me. I know. She's the wrong person to ask about me."

His gaze dropped for a moment, and I saw the calculation running behind his eyes.

"I'm not one to dig around in other people's business," I said. "But if we're talking about trust here, Dante, it's important we understand where everyone stands, don't you think? I'm just curious how far your relationship with Blair goes."

"Blair and I have some mutual benefits. But not a relationship."

Shit. But that doesn't explain her relationship with Harold.

"Mutual benefits?"

"Her father just bought a soccer team in Vegas. We go watch the races and place bets. She's…a bookie. Nothing that you're thinking of." Dante stood. "Do we have a deal?"

Blair is taking bets?

I nodded, rising slowly. "I think we do."

"Let's see where this partnership takes us then." We shook hands.

As he walked to the door, I followed, keeping my expression carefully neutral. I didn't trust Dante. I didn't trust anyone but Reese.

And I needed to tell him Dante was a suspect and a huge threat we had to contain.

I stepped out of my office, and there he was—Reese.

When our eyes met. The corners of his mouth turned up. I ran into his open arms, and we kissed.

"Hey, what are you doing here?"

He smiled. "Afternoon quickie."

I laughed, and his lips met mine with another soft kiss.

"I came to invite you to lunch. But I see you're busy." He glanced over at Dante, squinting his eyes.

I reached for Reese's hand, giving it a light squeeze, and I said, "Toby and Blair?"

Reese blinked, his mouth parting before he cleared his throat. "I was coming to tell you."

I sized him up. His eyes were dark, guarded. But I couldn't push him too hard now; not when Dante was watching.

"Thanks for the conversation, Dante. It was enlightening."

The mayor walked toward us, his gaze flickering between us, and I felt Reese stiffen next to me.

"Anytime, Mrs. Ashbourne," Dante drawled. He glanced at Reese for a split second, eyes narrowing, before he pushed off the doorframe, taking his sweet time as he walked past us. "See you soon."

CHAPTER 25
Reese

"ARE YOU POSITIVE?" I sucked my teeth, the sound echoing in the quiet room as I leaned back in my chair.

Nathan spread the papers out in front of me. "I am. The numbers don't lie, Reese. Money's been slipping through the cracks for years."

Frustration coiled in my chest. "*Years?* Be specific. How many years?"

He tapped one sheet. "Six. Maybe a few years before that is what my gut says. We're still finalizing numbers, but the earliest discrepancies go back to then."

We were losing money when Conrad was leading.

I leaned forward. "And you're telling me no one caught it? Not you, not the auditors, not a goddamn soul?"

"A few hundred here, a thousand there. Someone should have raised concern, but it was ignored." Nathan shifted, clearly uncomfortable.

"Should have," I echoed. My conversation with Jennie ran through my mind. "This is an inside job?"

"That's the most likely scenario. The patterns suggest someone with access, someone who knows your accounts well enough to avoid detection."

I tilted my head, studying him. "Someone like you?"

"If I were guilty, I wouldn't have brought this to your attention."

"Fair point." I leaned back in my chair, the tension in my chest simmering. "So, who's the most likely suspect? Give me names, Nathan."

He exhaled, running a hand over his neatly combed hair. "I can't point fingers without more evidence. But whoever's behind this has been careful. The amounts, the timing—it's deliberate with our losses and gains in the market."

"But if we were losing money when Conrad was here, he must have known this."

Did he try to stop it? Did he ignore it? If it wasn't that damn boat he cared about most, his money was the next thing. I was surprised he didn't know.

If word got out that someone was stealing from me, it would feed the narrative of *Reese can't handle the company. Reese isn't Conrad.*

"I want everybody interviewed. Fire the entire accounting team. Then go through every employee here, anyone who walked into this distillery—family, employees, partners, I don't care. No one gets a free pass."

If this was a setup, and someone was playing both sides, I couldn't let it go on. I was losing money every day, and I couldn't afford to lose any more.

"Make sure you cover all the bases," I continued. "I want this bastard's head on a spike. I don't care who you need to get involved. If we need to bring in outsiders, make sure they sign an NDA. Just find out what the hell's going on."

Nathan didn't hesitate. "Don't worry, Reese, we'll get to the bottom of this. Do you want me to contact your sister? Go over the resort's numbers?"

"Yes, tell her I sent you. She's had some concerns as well."

Nathan scribbled something down, but I barely noticed it. Laurene still hadn't said much to me since the confrontation in the gallery the other day. My distillery, Jennie, Laurene, the blackmailer, Conrad. Too many balls in the air, and I was juggling them all, barely keeping up.

"Get me answers," I muttered.

I stood up abruptly, the chair scraping against the floor, the sound like nails on a chalkboard. Nathan nodded and quickly left.

If I didn't find a way to vent this tension, to release it some-how, I was going to snap.

That's when I remembered.

There was a gym that had opened up not too far from here. I hadn't gone back to mine since, well, since everything with Blair and the blackmail started. It didn't feel like my place anymore. I'd passed it a few times, and honestly, it felt like a godsend right now. Something physical. Something that could match the chaos in my veins.

I moved toward the door, almost without thinking.

"Hold my calls for the rest of the day," I muttered to my assistant as I passed.

The elevator ride was slow, too slow, like the floors were moving at half-speed, and I couldn't stand it. Someone was stealing money from us. How could I have missed that? Hadn't I been trying to prove myself to everyone I could lead?

How would this affect my infused line? If they were stealing money, were they leaking secrets?

When the elevator doors opened, I practically stormed out, heading straight for my car, I pulled onto the street, weaving through traffic till the gym came into view.

I parked quickly, my hands already shaking, as I stepped out. *Slayer's Gym.*

Rap music blasted me the moment I stepped inside, along with the rhythm of fists hitting something. It was way different from the gyms I usually went to.

The walls were peeling in places, the floor scratched, and the smell of sweat and metal filled the air. The heavy door slammed behind me, and I turned the corner into the main entrance of the gym. The lighting wasn't soft or flattering, just harsh enough to make the sweat gleam off the fighters in the ring, the echoes of punches and grunts reverberating off the walls.

It was the kind of place that felt dangerous. And for some reason, that felt right.

"Can I help you?" a rough voice came from across the room, sharp and cutting through the noise.

I turned to see a tall, dark man with dreadlocks that fell down his back, with his arms crossed coming toward me, a deep frown on his face. His face was sharp angles, and his build was massive.

"We don't let fans up in here, partner. You gotta go."

I recognized him immediately. The tattoos, the intimidating presence, the aura of raw strength.

"Ronin Slayer?"

He didn't flinch, just narrowed his eyes at me, sizing me up. "Yeah, that's me. What the hell you want, rich boy?"

I didn't even blink. "I thought your gym was based in Oakland."

"Burned down." Ronin's jaw ticked. "Still, you should probably get your ass outta my gym now. Fighters only."

"I'm here to train. This where you do it?"

Ronin burst into laughter. "You? Fight?"

"Yeah, I fight." I leaned in, the corners of my mouth curling slightly.

His laughter died off as quickly as it came, replaced with a sharp, challenging look. "Alright. I'll give you a chance. Get in the ring, and we'll see if you last thirty seconds."

A rush of energy spiked through me, and that made me grin wider. Ronin looked me up and down before whistling and calling out to the guys in the ring, who broke apart.

"Go get your stuff, rich boy. I'm sparing you five minutes of my time."

I didn't need to be told twice. My hands were already itching for something—anything—that would get my mind off the mess I was dealing with. I turned and walked back to the parking lot.

I got to my car and froze.

The tires were slashed—completely destroyed. Every last one. The adrenaline faded, replaced by a bone-deep chill that sent shivers down my spine.

Less than five minutes.

That meant I was being followed. I whipped around, looking around the small parking lot. No one. Few cars. But I felt eyes on me, even if I couldn't see them.

I hadn't even noticed the note wedged under the windshield wiper until it caught my eye.

I grabbed the paper and unfolded it.

> *I'm getting tired of playing games. Laurene will publicly resign from her position at the art gallery. You're going to hand over 10% of Ashbourne Distilleries to a third party.*

I clenched the note in my hand, every muscle in my body tensing. The bastard wasn't playing games anymore.

And that's when my phone rang.

The sound cut through the thick silence of the parking lot. A distorted voice came through immediately.

"You got the note?" It wasn't even a question.

I could hear the low, steady breath on the other end. I gripped the phone tighter, my knuckles white.

"Yeah, I got it," I forced out, my voice low. "And if you think for one second you can control me, you're fucking wrong."

The voice chuckled. There was no humor in it. Just cold, clinical.

"You don't have a choice. Do what I say, or things get worse, Reese. Much worse. You saw what I did to Laurene. What else can I do to the rest of your family?"

The line went dead.
And I slammed my fist against the side of my car.

CHAPTER 26

Laurene

"WHERE ARE YOU?" I almost hung up on Gigi, but she'd caught me in a good mood—though that was fading fast.

"Serena said no already."

The car smoothly drove past the typical weekend shopping crowd; couples ambled along, their shopping bags swaying rhythmically.

"For good reason."

There was a sharp "Damn!" in the background, followed by the unmistakable clatter of dice hitting a table. Gigi's laugh was so loud on the phone, I had to pull it away from my ear.

I juggled my shopping bag, feeling the silky, lacy stuff inside. Reese's place was perfect for him, but it didn't exactly scream *home*. Not yet. Not without a few touches of mine. I smirked to myself, imagining his reaction when he saw what I'd picked out. He would be up all night drilling shelves and hanging paintings.

Except—lately, he hadn't been himself.

This past week, he'd been different—more withdrawn. Quiet. Checking his phone with a frown, then putting it down like it burned. Waking up before me, staring out the window with his jaw tight. And when he thought I wasn't looking, rubbing his temples like he was trying to keep something at bay.

I hadn't pressed him. Maybe I should have. It was the black-mailer. Things had been quiet lately, but the danger was still there.

I didn't know much, but I *did* know Reese.

"Come on, you can do this." Gigi's voice snapped me out of my thoughts. The sound of a loud crash in the background made me wince.

"Where are you *really*?" I asked again, my patience wearing thin.

"The studio."

"Studio? You can't sing or make a beat."

My driver slowed as we passed Élan Maison, the high-end home boutique I'd been meaning to stop by. Their window display showcased impossibly soft throws and crystal vases. I made a mental note to swing by later. But I couldn't shake the thought that whatever was going on, Reese was keeping me out of it.

And that scared me more than I cared to admit.

"Damn, you can't encourage me? What if I'm the new hottest female rapper?"

"You think Slick Rick's raps are too complicated. How the hell are you going to write a bar?"

"First of all, Laurene, you real loud for somebody that don't have a song out about them."

"I don't even wanna know what poor internet rapper you conned into making a song about you." I smirked.

"Second, *I* got star potential, okay? I'm *immortalized*. Don't be mad because I'm out here chasing my dreams while you're out buying bougie-ass throw pillows for your man's crusty-ass bach-elor pad."

"The dream of *this* week." I rolled my eyes. "But the answer is still no. Last time I watched Walter for you, I ended up in a ditch with a knot on my head and your little demon dog ruining my five-hundred-dollar skirt. Walter's gotta spend time with Auntie Serena or Uncle Erik."

"Now you know damn well Walter's been banned from Erik's house ever since he peed on his Star Wars figurine collection. I'm still paying Erik back for that."

I let out a sigh, staring at the boutiques blurring past the car window. "It's *your* dog, Gigi. Take him with you."

"Walter don't like loud music. It stresses him out," she said matter-of-factly.

I looked out the window and frowned. The gallery came into view, its black-and-gold sign shimmering.

"Why are we headed to the gallery?" I asked, leaning forward to address my driver.

"You have a reservation here, ma'am."

What? "The gallery is closed." Like anybody else, I did not want to be at work on my off day.

The driver didn't respond, but Gigi kept chatting on. That's when I noticed the red carpet unfurling from the front steps. Candlelit lanterns lined the path, their soft glow flickering in the early evening light.

"Uh, Laurene? You still there?" Gigi asked, but my focus was on what was in front of me. A faint strain of music floated on the air, growing louder as we pulled up. It wasn't until I saw the violinist standing on the stairs that my heart skipped.

"Is this for real?" I whispered to no one in particular.

"Absolutely, Mrs. Ashbourne," my driver said smoothly as he stepped out and opened my door.

"Laurene?" Gigi's voice carried on, but I barely heard her.

"No," I murmured, and hung up the phone as I stepped onto the red carpet. My eyes scanned the flickering candlelight reflecting on scattered rose petals leading up the plush, deep red carpet, and then the heavy oak gallery doors creaked open.

Reese stood there, framed by the warm light spilling out behind him. His expression was unreadable, but the flicker of a smile danced on his lips.

"Reese? What is this?" I stepped out of the car, and Reese began to walk down the steps.

"Just a little surprise."

"Surprise?"

He stopped just inches away. His eyes dipped briefly to the shopping bags tucked in the car.

"We didn't have a first date when you got back," he said, his voice soft, intimate. His gaze lifted back to mine, heat simmering beneath it. "I figured it was time to make up for that."

"This isn't a first-date vibe, Reese," I said, gesturing toward the red carpet, the candles, the violinist playing something achingly beautiful in the background.

He took another step closer, pulling me into him, his breath warm and slightly minty against my cheek.

"You're right," he murmured. "It's not. First dates are innocent." His voice dipped, rougher now. "And there's nothing innocent about what I have planned."

Taking my hand, he led me up the steps, and I could do nothing but be in awe. Did Arthur know? I hadn't seen anybody setting anything up.

Inside, the red carpet led straight into the big hall. Soft amber light filled the breathtaking space. Our main hall had been turned into an exhibition for *me*.

I felt a surge of recognition. Pieces from artists I adored flashed before my eyes.

"What did you *do*?" I asked, though I already knew the answer.

His lips curved into a slow, deliberate smile. "You've spent so much time curating beauty for everyone else. This is something curated just for you."

I saw Giotto's *Lamentation*.

"That piece should be in Italy."

Reese shrugged. "I had them send it over for the night."

We walked, my eyes glancing over more of the pieces. I saw *The Nightmare* by Henry Fuseli, and I shook my head. "That should be in Detroit, and that—"

I let go of Reese's hand, rushing over to look closely at William Blake's *Newton*.

"London."

I slowly turned, examining the pieces in the room. Paris. Amsterdam. Oslo. Minneapolis. Boston. Madrid. Every piece from every museum I'd wanted to visit was here. He'd brought all my favorite pieces from around the world and given me my own private gallery.

"How did you manage this?" I asked, voice trembling. "Some of these pieces are impossible to loan!"

"Impossible's never stopped me. Not when it comes to you," he said simply. "I wanted you to smile. To know there's not a corner of this world I wouldn't reach into for you."

"I…I don't know what to say."

"Every piece," he said, his gaze never leaving mine. "All you."

I blinked, letting his words sink in.

"I thought it was time to show you what I see." His voice was low, reverent.

Reese's hand found mine, and he led me farther down the corridor. Finally, we reached another entryway, and I froze as my gaze lifted to the sign above:

Laurene.

Reese tugged me along, and I covered my mouth with my hand as I blinked, taking it in. It was all photos of *me*.

I gasped when I saw the first picture—a closeup of me, with sunlight filtering through the leaves. Recognition bloomed in my chest. It was the week after we first started seeing each other six years ago. Reese took me on my very first hike.

I hated it; I fell in a creek. Reese laughed, then took the photo.

Another photo of me, in my art studio, paintbrush in hand, after sneaking him onto the property. Reese would sometimes just sit and watch me work for hours, and we'll be together in silence. I'd loved those moments.

The photos continued.

One of me dancing at a gala. A candid shot of me sitting on the edge of a bathtub in his old apartment, wrapped in a towel, staring off into the distance. Another from a secret trip we took to LA. In front of the Hollywood sign.

"Reese," I sighed, and looked at him as I pouted at the photo.

Me in his bed, on our wedding night.

The softness of the early morning light wrapped around me like a blanket, and I was curled up, my face peaceful, my eyes half-closed, the sheets surrounding me.

"This way," he said.

He led me into another alcove, and in the center of the room, a table for two was elegantly set up, with delicate white roses scattered across the floor.

He turned to me, and he had a boyish, nervous look that made me giggle.

"This is real, Laurene. Not for them—for me. I want you. All of you. I want *us*."

My breath hitched, his words sinking deep. *"Reese..."*

"I love you." Steady. Raw. Certain. "I didn't marry you because of them. I married you because I couldn't not marry you. Because even after everything, you've always been my person. Losing you"—his breath wavered, but not his conviction—"*was hell*. I didn't know how to breathe without you."

His fingers curled around mine, desperate, reverent. "I loved you when we built that community center. I loved you when you were with Tobias. I loved you when you were with my brother. Hell, I probably loved you before I even knew what love was—*I loved you*. When you were just the King girl I wasn't supposed to want."

I didn't wipe away the tear that fell from my eye.

He exhaled shakily. "But I did. I always did."

Reese's words shattered something in me. Broke me wide open.

"I know you fulfilled your deal with your mother. I know you probably hate every second of this arrangement. And if you want a gallery of your own one day, I'll make it happen. If you want to work here, we'll make that happen too. You can have it all. *All I need is you in my life. I need to know you love me too.*"

"Reese—"

"No, let me finish," he said, his grip on my hands firm but tender. "You don't have to choose between me and your gallery, Laurene. If you want it, it's yours. But if you walk away from all of it, I'll still be here, waiting. *I love you more than any of this bullshit.*"

I wanted this. God, I wanted this.

My breath hitched, my body betraying me, wanting to believe him, to let those words settle deep. But something about the way he was saying it—*the way he was looking at me*—kept my heart caught in my throat.

It wasn't just love in his eyes. It was something heavier. *Darker.*

Like he was bracing for impact.

"Reese…" I murmured, tilting my head, searching his face. "Why do I feel like you're trying to soften a blow I don't see coming?"

His fingers twitched against mine. Just a flicker of movement, barely perceptible, but enough.

"Laurene." He lifted a hand, brushing his thumb across my jaw, and for a moment, I thought he would say it—whatever it was, whatever was hiding beneath the surface of this moment.

But then, just as quickly, he shut it down. His expression smoothed over, the way it always did when he didn't want me to see too much.

"I just want you to know you have options," he said, voice quieter now. "That you're not stuck."

I couldn't stop the tears welling in my eyes, and I shook my head. "No. You don't get to put this all on me like I'm the only one making choices here."

He looked at me, startled.

"I want my gallery," I admitted. "I want the inheritance. I

won't lie about that. But I don't want any of it more than I want you."

I grabbed his collar, like I could keep him from slipping away. "You, Reese. It's always been you. Paris was hell without you. I could have had the world, and it wouldn't have mattered because you weren't in it. I was never perfect Laurene in your eyes, or what people in this town viewed me as—and thank God for that. With you, I can breathe. You have always *seen* me."

My voice shook, but I didn't. "You're the dream I was too scared to voice. Now I'm not afraid. I don't care about the strings, the expectations, any of it. This is what I choose. You are who I choose."

His hands slid around my waist, pulling me closer, his forehead pressing against mine as he exhaled a shaky breath. "Laurene, I—"

I silenced him with a kiss, pouring everything I couldn't put into words into that moment. His hands tightened on me, and when we finally pulled apart, his lips curved into a smile that sent my heart racing.

"You're stuck with me now," I said breathlessly.

"Good," he replied, his grin widening. "Because I wasn't planning on letting you go anyway."

His hands started to roam down my body and under my skirt. His fingers traced slow, lazy circles along my thigh, his smirk pure sin. I pulled away from the kiss, looking around us.

"Reese, we're in public," I hissed, heat rushing to my cheeks.

"We're alone in here."

I shook my head as he pressed kisses to my neck, and I was losing my grip on why this was a bad idea. "This is my workplace."

Suddenly, he stood, reaching over for me, and I instinctively clutched his shoulders as he swept the dishes off the table.

"Reese!"

"I need you."

I ran my hands firmly up his sides, feeling the heat radiating from him, my heart racing in response.

"Forget everything else," he murmured, stepping closer, the space between us collapsing. "Just be here with me."

"But what if—"

Reese didn't answer. Instead, his kisses trailed from my lips to my neck, his tongue teasing as he left unapologetic marks along my skin. My fingers gripped his shoulders, desperate for balance as his hands slid to my hips, pulling me closer.

"Fuck, baby." Reese's breath hitched and his fingers came up, brushing against my sensitive nipples, and I couldn't help but whimper his name. "Let me show you how much I appreciate this amazing dinner."

Reese dropped to his knees before me without hesitation, his gaze burning with intensity. His hands moved to my skirt, and in one swift motion, he tossed it over his shoulder.

His lips curled into a playful pout before he kissed me through the fabric of my panties, the soft pressure sending a shiver down my spine.

"I want to taste you so badly," he murmured, his voice low and full of longing.

"R-Reese…" I exhaled, a tingle spreading in my stomach, both nervous and eager.

Reese locked eyes with me the whole time, not even blinking as he used his teeth to slide off my panties. I bit my lip as Reese's tongue slid over my soaked folds, and I held on to the edge of the table tightly.

"Damn, you taste so sweet." Kissing his teeth, he grunted. "My dreams don't compare to this."

The second I felt Reese's tongue against my entrance, my thighs trembled, weak with anticipation. He moved slowly at first, as if savoring every moment, his movements deliberate. He found the exact rhythm that drove me crazy, and my hands curled through his thick hair.

"Pull. Harder."

I gathered a good enough handful and pulled harder and harder until he moaned. I felt his grin twisting against his lips before he started to slurp harder.

"S-spank it, Reese."

I felt him freeze for a moment, a shift in his tension as his breath hitched. Then a deep groan rumbled from his chest, the sound thick with desire. Then he spanked my pussy.

"Yes!" I exploded, and I could hear Reese's clothes falling to the floor before I felt him shift my body, placing my leg over his shoulder.

"Pretty body all just for me," he murmured. "Tell me you want me."

My eyes focused on him. "I want all of you, Reese."

I moaned, feeling his tip pressing inside me and the stretch of him. My walls gripped and enveloped his length, and I gasped as he stroked into me slowly. I reached up, trying to hold on, as my body jolted against the table.

Each thrust had me weak. *Stupid.*

"Y-yes, please. Right there, right there." I probably sounded pathetic, but I couldn't care less. My face scrunched up, twisting in blissful pleasure as he plunged into me at full force.

He was so deep, and I felt stretched, worn thin, dizzy.

Reese leaned down, grabbing my chin, pressing a wet kiss to my mouth. My thighs were shaking, vision spotty, sparks of white-hot electricity going all the way from my hazy brain. I shattered as he gave one *harsh* thrust.

"Reese!"

I felt him spilling inside me. We held each other, breathless, both trying to regain our bearings. His heartbeat thundered in my ear as I let my fingers trace the lines of his back, feeling more protected and loved than I ever had before.

CHAPTER 27

Laurene

THE SOFT MORNING light filtered through the curtains, casting a golden glow on Reese as he moved around the room, pulling on his shirt.

I lay there, naked beneath the sheets, watching the way the fabric stretched across his shoulders as he buttoned it up. He glanced over, catching me staring, and a lazy smile spread across his lips. "You're supposed to be sleeping."

"You're supposed to still be in bed," I countered, sitting up. The sheet slipped from my chest, baring me to him. His green eyes darkened, and his smile faltered, replaced by something hungrier.

In two strides, he was at the edge of the bed, kneeling before me, and I inhaled sharply when his mouth enclosed around my left nipple, hot and damp and gently pulling. Just as quickly he released me.

"I don't want you to go," I whispered.

His fingers traced slow circles along my waist. "I have to head into the office. More discussions about the missing funds, more excuses, more bullshit."

I leaned back slightly, my hands braced against his chest, my lips brushing his ear. "You're leaving me here, all alone?"

His hands tightened on my hips, his breath catching as he pulled back just enough to look at me. His gaze dropped to my lips, then lower, lingering shamelessly on my breasts.

"You're not playing fair."

"So?" I shot back, my nails grazing the edge of his collar. Then, with a growl of frustration, he pressed his forehead to mine.

"You're going to make me late," he murmured, his lips brushing against mine, but he pressed a quick kiss on my lips that left no room for protest. "Get some sleep. I'll be back later."

I huffed out a breath and flopped back on the bed, staring at the ceiling as I heard him shuffle around the room before quietly closing the door. The house was quiet, save for the faint rustle of the ocean breeze outside. I spent all day rearranging furniture and de-bachelorizing Reese's home, in Gigi's words, to make it ours. The sharp chime of the doorbell interrupted me.

Anxiety washed over me.

Nobody had called me. And we hadn't ordered anything that would get here this quickly.

I lowered the painting, cautious, and running to the kitchen, I grabbed a knife.

Tightening my grip on the handle, I made my way to the front door. Peeking through the peephole, I felt the tension in my shoulders ease, only to be replaced by confusion.

Jennie.

I hadn't really spoken to her since the wedding dress fiasco at the spa. Here she was, standing on my porch, holding what looked like a bottle of wine wrapped in a ribbon. Opening the drawer to the entry table, I dumped the knife, before exhaling deeply and opening the door. "Jennie?"

"Hi, Laurene. I hope I'm not bothering you?"

Her blue eyes were watery and nervous. Immediately the sympathetic part of me felt guilty. Jennie might have been a bit insensitive that day, but she wasn't a bad person. She hesitated, holding up the wine like a shield.

"I, uh, brought this. As a peace offering. For…you know, everything. Housewarming gift?"

"Thanks," I said finally, taking the bottle from her. "You didn't have to bring anything."

"I really am sorry about the spa. About the wedding dress. Reese talked to me about it, and I'm so stupid! I was out of line. And I just… I hate that we haven't talked since. I don't want to be that sister-in-law you hate," Jennie blurted out.

"Really, I forgive you. Let's just forget it, okay?"

She looked relieved and then she glanced past me, into the house. "Is Reese around?"

"No." I shook my head. "He's at work."

Jennie's face fell slightly, and she took a step back. "Oh. Well, I don't want to keep you. I just wanted to say—"

"Wait." The word escaped me before I could think better of it. Jennie froze, her hopeful eyes meeting mine. I cleared my throat. "Actually, I need to return some sheets in town. Would you mind giving me a ride? With everything I just still haven't bought a car—"

"Of course! I'd love to." Her expression brightened instantly. "My friend owns a dealership over in Monterrey, how about we go there after and see what he has?"

Her energy was infectious. I nodded, slipping back inside to grab my things. With everything going on, I needed to keep all my friends close.

Jennie was waiting for me in front of her sleek silver car. I offered to drive, but she waved me away to the passenger seat. Once inside, Jennie chatted animatedly about her baby shower theme.

"I think I want to go with something calming, like soft greens or blues," Jennie said. "What do you think?"

"Definitely calming," I agreed. I glanced in the rearview mirror and noticed a car behind us. At first, it didn't register as anything out of the ordinary. I shrugged it off and returned to our conversation about baby shower decorations.

After ten minutes, I glanced back again. The car was still there, closer now.

"Do you see that car behind us?"

Jennie looked back. "Maybe they're heading into town too?"

The car's dark, metallic sheen seemed to absorb the dimming light made it ominous. I leaned closer to the window, trying to see who was in it, but the tinted windows made it impossible to see the driver.

She flicked on her turn signal, moving into the opposite lane. But the car slowed too, hovering behind us.

We drove on, the engine's hum swallowed by the pounding in my ears. The car behind us didn't fall back. Didn't turn. Didn't stop. I glanced back again, pulse hammering. The driver was leaning forward now, like they were watching us, but I still couldn't make out a face.

"I think they're getting closer," I said.

Jennie's fingers tightened around the steering wheel, and car jerked slightly as she adjusted her grip. "Are you sure?"

Our car sped up and she moved back into the opposite lane, the car merged right along with us and sped up until they were right on our bumper.

"Maybe we should turn off somewhere?" I suggested, glancing down the road.

"There should be a gas station up ahead. Let's just get there."

Jennie turned right at the bend in the road, and the car followed.

"Shit," I muttered.

Jennie glanced back, and she just nodded anxiously. "Just stay calm, okay?"

But the car behind us didn't back off. Instead, it surged forward, pulling alongside us. My heart leaped as Jennie swerved trying to put distance between us, but the car pressed in, unyielding. Jennie laid on the horn, and my hand shot out, grabbing the armrest as the car beside us surged forward, its engine roaring louder.

"Just get us out of here," I told her.

She sped up, but the road seemed to narrow to one lane and both cars edged dangerously close to one another.

Then—

The roar was deafening as the car shot forward, veering into our lane and slamming on its brakes.

I screamed. Jennie slammed on the brakes, narrowly avoiding a collision as she jerked us back into the opposite, oncoming lane.

"I'm calling the police!" I said.

There was another curve in the road, and Jennie slammed her foot down on the gas, trying to get back over. From the fog and rain early this morning, I could feel the tires screeching, fighting for grip on the slick asphalt. My fingers scrambled for my phone, my breath coming in ragged bursts.

Then, without warning, the black car lunged forward, its front end ramming into us with a stomach-turning *thud*.

My body was thrown to the left, and the car's metal groaned. Jennie screamed, we swerved. The tires shrieked, fighting to hold on.

The car roared, its engine screaming, before slamming into us a second time.

We lurched, bouncing over the uneven ground as we veered onto the gravel shoulder. Ahead, the road split—our chance to lose them. But my phone slipped from my hand from the bouncing, falling to the floor with a *clink*.

"Just keep us on the damn road!" I gasped, forcing myself up and reaching blindly under the seat, my fingers scrambling for the phone.

Jennie made a sharp snap to the right, tires screeching as we barely missed the guardrail, the metal flashing by just inches from our side. The other car pulled back for a moment, but it didn't slow down—it roared forward again.

"Why aren't they slowing down?" Jennie's voice cracked, her

hands shaking as she glanced back, panic flooding her eyes. "What the hell are they doing?"

Before I could answer, my fingers found my phone, the black car surged forward, crashing into us, ramming the back of the car with a force that threw us violently forward. The whiplash knocked the breath from my lungs, and I screamed, my heart racing as I clutched my phone tightly.

Bam!

We took another hit, and Jennie was crying and screaming loudly. "They won't stop!"

Jennie swerved, left, then right, but the black car stayed with us, ramming us again, harder this time, throwing us sideways. I could make out only the silhouette of the person.

We skidded. My stomach lurched as the back end of the car slid to the side, nearly dipping into the ditch. My hands were shaking as I attempted to unlock my phone. The car groaned, burning rubber filling the air. The world around us seemed to tilt, the road narrowing as the black car pressed closer, faster.

I held my breath, gripping the seat, eyes flicking between Jennie and the rearview mirror, praying we could break free, as I pulled up keypad.

And then it happened—*wham!*

We spun out.

Time slowed down. I saw nothing but a blur—trees, road, sky—all of it spinning together in a dizzying whirl. We smashed into the guardrail with a appalling *crunch*. Thoughts left my brain. The impact threw me hard against the seat belt, my body snapping forward before slamming back into the seat. We careened toward the trees.

"No!" I screamed.

The crash was deafening—a violent roar that shattered the air and sent shards of glass raining down. I felt the car crumple around us. A piece grazed my cheek, the sting barely registering beneath the roar of blood rushing in my ears.

The car became a blur of twisting metal and shattered glass as it rolled, tumbling end over end. My body was thrown violently from side to side, every crash slamming me harder against the seat belt. My ribs ached, my breath knocked out of me.

My head slammed into the window, pain exploding through my temple. The world spun out of control, my stomach dropping with each dizzying roll. I tasted blood, metallic and sharp, filling my mouth, my pulse pounding in my ears as we continued to tumble.

My body jerked again as the car made its final, jarring stop, tilted against the trees, the engine sputtering like it was gasping for breath.

For a moment, there was nothing but the eerie silence that followed. The air was thick with smoke, the acrid scent of burning rubber and scorched metal. My lungs burned as I sucked in air, the taste of smoke and blood coating my throat.

I coughed violently, trying to focus, but my head was spinning, the dizziness pulling at me like gravity had doubled.

"Jennie!" I called. "Are you okay?"

I touched my head and I pulled my hand back to see it smeared with blood.

"Jennie!" I said again, turning to her.

She was slumped over the steering wheel, unconscious.

I fumbled with my seat belt, my fingers numb and clumsy. The belt finally gave way, my hands trembling as I reached for the door handle, but before I could move, a sharp pain shot through my side. I winced, gritting my teeth against it.

I pushed the door open with all my strength, the metal creaking in resistance, and slid out, collapsing to the ground. I pushed myself up, and then I saw it.

The other car, speeding away.

I squinted through the haze. I couldn't make out much, but a faded sticker caught my eye: a star peeling off the back window as it disappeared down the road.

The baby.

I rushed to the driver's side, hands shaking as I yanked the door open. My fingers fumbled over the seat belt latch. Finally, the latch clicked. The belt slackened, but when I tried to pull Jennie free, the dashboard pressed her down, trapping her.

"Help!" I screamed, my voice echoing in the stillness. "Somebody, please help us!"

I pushed and pulled at the twisted metal, every movement sending jolts of pain through my body, but Jennie was there and faintly breathing. The smell of gasoline mingled with the smoke, and I knew we didn't have much time

Luckily, the crash busted the trunk open, and among Jennie's knickknacks lay a heavy metal tire iron. I wedged it between the dashboard and the wreckage and gritted my teeth, pushing down with all my strength.

The metal shrieked in protest, but I kept pushing, using every ounce of energy I had left.

With a final, desperate heave, the dashboard shifted enough to free Jennie's legs.

Dropping the iron, I pulled her out, dragging her away from the car, and we collapsed onto the ground. My breath came in ragged gasps, but I needed to make sure Jennie was okay.

I forced myself to my knees, and I saw the blood between her legs.

Jennie needs to live. The baby needs to live.

I hurried back into the car, looking inside for my phone, and relief flooded me when I found it in the back seat and saw it had connected with the operator. I picked it up, hearing a voice on the other end.

"We've been in a car accident," I yelled, not knowing if someone was there. "My friend is pregnant, and she's bleeding. Please, we need help!"

"Stay calm, ma'am. Where are you?"

Relief flooded through me. I looked around, telling the dispatcher everything. I dropped the phone beside me, keeping the line open as I returned to Jennie's side. Her breathing was shallow, and I laid my hand against her belly, hoping to feel some sort of life there.

"Hang on, Jennie," I whispered, even as my own vision danced. "You're going to be okay."

Reese…

I heard sirens far off, then felt relief as the flashing lights appeared. I tried standing as paramedics rushed over; then, darkness.

CHAPTER 28

Reese

"WHERE THE HELL are my wife and my sister?"

I barely registered the heads snapping in my direction as I charged toward the reception desk, my heart pounding so hard it drowned out everything else.

Laurene. Jennie. The baby. My head was full of terrible what-ifs, each one worse than the last.

"Sir, you need to calm down," a nurse started, but my glare stopped her in her tracks.

"Laurene and Jennie Ashbourne," I demanded. "Where the fuck are they?"

"Your wife is stable, but please calm—"

I didn't let her finish. I couldn't lose them. I wouldn't allow it. I was *happy*. And life was fucking robbing me of that again. *You should have told her.*

"Take me to them!" I slammed my fist on the desk. "I need to see them."

"Relax, man." Erik's voice hit me, and I turned as he stepped out of the hall. He looked wrecked—his clothes rumpled, his face pale. "Don't call security, I got him."

I turned back, noticing the nurse's finger on the panic button. The thought hit me like a gut punch. *This is my fault.* If I'd told her they wanted me to give up ten percent of the distillery, and Laurene? They wanted her out of the gallery. *No fucking way*. I wasn't about to let them. I just wanted Laurene to not have to worry.

I had a plan.

"What the hell happened?"

I shouldn't have left. I should have stayed with her.

"You need to take a breath. Panicking isn't going to help them." Erik motioned for me to follow.

The sterile glow of the fluorescent lights flickered overhead. The walls were too white, too clean. My skin felt clammy. Conrad. The crash. *Crunch*.

I couldn't stop the flashes—the sharp sound of shattering glass, the metallic tang of blood in the air, his body crumpled, floating. It all came rushing back, punching the breath from my lungs.

Erik's hand clamped on to my shoulder and the acrid sting of antiseptic filled my nostrils, dragging me back to the present.

I set up a meeting with one of my old contacts—a private investigator who owed me a favor. I know we didn't want people to know. But this was bigger than us now, and I wanted a future with my *wife*. We couldn't have this following us.

We were going to set up a trap. A bait and switch. I'd pretend to give in to the demands—get the blackmailer to come us, I would insist that's the only way I'll give up control.

All we needed was proof. A face. A name. Something to expose them for good.

Then it would be over. But we didn't even get to that point.

The sharp beeps of monitors cut through the muffled murmurs of doctors and nurses, loved ones huddled around beds, the news playing on the waiting room TV. Everything felt too loud and too quiet at the same time, the sounds crashing together like a tide I couldn't escape.

Nothing had changed in this place since that day.

Every face I passed felt like one I had seen before—blank,

unfeeling eyes that had judged me when I came in with Conrad's body beside me on the gurney. I still remember that awful feeling—the sharp sting of loss, the total helplessness.

"Erik," I said, my voice strained. "I need to know what's happening."

I could still see Conrad lying there in my mind, motionless, a shell of the brother I'd known. *Please don't let Laurene look like that.*

"It was a car crash," Erik said. "The police are investigating."

My tires were slashed, and now a car crash.

"Laurie… What if Jennie—" I couldn't finish the sentence, couldn't let the reality of it settle in. The fear of losing her when I had just gotten her back. And I hadn't spoken to my sister since the wedding.

I felt so fucking stupid now for not speaking to Jennie over that damn dress.

"No." Erik placed a hand on my chest, staring me down. "Jennie's alive. My sister's alive. That's all that matters."

I exhaled only for a moment as we reached the doors of the hospital room, and Erik stopped. His hand rested briefly on my shoulder. "Lu's in here. Come down the hall to the left. I'll be there with Jennie. And your mom and Nina."

I glanced at him, my pulse quickening. "Harold isn't here?"

Erik's jaw clenched and he shook his head.

A cold knot formed in my stomach. Harold wasn't here—just like he hadn't been there when Conrad died.

Erik pushed the door open to reveal Laurene in the bed, her form small and fragile under the white sheets. Her arm was wrapped in a thick bandage, and bruises marred the side of her face. Her breathing was slow but steady, the rise and fall of her chest the only thing that kept me from losing it completely.

In the corner, Gigi was curled up, her shoulders shaking as she cradled Walter. The small dog trembled in her arms, his soft whines muffled by the sound of Gigi's sobs.

What surprised me most was Vincent and Yvonne standing

nearby. Vincent was stoic, his hands gripping the back of a chair so tightly that his knuckles were bone white. But it was Yvonne who truly shocked me.

Her face was…emotional.

The same face that usually was so cold now showed something raw and unfiltered. Her lips quivered, her eyes rimmed with red, as if she were holding back tears.

I turned to look at my wife. My chest constricted, twisting with an ache so deep it felt like something was tearing apart inside me.

My knees buckled, a wave of dizziness washing over me as I sank to the edge of the bed, my fingers trembling as they reached out. I brushed a strand of matted hair from her forehead, careful, afraid I might break her even more.

Tears burned the backs of my eyes, blurring the sight of her battered face, but I couldn't look away.

"I'm so sorry," I choked out, fear and guilt overwhelming me.

She stirred, groaning softly as her eyelids fluttered, and slowly she opened her eyes. They were fuzzy, unfocused at first, but locked on to mine, the relief in her gaze enough to make me choke back a sob.

"Reese…" Her voice was hoarse, but it was the most beautiful sound I'd heard all day.

"I'm here," I said, cradling her face. "I'm right here."

She closed her eyes. "I'm fine. Go see Jennie."

I shook my head. I couldn't leave her yet.

"I'm not going anywhere until I know you're okay."

"I'm fine." She tried to sit up but winced, sinking back into the pillows with a pained sigh, and everyone in the room sat up straighter.

"We're here with her, Reese," Noelle said firmly. My attention was so focused on Laurene that I didn't even notice she and Serena had been hovering near the bed.

"It's okay," Serena told me. "We're not leaving her side."

I leaned forward, placing a kiss on Laurene's lips. "I love you."

The thought that those might have been my last words to her felt like a cruel twist of fate.

"I love you too."

She sighed, leaning back.

"I'll be back soon." There was no response, just the steady sound of her breathing. I kissed her forehead once again, giving me the strength to step away, even though every instinct screamed at me to stay by her side.

Erik led me to Jennie's room, and I paused for a moment outside the door, my hand hovering over the handle. With a deep breath, I pushed the door open and stepped inside.

The hospital bed swallowed Jennie, her body motionless and disturbingly still beneath the thin white sheet. Her head was wrapped tightly in a bloodstained bandage, with only a few stray locks of hair poking out. The oxygen mask covering her face fogged faintly with each shallow breath, and IV lines snaked from her arms, taped to bruised skin that looked too pale.

Mom sat slumped in the chair beside her, her hands knotted together. She turned to me and her eyes were bloodshot, swollen, and rimmed with deep shadows. David, Jennie's husband, was on the other side, staring at his wife.

Nina stood behind her, arms crossed over her chest as though holding herself together. Her lip trembled, her face a pale mask of anguish.

I hugged my mom. "It's okay."

"I can't...I can't lose her. *Not again,*" she wailed, grabbing on to me as I approached.

I swallowed hard, my throat burning, as I pulled her into me, holding on like we were both drowning.

"We need her to wake up. She has to pull through." Her voice was a whisper filled with despair. "My little girl... My little girl."

I froze, seeing her flat belly.

Panic began rising like bile. "Where's the baby?"

"They had to do an emergency C-section," David said shakily. "But the baby is okay. She's alive."

"She?" The word stumbled out of me, disbelief and shock colliding in my chest. "It's a girl?"

David nodded, but the world felt like it tilted as a flood of emotions crashed over me—joy, terror, relief, and a fierce, unfamiliar protectiveness that rooted me to the spot. A niece. She was here. She was *alive.*

"Where is she? What's her name?" I asked.

"She's in the NICU. We haven't named her yet." His voice was thick with emotion. "I want Jennie to be part of that."

He didn't have to said the rest. *If she wakes up.*

"Can I see her?"

David's hand rested on my shoulder as he led me through the sterile hallways of the hospital, his silence heavy with exhaustion and unspoken fears. When we stopped in front of the NICU window, my breath caught. There she was—a tiny, fragile figure swaddled in a blanket, dwarfed by the machines and tubes surrounding her.

"She's a fighter. Like Jennie," David said softly, tears spilling from his eyes and down his face.

I stepped closer, my heart pounding as I leaned toward the glass.

"Hey there, sweetheart," I whispered, my voice trembling. "I'm your uncle Reese."

Saying the words felt like stepping into a dream I hadn't known I needed. My hand hovered over the glass, my fingers brushing against the barrier as if I could somehow protect her through it.

Her tiny fingers twitched, just the faintest movement, but it sent a rush of warmth through my chest. Tears stung the backs of my eyes as I swallowed hard.

This shit had to end now.

"You've got a whole family out here ready to love you, you know? We'll always be here for you. Always."

I stood there, transfixed, the rhythmic hum of the monitors fading into the background as the world narrowed to just her.

"She's perfect," I said.

David was gazing at his daughter with all the love in the world. Already a father who would do anything for his child. I know if I was him I would have been burning down this entire building, maybe even the town.

Fucking Harold.

The thought of him—of how he hadn't even bothered to show his face, not even a phone call while his daughter and his newborn granddaughter fought for their lives right now.

My fists clenched, nails digging into my palms as I stormed out of the room. The hospital doors slid open with a mechanical hiss, and the cold air slapped against my face.

When I reached my car, I yanked the door open so hard it groaned in protest, then slammed it shut with enough force to make the whole vehicle shake.

He's going to regret this.

The tires screeched as I punched the gas. It took a quick call to his assistant to discover he'd landed nearly an hour ago and had headed home.

I pulled up to my parents' house, tires screaming against the pavement as the car lurched to a halt. My chest heaved, the anger roiling inside me like a wildfire. I didn't even bother shutting the door behind me as I stormed toward the entrance, the slam of my boots against the ground echoing in the cold night air.

"Harold!" My voice tore through the silence, jagged and raw, but the mansion remained still, eerily hollow. I passed the grand staircase, fists clenched so tightly my knuckles ached.

"Where the hell are you?" I bellowed, the words ricocheting off the pristine walls. Each door I passed I slammed open with enough force to rattle the frames, but they all revealed the same thing: nothing. No Harold. No answers.

I stormed down the hallway, my voice cracking as I yelled his name again, frustration bubbling into something darker. And then the blackmailer flared in my head.

They'd done this. They'd hurt *my* family, and it all started with the goddamn accident.

With Conrad.

I rounded the corner and stopped dead in front of his door. *That door.* Always locked. Always closed. It stared back at me, mocking me, daring me to step inside.

A growl ripped from my chest, and before I even knew what I was doing, my foot collided with the door. The door splintered, the hinges shrieking before the door crashed open, slamming against the wall with a thunderous crack.

The room was still. Frozen in time. Dust coated the furniture, the faint smell of leather and stale air hitting me like a punch to the gut. Conrad's room, untouched, preserved like a damn shrine. The perfect façade for the perfect son.

"This is your fault," I hissed into the emptiness. "You did this. Because you were a fucking bastard."

My fists shook at my sides, nails digging into my palms.

"You were supposed to be my big brother. You were supposed to *protect us*. But instead, you just…left. You left us in all the bullshit!"

I staggered forward, grabbing the edge of the desk, my grip so tight it felt like my fingers would snap.

"Because of you, I lost the woman I loved. Because of *you*, there's a blackmailer. Because of *you*, Jennie and Laurene are in the hospital." My voice cracked, and I slammed my fist against the desk, the dull thud reverberating through the empty room.

"You ruined everything, Conrad. And you're not even here to fucking face it."

The words tumbled out in a choked whisper, my anger and grief bleeding together. My knees buckled under the weight, and I sank to the floor, my chest heaving as I gasped for air.

I forced myself to stand, trembling, and stared at the desk like it held all the answers I never got. My vision blurred with rage, and with a guttural roar, I swept the papers and books off the surface.

They scattered across the floor, a storm of forgotten memories and meaningless legacies.

It wasn't enough.

The anger clawed at my insides, demanding more. I turned to the shelves, yanking at the books, tearing them down one by one, their heavy spines crashing against the floor. The noise echoed in the silent room, a hollow, pitiful sound compared to the screaming in my head.

I will never be Conrad. I'll never measure up.

But it wasn't true.

I'll never be Conrad—because I'm so much more than he ever was.

I fought, not for glory, not for some twisted sense of approval. I fought to protect what mattered most. To protect Laurene. To protect my family. I fought for love, for something pure and real—something Conrad would've never understood.

He was a shadow, a ghost of who I never wanted to be. Cold, ruthless, never looking out for anyone but himself. And I...I was *alive*. I was me. I had purpose. I mattered. I've always mattered.

My hand found a framed photo on the desk—Conrad's smug, perfect face staring back at me. My grip tightened around the frame until the edges bit into my palm. With a yell, I hurled it against the wall.

The glass exploded into a thousand jagged shards, scattering across the floor like splinters of everything he'd left behind.

I glanced down and froze. A leather-bound book peeked out from beneath a pile of broken glass and crumpled paper. I picked it up carefully, shards of glass tumbling from its cover, and flipped it open.

The pages felt stiff under my hands. Then I saw it. The handwriting on the first page.

Messy, slanted, unmistakable.

Conrad.

My chest tightened as I scanned the words, the ink smudged in places, as though he'd written in a rush. The air seemed to still around me as I turned the pages, each one pulling me deeper into a part of him I'd never been allowed to see.

He had been keeping secrets too.

> I never thought I'd see the day where everything would feel so isolating.
> They expect so much from me. I've become a stranger even to myself.
> Every choice I make feels like it's for them, for Dad and the family, never for me. I'm simply a role to fill, a name to uphold. Somewhere along the way, I stopped asking myself what I wanted.

I turned the page and found another entry.

> I've buried so much—dreams, fears, even joy—so deep that I can't remember what they looked like.
> She sees me. No one else does. She brings me a kind of freedom I thought I lost.

I paused. Who was she? Laurene?

> I see myself, the man I've buried, in her eyes.
> With her, I'm not the heir, the leader, or the name everyone expects me to be. I'm just...me.
> When I'm with her, I can breathe again, free from the burden of Ashbourne Capital. She sees the parts

of me no one else even thinks to look for. I can't marry Laurene. To stand at that altar would be a betrayal—not just of her, but of myself.
Of the love I've found in someone else.

My jaw dropped as the words sank in. How the hell did he keep this from us? When did this happen? And who was she?

I can't live this life anymore. She deserves more. I know what I'm doing is wrong, but...it has to be done. I'll be there at the engagement party—I'll smile, toast, and pretend like everything is fine. By this time tomorrow, they'll be too busy cleaning up Reese's mess to even notice I'm missing. He won't even see it coming. I put everything on a backup file in Avalon, just in case she needs it. Reese is so predictable. He'll take the bait—he always does. Bringing him more into the company has been rough, but now it's worth it. A little nudge here, a word there, and he'll spiral out of control.
Everyone will look at him. I've planted everything I need to make it look like Reese has been the one mismanaging accounts, siphoning funds, and pulling reckless stunts with the company's name attached.
The paper trail is flawless. No one will doubt it's him.

My heart raced… No. He couldn't have. I was praying this

wasn't true.

> Dad will see him as the screw-up he always knew he was. The Kings will turn on him. He'll get the blame while I'm long gone with her. The money's ready, she's ready, and by the time the smoke clears, they won't even know where to start looking for me.
>
> Reese will be left holding the bag, and I'll finally be free.

The journal slipped from my hands.

Conrad.

Laurene and I had had a plan. But Conrad had a plan too.

All those years of rivalry, of resentment, and he'd weaponized them against me.

My pulse thundered in my ears as it all clicked into place. The missing money. The discrepancies in the accounts I'd been chasing for months. Every lead that felt like a dead end. Holy shit.

Conrad had planned to frame me.

My knees felt weak as I stared down at the journal in my hands, the truth staring back at me. All this time, I thought I was uncovering some external threat, some outside force threatening the company. But it was him. Conrad.

It wasn't enough for him to leave and disappear. He needed someone to take the blame for his mess.

Me.

CHAPTER 29

Laurene

"YOU DIDN'T HAVE to do all this," I said, eyeing the feast in front of me Noelle had brought. I pushed myself up higher in the bed, wincing as pain shot through my side.

"Hey, take it easy." Serena was at my side in an instant. She gently pushed me back down. "Relax. Lemme fix you a plate."

"I *got* it!" Gigi jumped up from her chair, rushing to the table to intercept Serena. "You've been in her face since she woke up. Let somebody else do something for once."

Serena shot her a glare. "Excuse me, but I've *been* here, making sure she's okay. Where were you? Off shopping for new shoes again?"

Gigi's mouth fell open. "Lu understands that I needed those Paloma Blossom Sandals to go with my dress for Coachella! At least I came back with snacks, which is *important*. Second of all, stop micromanaging!"

Walter, who'd been napping in the purse, woke up to bark.

"I've been meaning to try out some new recipes, anyway. And there's no way we were going to let you starve in here." Noelle sighed, stepping between them, eyeing them warily as she set another container of food on the table.

I glanced at the table, now crammed with food that smelled heavenly, and my stomach growled loudly.

"It's not that bad," I said, though the bland, rubbery pasta from last night begged to differ.

Noelle raised an eyebrow. "Laurene. That last tray had Jell-O cubes that looked like they'd been alive at some point. You deserve better."

Gigi and Serena ignored her and continued arguing.

"You came back with a half-eaten bag of chips and a chocolate bar." Serena frowned.

"*Both of ya'll,*" Erik's voice cut through the bickering. He stood in the doorway, arms crossed and eyebrows raised.

Serena and Gigi both froze, midglare, like kids caught raiding the cookie jar.

"Imma kick both of y'all out if you can't behave."

"I wasn't fighting," Gigi muttered under her breath, though she side-eyed Serena.

"You were *both* fighting," Erik said matter-of-factly, strolling over to the table. "Now, hand me that plate. I'll fix it."

"Why do you get to do it?" Serena demanded, though she took a step back, probably knowing better than to argue with Erik.

"'Cause I'm the oldest," Erik said. "And I'm not about to stand here listenin' to y'all argue over chicken and rice. Now, go sit down somewhere."

The countless bouquets and gift baskets crowded every available surface, their pastel colors and sweet floral scents filling the room.

"Did it double up in flowers up in here? I was gone for twenty minutes." Erik plated the food, looking around.

"Unfortunately, yes," Serena deadpanned, sitting back on the couch, pouting.

"They're from the whole town," Gigi said. "I hope people do the same for me. Not that I wanna be hurt and possibly break my nose. People just wanna check in on Laurene."

Erik snorted. "Right. Because they're *so* concerned about her well-being and not fishing for gossip about the crash."

Gigi rolled her eyes. "You know they're dying for the tea."

"They'll have to stay thirsty," Erik said firmly, shooting me a look. "No one's bothering you about this until you're ready, got it?"

I nodded, my chest tightening—not from the pain this time, but from the unexpected comfort of knowing my brother had my back. That *all* my siblings and Noelle had my back. It made that devasting moment just a little better.

The crash still played on loop in my mind, the screech of tires, the blur of headlights. It had all been so sudden, so violent.

Every movement outside my room had me on edge, and the hospital room felt more like a cage than a place for healing. I kept waiting for someone to slip through the door, for a face to appear in the window and finish the job.

The added security didn't help. It was hard explaining to my family it was just a *preventative* measure.

I lifted my spoon, ready to dig into the plate. The door to my hospital room slammed open, the sound so loud it made my heart skip a beat. Everyone jumped and turned to see Mama standing there, Dad trailing behind her.

Her eyes were hard, her lips pressed into a thin, angry line. "Laurene, did you see the news?"

"What news?"

"Change the channel," she barked, and Noelle scrambled to get the remote. She landed on the local news station and she turned it up for us to hear.

There was Harold, hands cuffed in front of him, being led into a Las Vegas jail.

"Reese said Harold was here," I said.

Mama shook her head as we continued to watch his face. His lips were pale and pressed in a grim line as reporters shouted questions at him. The camera panned, and beside him were two other familiar faces—Blair's father, Albert Sterling, Toby, and

Blair herself, all looking equally disheveled and furious as police marched them inside.

"Holy shit!" Gigi exclaimed.

The news anchor's voice filled the room, her tone laced with barely contained excitement.

"—arrests made earlier today in connection with a massive illegal gambling ring operating out of Las Vegas and tied to high-profile individuals. Harold Ashbourne, Albert Sterling, Blair Sterling, and Tobias Merrick were taken into custody on charges of money laundering, racketeering, and running an unlicensed gambling operation for the last few years. A whistle-blower on the operation revealed to authorities…"

Business.

Harold had said Blair was helping him with *business.*

"Your marriage needs to end. Immediately," Mama said.

I let out a breath, slow and measured, and set my spoon down. "Excuse me?"

"Laurene." Her voice was laced with cold pragmatism. "You know as well as I do that your marriage to Reese is more of a liability than an asset now."

I let out a short, humorless laugh. "A liability?"

"His father just got arrested like a common *criminal,*" she continued, like I hadn't spoken. "The Ashbourne name is about to be dragged through the mud, and yours will be right there with it. You need to cut ties before this gets worse."

"You mean before it affects the family," I said, voice flat.

"Before it drags *you* down," she corrected me. "Do you really want to tie yourself to a sinking ship?"

Something burned in my chest, anger and exhaustion and something too raw to name. "Reese is my husband."

"And? Your great-grandmother had five husbands! We're talking about survival. About the legacy we've spent generations cultivating. We cut the Ashbournes loose. Let's just void our deal with them and handle Dante another way."

Maybe she was right. Maybe Reese *was* a risk.

But he was *my* risk.

I sat up a little straighter, ignoring the ache in my ribs. "I'm not leaving my husband."

Mama's lips pressed into a thin line. "Laurene—"

"I mean it." My voice didn't waver. "I made vows, and I'm not breaking them just because it's inconvenient for you. I love him."

"Love?" She scoffed, and walked to the center of the room, standing at the foot of my bed. "I told you about love. Now you love him after a month? I'm giving you the easy way out. You never wanted to marry the boy. He was always a backup plan."

I looked at Daddy, hoping that he'd say *something*.

For a moment, he just watched, his eyes flicking between me and Mama. Then, he exhaled through his nose and turned to Mama.

"Yvonne." His voice was even, but there was an edge underneath. "Laurene's made her decision."

Mama barely spared him a glance. "She's emotional. She isn't thinking clearly."

"She just survived a car crash, Yvonne. I think she's thinking clearer than most people would be in her position." Daddy stepped forward, planting himself between us. "It's her decision."

"Vincent." Mama looked at him, shock across her features, and her gaze went from him to me and back again. "Do you realize what's at stake? Dante just approved the redevelopment of downtown. He's bypassing us, we've just lost millions."

"Like the deal you wanted to force him that would have eliminated all the other businesses and families? Augustus King wanted this town for *everyone*, not just us," I snapped.

My siblings all looked at her, even Daddy. She had the gall to look crazy.

"He told you that? It was private—" Mama said.

"I'm not focused on deals right now," he cut in. "Laurene isn't a child. She understands the consequences." His gaze flicked to me.

"I've allowed you to dictate us for years, Yvonne. It stops now. And if she's willing to stand by Reese, then we need to respect that."

Mama scoffed, stepping closer. "Respect?"

"Yes, *respect*," he said. "We didn't raise our children to be weak. We raised them to be smart, to be independent, to make their own choices. And she's making one now."

Mama's nostrils flared, and she turned to me. "You can find another man, sweetie."

I shoved the blankets off and swung my legs over the side of the bed. Erik quickly came to my aid, and I held his hands. A sharp pain shot through me but I kept moving toward Mama.

"Laurene—" Daddy started, stepping toward me.

I needed to stand for this. Needed her to see me, not just as her daughter, not as a piece on her chessboard, but as a woman making her own damn choices.

"And what exactly do you think this little display is going to prove?" Mama arched a brow, unimpressed. "You had sex with him, and now your emotions are all twisted up?"

Daddy exhaled sharply. "Yvonne—"

"What? Am I wrong?" Her eyes flicked back to me. "Love don't pay settlements, don't protect us from scandal, don't undo a business deal already in motion."

I clenched my fists, my nails biting into my palms. "This marriage was *your* deal. Not mine."

"And you agreed to it."

"Because you *forced* me into it!" I tried to breathe slowly. "You really think I'm just gonna throw him away for your fucking *ambition*?"

Mama's eyes flashed. "Watch your mouth—"

"No." My voice was steady, sharp. "I've spent my whole life watching my mouth. Watching my steps. Doing what I was told, *marrying* who I was told. I let you rip me away from him once. I let you *win*." I swallowed, my chest rising and falling too fast. "But I never stopped loving Reese. Not when I was pretending to hate him. Not when I was sneaking around with him. Not when I was lying to myself for *you*."

Mama's nostrils flared. "Laurene—"

The door opened again, and we turned to see Reese as he stepped inside, looking rough around the edges. He froze as his gaze swept over the room, wary. And then he saw *me*.

I shifted, and my body betrayed me. I stumbled. Before I could catch myself, Reese was there, crossing the room in three long strides, hands firm on my waist, steadying me, pulling me from Erik. His grip was warm, solid—*home*.

I shook my head, my eyes never leaving Mama. I *wanted* him to hear this.

"You made me choose the family over my own damn happiness before. And I did it. I bled for this family. I sacrificed for this family. I let you carve me into the perfect fucking daughter. And you know what?" I let out a bitter laugh. "I don't want it. Not like this. Not if it means choosing pain over love. Not if it means ending up like you."

I looked over at my siblings. Gigi looked scared and awed. Serena was a mix of surprise and maybe some disappointment. Erik nodded at me, grinning.

"I'm done," I said to Mama, voice stronger now. "I don't want my inheritance. I don't want a fucking *dime* from you. And I *never* want to see you again until you can look me in the eye and *apologize*. Until you get help."

Mama stood there blinking at me.

"Get out."

She glanced toward my siblings, searching for someone—anyone—to side with her, but none of them moved. They stood behind me, silently.

Mama's gaze flicked to Daddy, a silent plea for him to intervene. But he didn't. Not this time.

"Vincent?" she snapped, but he only shook his head.

"This has been a long time coming, Vonnie…"

And then she stormed out, the door slamming shut behind her, leaving a heavy silence in its wake.

I didn't feel the relief I expected. Instead, it was like I had just stepped off a cliff. The freefall was terrifying, but also exhilarating. I was *free*. Free from her, from everything that had kept me tethered to a family that never understood me.

My legs buckled underneath me. Reese was there immediately, his strong arms catching me. His face was drawn, concern flickering in his eyes, but there was a quiet strength in him. The kind I had always needed.

"Are you okay?"

"I'm fine," I whispered, the words barely coming out, my throat tight.

I looked over at my family.

"Holy shit, I think I just pissed myself," Gigi finally said.

Erik nodded. "I think I gotta agree with G."

Serena only stared at the door Mama left through.

Reese gently helped me to the bed. I sank into the sheets, exhaustion suddenly flooding my body. He sat beside me, watching me closely, his brow furrowed.

"You meant those words," he said, his voice quiet but heavy with meaning.

"Yes, I meant them," I said. "I'm done with all of it. I can't live for them anymore. I'm living for *me* now. For us."

Reese's eyes softened, and he leaned in, brushing his lips against mine. It was tender—*real*. And for the first time, I felt like I was exactly where I was meant to be.

"I just want to rest. With Reese."

I looked back at my family and Daddy nodded.

"We'll leave you two alone," he said softly and made a movement with his head at my siblings.

Erik stepped up next, offering a fist bump. Gigi gave me a quick, nervous smile, Noelle gave me a thumbs-up, and Serena's eyes softened before she turned to leave.

"No way I can go home. Erik, can I come stay with you?" Gigi asked.

Erik turned back around, looking at Gigi and then at her purse with Walter. "I told you your mutt ain't welcome in my house.

"C'mon, let that go! I've almost paid you back."

"You paid me ten dollars. That collection was worth *fifteen thousand dollars.*"

Gigi stomped her foot. *"Pleeeaaase?"*

Erik ignored her with her on his heels.

And just like that, they were all gone. It was just Reese and me.

Alone.

"How are you dealing with everything? With your father?"

Reese's face tightened, and I could see the pain flicker in his eyes. And something darker crossed his expression, like a storm rolling in.

"The blackmailer contacted me again," he said.

I swallowed. This was what I had been afraid of. "What do they want this time?"

He clenched his fists.

"Twenty million, in two days. Or we'll be dead this time."

CHAPTER 30
Reese

CONRAD'S JOURNAL felt like it was burning in my back pocket as I began pacing in Laurene's hospital room. My pulse was a steady roar in my ears, my head pounding from too much —too much shit, too many lies, too many goddamn problems stacking on top of each other.

"T-twenty million?" Laurene echoed, her voice barely above a whisper.

She exhaled sharply, gripping the sheets. "Reese, this is becoming too much."

I let out a bitter laugh, shaking my head. "Tell me about it. And that's not even the worst of it."

Her eyes snapped to mine, a flicker of fear crossing her face, but she masked it quickly. "What do you mean?"

I stopped pacing. My hands felt cold, my chest tight, but I had to say it. I couldn't hide from this anymore.

I pulled the crumpled note from my pocket and threw it onto the bed. The ultimatum. Laurene stared at it, disbelief written all over her.

"I should have told you. I—I never wanted you to get hurt. If I had told you sooner. Then I got the call about the accident—"

Her eyes snapped back to mine. "Wait. You mean… You're saying this is *your* fault? That I got hurt because of you?"

"I didn't think it was gonna escalate!" I rushed to her side, my voice desperate, raw. "I never meant for you to get hurt. I just…I thought I could handle it. I hired a PI. But now…now I can't even think straight."

Laurene looked away, struggling to steady her breathing. The tears came now, unbidden, and she wiped them away hastily. "Well, I wish I knew that before I gave my inheritance away. But how much worse can it get?"

I stopped pacing and pulled the journal from my pocket, tossing it onto the bed.

"Conrad," I said, voice flat. "He was stealing from the company. Millions, probably. And he was gonna pin it on me."

Her breath caught. "What?"

"It's all in there." I nodded at the journal. "Numbers. Transactions. A whole fucking plan to make me the fall guy while he walked away clean. But where he was sending that money? I don't know."

Laurene reached for the journal with trembling fingers, flipping through the pages, her eyes darting over the handwriting. I saw the moment it hit her, the way her shoulders tensed and her expression tightened.

"He was going to frame you," she murmured, looking up at me. "He—Reese, he was really gonna do it."

I used to think that one day, despite everything, Conrad and I could fix what was broken between us. Yes, he stole my ideas, but we weren't always like this—hateful, distant. As kids, we were brothers. Then I hit my teenage years, and suddenly Conrad became Dad's perfect shadow. *Yes, Dad. I agree, Dad.* Harold's own fucking robot.

Now he wasn't fucking redeemable in my eyes.

"Yeah." My voice was rough, edged with something I couldn't push down. "He spent years treating me like I was a fucking disgrace. And the whole time, he was the one stealing from the family. From me."

Laurene stared at the journal like she wanted to burn it. "Reese, this wasn't your fault."

"Yeah? Tell that to the part of me that would fucking kill him if he wasn't dead already."

Laurene leaned forward on the bed, catching my hand.

"Then scream," she whispered. "But you're not carrying this alone."

I let out a slow breath, flexing my fingers against hers.

"I'm investigating everything now—where the money Conrad stole went, who else was involved. I've frozen all the company accounts. No one's touching a damn cent until I know the full damage."

"But we have to pay off the blackmailers." Laurene swallowed.

I stiffened. "No, we don't."

"Yes, we do." Her voice was softer, but unshakable. "They aren't going away, Reese. Look at me!" She gestured to herself on the bed.

"I'm not handing over money to some faceless bastard when I don't even know what the endgame is. Twenty million? Who's to say it stops there?"

"There's nothing else we can do. They could have killed me and Jennie and the baby."

Every instinct in me rejected giving in to their demands, but I knew Laurene had a point.

"I have the ten million from Dante."

I stopped cold. "From *Dante*? Since when are you friends with him?"

She straightened. "Recently. I made a deal with him."

"A deal for ten *million*? For what?"

"For my help when the time is needed."

I made a face. "What the hell does that mean? Now we're friends with him? He's still a suspect."

"It means we have some money."

I let out a sharp, humorless laugh. "So instead of being tied to your parents, you decided to owe Dante Castillo?"

She lifted her chin. "He keeps secrets."

"He keeps secrets because he's the fucking devil," I scoffed.

"He came to me with a blackmail photo, and instead of using it, he warned me. Maybe he's not as bad as you think."

I let out a sharp, humorless laugh. "Come on, Laurie. He's a predator."

"He didn't have to help me."

"No, he didn't," I agreed. "Which means when he *does* come to collect, it won't be something as simple as a check."

She lifted her chin, unwavering. "And we don't have twenty million."

"We have the money. Just not for these thieves. I think it's time we call in the law."

"No," Laurene exhaled. "This can't get out, it will ruin us. Our image and everything."

"I can't stand around and let you get hurt. What if they go after your family? My mom? More people we love getting hurt?"

We stared at each other, neither of us willing to back down.

Then my phone buzzed. I glanced down. A message.

Plane's ready.

Laurene saw my face shift. "What?"

"I'm going to Vegas," I said.

She nodded, sitting back on the bed, "Go. I'll be fine."

I didn't want to leave her. Not now. Not when we were in the middle of this shitstorm.

"You need to have this talk with your dad. Once and for all. This time, he doesn't control you. Don't let him handle you. We'll figure it out when I get back. My family is here. The security is here. I'll be fine."

She didn't have to worry about that. He would never, ever hurt me again.

She reached for my hand, threading our fingers together. "Just remember why you're going. Not for him. For *you*."

For the company. For the mess Conrad left. For the damn truth.

I stepped closer, brushing my fingers against her jaw before tilting her chin up. "Don't leave this room or the hospital without security. We'll discuss what to do when I get back."

"I won't."

"I mean it, Laurene."

"I promise."

I brushed my thumb along her jaw, then let go.

And I walked out, hoping I'd survive the fucking wrath of Harold and his mess.

The dry air felt rough and irritating on my skin. The jail loomed ahead. My legs were restless, like I couldn't decide if I wanted to stand still or pace until my feet bled.

The city buzzed in the distance, the sound of traffic and life and all the bullshit that went with Vegas, but here, it was dead quiet. Just the faintest breeze kicking up dust and the distant whine of a siren that seemed to echo inside my skull.

After doing business with my clubs in Vegas for so long, you get to pull enough favors, and Harold should have been walking out those doors twenty minutes ago.

Hell, I didn't want to have this conversation, but there was no way I was letting him walk out of there without facing the truth. Without facing me. I sat in the back of the car, flipping through the document that Nathan sent, all fucking there in black and white.

Page after page, the numbers bled together—fractions of a million here, a couple hundred thousand there. But adding it up? It was a fucking fortune: $32.7 million.

That was how much had disappeared under Harold's watch over the years. He wasn't just gambling; the man was a fucking addict.

The bastards had been bleeding Ashbourne Capital dry.

Harold and Conrad had been taking money separately. Harold hadn't done it alone. The board. The very people who were supposed to protect the company, had been funneling funds, shuffling numbers, masking withdrawals under bullshit expense reports.

Conrad's theft went further. He'd been taking money and sending it to this sperate account. Harold hadn't known nor did I. The money had been going to this account up until I cut off funds.

Nathan was looking into information on this account and how this person had access.

Anyone who helped Harold had been fired, and I planned to ruin all their damn careers and reputations. They wouldn't be able to work at the fucking liquor store when I was done with them.

"Mr. Ashbourne," my driver said.

I looked up as the door creaked open, a grating sound that sliced through the air. And there he was—Harold.

He looked smaller somehow, like the weight of the last few days had chipped away at him, but there was still that damn arrogance he carried.

The bastard had ruined everything, and for what? A few high-stakes poker games?

I set the tablet down, stepping out of the car.

"Reese." His voice was rough, like he'd been chewing on gravel. "I'm surprised you got me out of here. Least you can do."

"Don't," I snapped.

He stopped a few feet away from me, and he must have seen my expression, because this time he tried to look sheepish. "I know you're upset—"

Before he could finish, I punched him. He stumbled back,

eyes wide with pain. He clutched his jaw, his face twisted in a mix of surprise and anger.

"Reese, what the hell—" he started, but I didn't let him finish.

"You're a horrible father, husband, and overall fucking lousy human being," I said calmly.

His hand dropped from his face, and I could see the anger flaring in his eyes now. "I'm your father—"

My fist slammed into him again, the force of the blow sending a jolt up my arm. Harder. This time, the bone shifted beneath my knuckles with a sickening crunch; I felt the give of cartilage as he staggered, crumpling to his knees. A steady stream of blood dripped from his mouth, staining his chin.

He spat to the side on the pavement.

Conrad's journal explained everything. Reading on the plane, I learned Conrad had been just as overwhelmed with Harold's ridiculous expectations. He'd wanted to get away from the family for a long time. So he planned to take the money and run.

"That all you got, boy?" His voice was taunting. "You think this makes you a man? Hitting your old man like that?" He sneered, wiping his mouth with the back of his hand. "You're just like me. No better. No different."

That was the thing about men like Harold.

They never took responsibility. Never admitted they were the problem.

I thought about Conrad. About the way he crumbled under the weight of Harold's expectations, the way he broke, and instead of fighting back, he chose to save himself.

No, I didn't forgive Conrad. But I understood him now.

And Harold—Harold was the reason for all of it.

Crack.

My fist crashed into his jaw one last time, harder than before, and he went down. *Hard.*

For Conrad.

For everything Harold took.

For everything he ruined.

I stood over him, my breathing slow and controlled, watching as he groaned, shifting onto his side. He wouldn't get up quickly—not this time.

"I'm nothing like you."

"You're weak," he snarled, lying on his side he looked up at me. "Look at you! Always emotional! Always reckless!"

"You've been lying to us for years. You ruined everything. You dragged Mom into this scandal, you used Conrad, and you didn't even go see Jennie or your granddaughter in the hospital. That's a selfish man, not a man who cares about his family."

"I did what I had to do." His voice was low, like he was trying to reason with me.

"Bullshit!" I shouted. "You did what you *wanted* to do."

"You don't know the whole story, Reese."

"I know enough," I shot back. "I know enough to see you for who you really are."

"Then hit me again, big guy. Since that's all you can do?"

"Yeah, I could hit you again. I could probably fucking kill you, but I won't. You're not worth it. No one is gonna push me there again," I said, my voice steady, almost calm. "Because what would that do, really? You'd still be the same sad, broken man. I know the truth now, Harold. I know everything."

"What the hell are you talking about?"

I reached into my jacket pocket and pulled out Conrad's journal, the worn leather cover rough against my fingers.

"This," I said, holding it up for him to see. "Conrad kept a record of everything. Your lies, your manipulations, how you tried to control us and shape our lives the way you wanted. He wrote it all down."

Harold's eyes widened slightly, the confidence in his posture wavering. "You think a few scribbles in a notebook mean anything?"

"You pushed him to the point where he was stealing money from our company, framing me, and cutting you off. He was gonna run away, did you know that?"

Harold looked shocked.

"Yeah, your golden son wasn't so perfect. He fucking hated you. He thought just like me what a fucking cancer you are."

His head dropped to the ground, his chest heaving, and I saw the blood drips fall slowly. *Plop. Plop. Plop.*

"Get up," I growled, barely able to hide the disgust in my voice.

With a groan he pushed himself up to his knees, making a show of shaking and falling back down, but I didn't care, I watched him till he stood at his full height looking at me.

"Why were you gambling, Harold?" My voice was steady. "Blair was involved in this too? How'd she fit in?"

His eyes flickered to mine—guilt, regret, fear all tangled up in the look he shot me.

"Blair took my bets," he muttered. "She—she got me in contact with her father. Thought I could make more, but I lost more than I won. Couldn't stop. I thought I could get out of it, but…but I didn't. Toby got in on it. Said he knew some people in Dubai that could double my odds."

I took a step closer, closing the distance, and I saw his eyes widen.

"You're gonna pay back every fucking cent, Harold. All thirty-two million you stole. And I don't care if you have to pawn every fucking thing you owe or hit the blade, but you will pay Ashbourne Capital back."

His face fell.

"Ashbourne Capital belongs solely to me and Jennie now. You'll forfeit all stocks, investments, and equity in the company. You don't get a say in anything related to our business anymore."

"I fucking made this company!"

"I could sue you. But I'm letting you bow out with ease you don't fucking deserve. You either go to jail for your crimes or you go to rehab. If Mom wants to divorce you, you'll accept it with no resistance, and if she doesn't, you go to every fucking marriage counseling session. If you miss a single one, I'll be right back on your ass like a tick."

Harold glared at me.

"What will it be?"

"You think I'm going to let you take everything from me?" he sneered. "You're just a kid playing at being a man. You don't have what it takes."

"Maybe not," I replied, my tone unwavering. "But I have a wife whose side I need to be back next to. I need to make sure Jennie and your *granddaughter* survive. I can be the man you and Conrad couldn't be. All this ends with me."

Finally, he gave me a look, one of pure defeat. "Fine. I'll sign it over. Just…I want to speak to your mother. Explain everything to her first."

I just nodded once, and without another glance, I walked to my car and slammed the door. The driver took off immediately, leaving Harold standing there in the dust.

The phone buzzed in my pocket. I looked at the caller ID. Nathan. I answered it without a second thought, leaning back in my seat.

"Reese." Nathan's voice crackled over the line. "We found something else."

"What?"

"It wasn't just Conrad and Harold," Nathan said.

I could feel the hairs on the back of my neck stand up. "Who else?"

There was a pause, and I could almost hear Nathan swallowing on the other end.

"Your mother, Reese. She's been taking money too."

CHAPTER 31

Laurene

"HELLO, Laurene. Looking as beautiful as ever." Dante stepped in my room holding a bouquet of flowers.

"Don't lie to my face," I muttered, switching off the TV, some reality dating show Gigi had insisted on putting on for me.

"Late to the party," he remarked, glancing at the flowers all around the room. "You've got quite the collection, I see."

"What brings you here, Dante?" I asked, not bothering with pleasantries.

"Just checking in, making sure everything's alright. Did you like what I did?" He gave a small, inscrutable smile, and placed the bouquet on my bedside table as he took a seat next to the bed.

I blinked, thinking about the news with Harold.

"That was you?"

"We're partners, remember, and you've been through a lot recently. Of course I kept my name out of it, but…"

"Partners don't lie to me about their involvement. Especially when my father-in-law is involved."

Dante's eyes flickered with something. Amusement? Annoyance? Hard to tell, but he didn't look caught off guard. "You know the game, Laurene. There's always a bigger play. A bigger plan. I rather you found out on your own."

"Cut the crap," I pressed, sitting up straighter. "I don't know if we can be partners anymore. I can't trust you, truly. You may be worse than my own mama. Playing games."

He remained cool, his gaze steady. "The Kings will always be Lush's first family. Don't worry about it."

I narrowed my eyes. "You're hiding something bigger. I don't know what it is but I don't wanna be involved."

"I didn't come to fight with you, Laurene," he said finally. "Only to let you know the money you requested is officially yours."

He uncrossed his legs slowly, crossing them the other way.

"I'm hoping that shows my loyalty and commitment to this partnership. I cut off something lucrative for me, because I knew it would hurt you."

Before I could respond, a knock at the door interrupted us, cutting through the tension like a blade.

"Come in," I called, irritation creeping into my voice.

Maybe Reese had been right about Dante.

The door opened, and Nina stepped inside. She froze when she saw Dante.

"I'm so sorry," Nina stammered, her eyes bouncing between the two of us. "I hope I'm not interrupting anything."

Dante's gaze immediately narrowed on her.

"No, you're not interrupting," I said. "What is it, Nina?"

She seemed to straighten, forcing the surprise off her face as she gestured behind her.

"I just spoke with the doctor," she said. "They're discharging you, Laurene. Reese asked me to come and help you get home."

"They did?" I sat up straighter.

Nina nodded. "Yes, everything's been cleared. Unless you want me to call your family or Noelle?"

"No, you don't have to," I said. I felt guilty for the trouble I had already caused and how much time my family had spent by my bedside, so having Nina here was actually quite convenient. All I wanted was the soft sheets and the familiar scent of home and our bed.

"Let's catch up later, Dante," I told him.

Nina nodded as she reached for the door handle and stepped out. "I'll just get the car ready for you."

I dragged myself out of bed. "Thanks for the cash, Dante. You'll get that back in your account soon."

I kept my gaze locked on his as he stood, his eyes unreadable. Then he nodded and left the room, and I heard the door opening and closing. I took a deep breath, squared my shoulders, and started changing. I didn't notice the door open again until I heard the soft shuffle of footsteps behind me.

"Thanks again for this, Nina."

I turned and I froze when I saw her gun pointed at me.

The Accident

TEN MINUTES BEFORE THE CRASH—SIX
YEARS AGO...

The night air throbbed with the bass of the music, carrying the sharp tang of salt and the sweetness of spilled champagne.

This was it.

We were finally gonna do it.

That yacht was a shining streak cutting through the black Pacific. The wind caught my silk dress, brushing it against my thighs as I stood by the railing. Goosebumps prickled my arms, but I couldn't tell if it was the ocean breeze or the weight of what Reese and I were about to do.

Breathe, Laurene.

With a sigh, I turned and watched the yacht club, the glittering lights reflecting off the water. I twisted my engagement ring, feeling its smooth surface under my fingers.

Can I really do this?

Yes. No more secrets. No more lies.

I turned to find Reese standing there, his face pensive. He stepped closer, his fingers brushing my arm, sending a fiery, dangerous shiver down my spine. "Are you sure you can do this?"

No. I was freaking out. Terrified. What would Mama do? I

didn't even want to go there. But I couldn't marry Conrad. I couldn't go along with her plan.

"We said we'd do this tonight, so that's what we're doing."

He hesitated before putting his hand on mine. "Nothing's gonna happen that we don't want."

A bitter smile twisted my lips. "We're blackmailing Conrad into calling off our engagement so I can marry you. Do you really believe that?"

His jaw ticked, but he didn't argue.

I glanced left and found Blair staring directly at us. Her gaze latched on to me, unblinking, unreadable. The knot in my stomach tightened. I yanked my hand away from Reese.

"I need to fix my makeup again."

I had fixed everything after our encounter in the bathroom earlier, but I just had to make sure.

I stumbled back, my heel catching on the slick deck, but before I could fall, a hand clamped around my wrist.

"Whoa, easy there," Nina said, steadying me. "Are you okay?"

I forced a smile. "Perfect. Excuse me."

The stairs felt endless as I descended into the lower deck, my breath coming fast, uneven. The moment I stepped onto solid ground, I braced myself against the nearest wall, pressing a hand to my chest.

What if this all fell apart?

For two years we'd managed to keep our relationship a secret, and soon it would be out. I just prayed I was right in my assumption that Conrad hated this engagement just as much as me. I didn't know the exact pressure Harold was putting on Conrad, but if it was how Mama was treating me, I was fucked.

And me—God, what would people say when this got out? That I was reckless, stupid, selfish? That I destroyed my own engagement, my own reputation, my family's reputation, just to crawl into bed with the one person I was never supposed to love?

But what if, for once, I stopped caring? What if I let Lush burn behind me? Leave my parents, leave the expectations, leave behind the version of me that never felt like enough?

My nails dug into my palms. The thought was huge, scary, and irresistible.

I gulped and straightened up, smoothing my dress. No. I couldn't lose it now.

I stepped forward, deeper into the dimly lit hallway, the low hum of the yacht's engine beneath my feet grounding me. I just needed a moment.

But then—footsteps.

"Laurene…"

Conrad was standing behind me. His cold blue eyes gave nothing away as they looked me over, his dark hair neat despite the wind. He was just steering the boat. So why the hell was he down here?

I straightened up, trying to relax. "Hey, what's up?"

"I could ask you the same thing."

I lifted my chin. "I just needed a moment."

He hummed as he drew near, his expensive cologne mingling with a hint of alcohol. "Funny. So did I."

My pulse kicked up. His face was blank, but there was something in his eyes—a deadness.

"Wasn't our kiss good?"

I swallowed. "Was there a reason you had to pull that?"

"You're going to be my wife," Conrad said. "What do you think we're going to do on the wedding day?"

"About that—"

"Look, look." Conrad raised his hands. "I haven't been the most charming version of myself. I understand. You're not a bad-looking woman, Laurene. But let's just keep any of that push-back and back talk to a minimum in our…arrangement."

I blinked. "Excuse me?"

He exhaled angrily, like I was exhausting him.

"I'm going to have it all. A mansion, a high-paying job, a

beautiful wife—and I'm going to hate every second of it." His lip twisted up. "I'll hate waking up in that house to greet my nosy neighbors, hate driving to my soul-sucking job, and especially hate going home to you every night. You'll leave me leftovers in the fridge and kiss me good-night before bed, and I will stay up every night wondering how to escape this fucking limbo."

I straightened.

"But guess what?" He got super close, and I smelled alcohol on his breath. "We'll do it. I've…made some mistakes. But that's being fixed. This is my life, and I'm staying here. Because if we don't act together, that fucks up everything I've done and am trying to fix. And, Laurene, I don't let anyone fuck up my plans."

A cold sweat broke out along my spine. "Then don't do it."

He cocked his head. "What?"

I breathed slowly. "You just said it yourself. You don't want this. Why don't you just walk away?"

Wasn't this exactly what we needed? Was Reese right? Would it really be that easy?

"You think I can?" he asked. "Laurene, sweetheart, this isn't about you. It's not even about me."

I frowned. "Then what is it about?"

"That is all I have."

"What does that mean?" I asked carefully.

He shrugged. "It means the money, the power, the family name—it's all tied to this. You, me, the pretty little life our parents arranged for us. I thought I didn't want it. But I do. I change my mind, and I can fix things and if I can't, somebody has to take the fall."

Go ahead, tell him.

"You know, Conrad, I'm starting to understand why you're so desperate to keep this engagement."

He squinted, but said nothing.

I leaned in, keeping my voice calm. "You've been stealing Reese's ideas. And you've been getting away with it."

For the first time, I saw a flicker of something in his eyes—a little tension, a slight tightening of his jaw.

"How did you find out?"

"Why? You and Reese could work together and be something—"

"I don't *need* his ideas. Hell, I don't even need him. The only reason he's still right there for now is because it'll look bad if I throw him on his ass. Is that all you know?"

I held my ground, refusing to let him break me. "You think I'm just going to sit back and let you ruin him?"

"Why are you worried about my brother? Is it—"

He recoiled, his eyes wide with shock as he figured it all out.

"Yes, Conrad. Me and Reese. Sleeping together. For a long time now."

Until then Conrad had been controlled and cool, but it was like his face cracked. A searing ugliness crossed his features, and I took a cautious step back.

"Did he put you up to this?" he hissed, voice laced with venom. "Was this his idea? His way of getting back at me? Fucking my *fiancée*?"

I sucked in a sharp breath. "I'm *not* your fiancée."

His fingers tightened at my waist, digging in.

"You *are*," he murmured. "Until I *say* you're not."

I shook my head, ready to go back upstairs, and he grabbed me.

"That's fine. Fuck him for now, but that won't happen in our marriage. I'm thinking of having him fired. He's nothing but a liability. I'll make sure they see him as a failure, someone who's been holding the company back. Fuck, I got feet and changed everything only for him to fuck me over? He'll never work in this town again, and face it, Laurene, you're far too prissy to love a poor man."

My breath hitched. "You can't do that."

He reached out quickly before I could respond, fingers

brushing my jaw in a mockery of affection before gripping my chin hard enough to make me gasp and force my neck back.

"You can either walk down that aisle and smile pretty for the cameras, or you can watch everything crumble—your family, your name, that little empire your mother built, and your beloved Reese." His grip tightened just enough to make my eyes sting. "And if you think I won't make it happen, I dare you to test me. You will marry me, you will like it, and you will end it with him."

I jerked my face away, my heart hammering. "Go to hell."

I didn't see it coming.

One second, I was standing there, my pulse hammering, my brain screaming at me to run. The next—

Pain.

Conrad shoved me—hard. My back slammed against the wall, the impact rattling through my bones, knocking the breath from my lungs.

I let out a strangled gasp. My fingers scrambled for something, anything, to grab on to, but there was nothing but smooth, polished wood.

Conrad came closer; I felt the heat radiating off him. Whiskey was all over his breath as he yanked me by my dress.

I pushed, but he was solid muscle and pure anger. He didn't budge.

"I will not be second-best to Reese. I'm first. I've always been first. Do you understand?" he whispered.

I gulped, short of breath, heart racing.

"What the fuck do you think you're doing?"

And then Conrad let go.

I stumbled forward, gasping, and when I lifted my head —Reese.

Standing at the top of the stairs. Face thunderous. Jaw clenched.

He glared murderously at his brother.

Conrad barely smirked before Reese moved.

He was on top of him in a matter of seconds. A crack echoed as Reese's fist slammed into Conrad's jaw.

Conrad staggered back, a snarl ripping from his throat. He braced himself against the wall, eyes wide, still stunned by Reese's punch. Then, his hand rose to his lip, smearing the dark, sticky blood.

And then he laughed.

"Wow," he breathed, rolling his jaw. "So that's how it is, little brother?"

Reese didn't answer. His whole body was coiled, ready. His hands, clenched at his sides, twitched with barely controlled rage, his knuckles white.

"You're pathetic," Conrad sneered, stepping forward. "We really got fucked when Mom gave birth to you. You can't lead. You don't listen. You fly off the handle each and every time. Now, you're slumming it with the woman they gave me? You think you get to *win*?" He let out a sharp breath, his eyes wide. "You're just a fucking nobody, Reese. Do us a favor and get the fuck out this family. And once I get back up there, I'm turning this boat around, and we're going home. Then I'm telling Mom and Dad *everything*. Let's see how long your little fantasy lasts then."

"No," I breathed, heart stopping in fear.

Conrad barely looked at me. He shoved past Reese and stormed up the stairs.

"Conrad, *don't*," I called out, but he was already gone, taking the steps two at a time.

I spun to Reese, breathless. "Stop him."

Reese didn't hesitate. He ran up the stairs after him, and I followed.

Conrad shoved past everyone to get to the helm where Nina was, totally unaware of the trouble brewing.

Reese lunged.

He grabbed Conrad's shoulder, yanking him back just as he reached the helm. Nina screamed. Conrad spun around, swinging. But Reese dodged, catching his wrist midair and slamming him back. The yacht jerked from the sudden weight hitting the helm.

People gasped.

Heads turned.

"We don't need to do this, Conrad," Reese said.

"You want to know why you've always been a fucking disappointment?" Conrad sneered and stepped closer. "Because you never *listen*. You don't shut up long enough to realize that no one —*no one*—cares what you think."

Reese gritted his teeth.

"If you just listened instead of running your damn mouth all the time, then maybe Mom and Dad would have loved you. Maybe Dad would've trusted you with something real instead of just *tolerating* you."

Reese's eyes flashed dark, but he didn't flinch. "That's funny, because last time I checked, you don't do shit without Daddy's approval. Or have you convinced yourself you're actually in charge?"

"You see everyone here?" Conrad whirled around to face the crowd. "They're here for me. Me! Not you. Never you. That's how it is and will always be."

"You mean they're here for Dad's money. Same as you," Reese said.

"You know why we were never close? Because I never wanted to be associated with a fucking disappointment." Conrad leaned closer. "You always needed saving, Reese. From Dad, from school, from yourself. Pathetic."

Reese's jaw clenched. "Maybe if you weren't such a selfish, spineless bastard, I wouldn't have had to do it *alone*. I wanted my brother to love me, was that wrong?"

"Save the sentimental bullshit, Reese. Because if you were in my spot, you wouldn't do the same thing as me?" Conrad chuckled.

Reese moved forward. "And what does that make you?

Scared? Dickless? You rather take the easy way." His laugh was bitter. "You can steal my ideas, take my job, hell, you can *try* to be me—but you'll always be nothing more than a fucking fraud."

Conrad lunged forward, yanking Reese's shirt collar, the sound of ripping fabric tearing through the sudden silence. "Say that again."

Reese shoved him back. "Fraud."

Conrad *snapped*. With a merciless thud, he collided into Reese, the combined weight sending them both crashing into the wooden wheel with a splintering sound. Their weight yanked the wheel hard to port.

The yacht tilted, throwing everyone off-balance with a earsplitting creak of the hull.

Screams.

The second punch landed, Reese's fist meeting Conrad's jaw, sending a spray of blood arcing through the air as Conrad's head snapped violently to the side. Conrad stumbled, recovering in a flash, and connected with a vicious right, his knuckles cracking sharply against Reese's ribs. Reese grunted in pain.

Someone shouted, "Jesus Christ, stop them!"

Reese grabbed Conrad by the front of his shirt and drove him back, slamming him against the mast. The impact made the sail snap, ropes whipping dangerously overhead.

Conrad laughed through clenched teeth, blood on his lip. "Hit harder, little brother."

"Reese! Don't!" I shouted.

He landed another punch—this time to Conrad's stomach, making him double over. But before he could land another, Conrad twisted, using his weight to shove Reese back. The music cut out.

"Shit! Watch the wheel!" someone shouted, but the fight was moving too fast.

Conrad charged.

He tackled Reese, the force slamming them to the ground.

The wood splintered under their weight. Reese grabbed Conrad's collar and flipped them over, landing on top. He drove a fist into Conrad's face, then another.

And another.

But Conrad caught his arm and headbutted him.

A sharp, pained groan ripped from Reese's throat, his face contorted in agony. His hands went to his face, just enough for Conrad to roll them over, pinning Reese down. His hands clamped around Reese's throat, squeezing hard.

"You don't get to win," Conrad growled, his voice a low, venomous hiss. "You never get to win."

Water splashed over the side as the boat jerked dangerously close to the rocks.

He grabbed Conrad's wrist, trying to pry him off, but Conrad was unshaken, his grip tightening.

The yacht swayed hard again, nearly knocking them both over. More screams. More chaos.

"Conrad!" I turned to see Nina screaming.

A sharp, splintering *crack* echoed through the deck as the yacht teetered, too close to tipping, and people screamed—some scrambling to grab on to the railing, others falling into each other like pins.

"Let—go—" Reese gritted out.

But Conrad didn't listen.

I couldn't just *watch* this. I couldn't.

"Conrad!" I shout, my voice barely reaching over the crashing waves. "Stop!"

But it was no use. He was lost to rage. He didn't hear me. He didn't care.

I surged forward, my feet slipping on the slick deck, but I forced myself to push through. I reached out, my fingers gripping the back of Conrad's shirt, trying to pull him off Reese.

But Conrad was solid, like a damn boulder.

I pulled harder, determined to break this up before it was too late.

The yacht swayed again, more violently this time, and I lost my footing, stumbling backward.

"Laurene!" someone shouted as I was knocked off-balance.

But I wouldn't give up. Not when Reese needed me.

I lunged forward again, reaching out just as Conrad shifted his weight, his attention still solely on Reese. I grabbed his arm, pulling, yanking, using every bit of strength I had left.

Then my fist slammed into the side of Conrad's jaw, the contact jolting through my arm, pain flashing up my wrist. But I didn't hesitate. I swung again, landing another punch to his ribs, a satisfying grunt escaping him.

But then—

Conrad shoved me back, his eyes flashing with fury.

That was all the distraction Reese needed.

He slammed his knee into Conrad's side. Conrad grunted, his grip loosening just enough, and Reese punched him in the throat.

Conrad choked, stumbling back, grasping at his neck.

The boat jerked again, and this time, it felt like it might just capsize.

But no matter how bad it got, I couldn't tear my eyes away.

. But then my eyes locked on to the distant shoreline—and my stomach dropped like a stone.

The lighthouse. Its beam cut through the darkness, rotating like a warning, illuminating the jagged rocks below.

We were heading straight for them.

Reese didn't hesitate. He shoved him off. And Conrad went staggering back into the rail. For a moment, he teetered.

The rocks rose up out of the water, sharp and unforgiving, just beyond the light's reach. We were going to crash—I could feel it.

"Reese!" I screamed, my voice breaking through the chaos.

"Laurene!" Reese turned to see the imminent crash. He let go of Conrad, and started to run to me.

And then—*bang*.

The boat crashed into the jagged rocks, the impact shattering the night air with a deafening crack. I heard the wood splintering, breaking apart under the force. The boat jerked violently, and for a moment, everything was disoriented, as if the world itself was tilting upside down.

I heard a scream—Nina? I didn't know. It didn't matter. Everything was spinning.

The last thing I saw was Conrad's wide, shocked eyes before he went overboard.

A splash.

A crunch.

Then silence.

And Conrad was gone.

CHAPTER 32

Laurene

"NINA, what the hell are you doing?"

She held the gun steady, her eyes icy. "Be quiet and do what I tell you."

I swallowed, my voice shaky, but I pushed through. "What do you want from me?"

"What do I want?" She stepped forward, the barrel of the gun still locked on me, and she laughed. *"Everything."*

I backed up, not taking my eyes off her.

"Move again, and I'll shoot," she warned.

"What are you talking about? What did I do?"

Her eyes hardened as she took another step closer. "You killed Conrad. That's what you did."

The words hit me like a punch in the gut. My breath caught in my throat, my heart racing as I processed what she said. "What? I didn't—"

She swung her free hand, palm colliding hard with the side of my face. My head whipped to the right and a sharp pain radiated through my temple.

"Shut the fuck up." Nina's eyes were wild, almost unrecognizable. "Be cool, Laurene. You don't want this to get messy."

I stood there, dazed, my face burning with the sting of her slap.

"You're going to do exactly what I tell you, or I swear to God, it'll be your funeral next."

Her fingers tightened on the gun, and I locked my eyes on the barrel, terrified that one wrong move would be the end of me.

"Now walk."

I walked. As I stepped out of the hospital room, I glanced toward where the security detail usually stood—but they were gone. The hallway was quiet, too quiet. No guards. No Reese. No one.

"Where are the—"

"Getting rid of them was a nightmare," Nina cut in, sounding weirdly happy about it. "But I managed. You're welcome."

Welcome? I bit my tongue.

I forced myself to walk steadily past all the nurses and doctors, who were busy with other things. A conversation about a patient's vitals. The beep of machines in nearby rooms. A clipboard tucked under an arm. Life moved on around me like nothing was wrong, like I wasn't walking toward something I might not survive.

The elevator doors slid open. I hesitated for half a second— long enough for Nina to push me forward.

"Inside."

I stepped in, and she followed, close enough that I could feel the heat of her breath at my shoulder. The doors shut with a soft *ding*, sealing us in.

The metallic walls reflected us back—me, standing stiff and controlled, and Nina, standing behind me, the gun hidden from anyone who might see. But I could see it. The black shape against my back. The slight shake in her fingers.

I had only a few seconds to figure it out before we hit the ground floor. Before she got me outside.

Outside meant fewer people. Fewer distractions. Fewer chances to run.

I needed to act *now*.

The numbers above the doors ticked down.

Nine.

Eight.

Seven.

Nina shifted behind me, adjusting her grip.

Six.

Five.

I had to do something.

Four.

Three.

I exhaled slowly, schooling my voice into something careful. "Nina—"

"Shut up," she snapped, pressing the gun harder against my back.

Two.

One.

The doors slid open.

"You don't have to do this."

Nina shook her head. "Too late."

The cool night air rushed in from the hospital's main entrance, but it didn't soothe the fire burning under my skin. My pulse pounded, my instincts screaming at me to run, but before I could take a full run—

Pain exploded at my scalp.

I gasped as Nina yanked me back by my hair, her fingers twisting at the roots, sharp and unrelenting.

"Not so fast," she hissed, her breath hot against my ear.

She forced me across the dimly lit parking lot, dragging me toward a sleek black sedan, and I saw the dents in them.

She'd been the one that hit us.

"Get in the car." She shoved me toward the driver's side. "Drive."

She slid into the passenger seat, the gun pointed directly at me.

I swallowed hard, gripping the wheel. My mind raced, searching for an opening, a way out. But she was too close. And I didn't doubt for a second she'd pull the trigger if I so much as hesitated.

"Where?" I asked, barely a whisper.

Nina smirked.

"I'll tell you."

The directions were short and clipped, forcing us farther and farther from Lush. The city lights faded behind us, swallowed by the thick woods lining the road. I gripped the wheel, my mind racing.

Finally, we turned onto a gravel road, the tires crunching as we pulled up to a secluded cabin. It was old, the wood darkened with time, but something about it sent a jolt through me.

"Out."

I crept up, eyes glued to the place, my stomach churning as we got closer to those steps.

Then I saw it—the faintly carved emblem by the door.

Ashbourne.

"Hurry up," Nina hissed, her fingers tightening in my hair as she forced me up the steps. Her eyes flicked around, scanning the trees like she expected someone to be watching. The door creaked open, and the second I stepped inside, my breath caught.

The cabin wasn't abandoned.

A fire crackled low in the stone fireplace, the scent of burnt wood and something faintly spiced hanging in the air. A jacket was slung over the back of the couch, boots tucked neatly by the door.

"Sit," Nina ordered, shoving me toward a worn wooden chair in the middle of the room.

My gaze flicked to the table beside me, where two plates sat, remnants of a meal still clinging to them. The silverware was stacked, a half-full glass of wine and a half a cup of milk still waiting to be finished.

"Why are you really doing this, Nina?"

"I already told you," she snapped. "You killed Conrad."

"Has it been you the entire time?" My voice was quiet but steady. "The notes. The photos. The threats…" I swallowed. "The car crash?"

Nina's expression filled with satisfaction. "You and your damn family, pushing him, controlling him, suffocating him until there was nothing left of who he was. You were his fiancée. Not me. And you never deserved him."

My engagement to Conrad had been more of a formality—it had never been about love, not for me. But for Nina…

"He *loved* me," she hissed. "Not you. Never you."

Oh my God.

"How long?"

Nina's fingers flexed on the gun, her jaw tight.

"Longer than you," she said. "Long enough for him to *need* me before you ever got your claws in him."

I stared at her, the pieces clicking into place.

Did Reese know? Pauline? Harold or Jennie?

My stomach turned. "When, Nina?"

Her lips curled into something almost smug. "Eight years ago."

I felt the floor tilt beneath me. That meant—

"And yet, you got to be the fiancée."

"How? When?" I asked. Why hadn't Conrad come forward with her? Why did he agree to marry me?

Nina began to pace in front of me. Swinging the gun back and forth in her hand.

"Two years before…*you*, he hired me as an assistant. I was just a nobody fresh out of school. But I was smart, and I was *good*, and he saw that." Her voice dropped, turning almost dreamy. "It started slow. Late nights. Takeout in his office. A hand on my back when I did something right. Then one night, we were celebrating a big deal, just the two of us, I kissed him first. I knew he wanted me, but he wouldn't cross that line—so I did it for him."

I clenched my jaw, heart pounding.

"That night was the first of many. We were careful. Secretive. But when we were together, it was real. I knew him in a way you never did."

"Then why did you both never take it public?"

"You think I didn't *want* to?" she snapped.

I held her gaze, ignoring the way my pulse hammered in my throat. *Keep her talking. Keep her distracted.* "So why didn't he?"

"Because he couldn't. Harold made that clear. He had a plan for Conrad, and I was never part of it. Conrad had to marry someone with money, not a poor girl from Kansas like me. He told him—straight to his face—that if he married someone like me, he could kiss the company goodbye." Her lips curled. "But *you*? You were perfect. Lush royalty. You had the name, the connections, the pedigree."

The gun in her hand wavered slightly as she spoke, her fingers tightening and loosening around the grip. *What a fucking bastard.*

I shifted slightly in the chair, careful not to move too fast. "You think I *asked* for the engagement?"

"Conrad had a plan. He was gonna get us out of here. He was giving me money... Then it stopped." Her head snapped toward me, eyes narrowing. "The second he put that ring on your finger, he changed. Stopped calling. Stopped looking at me like I was *his*."

"We were trying to find a way out," I told her. "Reese and I."

"You ruined everything! You destroyed my life, and now you're going to pay for it!"

"I'm sorry, Nina. Truly, I am. I didn't know. Maybe all of us could have come to an agreement or helped each other out—"

I took in the room around me as Nina ranted, searching for

any clue that might give me an out. My gaze fell on an old family portrait on the wall. The Ashbourne family, all smiles.

"So why stay after the accident?"

Nina froze for just a moment, her eyes flickering to the portrait as if she could see Conrad's ghost haunting her. She didn't answer right away.

"Conrad left me millions," she said at last, her voice almost wistful, but her eyes were hard as stone. "Took it from the company. He left this cabin for me too. But I'm running out of money. I have a lifestyle to maintain."

My stomach churned.

"And you want to know the best part?" She took a step closer, pointing the gun at me again, the barrel steady against my chest. "I've been stealing from the company. Pauline gave me access to all the books. All the accounts. I was pulling money from every angle I could—nobody noticed. Till Reese stopped things. That's when I demanded my twenty million. So where is it, Laurene?"

Shit, Reese had been right to not pay.

I steadied my breath, looking directly into her eyes. She was broken—there was no question about that. But there was something else beneath her anger. Something raw. Desperate. Maybe, just maybe, I could get through to her.

"Nina," I said gently. "You've been through hell, I know that. But taking me isn't going to fix anything. It won't bring Conrad back. It won't make anything right."

"You don't get what you've done. What you took from me. He was mine."

"I didn't take anything from you." I shook my head. "Conrad...he loved you. But he was trapped, Nina. Trapped by the same things I was. We were all trapped."

The gun wavered just slightly in her hands, but the fire in her eyes remained. "And Reese? What about him? He hated Conrad. I'm sure that's what you two planned, kill him off?"

"No, Nina. That's not what happened." I was trying to stay

calm, trying to make her understand. "We just wanted Conrad to end the engagement. He took it too far."

Nina's face twisted, disbelief flashing across her expression, but she didn't lower the gun. "Liar."

I caught the glint of something on the table—a knife resting just inches away.

"On the boat, when I went downstairs, I needed a moment to myself before we told him. When I came out the bathroom, Conrad was there. I thought I could convince him. Conrad said no. That's the truth."

"That's a lie."

I shifted slightly in my chair, careful not to draw attention to my subtle movements toward the knife.

"He said he wouldn't lose the life he had."

Nina's face twisted, confusion and rage battling for dominance. "You're a liar. Before we got on the boat, he told me he wanted out. He said we'd be free together. He promised me."

"Nina—"

"You did something. You and Reese—he wouldn't have changed his mind. Not unless you forced him to."

I could see it now—the way she was *breaking*, piece by piece.

"You backed him into a corner, didn't you?" she accused, stepping closer. The gun shook, but her voice sharpened. "You turned him against me."

I shook my head. "No, Nina. That's not—"

"Shut up!" She slammed her free hand against the wall. The gun jerked with the motion, and for a split second, I thought she was going to pull the trigger. "I know what I heard. I know what he told me. And you—you're just trying to twist it."

I swallowed hard. "I think you're grieving, Nina."

"So that's what you're saying?" Her voice dropped, low and lethal. "That Conrad turned on me?"

I didn't move. Didn't breathe.

"Why else would he have said no? Why he wouldn't have agreed to our deal? Unless he had another plan," I said.

"Conrad loved his life, and he might have loved it more than you."

The gun wavered—it moved like she was deciding whether to aim it right at my head or heart.

"You think I don't see what you're doing?" she whispered. "You're trying to get inside my head, make me doubt him."

She started pacing, sharp, jerky movements, her free hand pulling at her hair.

"He wouldn't do that to me. He wouldn't." Nina's head snapped toward me, her entire face contorted in fury. "Say it!" she screamed. "Say that Conrad didn't turn on me!"

My heart slammed against my ribs. If I lied, she might see through it. If I told the truth—

"Maybe he was never going to leave with you. He loved his status. Would he give that up for you like you thought?"

Her breath caught.

"Maybe he wanted you to believe that," I continued, "so you wouldn't question what he was really doing."

"Stop it."

"Maybe Conrad was only telling you what you wanted to hear."

"Stop it!"

Her hand jerked—her finger pulling against the trigger just slightly.

I swallowed, forcing my voice to stay calm. "He stole money, Nina. He stole Reese's ideas. That was never about you. He said he changed things, maybe he wanted to give the money back and stay? This life is the only one he knew."

"You don't know that," she whispered.

I tilted my head. "Neither do you."

Her lips parted, and for a second, I could see her working through it—every possibility, every question she never let herself ask.

Then, I struck.

"But Reese does. He found Conrad's journal."

Her entire body snapped taut.

"If you want the truth, you need his journal. Maybe Conrad did plan to run off with you, but he changed his mind at some point. Maybe he was gonna tell you or not," I said, voice quiet but firm. "You need to know what he wrote."

Nina's fingers twitched around the gun, and she lowered it slightly. I launched myself sideways out of the chair, my arm swinging out to grab the knife.

Bang!

A deafening gunshot ripped through the air. The bullet punched into the wooden chair where I'd been sitting.

Too close.

I crashed into the table, grabbing the knife. I twisted on the ground, the steel handle cold in my fingers. Nina was already turning back toward me, her face twisting in rage.

I swung.

The knife sliced through the air, catching her across the arm. A shallow gash, not deep enough to stop her, but enough to make her scream in pain. She staggered back, clutching her arm in pain, and I lunged forward, our bodies colliding with a thud. Hard.

We hit the floor, and the gun skidded across the wooden planks. Her long nails dug into my skin, leaving burning red marks as her knee smashed into my ribs. I started to lift the knife, but she grabbed my wrist and pulled it away. I twisted, feeling the muscles in my back strain as I used my weight to roll us over. The cabin spun. Nina was under me, and I was on top.

I drove the knife down.

Her fingers closed around my wrist, a surprising firmness in her grip. We struggled, arms shaking, the blade inches from her throat. I pressed down and she dug her fingers into me; it was scary how strong she was, even hurt.

"Fucking die!" she screamed, bucking beneath me.

With a sharp twist, she wrenched my arm sideways, and I heard a sickening crack. The knife slipped from my grasp. A cold wave of fear washed over me, and my stomach lurched violently.

Then she punched me square in the jaw.

My head snapped back, vision blurring for a split second.

That was all she needed.

With a sudden, harsh shove, she sent me tumbling. I hit the floor, gasping, but I was already up and moving. I scrambled for the knife, and she went for the gun.

I'm not dying tonight.

I grabbed the knife, twisted—and drove it into her side.

A gurgle escaped her lips, as the gun clattered to the ground. For a second, neither of us moved. Her fingers trembled against her side, blood pooling beneath her palm.

I took a shaky step back.

"I can't die, Laurene." She turned her head. "I can't... My son."

What the fuck?

"Your son? What son?"

She nodded, and she stumbled, clutching the knife in her side.

"Conrad's son," she rasped.

Conrad's son?

Conrad had a son. A child.

She lifted her blood-soaked hand, as if to reach out to me. "I never meant for any of this to happen."

I took a step back. She was still standing, but then a moment of evil clarity appeared in her eyes, and Nina's gaze flicked to the gun on the floor.

I bolted.

The door burst open behind me as I hurled myself through it, my balance breaking. I tumbled down the stairs, my knees slamming into the dirt, but I barely felt it. Adrenaline burned through my veins.

A gunshot cracked the air.

I flinched, ducking instinctively, but I didn't stop.

My legs were already driving forward, knees pumping high, feet tearing through the thick, clawing underbrush. Thorns scraped at my skin, twigs snapped underfoot, and dry leaves crunched as the woods swallowed me whole.

I heard Nina behind me. "You can't run away!"

Another shot rang out, the bullet whizzing past me into a tree.

I had to live. For my siblings, for the dream of owning my gallery, for Reese. I envisioned a future with him: kids, a house, growing old together.

I couldn't let her win.

The staccato bursts of gunfire echoed around me, and I wondered how many bullets she had left as I ducked and dodged. I crashed through the clearing, lungs on fire, sweat blurring my vision. Each breath was like swallowing glass, sharp and ragged. The only thought pounding in my head—I had to make it to the road.

Back to town. Back to someone. Anyone.

I burst through the tree line, and my feet hit concrete, but I was moving too fast—I stumbled and pitched forward, hitting the ground. My palms scraped against the rough pavement, skin tearing. Dazed, I lifted my head—just in time to see the blinding glare of headlights bearing down on me.

Tires screamed.

The car swerved, skidding across the asphalt, missing me by inches. The wind from it blasted against my skin, the scent of burnt rubber choking the air.

I pushed myself up, turning to see the car skidded to a halt, into the ditch on the side of the road.

Then the door opened.

Reese.

And beside him, Dante?

A sob clawed up my throat, but no sound came out. My body locked up, torn between relief and the sheer terror still clinging to my skin.

"Laurene!"

He was already moving, his feet pounding against the pavement.

Before I could blink, he was in front of me, kneeling, his hands gripping my arms as he lifted me to my feet. Heat radiated off him, his chest rising and falling just as fast as mine.

"Nina," I gasped, my voice barely above a whisper. "It's been Nina the whole time."

I turned to Dante, and there were no sly looks and grins. He looked both relieved and horrified to see me.

Reese looked back at him and said, "He stayed at the hospital. He saw her take you just as I got there."

Then—*crunch*.

My blood ran cold.

Nina.

She lurched forward from the tree line, her body swaying, a grotesque silhouette against the moonlight. Blood soaked her side, dripping in thick rivulets down her arm, but she barely seemed to notice.

With an eerie slowness, she reached down, fingers curling around the hilt of the knife buried in her flesh. She yanked it free. The sound—a nasty, *wet* suction of steel leaving muscle—turned my stomach.

A wicked smile stretched across her lips, her hand shaking violently as she lifted the gun.

"No!"

The shot rang out.

Reese thrust me aside with a grunt, the force knocking me off-balance. I hit the ground hard, just in time to see the bullet punch into his chest.

No.

A strangled scream ripped from my throat. Reese stumbled, his body jerking from the impact before crumpling onto the concrete. Blood spilled beneath him, dark and spreading fast.

"Reese! No—*no!*" My voice cracked, panic choking me as I scrambled toward him.

Dante was already moving, his attack so sudden that Nina barely had time to react. He tackled her to the ground, the gun flying from her grasp as they tumbled, the dirt spraying up around them.

But it didn't matter.

Not while the shallow, rasping sound of Reese's breath filled the air.

His eyes were hazy, unfocused, but they found mine.

"Reese, please," I begged. "Please, don't—don't leave me. I love you, stay awake. Stay with me, baby."

His trembling hand weakly reached for mine, his skin cold and clammy.

"I love you too," he breathed, the words barely audible. A sudden darkness clouded his eyes; his hand, growing cold and still, slipped from my grasp.

A cacophony of sirens filled the air, growing louder and closer, a desperate, hopeless sound, but it was agonizingly too late.

CHAPTER 33

Reese

"WHY WON'T HE WAKE UP?"

I fought to focus, but my brain was all fuzzy. I was so tired, and the darkness was so comforting. But I didn't need to open my eyes to know who it was. Laurene. She sounded fragile, barely holding it together.

Papers shuffled quietly; someone was looking through a document. "Your husband lost a lot of blood."

"Oh lord, he gonna die!" Gigi screamed, and immediately I heard the room calming her down.

"Please, Gigi, we don't need that right now," Serena snapped.

"I can't lose him," Laurene murmured. I felt the pressure of her hand wrapping around mine, the warmth of her touch grounding me. "I can't, please."

"Lu. You need to get some sleep. You've been here for three days," Erik said.

"He gonna die!" Gigi wailed again, and this time Walter started to howl.

"*Georgiana,*" Vincent snapped.

Three days? My mind was all over the place, like a broken puzzle.

Nina.

I rushed to our Vegas office after leaving Harold, and Nathan showed me my mother's transactions. A quick call to my mom confirmed it all. She had trusted Nina, let her have access to her accounts for years, never realizing Nina had been siphoning cash from us, hiding it right under our noses.

"Can't you wake him up, Doctor?" Gigi said.

"You've been asking that question for the past hour, Gigi. The answer's still the same," Serena snapped. "He'll wake up when he's ready."

"I'm just saying! Shine a flashlight in his eyes? Give him those poppers? Stick a thermometer up his butt?" Gigi said. "I can get him awake."

"*No!*" the room shouted and suddenly the bed rocked dangerously and commotion happened before everyone quieted down.

"The bullet came close to his heart. It was an intense surgery." The doctor's voice was steady, but I could hear the weight of it. "He just needs to rest."

"But he's not gonna die?" Noelle's voice was soft as she asked, and Gigi made a sound of agreement.

"No. For the tenth time, no." The doctor's voice was firm.

"This is embarrassing," Serena muttered.

I wanted to say something—anything—to assure them all. But the words wouldn't come. My mind was trapped and my eyes were closed.

Nina had been too close, too involved for years.

How had we missed it? How had I missed it?

"How about *I* wake him up since he wanna take his time?" Gigi said, and I felt something shift on my right side. Suddenly there was a violent shake to my shoulders, and I felt myself be lifted and then everybody was shouting and Gigi was arguing back. "He ain't dying up in here and haunting our family! I rebuke it."

A groan escaped me as I plopped back down, and I tried to force my eyes open.

Light bled into the darkness, soft at first, then too sharp, too bright. I blinked sluggishly, the world around me a mess of shifting, distorted shapes—blurry outlines stretching and bending.

Slowly, the room began to come into focus, the outlines of faces forming, and the entire King family and Noelle were staring at me with wide eyes.

I turned my head just enough to see her.

Laurene.

Her smile was the first thing I saw, soft and warm, her brown eyes glistening with unshed tears.

I could feel my lips curve into a smile, instinctively, and despite the pain in my chest, I couldn't help it. "Damn it's good to see your face, Mrs. Ashbourne."

Laurene let out a breathless laugh, as she cupped my face. "You scared the hell out of me."

Before I could answer, her lips crashed into mine, warm and desperate, stealing the breath right from my lungs. It wasn't soft. It wasn't careful. It was everything—relief, fear, love—all pouring into one kiss that deepened as I pulled her closer, ignoring the pull of pain in my chest. Her fingers tangled in my hair, my hand sliding over her waist, and for a moment, the world faded into nothing but the heat between us.

Then—

A loud, pointed *ahem* broke through the air, followed by an exaggerated groan.

"Oh my God, get a damn room," Gigi drawled, sounding both amused and disgusted. "He just woke up, can he breathe first?"

A chorus of muffled laughter followed, and Laurene tore herself away, her cheeks flushed as she shot a glare toward the door. "You could leave."

Gigi smirked, arms crossed. "Can I just say, my method woke you up. Everybody in here needs to give me an apology."

The room erupted in chatter.

The doctor's voice cut through the chaos. "Well, now that Mr. Ashbourne is awake, be easy with him. He needs rest."

He gave us a final glance before leaving the room.

I turned to Laurene, my gaze locking with hers.

"What happened with Nina?" My voice was rusty, barely a whisper.

Her face softened, and I could see the pain in her eyes. "She's in jail. She's not going anywhere."

I let out a sigh of relief.

Before I could get a word in, the door creaked open. My mother stepped in. "Finally! Look who's come to see you."

From behind her, David wheeled in Jennie.

Bruised and battered, but alive. No tubes, no IVs. Just her, looking stronger than I expected.

"Wow," she said with a weak smile. "I thought I looked bad."

Everyone laughed, including me, despite the pain.

But then, something caught my attention. Jennie wasn't just holding on to the wheelchair. No, she was cradling something in her arms—something small, wrapped in a soft, pink blanket.

I blinked.

"Meet your niece," Jennie said as she rocked the baby gently in her arms. "Faith."

The room seemed to quiet for a second as I took in the sight of the tiny girl, her face still partially hidden beneath the blanket. My niece. Faith. A fragile piece of our future.

David moved the chair closer to the bed, and Jennie carefully positioned the baby so I could see her better. The little one's blue eyes fluttered open for just a moment before closing again. I couldn't stop staring.

Laurene's hand rested lightly on my shoulder.

I reached out with trembling fingers and touched the baby's teeny hand, marveling at the softness of her skin.

"I don't think I've ever been this speechless," I muttered, still looking at the baby in awe.

"Don't get too attached to the quiet, Reese. She's mine," Jennie teased, and offered her to me. "Wanna hold her?"

I nodded, the baby's gentle scent filling my nose as I carefully accepted her into my arms. I watched her chest go up and down. I looked up, and Laurene was smiling back.

"I love you," I told her.

Laurene's eyes softened, and she reached out, her fingers brushing the baby's cheek.

"We made it," she said, her voice barely above a whisper. "Against everything—we *made it*."

Conrad. Yvonne. Nina. Harold. The weight of the past, this town, all the forces that tried to tear us apart.

And yet, here we were, still standing.

The world hadn't won. We had.

And as I looked at Laurene, at the life we'd fought for, I knew this was only the beginning.

CHAPTER 34

Laurene

MONTHS LATER...

A LOW HUM OF CONVERSATION, punctuated by laughter and the clinking of champagne flutes, filled the gallery. The surrounding walls were adorned with pieces from local artists mixed with the masterpieces.

"Laurene King," a voice called from behind me. I turned to see an older woman, dressed impeccably in a tailored black suit, her cane hitting the floor steadily. "You've truly outdone yourself this time."

"It's Laurene Ashbourne now, Mrs. Fontaine," I said. "Thank you for coming. How is the *Lush Chronicles* doing?"

She raised her glass. "Perfect! I have great things to write. You are just what we needed here in Lush. Your grandfather Benjamin would be proud."

I let myself take it all in—the crowd, the art, the strange mix of pride and vulnerability tightening in my chest. This wasn't just an exhibit; it was a declaration. A way of saying, *I'm still here.*

Then I saw him.

Reese stood near the back of the room.

He wasn't in a tuxedo like the others. Reese wore a black blazer and crisp, unbuttoned white shirt, showing skin. The slight shine on his polished black leather boots caught the light, and I thought again about how sexy my husband was.

He stood there like he owned the space, one hand casually tucked in his pocket, the other holding a drink he hardly touched. His eyes were on a painting in front of him.

I calmly walked over, despite feeling a jumble of emotions.

"Where have you been hiding?"

"The exhibit is amazing, baby." He turned, his green eyes locking on to mine.

His gaze softened, and without a word, his hand slid around my waist, pulling me in flushed against him. The air between us thickened as his other hand cupped my face, his fingers brushing against my skin like he was claiming it.

Then, he kissed me—slow, deliberate, and almost too soft at first, as if he were savoring every second. I melted against him, the heat of his body seeping into mine. The kiss deepened, and for a moment, nothing else mattered. But as much as I wanted to stay, I pulled away, the air between us now crackling with something far too dangerous to ignore.

"Careful, Reese," I whispered, looking at his chest. He was still healing.

"I'm fine," he murmured, his thumb wiping some of my gloss of his lips. "Just needed that."

Gigi shrieked, and when I looked, she was glaring at Erik. Noelle, standing close by, was trying not to laugh.

"We need more wine! Greedy-ass Erik drained it all." Gigi stormed past, holding an empty glass.

Jennie and David stood before a large abstract canvas nearby. Jennie held Faith close, her peaceful face nestled against Jennie's chest, tiny fists curled up adorably.

Reese and I strolled toward a massive bronze sculpture, the smooth, soulful sounds of live jazz filling the air.

"I hope you know I just made a sizeable donation," Reese said as he tilted his head, looking at the sculpture.

I lifted a brow. "Oh really? And to what cause, Mr. Ashbourne?"

Reese glanced at me, a smile on his lips. "The gallery, obviously. You've been busting your ass to make this exhibit happen, and I wanna support the arts and my wife."

I felt a smile pull at the corners of my own lips, but I fought it back, crossing my arms and keeping my cool. "I see," I said slowly. "And I have to thank you in some kinda way."

A wicked glint filled his eyes.

"Hmm… There are some ways. Preferably with you naked. But I care about you—what matters to you."

I laughed, hugging him tighter but being mindful of his wound.

Nina was in jail for blackmailing, stalking, and almost killing Jennie, Faith, Reese, and me. She'd likely never see the outside world again.

I glanced around the room and found Pauline standing near the far corner, a little boy beside her, about eight years old, holding her hand. His hair was dark brown, tousled in that playful way, and his face carried a mix of both his parents—Conrad's strong jawline and Nina's features, but his eyes were exactly like Reese's.

Green and full of life.

That was why Nina had demanded the money.

She'd been raising Alex in that cabin, homeschooling him, and no one had ever known. A DNA test had confirmed it: Alex was indeed related and Conrad's son. Pauline had adopted him, and hopefully when Harold was done with treatment, he'd get to meet his oldest grandchild.

My heart ached for Alex; he had been caught in the crossfire of his mother's choices. But Jennie and Reese were helping raise him, my family would help too, and he would never experience what his father had felt.

"Laurene." I turned to see the mayor approach.

"Dante," I greeted him. "It's good to see you."

Dante had helped in ways I hadn't expected. I still didn't fully trust him, but he'd been an ally. Just like he'd said from the beginning. Something was brewing, and I figured it was best to keep him close.

"Congratulations on the exhibit," he said, his gaze flicking around the room. "Impressive work. Tourism is up in town. You sure I can't pull you away from Arthur and have you run our tourism department?"

"No, but thank you."

"It was nice seeing both of you." He nodded at Reese, who, to my surprise, nodded back. "Looking forward to working with you *again*."

The "again" hung in the air between us.

As he turned and walked away, my thoughts briefly shifted to the guilt that always seemed to follow me when I thought about the ten million I'd originally taken from Dante. I'd given it back, of course, but the weight of it lingered—especially since I knew it could have gone against my mother. But I couldn't shake the feeling that I'd walked too close to a dangerous line.

On the other hand, thanks to Daddy, I'd been able to receive my inheritance no strings attached and even more.

Arthur had even surprised me. I'd gotten a bonus during my recent employee evaluation—a substantial bonus. Money was soaring again, and I had more than enough to start my gallery.

"Did you ever think we'd have this?" he said, motioning to our family across the room.

"I didn't," I admitted, my heart swelling with warmth. "But look at us now. A happy ending."

Reese's new line, Rebel Spirits, was doing amazing. His infused liquor flowed freely at the party, and I watched as the guests enjoyed their drinks. It was going to be successful.

I grinned, reaching up to kiss him.

Arthur appeared. "Laurene, it's time for your speech."

"You got this, baby." Reese kissed me again.

I slipped my hand from his and made my way to the small stage at the front of the room.

"Good afternoon, everyone," I began. "Thank you all for being here today. This exhibit is incredibly special to me, not just because of the talent behind the works, but because of the stories they tell."

As I spoke, I let my gaze wander over the paintings, taking in the faces, the art, the life that filled the gallery. This was my sanctuary, my place of strength.

"These pieces are more than just art. This collection is a testament to the power of art to heal, to inspire, and to connect us in ways that words often cannot. Each piece on these walls represents a journey. These artists have created something truly remarkable for us to experience today."

I glanced over at Reese, finding him in the crowd. His presence gave me strength, grounding me in the moment. I continued, feeling more confident as I spoke.

"As a curator, my role is to bring these stories together, to create a space where they can resonate with each of you. Today, I hope that you find something in these works that speaks to you, something that challenges you, or even something that heals you."

My voice remained steady as I spoke. I could hear someone's heels clicking on the floor. I looked over to the entrance.

Mama was standing in the doorway.

The sight of her in that moment caught me off guard. My heart pounded, but I continued speaking.

"I have one more thing I want to share with you all." I cleared my throat. "It is with great honor that I announce today that the gallery has become the second major donor to the King Foundation for Change. After nearly six years, my family's foundation will be reinstated in honor of my grandfather, Ben."

The crowd clapped, and I glanced over at my parents. My mother's expression shifted, a quick, visceral change. Noelle, my sisters, Erik, and Reese's family cheered.

I'd changed my mind. Lush was my home. Lush was in *me*. That meant I was going to make it a better place like all the Kings before me. It might be better. With Daddy's blessing, in addition to my job at the gallery, I would be the president of the nonprofit.

Also, I liked working with Arthur and the team. My own gallery could wait for now.

"I also want to thank my family for their unwavering support in everything I do, especially my husband, Reese, the love of my life."

A warm, genuine smile spread across Reese's face.

"And to all of you here today, thank you for being a part of this moment. It's your presence and your belief in what we're doing that makes it all possible."

With that, I stepped back slightly, giving a nod to Arthur and the gallery team. The room applauded, and I felt a surge of pride. Reese instantly swept me into his arms once I stepped off the stage.

"You were perfect," he whispered, making me blush.

But I looked back over my shoulder at Mama, who had turned and was staring at the *Unequal Marriage* by Vasili Pukirev.

I patted Reese's shoulders. "Excuse me."

I walked slowly. Mama's back was to me, her posture still stiff. I stopped a few feet away from her. A long silence hung between us. I studied the painting in front of me and I wondered if that's what she saw when she looked at me—her finest artwork.

"You did a good job," she said finally. Clipped.

I nodded. "Thanks."

For a moment, she stood there, quiet. Slowly, she turned to me, her expression unreadable.

Then, as if the dam had finally broken, her face relaxed.

"I'm sorry," she said, her voice raw in a way I hadn't heard in years. "For everything. For pushing you to be perfect all the time. For not seeing you as a person, as my daughter, but as some…some pawn in this game I was playing."

Her words came out in a rush, and I stayed silent, letting her speak.

"I didn't handle Grandpa Ben's sickness, his death, the way I should've," she continued. "I was scared. I was hurt. And all I could think about was keeping our family together—keeping us on our throne. But I pushed everyone away in the process, didn't I?"

"You did."

"I've been so damn wrong, Laurene," she said, her voice thick now. "It feels overwhelming right now. Choosing where to start to fix things. I know I have to apologize to everyone at some point."

I nodded slowly, not trusting myself to speak. She was finally admitting it, but I had so much more to say.

"I'm so proud of you," she whispered, the words almost like a prayer. "You're the best woman I could've ever hoped you grow into. You did it all on your own. You've made our legacy proud."

I swallowed hard, my throat tight, and a tear escaped my eye.

"I don't know about therapy… I'm considering it. Right now I'm meditating, speaking with somebody *informally*. No therapists yet. When I'm ready I'll go."

"As long as you make the change," I said, and then Mama stepped closer, and before I could say anything, she pulled me into a hug.

I froze, every muscle in my body locking up. The shock hit me like a punch to the gut. This was the last thing I expected. The last thing I ever thought she'd do.

My mind screamed to pull away, but my body didn't move. I just stood there, my heart pounding in my chest.

You know what to do, my conscience said.

Slowly I lifted my arms, and hugged her back.

I don't know how long we stood there, but when we released one another, I saw a tear fall from her face.

"Excuse me," Mama said, wiping it quickly. She brushed past me and I watched her go, disappearing into the crowd and around a corner.

I felt Reese's arms around me. "Everything okay?"

"Perfect," I nodded, my brain reeling.

"Since you are the curator, I think I need a VIP tour of the collection, beginning in your office."

I couldn't help but laugh softly, rolling my eyes. "You really can't resist, can you?"

He leaned down and I kissed him again. "Let's start in my office, but I may have to end it early if you make a lot of noise."

"I'll be quiet." He grinned.

I was home.

Finally, where I belonged.

With him.

Epilogue

A YEAR LATER...

"A GIRLS' brunch, at last!" Noelle exclaimed, relaxing.

It was one of those rare heat waves in Northern California and everyone was out and about. Tourists filled the beach. Boats filled the marina and beyond.

"You think they can give us some shots?" Gigi frowned as the waiter placed another glass of wine in front of her, her oversize sunglasses perched atop her head. Walter barked excitedly from the high chair she insisted the staff bring out for him.

"Girl, it's a brunch. Ain't nobody doing shots," Serena said dryly, stirring her cappuccino despite the heat.

"Oh, so now you're a saint?" Gigi shot back, her perfectly arched brow lifting. "I seem to remember somebody dancing on tables at *that* New Year's party."

"*Years ago*, and you drugged me," Serena said.

"Drugged? Girl, it was *gin*. And I told you before you drank it that gin will fuck you up, but nooo, you had to have three glasses and then you were twerking on Mrs. Dupont's geriatric husband."

I snorted, covering my mouth, and Serena glared over at me. "I'm sorry, but that was funny."

"We came here to celebrate, or did I turn down my Grammy-winning rapper's offer of an all-exclusive trip to Madrid for nothing? Let's party! We've made fucking accomplishments this year."

That was true. The gallery was thriving. The town was raking in money. Reese and I were better than ever. Arthur had told me just last week that I had turned Lush into a destination, his grin so wide it could've cracked glass.

And the King Foundation for Change?

Just hit its one-year anniversary. The gala we hosted last month raised over half a million dollars, doubling the number of scholarships we could award this year. I just knew Grandpa and Augustus King would've been proud.

My phone buzzed, interrupting my thoughts, and Reese's name lit up for the fifth time.

"You know he's gonna find you sooner or later." Noelle raised a brow and sipped her mimosa.

"So?" I replied, dropping the phone back into my purse. "I need a break. I told him to go ride his bike or something."

"Married life, couldn't be me. I like my freedom." Gigi sniffed.

I reached for my drink and looked at Serena, ignoring G. "How's the acquisition going?"

Serena's mouth thinned, and she looked back down at her cappuccino. I knew running King's Development had been Serena's pride and joy, but lately I heard less and less about it.

"Ass," Gigi said, taking another sip of wine and winking at Serena. "It's *ass*, and she ain't even tell Mama yet."

"Mind your business. You don't even have a job," Serena snapped.

"My parents are millionaires." Gigi swatted her braids over her shoulders. "My only responsibilities are looking good and shopping. Don't blame me 'cause you wanna be all independent and shit. I'm soaking up *all* my nepotism."

My phone buzzed on the table again. Reese, again.

"Girl, if he's called you one more time..." Gigi swirled the last bit of mimosa in her glass. "Y'all good, right? Or should we be worried? I can't be a child of divorce."

"We're fine," I said quickly. "He's just…being protective after everything."

"He's being *clingy*," Gigi quipped, sitting up straighter. "Noelle, can you put a tracking device in Laurene's phone or something for him? So he doesn't keep killing our vibe?"

Noelle rolled her eyes, the corners of her lips twitching in amusement. "I have better things to do than that."

"Like what?" Gigi asked.

"Like trying to track down my biological parents."

"*What!*" my sisters and I screamed. I knew years ago Noelle had been interested in her birth parents, but the McKenzies adored Noelle, and after a while she stopped bring up searching for them.

"That's…big," I said softly. "Have you found anything?"

"Not yet. But I'm making progress. It's hard but I'm slowly pulling records. It's a lot of reading and tossing out junk. I just —" She paused, letting out a small breath. "It's important for my doctors to know."

"You're gonna find them," I said, reaching out to squeeze her hand.

Before Noelle could respond, her phone buzzed loudly this time.

"Speaking of unstoppable," she muttered, checking the screen. "If Adam calls me one more time asking for a meeting—"

"It's not Adam," a deep, familiar voice cut her off from behind us.

I turned, and there was Reese.

He looked pissed…and sexy.

His jaw was tight, his green eyes dark with something unreadable, but the slow, deliberate way he held himself sent a thrill down my spine.

"Hey, baby," I said, trying and failing to hide the surprise in my voice.

"Don't sweet-talk me," he said, leaning down to kiss me before glancing at the others. "Ladies."

"Hi, Reese," they all said simultaneously, and I glared at each of them.

Traitors.

"You're not answering my calls." Reese frowned as he picked up my glass. "That better not be wine you're drinking or that's a spanking."

I flushed in embarrassment. *"Reese!"*

"Gag." Gigi made a face.

He took the glass out my hand and took a sip.

"Oh, cranberry juice."

"Cranberry juice?" Gigi said and she glared at me. "I thought we were throwing back mimosas?"

"I—"

"Laurene's pregnant," Reese said, downing the rest of my drink.

The table went completely still for a moment. Then, Gigi's face lit up, and she let out a loud, dramatic scream that shook the entire patio, and a waiter nearly dropped a tray.

"What?" she yelled, sitting up straight, her hands flying to her mouth in excitement. "Oh my God, Lulu, you're pregnant? Wait, does that mean I gotta start shopping for my future niece?"

Noelle's face broke into a wide smile, and she threw her arms out across the table to hug me. "Oh, honey, you're gonna be a mama!"

I opened my mouth to said something, but Gigi was already going off, making plans.

"I gotta get her all the flyest little outfits. Like, we're talking the cutest little designer onesies. Chanel, Gucci, Prada! Nothing but the best for her, oh my. I need to fly over to Rome and get Isabella to make a custom bootie set—"

Serena raised a brow. "It could be a boy, you know."

"Doesn't matter. I'm making sure my niece or nephew is the freshest baby on the block, okay?" She had her phone out and was typing rapidly. "Don't worry about nothing when it comes to clothes!"

Noelle clapped her hands, almost spilling her mimosa. "This is *so* exciting! Someone needs to tell Erik. Oh, you better believe I'm throwing a baby shower for you. Whatever you need, I'm in. I can try my new recipes…"

Serena gave a small smile. "I'll find a new house for y'all immediately. If you want me to manage the foundation while you're on maternity, no worries."

"You guys are crazy," I muttered, my voice tight with a mix of nerves and relief.

Noelle, Gigi, and Serena were already making plans and arrangements, and Reese leaned down into my ear.

"Come on," he said, pulling me gently to my feet. "Let's get you home. You need to rest."

He took my hand, and I let him lead me out of the café, which my sisters and Noelle didn't even notice in their heated debate. The salty air from the ocean, just a few blocks away, teased the breeze as we walked toward his car.

Reese's arms wrapped around me, and when we reached his sleek, dark car parked at the curb, he paused and turned to face me.

"You couldn't keep it a secret for a few more weeks?"

He shrugged. "I couldn't help myself."

I rolled my eyes, but he grabbed me by my shirt, pulling me flush with him.

"I love you," he murmured, his voice low and full of something raw, something real.

His hands gently cupping my face as he guided me into his arms. His lips were warm, soft, but urgent against mine.

I loved this man with every inch of me.

"You and me," he whispered, his voice full of promise. "Our next adventure."

"Together," I murmured, feeling the truth of it settle deep in my bones. "Our next adventure."

Serena

I reached for my drink, fingers cool against the glass, and glanced back at the table.

Gigi was animated, as usual, her voice a high pitch that barely registered in my mind. Noelle was nodding along, both already deciding baby shower themes for Laurene.

But my thoughts…well, my thoughts were far from this brunch.

The pressure from King's Developments was overwhelming. It fucking hurt to admit that. I didn't fail. I never failed. That wasn't what a King did—and I wouldn't start now.

My mind swirled with numbers, strategies, and risks. I could hear Mama's voice in the back of my mind, sharp and commanding, reminding me that success came at a price, that there was no room for weakness, no room for anything but *perfection*.

And somehow, despite all the years of trying to break free from her shadow, I was still that little soldier my siblings thought I was.

I hated it.

I hated that I was always the one holding it all together, the one who had to shoulder the burden of it all while the others went off and did their own thing, blissfully unaware.

But me? No one asked if I was okay. I was the one who kept everything in line.

And damn it, I was tired.

Even now, I could feel the anxiety twisting in my gut, the fear that it was all unraveling faster than I could control.

And then he walked into my line of sight.

Miles Whitmore.

It was like the universe was laughing at me, testing how much longer I could hold on before I fucking snapped.

I averted my gaze before I slowly glanced back over, watching him as he swaggered across the patio. My pulse quickened despite myself, my chest tightening. We had a history, one I couldn't escape, no matter how many years had passed. No matter how much I told myself I was over it.

I took a slow sip from my glass, forcing my eyes to stay down, to focus on the foam in my drink. I didn't need to look at him. Not now. Not ever.

But damn it, I wanted to.

I wanted to tell him that it never got better, that my feelings for him never truly went away, that I could never let go. I wanted to scream at him, to tell him how I resented everything that happened between us, how much I hated him for making me feel like I couldn't move forward without him.

I couldn't.

He was my brother's ex–best friend. He didn't belong in my life anymore. I had to play this cool. I didn't get emotional like my siblings. Emotions had no place in my life.

There was only success, and that was my only compass.

"Serena." Noelle's voice broke through my thoughts, and I forced my gaze back to her, a tight smile pulling at my lips. "You okay?"

I nodded, my traitorous gaze shifting back over to Miles again. He was talking to someone, but his eyes flicked over to me, that damn smirk on his face, the one that made my heart twist and my stomach tighten.

Without thinking, I stood up abruptly, the chair scraping against the stone floor behind me, loud enough to make everyone pause.

"I have to go."

Before either of them could protest, I turned on my heel.

"Serena!"

I didn't look back, didn't slow down. I needed to be away from here, away from the place where everything felt out of control, where every thought seemed to lead back to him.

"Serena— Goddamn it, *Sunny*!"

Not that name.

I felt his hand on my arm, and he spun me around. My heart slammed against my ribs as I came face-to-face with him, breathless, furious, too close.

"Let go of me," I hissed, but my body already betraying me, too tangled in the pull between us. "Don't call me that. I told you never to call me that again!"

"You're running again," he said, his voice rough. "You think that's gonna fix anything?"

I shoved at his chest, but he didn't move. He just stood there, holding me captive with that maddening stare, like he knew me better than I knew myself.

He probably did.

"I'm not running," I bit out. "I'm leaving because I don't have time for this. For *you*."

For a second, I thought he was going to pull me back into him. Instead, he pushed me against the wall of a nearby building, trapping me between him and the cold stone. The rough texture of the wall scraped against my skin, but it barely registered as he leaned in, his breath hot against my ear.

What would people say if they saw me, Serena King, speaking with *the* Miles Whitmore? The scandalous Whitmores. Our ex-friends.

"Stop lying to me, Sunny," he growled, his voice thick with

frustration. "You want me to stay away, but you keep popping up everywhere I go. Coincidence?"

I shoved harder, trying to push him off, but it only made him press closer, his body like a furnace against mine mixed with the already scorching heat.

"No," I gasped, fighting to break free. "I told you if it's not about business, we don't speak, and even that's limited."

He jerked his head back, looking down at me with disbelief and something else—something dangerous I couldn't quite name.

"You're the one who won't let it go, Serena. Why the fuck were you at my house last week, then?"

I didn't want to hear it. That had been a mistake. A moment of weakness. I didn't give myself that often, and I wouldn't again.

"I'm not here to help you or your company or whatever game you're trying to play."

His expression flickered. "Last time I checked, your company's got a hell of a lot more to lose than mine, or was that little visit just attempted sabotage?"

I laughed, but it wasn't a real laugh. It was sharp, biting. "Your company is already on the brink of bankruptcy. You aren't a threat. It's called playing with your meal."

The words hit their mark. I saw the muscle in his jaw tense, his fists clenching at his sides. I couldn't help the twisted satisfaction that rose in my chest.

"Then tell me," he said quietly, his eyes locking with mine. "Tell me you don't feel anything for me anymore. Let's have full-blown war, Sunny. Tell me what you want. When I leave this time, I won't have mercy on you, your family, or King's Developments."

The words hung between us like a challenge, and I knew—*I knew*—that I couldn't lie to him. Not this time. Not when he was so close, and the heat of his breath mingled with mine, drawing me into a place I could no longer ignore.

So I didn't.

Instead, I stared up at him, my heart racing in a way that terrified me more than anything.

"I don't feel anything for you, Miles." Fire raced through my veins. "I *will* destroy you. Every. Single. Bit. Of you. You'll wish you took Erik's warning and left town."

And that was the most honest answer I'd given anyone in years.

The King Family Saga Continues…
Lavish

Want more of Laurene and Reese's happily ever after? Get the exclusive bonus content here!

There's more to explore!

Pacific Grove University Series

It Started with a List – A bucket list, a loner, and an unexpected romance.

It Started with a Dance – A fake dating deal that turns into something real.

Standalone Romance

The Last-Minute First Lady – A whirlwind marriage, political scandal, and family drama.